ALSO BY MARIE RUTKOSKI

Real Easy

The Hollow Heart

The Winner's Curse

The Winner's Kiss

The Midnight Lie

The Cabinet of Wonders

The Celestial Globe

The Jewel of the Kalderash

Shadow Society

ORDINARY LOVE

ORDINARY LOVE

MARIE RUTKOSKI

ALFRED A. KNOPF
NEW YORK
2025

A BORZOI BOOK
FIRST HARDCOVER EDITION PUBLISHED BY ALFRED A. KNOPF 2025

Published by Alfred A. Knopf, a division of Penguin Random House LLC, 1745 Broadway, New York, NY 10019.

Knopf, Borzoi Books, and the colophon are registered trademarks of Penguin Random House LLC.

Library of Congress Cataloging-in-Publication Data
Names: Rutkoski, Marie, author.
Title: Ordinary love : a novel / Marie Rutkoski.
Description: First United States edition. | New York : Alfred A. Knopf, 2025.
Identifiers: LCCN 2024033304 | ISBN 9780593803264 (hardcover) | ISBN 9780593689134 (paperback) | ISBN 9780593803271 (ebook) | ISBN 9781524712846 (open market)
Subjects: LCGFT: Romance fiction. | Queer fiction. | Novels.
Classification: LCC PS3618.U789 O73 2025 | DDC 813/.6—dc23/eng/20240719
LC record available at https://lccn.loc.gov/2024033304

penguinrandomhouse.com | aaknopf.com

Printed in the United States of America
1 3 5 7 9 10 8 6 4 2

The authorized representative in the EU for product safety and compliance is Penguin Random House Ireland, Morrison Chambers, 32 Nassau Street, Dublin D02 YH68, Ireland, https://eu-contact.penguin.ie.

For Becky Rosenthal

The river where you set your foot just now is gone—those waters giving way to this, now this.

—HERACLITUS, LATE SIXTH CENTURY BCE

ORDINARY
LOVE

1

The earth was full of stones but she liked prying them out of the ground. Emily's gardening knife scraped their edges. Some stones were flat and could be added to the rock wall bordering the property; others had set their long, sharp teeth deep into the dirt. She wiggled rocks out of place but stopped when she heard the distant splash of the children.

Their voices were happy. She didn't want to overreact. Jack said she always overreacted. She stifled the instinct to go around the house to the backyard and scold the children for swimming without an adult present. She didn't want to be an oppressive mother. They were good swimmers. If they needed her, she was close by. It's crazy, Jack often said, the way parents constantly monitor their kids. It wasn't like this a generation ago. Let them play.

They had tolerated the traffic on the drive upstate, had tolerated Jack waking them early on a Saturday. He had carried them down the staircase of their Upper East Side town house, one sleepy child in each arm. Stella's dreaming mouth was open as she rested her strawberry-blond head on Jack's shoulder. Connor was too big, really, to be carried, his long, thin legs knocking loosely against Jack's strong ones as the trio descended the stairs. Jack's smile was contented and proud, as though this moment with his children in his arms was a long hike with a vista at its end. "You can eat breakfast in the car," he had told them, "and jump right into the pool when we get there. This might be the last warm day of fall, so let's enjoy it." Connor and Stella had flung themselves from the car, slammed through the pool gate, and jumped off the diving board. Emily's dive was a clean slice. Jack chose not to swim. He went into the guesthouse, crowbar in hand.

That was hours ago. Emily set a daffodil bulb into the pocket left in the ground by a rock, pushed dirt into the cavity, and straightened. The splashing on the far side of the main house grew louder. Earlier, Connor and Stella had gone inside, teeth chattering, to change into last year's Halloween costumes: a pirate for Connor and a pink cat for Stella. Now, though, they called to each other over the slap and scatter of water.

Unable to ignore her unease, Emily set down the gardening knife and stepped out from under the maple. She walked toward the backyard. A bird sang. Her pace quickened.

No one had wanted to go upstate except for Jack. He had work to do, he said. There was a leak in the roof of the guesthouse: a yellow stain on the ceiling. Last weekend Jack had broken into the drywall to find dead chipmunks that had eaten through the fluffy pink insulation and clawed the studs. He removed their carcasses from the holes he had made and took photos of their brown husks, their big teeth. He made the children come look and placed a skeleton into Connor's open hand. "See what they did to our house?"

"Not our house," Connor said. "The guesthouse."

"I'm going to get them," Jack said. "Every last one."

"Bad guests!" said Stella.

"Exactly." Jack boosted Stella so that she could peer into the ceiling's hole, insulation pulled from its gut like intestine. "Bad guests!"

"We could hire someone," Emily said, not hopeful. When Jack began a project he finished it.

"Why, when I can do it myself? Or do you think I can't?"

He worked on the guesthouse while the others swam, until the children grew bored and hungry and left the pool to eat hot dogs in front of the TV in their costumes. She had thought that was where they were, watching cartoons while she gardened. She had thought that she'd locked the pool gate, but she must not have. Connor and Stella shouted, then only Stella, whose shout became a word that changed Emily's worry into fear: "Mommy! Mommy!"

Emily ran across the grass.

The children barreled into her before she turned the corner of the house. She clutched them. Stella's cat suit was dry, but Connor was soaked, his brown pirate's jacket now black and heavy with water.

"Are you okay?" she said. "What's wrong? Connor, why did you swim in your costume?"

"He didn't!" Stella said.

"Daddy threw me into the pool," Connor said.

"What?"

Connor's wet eyelashes were spiky. His spindly body, tall for ten years old—he was in the ninety-seventh percentile for height, tall like his father—was shaking. He coughed, then couldn't stop coughing, even when Emily rubbed his wet back. Finally, voice thin, Connor repeated, "He threw me into the pool."

The air was quiet. Emily noticed, as she should have noticed before, that no thumping or clattering came from the guesthouse. "He was playing with you?"

"No," Connor said.

"No," Stella said, more firmly.

It had happened like this: from the playroom, the children had seen Jack dive into the pool. As he did laps, they snuck into the pool area, past the open gate. "To surprise him," Stella said, taking over the story when Connor stopped. Stella was much shorter than her older brother, eyes a muddy green, and angry—at Emily.

Her daughter's silent accusation struck home: Emily couldn't protect anyone, not them and not herself. She hadn't been there when it had counted. She wanted to explain her exhaustion, how every moment counted in the company of Jack because each one was a crisis or the incubation of crisis—or things seemed fine, and Jack was happy, even joyous, yet she had learned not to be fooled, so the crisis coursed inside her: electric, perpetual. Yes, she had been planting flowers. Neglectful, selfish. As if anyone cared what grew in the spring. But she couldn't always be on alert. She wanted to describe the fatigue, the defeat, how it wasn't possible always to know where to be and when, what to do, how to do it, how to prevent or soothe or deflect her husband's moods, when to heed her anxiety, when to suppress it. She didn't know exactly what had happened at the pool but knew enough. Connor was crying but she almost couldn't tell because he was soaked. Water ran from his hair down his forehead. He wouldn't look at her. Stella looked nowhere but at her. When had Stella first looked at her like this, as though Emily weren't her mother but a cardboard imposter, a rip-off?

Stella told the story of what had happened at the pool. Connor had asked Jack a question and was ignored. He asked again, was ignored again. He began splashing Jack, who lunged from the pool, grabbed Connor's arm, and yanked him underwater.

"Is that it?" Emily said.

Connor was silent.

"Yes," said Stella.

Connor said, "When I was underwater, I didn't know if I would come up."

"But you did? Right away?"

"Yes," Stella said. "Daddy let him come up right away." Stella was no longer angry, but chastened, worried that her anger would be to blame for what might come next. "It's okay."

"Is that true?" Emily asked Connor.

"Almost right away," he whispered.

"Stay here," Emily told them.

She went to the backyard, where Jack stood at the pool's edge, toweling off, his red hair like a lit match. He saw her expression and rolled his eyes, letting his gaze slide deliberately over the heated saltwater pool with its deep bottom and sides the smooth gray of a dolphin; the cherry trees that, a few months earlier, had blown pink confetti over the velvet lawn. His gaze invited her to behold the acres that they owned, the woods where the children liked to gather wild blueberries from an overgrown island in the lake. Sometimes they startled a fawn waiting in the marshy bushes for its mother and sent it splashing into the water, startling frogs in turn. Jack looked at the eighteenth-century colonial farmhouse with fireplaces large enough to roast a pig; wide-board oak floors scarred beautifully by time; Dutch doors; the porte cochere with its fluted columns, built to shelter a horse-drawn carriage from weather. Come winter, this scene would be crystalline, trees bare and frosted, snow scalloped into drifts like thoughts that start small and then amount to something. Jack would turn on the radiant heat beneath the kitchen floor's blue-and-white Portuguese tiles. Her slippered feet would warm. She would relax until Jack looked at her, exactly as he looked at her now, expression fascinated, betrayed, alive with an unbelieving disappointment that said, *Here we go again* and *Nothing will be good enough for you.*

Jack said, “It was a game.”

“It wasn't.”

“Connor needs to learn how to behave. What do you want, for him to grow up with no respect? You didn't even ask what happened. I'm not the problem here, Em. You act like I'm a monster for playing with my kid.”

“You can never do that again.”

He whipped the towel from his hair. The sun was bright in his hair, bright in her eyes. “Who are you,” he said, voice low, streaked with menace and hurt, “to put me on trial?”

They had been dating for five months when he leaned over the boat to dip one half of a cut tomato into the Mediterranean, lifted it, dripping, and squeezed lemon over it. He had used a serrated knife; the tomato's edge was ragged. The deck tipped gently beneath her as she accepted the tomato, its red bowl overfull, reddened seawater running down her arm. Beyond him lay Li Galli: three islets, the largest one knuckled like a finger whose gesture was hidden below the water. “Look at you,” he said. “How did I get so lucky?”

Emily's white bikini accented her flat, tanned belly. Her blond, wet rope of hair stuck to her breast. She had the sense that her beauty was a story told about her and she wasn't its author. She didn't know how to make her beauty mean other than what people decided that it meant, yet its value was obvious: a currency she possessed even though she was poor.

The soles of her feet burned against the deck. Hours earlier, they had been cool on the terra-cotta tiles of the villa that Jack had rented in Positano. One wall in the bedroom was formed by the side of the bare cliff, rugged and chill to the touch. On the terrace that morning, a housemaid swept bougainvillea petals into a vivid pink pile. The brush of the broom echoed the waves against the rocks below.

At first, Emily had felt uncomfortable with how much Jack spent on her. Lavish gifts. This vacation. But he urged her to let him. He wanted her to see how much he loved her, which made the luxury he offered hard to resist. And why resist it? She felt elevated, relieved of care. Dazzled. Her beauty allowed her to enter a more valuable kind of beauty—this boat on the sea, that villa on the cliff, the ease of a life maintained by others. The bliss of never having to worry about how to pay. Emily wasn't merely an example of beauty, or its witness; she now lived inside it. She belonged, and it belonged to her.

Earlier that week, they had taken the ferry to Capri and swum in grottos whose spectral light painted their bodies blue, then went to Pompeii because she had studied Classics and wrote her senior thesis on Etruscan mirrors. The plaster casts of the volcano's victims didn't haunt her. The frescoes in the brothel held her attention but she forgot them later. What stayed with her, out of all the relics of Pompeii's long dead, were the empty fountains in homes for the wealthy. She imagined the fountains as they once were: the chandelier of water, the calm before catastrophe.

The volcano killed the rich, too. This was a lesson from the past. Emily shouldn't let herself be carried away by how nice Jack made life by having money and loving her. Nothing lasted forever. No one was immune from tragedy. Pliny the Younger had written about the indiscriminate disaster of the volcanic eruption, seen from across the Bay of Naples, its cloud like an umbrella pine. The air after Vesuvius's eruption had been so hot that it could turn brains into glass. She should remember that. Wealth's protection was not perfect.

But it felt perfect. After the excursion to Pompeii, Jack opened a bottle of Barolo on their terrace and told her that it was a superior vintage. It was delicious. The sea below was silver. He ran a large hand over the Oscar de la Renta dress he had given her. It was hard not to get carried away, because he *wanted* her to get carried away. It made him happy, and his happiness—like his wealth, his love—felt good. "I can't imagine my life without you," he said. She blushed with delight.

One night, Jack sailed their boat to Praiano, a village tucked into a cove, where they dined in sight of the black sea and begging cats. Clamshells littered Jack's plate. Emily had thought that maybe it would happen then, but it didn't. It didn't happen when they sailed back to the house, even though the Milky Way floated above them like a vast bolt of metallic fabric. The time was right, but it didn't happen then either.

Jack pointed toward Li Galli. "That's where the sirens sang to Odysseus," he said, which she knew. She was touched by his effort to please her. Jack was a romantic. She had been reading *The Odyssey* when they first met. "Go on," he said. "Eat."

She bit into the tomato. It was salty from the sea and tangy from the lemon. Its taste unleashed a memory. It tasted like her first kiss, at seventeen, almost four years before she met Jack, but it was as if she had been an entirely different person then. On a hot day, she and her friend Gen had gotten lemonade and sat on the back of Gen's pickup truck, watching a storm blow in. Gen's hair had been wild in the wind. Gen shoved her hair out of her face. Emily leaned to kiss her, and they stopped being friends.

In the gently rocking boat, Jack went down on one knee, a smile on his handsome face, the diamond beaming from its box. She couldn't breathe or move: one hand clutched the gunwale, the other held the tomato so lightly that it might fall. She was crying even before he asked her to marry him.

A castle with a vineyard in the Loire Valley, roses planted amid the vines to draw aphids from the grapes. The flare of poppies in the far, high grass. A powder-blue vintage car. A piece of paper in her pocket: her Something Old. When Emily had protested, saying that a destination wedding would be too expensive, that some of her friends couldn't afford to come, or her parents, Jack had said he would pay for their travel and lodging. Of course he would. He wanted everyone she wanted to be there.

Her mother drained her glass of champagne. "Where's Gennifer Hall? Your other high school friends came."

"Gen couldn't make it."

"She turned down a free trip to France? What a dum-dum."

Emily wished that Jack were by her side. Where was he?

Her mother said, "I thought she was your best friend."

"That was a long time ago." Emily's mother didn't know that Gen had become more than a friend. Jack did and, once he recovered from the surprise, found the knowledge unthreatening. Emily wished that Jack would save her from this conversation. She didn't want to talk about Gen, whom she had invited at the last minute, yet who never would have come.

A warm hand touched the small of Emily's back. She turned gratefully into Jack's kiss, the drift of his hand. He had been looking for her, just as she had been looking for him.

Jack dropped the towel to the pool's edge. Water snaked down his neck and trickled over his hard chest. "You think you can tell me how to raise my son? How dare you criticize me, after all I've done for you?"

2

It's a studio apartment," Emily told Jocelyn.

Jocelyn set down her latte. "A *studio*," she repeated. Plush curtains partially shielded their table from the rest of the tearoom, whose center was marked by a pyramid skylight so luminous it was as though the chunk of glass had been mined from the sun. The waiter set three desserts in front of Jocelyn: a lemon tart with meringue, an opera cake dressed in ganache, and a crème caramel. Jocelyn had been unable to decide what to order and so had chosen several options. She took a bite of opera cake.

"Jack controls our finances," Emily said. "I have a separate account that he puts money into but it isn't much."

Jocelyn shook her head in dismay, tucking a black lock of hair behind her ear. "You need a lawyer."

"It's a separation, not a divorce." It was important not to escalate. Escalation never worked because Jack's capacity to escalate was greater than hers. She had mentioned a lawyer and he had said, "Fine, get a lawyer, and I'll get a lawyer. I have more money, so we'll see who wins."

Jocelyn rested her narrow hand on Emily's. Jocelyn wore a white linen shift that accentuated her flawless, light brown skin. There was nothing ostentatious about her except the diamonds, yet they, too, possessed a simplicity, one that mesmerized, their size stopping the mind and setting it to rest as they silently explained the restful futility of trying to guess their worth. "New York law is fifty-fifty. You get half of everything, unless you signed a prenup."

Emily had signed a prenup. She had been twenty-one and full

of optimism. The freshly printed document was warm, like bread out of an oven. "I don't want to do this," Jack had said sheepishly, "but my parents insist. They say the terms are fair, if you really love me." She did. Divorce seemed impossible.

"You get nothing?" said Jocelyn. "Even mobsters leave their wives something." She reached for her phone. "Regardless of a prenup, he needs to provide for the children. I'm sending you the name and number of a lawyer. Use it." If Emily had remained true to the ambitions of her youth and had gone to law school after college, she might have been able to represent herself in a divorce, or have colleagues advise her. She would have had her own income. What was she supposed to do with a degree in Classics? Her elite education was useless. Her mother would laugh. But it had made sense when she became pregnant with Connor to forget about law school. "You don't really want to become a lawyer," Jack said—and she didn't. "Classics is your passion. Law would just be to pay the bills. You don't have to worry about that anymore." Jack wrote a check that vanquished her undergraduate debt. He framed her diploma and hung it on the wall. When guests came, he asked Emily to translate its Latin for them. He liked to explain to people that while everyone who graduated from Harvard received a diploma in Latin, not all of them could understand, as Emily did, what the document actually said.

"A studio!" said Jocelyn. "Where do the kids sleep?"

"It's furnished. There's a bed. We share."

Jocelyn took a bite of crème caramel and frowned, setting down her spoon with a dissatisfied *clink*. "All this over a little dunking in the pool?"

"It's not just the pool."

"I've seen this happen before. It's always the same. A wife decides she's done and she has her reasons, but by the time she's proven her point it's too late. He'll find someone like you but younger and as accommodating as you used to be. And you will be alone."

"I'll have Connor and Stella."

"You think he's going to let you keep them? Even if he does, they'll grow up—sooner than you think. Listen, Jack adores you. He never looks at another woman. It's only you."

Emily knew. The knowledge sat inside her like an extra bone: hard and jutting at a wrong angle. She looked away from Jocelyn, who assumed that adoration was always a good thing. Emily had believed that, too, at the beginning of her marriage. "He gets angry when he thinks his level of love isn't returned."

"So would I!"

"He can be manipulative."

"Marriage is full of manipulation. I manipulate David all the time. He insisted we have our gardener plant sunflowers. Sunflowers! So common. I told him, 'You're right! Let's have some yellow in our palette. How about zinnias?' David was very proud of himself, and since zinnias are annuals they'll be dead after the first frost, so everyone wins. Are you telling me that you never manipulate Jack?"

"I can't anymore."

"Maybe you can work this separation to your advantage by reminding Jack of what he stands to lose. Just don't go too far, because if you divorce, someone will snap him up and you'll be penniless. Honey, wait! I have an idea. My apartment!" Jocelyn owned a two-bedroom apartment in the Village that her parents, who lived in Beijing, had given her when she turned eighteen and moved to New York to attend Columbia. She hadn't lived there in years. She and David lived in a West Village town house decorated in elements that matched Jocelyn's looks: creamy marble, abundant light, a sculpted oak staircase with black risers and a black banister that curved, at the bottom, into such a sensuously smooth newel that to let go of it was like forgetting a nice dream. "My renters broke the lease. Never again am I renting to college students. Why don't you stay there?"

Shame thickened in Emily's throat. She couldn't afford Jocelyn's apartment.

"For free, of course," Jocelyn said, which made her generosity worse for Emily, because she needed a godsend and Jocelyn didn't. She wished time weren't a straight line, that it could be bent, amended. Why can't we go back and make different choices? Why hadn't she foreseen the troubled course of her marriage? Jack had seemed to be the best thing that could have happened to her. His proposal in Italy was a moment of great happiness. To go back and say no to him would undo her current life, unmake her children, her very self. But at least she could have chosen to have a career.

As soon as that thought occurred, though, Emily recognized that a career would have been no solution. How much sooner would her marriage have soured, if she had been more equal to Jack financially and professionally, and therefore, a threat?

She couldn't untangle the past and the present and what could have been. She told Jocelyn that she had already signed a year's lease on the studio.

"Emily, this is not *La Bohème*! Are you going to sing in a garret until you die of consumption? People like us don't live in studio apartments."

She had never been like Jocelyn, only masquerading as someone like her. It had worked, for a while. It had been nice, until it wasn't.

"Fine," Jocelyn said. "My renters left behind a twin mattress. Accept *that*, please. For Connor."

"Okay. Thanks."

The waiter came with the bill. Emily looked at Jocelyn's half-eaten cakes and put down her card.

"Don't be absurd," Jocelyn said.

"I can afford cake."

"This studio life of yours isn't forever. Go home to him, or call that lawyer and get what's yours."

"I'm grateful to you."

Jocelyn gave her a smile. "It's nothing."

The mattress was heavier than Emily had thought. She and Connor carried it from the apartment while Stella, who walked beside them, enjoyed the stares of passersby. Jocelyn's apartment was only six blocks from the studio, a distance that had seemed manageable at first. Her arms ached. Connor got underneath his end and ported it like a canoe. “I’m proud of you,” she told him. She couldn’t see his face.

A few blocks from the studio, as they were walking past the brass triangle whose angles were no longer than a ruler and marked the smallest piece of private property in New York City, a man in gym clothes offered to help. Emily’s relief when he lifted Connor’s end from the boy’s shoulders was as welcome as stepping into a fresh lake on a hot day. He helped her carry it to the building’s lobby.

Connor was furious. “I wanted to help.”

The man gave Emily an awkward smile, plugged in his headphones, and left.

“You did help,” she told Connor.

“I wanted to help the whole way.”

“But you didn’t need to.”

Stella sat on the lobby bench, rhythmically swinging her white sandals as Connor shouted at Emily.

In high school, she liked to run. She wasn’t very fast but good enough to make the track team. She imagined wings pinned to her ankles: the talaria of Mercury, messenger of the gods. Sometimes that helped to propel her past the finish line. Emily had a second-place ribbon tacked to her bulletin board. The early hour of track practice pleased her: the cold and the brittle grass. A white sky. The coach’s whistle.

Track tryouts were in October, with not long to go before the sky dumped snow everywhere and practice moved indoors. Emily was a senior, her place on the team secure. She watched a few juniors line up. Gen Hall pushed one foot, defiantly, right up to the line. She wasn’t wearing proper sneakers. They were ragged Converse, the toe of one shoe open like a mouth. The coach blew his whistle again. It became instantly evident that Gen was faster than the other juniors, faster than Emily could ever be, faster than the entire varsity team. Gen flew.

“How long do we have to be here?” Stella snuggled up against Emily under the sheet.

From his mattress on the floor of the dim studio, Connor eyed her. He wanted to know, too.

"Until I figure things out."

"What if," Stella said, "we got lost in a big snowstorm?"

"I would save you."

"What if you couldn't?"

"I would."

Connor said, "You can't do everything."

"Okay, if I die in the blizzard, eat me until help comes." She was frustrated by their worry that she couldn't protect them, even though this was her worry as well. "I'll make sure I die before you starve."

"Ew, no!" Stella said.

"I want you to." Emily didn't like her stern tone but couldn't help it.

"I wouldn't," Stella said. "I would sleep next to you in the snow."

Emily held Connor's gaze. "Promise me you would. Make Stella eat me, too."

"Okay," Connor said softly. "I promise." His eyes glimmered, and Emily was instantly sorry. She wanted to say so, except an apology might make her seem even more incapable. "It wouldn't come to that," she said, her voice gentle. "I would find a snowbank against a break of pines. I would peel bark from a tree to make a shovel and dig into the pile of snow until I hollowed out a little snow house."

"Like an igloo?" said Stella.

"Yes. We would slide inside and keep each other warm. I'll stay awake while you sleep. I'll keep watch so that the falling snow doesn't cover the opening. When the snow stops, I'll drape my scarf over the lowest pine branch to mark where you are and I will go for help."

Stella said, "I don't want you to go."

"Then I'll stay and make a fire."

"You have no matches, Mommy."

"I'll find a dry stick and a dry flat piece of wood. I'll rub the stick against the hearthboard until there is enough friction to create a spark."

"Hearthboard?"

"The flat piece of wood."

"I don't think this will work."

"I read about it in a book."

"Um, yeah, that's why it won't work."

"I'll pull feathers from my down jacket for tinder and touch them to the ember. I'll add dry pine needles to the tiny fire, then sticks."

"It could maybe work," Connor said quietly from the floor.

Encouraged, Emily described how she would hunt for them, and it began not to matter whether she could do the thing that she planned. The plan was enough. For each question, she had an answer until the children's questions were less critique and more collaboration, and the three of them lived in the snowy woods together. She was describing the arrival of spring when Stella fell asleep.

"Spring means bears," whispered Connor.

"I see a bear," Emily said. "It lifts its nose and scents the air." Connor was half afraid, she knew. "The bear won't attack."

"Why?"

"We are stinky after all this time. The bear smells no soap. No shampoo. No perfume. We don't smell human. The bear thinks, *That is a bear smell: a deep stench*. It lumbers away."

"Is that the end?"

"Do you want it to be the end? It's spring. We can find our way back to the path."

"And go home?"

Emily said, "Maybe not yet."

The city light from the window fell away from Connor's face as he turned onto his side and into shadow. "It's not so bad here."

Emily closed her eyes. Before sleep, when imagination started to slip from control and she could no longer be responsible for what she thought, was no longer building a story but letting one build inside her, Emily saw snow: a field of it. There were no woods. No bear. No children. There was only Emily, and even Emily didn't seem fully there. She looked down and saw no hands, no trace of herself. A dark blur moved across the horizon. It was a runner, feet so fast that they didn't dent the snow. The runner was a swift blade that split white ground from white sky. The runner was Gen.

3

I remember you," Gen told Emily after their first track practice. The October air was cold, the grass brown, but Emily's face was hot and her breath fast. Running with Gen had been like keeping pace with a streaking deer. Emily was thirsty and annoyed and her body felt like a hot-water bottle.

She remembered Gen, too, from elementary school, but Gen's openness, her light smile—as if practice had been a pleasure and so was Emily's company—made her pretend that she didn't. "I don't think so," Emily said. "You're a junior." A full grade behind Emily. They had been in the same year in fifth grade, but something must have happened after they went to different middle schools.

"Yeah, but I've decided I'll graduate this year."

"You can't just *decide* that." The other girls on the team had gone ahead of them to the gym entrance. Emily watched the heavy doors slam shut. A raven picked its way through tough grass. Emily made her tired legs move more quickly, eager for the conversation to be over, but Gen lengthened her stride.

"I want to be class of '96. I don't mind extra work." Gen was stupidly tall, and although her shoes were falling apart, her graceful pace made Emily think of paintings of gentlemen from bygone eras, the kind on paperbacks like *The Age of Innocence*. "Are you always this way? Do you not like me, or do you not like someone being better than you?"

The words—said with no resentment, only curiosity—brought Emily to a halt.

"At this one thing," Gen amended, her smile still friendly. "It's just running. It's not everything."

"I don't remember you being this chatty."

"So you *do* remember."

Emily felt embarrassed. Gen was right: Emily was angry because she had been bested. She had tried as hard as she could to run fast and even though she didn't usually care much about track, there had been something gallingly elegant about Gen's swiftness, the way it had made Emily feel leaden, earthbound. Although before Emily had pretended not to know Gen because she had wanted to end the conversation, now she didn't want to talk about how they once *did* know each other, as little kids, because she worried, suddenly, that she might shame Gen by discussing the circumstances . . . even though that was clearly what Gen wanted to discuss.

Gen said, "I used to be shy."

In fifth grade, the new girl who had arrived midyear wasn't in Emily's class but was in her lunch period. Genny Hall had sharp elbows, long legs, and bony knees. Her lunch tray was bare except for a blue carton of skim milk. She opened it and drank so quickly that Emily thought that the girl might throw up.

Emily sat next to Meredith, who had Lunchables and a Hostess cupcake in her My Little Pony lunch box. Meredith ate the cupcake like the commercial instructed: first, the icing, then the cake, then the creamy middle that she squashed with her tongue. Emily didn't have a lunch box but always decorated a brown bag before school, writing in painstaking cursive so that it would look adult: *Have a Great Day, Emily!* Her mother had decorated the bag like that for the first day of school but hadn't since. Inside was a peanut butter sandwich, which Emily made every day because she didn't know how to make anything else. She cut off the crusts and told her friends that she was obsessed with peanut butter, it was her favorite.

Kim could do fishtails and braided one into Meredith's hair. She clipped the bangs back with a butterfly barrette. "Fuh-*reak*," Kim said. Emily, for a moment, thought that Kim meant her and worriedly glanced down at the sandwich in her hands, but Kim meant the new girl, who had ripped open the milk carton and was licking the waxed inside.

That night, at home, Emily leaned against the fake wood paneling of the family room, torn between savoring the last few pages of her library book and consuming them. She thought of the girl licking the inside of the milk carton. Emily turned the pages more slowly. The end came anyway. She closed the book and looked at the ceiling, trying not to blink.

"What's wrong?" Her mother poured Sweet'N Low into her coffee. "What have you got to cry about?"

Emily glanced down at the book cover with its illustration of a Pegasus. She rubbed the wetness from the cover's plastic casing.

"Oh, Em." Her mother sighed.

Emily wondered if the school library would fine her if she kept the book and claimed it had been lost. Maybe they didn't fine children. Maybe she could keep it for free, forever. "I know it's dumb. I know a Pegasus isn't real but I wish it was."

"You're right," her mother said. "That's pretty dumb." She wiped Emily's cheek and told her to turn on the TV. They adjusted the antenna. CBS came through nice and clear. There were cartoons. Emily's mother put an arm around her and fell asleep on the couch. When a commercial came on, one Emily knew well, about an old car that was still worth money, she thought about how skim milk was five cents cheaper than whole.

The next day at lunch, Meredith complained about their teacher, who had made them plant grass seeds in Styrofoam cups. The entire class was insulted. "That is so kindergarten," Meredith said at lunch. "We are not *babies*."

"Yeah, fuck photosynthesis," Kim said, delighted by her daring. The other two laughed to please her. At a nearby table, empty save for her, Genny looked up from her torn-open milk carton. Emily said that she agreed with Kim. "Grass is boring. I like flowers."

"Gennifer Hall is staring, oh my *God*," said Meredith. Emily felt the prickle of the girl's gaze.

At library hour, Emily went to the history section and found Genny Hall hidden between the stacks, just as Emily had seen her hide earlier that week. Emily thrust a baggie with a peanut butter sandwich at her. That morning, Emily had made two. Silently, gaze down, Genny took the sandwich.

Every day they had library together, Genny accepted a sandwich. At lunch, she drank her milk like a normal person and some days didn't buy it. Weeks later, when the cold meant business and snowy boots squeaked down the orange halls, Emily put her hands in her coat pockets at dismissal, looking for her mittens. Something small, flat, and rectangular fell from her pocket to the ground.

It was a packet of marigold seeds. The price was printed on the top right corner. Emily did the math. Six days of skipped milk could buy a packet of marigold seeds.

On the track field beneath the dimming sky, Emily studied Gen, who still seemed underfed—not so much in her body, though Gen was lanky, her features angular, but in the way she looked at Emily expectantly, large eyes dark and growing darker, because even though it was only four o'clock, this was autumn in Ohio and soon it would be dusk. Despite how hot Emily had been after practice, sweat had chilled on her skin. The wind picked up, juggling a tree's yellow leaves. She shivered.

"You're cold," Gen said. "Let's go inside."

The attentiveness surprised Emily. It made her wonder what else Gen noticed, what else she was thinking. When they reached the gym doors, Gen said, "Where did you plant the seeds?"

"I didn't."

"Oh."

"I liked them too much," Emily said in a rush. "If I planted them, they'd grow but then they'd die. I liked imagining what they'd look like better than seeing what they did look like." She still had the packet. It was in her desk drawer at home, mixed in with birthday cards from her father.

"That's nice," Gen said.

"It is?"

"Yeah. Save them for when you need them."

"Okay."

"Do you want to go running together?"

"At practice?"

"Just us."

That was October. In June, Emily's legs were tangled between Gen's in the flatbed of Gen's pickup truck, the metal hot beneath her skin. Summer slid into September and Emily was moving into her double in Thayer Hall at Harvard. Emily's roommate, brash and lively, ordered pizza and asked questions that were inappropriate yet endearing, because they were predicated on the assumption that she and Emily were already friends. "Let's get the basics out of the way," Florencia said. "How many guys have you slept with?" When Emily said none, Florencia shrieked, "You're a *virgin*?"

"I didn't say that."

Florencia wanted every delicious detail.

4

It wasn't much but Emily had thought it would count for something: two years' experience cooking at IHOP on weekends and during summers, fingers gummy from maple syrup, watching pancake batter bubble with holes as it cooked on the griddle. Years later, at a beach on Ile de Ré, she and Jack went clamming. The tide withdrew, exposing muddy sand. They squelched over it, wicker baskets in hand, searching for bubbles that signaled life below, and dug down for clams the size of peach pits.

In high school, at seventeen, gooey bubbles meant it was time to flip the pancakes. In Cambridge, when she was twenty-one years old and it was her senior year of college, IHOP meant nothing and the clams hadn't happened yet. Restaurant managers in Cambridge and across the river in Boston told her over the phone that they had all the waitstaff they needed. Others didn't return her call.

Florencia, who concentrated in English and was reading *Ulysses* in bed, glanced through the open door between their rooms as Emily hung up. "Did you know that potatoes aren't native to Ireland?" Florencia said. "They came from South America. My professor, though, says the potato in Leopold Bloom's pocket is a symbol of Ireland. My friend, that potato is not a potato. It's in Bloom's pocket when he's lusting after Gerty MacDowell. Let me tell you what that potato means: stately, plump, postcolonialist *dick*."

"It's impossible to get a job off campus."

Florencia didn't ask why she needed one or point out that

Emily already had a work-study job at Widener Library. Florencia set *Ulysses* aside. "I always wondered who was smarter but now I know it's not you. Don't *call* them. *Show* them." They went to the computer lab in the dorm's basement and looked up high-end restaurants.

Emily took the T across the river and walked through Boston's snowy Common. She entered Sirocco in Beacon Hill, where the restaurant's manager, a woman with a tight bun, looked at Emily and said, "You are not a cook."

"I can do prep."

"You are not back of the house. You are front of the house." The manager told Emily to stand behind the bar, which glowed with topaz vessels and turquoise gin. A pear-shaped bottle held a pear that slept like a fetus in clear brandy. Florencia had been right: the manager said, "You look amazing. Can you start on Friday?" The manager didn't ask whether Emily knew how to make cocktails (she didn't), only if she was a quick study (she was).

She learned the arctic burn of a cocktail shaker filled with ice and how to foam egg whites. One night, she peeled the rind of an orange so that its ribbon wrapped around one large ice cube in a glass of bourbon and placed it in front of a man who introduced himself as Jack.

"So he's hot," Florencia said.

They were supposed to be studying. Emily had a copy of Herodotus open on the café table and Florencia had been snickering her way through Pepys's diary, periodically interrupting Emily's reading to report on the diarist's affair with the woman who combed lice from his hair, yet how the sexiest thing ever for him seemed to be when he boarded a merchant ship and saw bags of rubies and other riches. " 'Pepper scattered through every chink, you trod upon it,' " Florencia had read out loud. " 'In cloves and nutmegs, I walked above the knees.' Treasure was his kink. He's practically coming all over the page. Don't get me started on when he buries gold in his backyard and can't find it later. Hilarious!"

The skinny, blond-bearded waiter looked offended when Emily asked for hot water to refill her teapot. Emily didn't blame him. She knew what it was like to work for tips. She was embarrassed that she hadn't ordered more. Florencia ordered falafel.

Café Algiers was packed with students preparing for finals. Emily and Florencia had arrived early to claim a table upstairs and had been there for hours. A snowfall that had begun when they arrived had stopped. Outside, snow lay in thin scarves draped over the tilted gravestones from the sixteen hundreds. Emily drank her watery mint tea. Her father had refused to pay for college. He had two more children, Emily's younger half sisters from his second marriage. She understood, didn't she, that he had already divided marital assets with her mother in the divorce, and if Cheryl had spent everything, well, that wasn't his fault, was it?

The waiter stuffed his order pad into his apron and went to the next table, his narrow shoulders slouched, his body like a doodle drawn in the margins of a notebook. "I dare him," Florencia had said, not especially quietly, "to tell us to leave."

Concentration broken, Emily had closed her book and told her about Jack. Yes, he was hot: face noble, jaw wide, mouth nicely cut. His red hair was short enough to qualify as professional yet long enough to ignite into a fiery mess when he ran a hand through it.

"Redheads experience pain differently." Florencia was full of random facts—or pseudofacts that she announced with such casual surety that their truth took second order to her confidence. "They have a higher tolerance for pain. It's all about their melanocortin 1 receptor gene. Is he freckled?"

"No, tanned." His oxford blue shirt had been unbuttoned at the neck. He had smiled at her when she handed him the square-cut glass, his teeth very white against his skin.

"Tanned, in this weather? Tanning-bed tanned? Orange undertone, pale around the eyes from goggles? You white Americans are always doing weird shit to your skin."

"No, he looks good."

Florencia slapped the table. A girl at the nearest table, textbook open, gave them a dirty look. "Then he's *rich*. Caribbean vacation, probably." After Thanksgiving break, a select group of students had returned to campus with deep tans. Florencia had pointed them out over dinner in their dining hall: "St. Barts, Abu Dhabi, hmm, Punta del Este, I bet." Florencia was rich, too, born in Buenos Aires to landowning scions.

Emily told Florencia about the hundred-dollar bills. Twice now, Jack had come to Sirocco's bar, ordered an old-fashioned, and left a crisp one-hundred-dollar bill as a tip. "Do you think it means something?"

"Duh."

"What should I do about it?"

The waiter returned, bearing two plates of falafel and hummus dusted with za'atar. Emily said, "But I didn't—"

"I did," Florencia said. "I'm buying. Emily, stop. It's not even me, okay, it's my parents. They're buying and they won't notice and if they did, they would be glad. As for what to do with Jack, easy: pocket the money. You are under no obligation to him. Has he asked you out?"

Emily shook her head. "You think he's trying to buy sex."

"Only a teenager thinks two hundred bucks will buy him sex."

"So he's just being nice."

"I didn't say that. What do you think of him?"

Emily considered the question as she ate the falafel. She tried not to think about the warm gift of this meal. Kindness always made her eyes sting. She remembered Gen's marigold seeds sliding inside their packet, their soft, costly rattle.

Was Jack nice? She couldn't tell. He was friendly, not pushy. He didn't linger at the bar or try to pull her attention away from other customers. He had come to Sirocco two Fridays in a row. In town for work, he had said. He was older, Emily guessed, by about five years. His eyes were gray, the color of an empty mirror. He sometimes rubbed his bright stubble when he checked his BlackBerry. He had offered his name, and when she gave him hers, he shook her hand, clasp quick and firm, palm cool from holding his drink.

"If you like him," Florencia said, "it would cost him way more than two hundred."

"I'm not interested in that." By senior year, Emily had learned that there was a market for girls like her, on campus or off, in various ways. She knew other students on financial aid. A barrel-bodied guy down the hall worked on a fishing boat every summer in Alaska, making tens of thousands of dollars that he buried beneath the sand where he pitched his tent when he came to shore. He sold his sperm regularly and told her that she could get big money for her eggs; people paid extra for Harvard genes. She dismissed the idea, just as she ignored rumors about girls who were sugar babies ("Not the same as prostitution!"), not because she thought it was wrong but because she wanted to get by on her own, and if someone were to say, But this *is* your own, your own eggs, your body, she would feel a lonely, condensed anger, like a stone pendant knocking against her chest with each swing of the chain, and remember her mother's tired expression when she learned where Emily was applying for college, and how that expression had hurt. Much later, when Emily had children of her own, she would think that maybe her mother's face hadn't shown skepticism about Emily's chances, only the resignation of someone being left behind. But as a teenager, and for many years after, Emily was sure that her mother believed that she wasn't good enough for Harvard. Gen's reaction had been very different. When Emily had told Gen her top choice for college, Gen nodded knowingly, her breath rising white over the track field as she said, "I'll miss you when you go."

Emily wasn't willing to trade her body. In loving Gen, Emily had already given away too large a part of herself before she understood its worth, and was too young to know that she wasn't alone, and that people did this in all kinds of ways. Emily was also just old enough to dread another self-betrayal, and not old enough to know its inevitability.

Florencia said, "I'm not trying to *sell* you. Just acknowledging basic facts about pretty blondes in a capitalist society. Did you know that in late-seventeenth-century Italy you could buy interactive, lift-the-dress drawings of courtesans?"

"I'm going to study now."

"Maybe this Jack will be your one true love."

Emily opened her book.

"Make you forget your broken heart."

"I'm reading," Emily said.

"Make you forget all about Dillon."

"I never cared about Dillon," Emily said, which was true.

Florencia sighed.

"He didn't break my heart," Emily said. "Gen did."

"I know. I'm just pretending that he was the one to do it, because he kind of sucks, so it'd be easy to say, Emily, he's trash, forget him. But you actually forgot Dillon the moment you met him."

"*You* made me go out with him."

"I have terrible taste in men. Never listen to me where they're concerned." Yet weeks later, when Emily introduced her to Jack and Florencia pronounced him perfection, Emily believed her, because Emily agreed, and it was what she wanted to hear.

5

The Friday after studying at the café with Florencia, Emily was summoned to Sirocco for an extra shift. It didn't matter that final exams began the following week. Another bartender had called in sick. The manager made clear to Emily that her job was on the line. Emily bundled up and shoved stacks of index cards labeled with conjugations of Greek verbs into her backpack. Wind cut through her hat as she walked down Mass Ave., footsteps rapid over brick sidewalks glazed with ice. The cold grasped her in its fist until she took an escalator down into the T, where the sugar-and-coffee smell of the station's Dunkin' Donuts wrapped her in an extra layer of subway warmth.

She caught the Braintree train, remembering how tentative she'd been taking the subway for the first time, sure she'd get lost, especially when red line trains from Harvard Square into Boston had different names and went different places, but then she had learned that the terminus meant little, because she probably wouldn't go that far, whether it was Braintree or Ashmont. Emily had written to Gen about that, including an annotated map of the T in the letter's envelope. She had circled the Longwood Medical Area stop and wrote about how everyone she knew at Harvard had had braces in high school, so when she discovered that her student health insurance included dental, she took two trains and a bus to ask a campus dentist if she could get the braces she'd never had. He said that her teeth were perfect. She was disappointed. It was as though she had been told that there was no point trying to catch up to her new friends. Emily circled the map where she had gone ice skating with Florencia at Frog Pond. She circled the T stop for the art museum with orange nasturtium trailing down its interior courtyard and a hall that had held Rembrandts until thieves cut the canvases from their wooden frames. The paintings were rolled and taken away. *Who is the frame and who is the canvas?* she almost wrote, but knew the answer. Gen was the missing canvas: a huge emptiness in Emily's mind, which was the frame. It wasn't until after Gen's awful visit to Harvard later that year that Emily considered that Gen could be the thief, too, and the knife.

The train emerged over the Charles River. The water below was as dull as stone.

At Sirocco, Emily pulled her hair into a ponytail, tied her black apron, and taped the index cards with ancient Greek verbs behind the bar. She hid her copy of *The Odyssey* in the refrigerator. It was happy hour, but slow enough that she could read an index card when she reached for the soda gun. One couple left the bar to sit at their ready table. A man's suited companion arrived and ordered a margarita, which was every mom's favorite special drink in Emily's hometown and clashed with the serious tone of the two men's low conversation. Emily scrunched the rim of a cocktail glass into salt. The men's faces reminded her of the WWII soldiers in *Saving Private Ryan* as they contemplated a blown-out church in Normandy. When they were dating, Dillon had suggested he and Emily go see that movie. He had suggested it ironically, as a low-class alternative to the Kieślowski retrospective at the Brattle. She agreed to spite him, then regretted it when he held her hand throughout the gunfire.

After her breakup with Gen, she had thought she might as well date Dillon, who was objectively cute and had told everyone that his resolution for '98 was to ask her out. The idea of dating another woman made her want to look for the nearest bomb shelter. Nothing had been better than being with Gen—until the end. It had been the kind of disaster you should have known was coming by how much you needed it not to be one. Maybe being with a woman would always be that way: too good, then too sad. So there she was, sharing a Coke with Dillon, watching a movie about being brave.

As the Tom Hanks character recalled his wife cutting roses in their garden, Dillon drew Emily's hand across his lap and positioned it on his erection. She pulled away. He told her not to be a prude. They had been dating for a few months and hadn't progressed beyond making out. He wanted to know why she wasn't interested in more. She said, "Maybe I just don't like you enough." He said, "You're cruel, you know that?" He stood, his face bathed in the projector's shifting light, eyes squinted as though she had punched him. He thudded up the aisle, head swinging back once to see if she was following. She stayed until the end of the movie, when Private Ryan became an old man who wondered if he had been good enough to have been worth saving. She loved it.

The suited man at the bar accepted his margarita and turned back to his companion. They were probably talking about stocks or a new dot-com company.

Then Jack came in, beating snow from the black wool shoulders of his coat. He smiled at Emily from the door, checked his coat, and came to her. He sat, hair damp with melted snow, and ordered an old-fashioned. The two serious men left, and Emily predicted that Jack would say, *It's cold out there!* or *It's really coming down*, or another dull and harmless phrase that might clear a path between him and his obvious object of interest: her. But he took his drink with a simple thanks and opened a newspaper. The facing page showed an article about the Y2K bug. Emily retrieved *The Odyssey* from the fridge. He noticed, raised one brow, then ignored her. She ignored him, turning the chilled pages, reading about Odysseus's bow. Jack slid a new section from the paper's fold. He had an unusual way of reading: he held a flat blank sheet of paper over a portion of the text and shifted it lower as he read. He must have been reading line by line. Emily didn't want to be curious about him, so she returned to her book. They pretended the other didn't exist until Emily forgot that that was what they were doing and stopped pretending, the book no longer cold in her hands as she read intently. She was startled when he asked for the check.

Again, he left a one-hundred-dollar bill. It made Emily mad. She didn't like the pressure of trying to figure out what he meant by his stupid tip. She pulled the bill from the server book and set it down on the bar. With one finger, she pushed it toward him. "Why?" she demanded.

He pushed it back. "Why what?"

"What do you want from me?"

"Nothing. It's a tip."

"That's not a tip. It's too much."

"Not really."

"So you tip every server like this?"

He laughed. "Just the rude ones."

"What are you, made of money?"

"That's an odd expression, isn't it? Like if I cut myself, I'd bleed pennies."

Surprise interrupted Emily's irritation. She imagined, vividly, what he had just said. She imagined dimes shed as tears. She reached into his chest and pulled out a paper heart.

"The tip doesn't mean anything," Jack said. "I like to think about what you will do with it. I think about it when I'm on the train from New York or sitting through my parents' endless dinners. Sometimes I think, *She will buy a scarf.*"

"For a hundred dollars?" No one would spend so much on a scarf.

"Or I think, *She has a dog. She will buy dog food.*"

"What kind of dog do you suppose I have?"

"A loyal one."

"What else do I buy?"

"Dinner with your friend. You treat her, and gossip."

"About you?"

"I would never presume to know your secrets. I honor the sanctity of girl talk."

"Pretend we talk about you. Do I say nice things?"

"I hope so."

"Maybe I have a boyfriend, and I'm treating him to dinner." She had dated a few guys after Dillon but couldn't bring herself to sleep with any of them. They were too boring.

"Maybe you do. Take the money. You're doing me a favor. If the tip means anything, it's a story I tell myself about how you enjoy it."

Although at first it had been disconcerting to imagine him imagining her—all those alternate Emilys taking actions in response to his own—she found that she liked his boyish smile. She liked that she occupied his mind. She enjoyed being the center of his game. This man was not boring. "I'll tell you what I do with the money."

"I'd rather you didn't."

"Ruins the fantasy, does it?"

He held up one pleading hand. She felt the force of his good looks. He said, "How about we stop right there."

Why stop, when she was already appreciating the clean, hard lines of him, offset by the soft play of his hand raised in defense? She liked his pretense of vulnerability, perhaps because some part of it was real. It had to be, for him to think of her so much, to return to the same bar and leave the same tip, with the habit of ritual. She said, "I save the money."

He placed his hand flat against his chest. "You're breaking my heart."

She smiled. "Do you want to go out with me?"

6

Jack hired a wedding planner, telling Emily that she should relax. "Do the fun parts. Choose the flowers and music." Yet he couldn't quite relinquish control to the planner and kept presenting Emily with new possibilities. Near the castle that would be their venue was a hotel built into the ramparts of a medieval wall surrounding a nearby village. Wouldn't that be great for guests? He'd book the entire hotel. Since the castle's vineyard produced wine, a wine tasting for their guests the day before the wedding was in order. He would arrange it. Emily was blown away by his attention to detail. Black truffles would be in season, so he wanted to structure the menu around them. Truffle mousseline served on Parmesan crisps as hors d'oeuvres, followed by truffle risotto, then quail braised in wine and festooned with shaved truffles.

"Will there be truffle dessert, too?" she teased. They were having coffee in bed in his apartment in New York's Financial District. His apartment was so large that when she'd go to another part of it, she would forget her purpose along the way. She lost books, her keys. It was an incredible space but felt like the architectural expression of PTSD, where things vanished like bad memories. "Maybe we should serve truffle ice cream, or truffle crème brûlée."

His expression tightened. "I'm working hard here, Em."

She was taken aback by his sudden displeasure. "But you don't have to."

"I'm doing this for you."

She guessed what the problem was, and then his irritation moved her, because it was, at its core, concern: a dedication to making everything perfect. He wanted everyone to be pleased. Impressed. No one else had tried so hard to make her happy. "It was a bad joke." She caressed his cheek. "Who's this really for? You know it's not for me. We can get married at city hall."

"But you deserve the best."

"I *am* getting the best. You are the best."

His expression softened.

She said, "This is about your parents."

"I want them to love you."

"A splashy wedding won't make them love me."

"It would help."

"It's just one day." Well, three, if you counted the wine tasting the day before and a champagne brunch the day following. "Even if they're happy for the wedding, when it's over, they'll go right back to thinking I'm not good enough for their son."

He turned to kiss her palm. His smile grew. He slid the strap of her camisole down her shoulder. "You're the only one for me."

"Say you're sorry you got mad at me for no reason."

"So sorry." He pulled down her pajama bottoms and it felt good to show how much she wanted him. It made her feel powerful to have changed his annoyance—an understandable one—into mutual understanding.

Afterward, he said, "Tell me about the dress."

"That's bad luck."

"Tell me without telling me."

Emily's mother had refused to come to Boston, even though Jack had booked an appointment at the most exclusive bridal shop in Back Bay. He had envisioned her mother helping choose the perfect dress, then the two of them having mimosas at brunch. "That kind of thing is not for me," her mother said over the phone.

"But it would be nice," said Emily.

"For who? You want me to get into a flying tin can and come all the way to La-La Land to help you pick a dress? No thank you."

"La-La Land means Los Angeles."

"I don't need you telling me what things mean. You won't like the dresses I like. It's your wedding. Choose your own dress."

Emily asked Florencia to come to the appointment instead. Emily wasn't sure what was worse, her mother's refusal or that her mother had been right not to come. The sting of both was almost forgotten in her relief to be unburdened by her mother's presence. Florencia gasped dramatically and insisted on seeing the veil. Why had Emily even asked her mother?

"Florencia said I looked like Grace Kelly," Emily told Jack.

"You do," he said in wonder. "Princess Grace. Don't marry a prince in Monaco, Em."

"I won't."

"Don't marry anybody but me."

The reception was large, of course, filled with Jack's extended family and his parents' connections, peppered with Emily's friends from high school and college. Emily was supposed to say hello to everyone individually but was starving. She felt as hollow as an empty vase. She decided to do the bridal duties after dinner. French burbled in the background as servers brought each plate, the food artfully arranged. After dinner—during which Jack's mother made a chilly toast that dwelled on Emily's humble origins in Ohio while forgetting the basic particulars ("She grew up in the middle of nowhere in Iowa") and showcased Emily's academic success in order to dismiss it ("Of course her greatest accomplishment was stealing my son's heart")—Jack kissed Emily's cheek. Then the clinking of spoons against crystal invited him to kiss her deeply on the mouth. He murmured in her ear that he needed to make his rounds. Maybe she should do hers?

She agreed, and without meaning it to be a lie, slipped instead out of the castle and onto the grounds. She was alone except for a crew setting the dance floor into place on the grass. Insects sizzled loudly in the plum dusk. Emily expected to see fireflies but there were none. They weren't common in France. It surprised her that a country that appeared to have everything desirable could lack what she had always had. Ohio summers were full of fireflies. She missed them: their intermittent light, their unmappable movements, their ignorance; they didn't know that humans watched them, or found them pretty, nor did they care.

Her bare shoulders felt cold. A violinist tuned his instrument. Another joined him. She reached into her pocket and touched the rigid paper there. She remembered its printed words, its image. She would have taken it out and looked at it in the fading light, but was glad that she didn't, because someone said her name, the voice immediately recognizable.

It was as if, by thinking of her, Emily had conjured Gen Hall.

"I didn't mean to startle you." Gen's large eyes were darker than usual under the deepening sky. She bit her lip in an apologetic grimace and rubbed the back of her neck. Her light brown hair had been cut since Emily saw her last. If it hadn't been tied back into a short ponytail, it would have barely brushed the shoulders of Gen's rumpled suit. She wore sneakers. Her white shirt was unbuttoned low. This was before Gen became famous, her careless look iconic. "You're not speaking, Emily. Are you mad I came? You invited me."

"I didn't think—"

"Oh, I know, me neither. But I wanted to be here for you. Your big day."

"I didn't see you earlier. Not at the wedding. The dinner." Emily remembered—rapidly, horribly—every public moment of the procession, the vows, Jack's possessive kiss.

Gen widened her eyes in what could have passed for amusement but had a harder quality. "You have a lot of guests. I'm easy to miss."

A woman emerged from the glowing lantern of the castle and picked her way in heels toward them across the gravel. The violins played the opening melody of a piece that was familiar and should have been easy to name. Gen smiled at the approaching woman, whose soft features and slim mouth were happy, her black eyes shining. Gen introduced her as Maiko, her girlfriend. Maiko slid an arm around Gen's waist, inside Gen's suit jacket, and offered the other hand to Emily. Maiko's hand was warm, which let Emily know that her own was freezing. Maiko's black hair was buzzed close to the head in a way that made her beauty inevitable, incontrovertibly real, as though Emily were made of plastic: the painted bride topper on the wedding cake.

"I came because I wanted to wish you well," Gen told Emily.

"Congratulations!" Maiko said.

To Emily, Gen said, "Don't you wish me well, too?"

Maiko nudged Gen. "Of course she does."

What had Emily expected when she had mailed the invitation? At the time, she had been hopeful, and had thought that she wanted to revive their friendship. Now she recognized her self-deceit. She and Gen had never really been friends. They had wanted each other too much. Emily loved Jack, but it wasn't as simple as what she had had with Gen, which felt long ago yet fresh at the same time: Gen's mouth, her accurate hands, the way her mind challenged Emily's, the easy collaboration of their conversation. And being with Jack wasn't as complicated as it had been to love Gen. Emily knew—she couldn't forget—that she had hurt Gen the night Emily's father had taken them to dinner, that summer after graduating from high school. Emily's father had been cruel to Gen. Emily had let him. She hadn't known, before then, how useless apology could be. She hadn't known how useless forgiveness could be, because Gen did forgive her, or had said that she did. And it seemed that she *had*, until Gen visited her at college. Gen spent one night in Emily's dorm room, their bodies crammed eagerly against each other in the narrow bed. Then Gen packed her things and left.

Standing on the gravel, the castle behind her, Maiko at her side, Gen waited for an answer to a question Emily had almost forgotten. Did she wish Gen well? "You know that I do," Emily said, and it was achingly true.

Late morning light varnished the interior of the castle's carriage house. Emily stood at the window, studying the far-off collection of antique biplanes parked near the vineyard.

Jack stirred in the bed, finally awake. He reached to the floor for Emily's wedding dress and frowned when something unseen crackled between his fingers, an object hidden amid the white folds. Eyes blurry from sleep, he searched through the tulle and silk to find what had made that sound. He reached into the dress's pocket. "What's this doing here?"

"It's nothing," Emily said, and took the packet of marigold seeds from him.

7

I've been patient
I said I was sorry
I've been a jerk but it would help if you acknowledged your own part in this

Texts from Jack came multiple times a day, buzzing Emily's back pocket as she tidied the studio, shopped for groceries, and dropped the kids off at their private school, avoiding the other moms, who probably already knew about Jack and Emily's separation. Jack's texts were more error-free than most people's. He always used spell-check after dictation; many times she had watched, her chest tight with loving compassion, as he corrected texts so that no one would see traces of his dyslexia. Even when another partner at his hedge fund sent messages that made Jack throw his phone against a wall, he would pick up the phone, brush it off, and craft a careful response. He used to ask Emily to check his outgoing messages and emails, but that had been earlier in their marriage, before the one time that Emily had offered before being asked and was told, "What makes you think I need your help?"

Emily's phone buzzed again.

I love you
I miss you
Em, please
Come home

It's been a month. Aren't you tired of living in that little shithole
I want to see the kids
You can't keep me from my children
Don't ignore me
You are my wife
You are my everything
My heart is always on my sleeve for you
How can you throw our life away
I bet your happy now
I'm alone and sad just like you wanted
Are the kids ok
I miss them
They need there father
Can I see them this weekend
Can I see them next weekend
Call me
Call me
Drop them off at our house Saturday morning at 10 am or my lawyer will fucking make you

When Connor was born, he had trouble nursing. He latched badly, and Emily's nipples cracked and bled. He didn't gain much weight during those first weeks. Jack weighed him every day in a gold-trimmed porcelain cake pan balanced on a baking scale. Connor's pediatrician blamed Emily's milk flow and told her to pump after every feeding to boost her supply. "That's eight times a day," Emily said, stunned, close to panic. "Every three hours." She had already tried pumping, which required at least another half hour to get a few milliliters of milk. Pumping hurt even more than breastfeeding. "I can't."

The pediatrician said, "Don't you want your baby to thrive?"

Emily suggested formula to Jack.

"But milk is best," he said.

"If we bottle-fed him, you could take a turn."

"I'm already holding down the fort, Em. I have to be able to work, and to work I need sleep. We can't both be out of commission. Otherwise, I can't take care of you."

Emily's breasts were rocks, her nipples points of fire. She didn't think she'd had more than two consecutive hours of sleep. "What about one bottle of formula during the night? We could hire a night nurse."

Jack—bewildered, disappointed, yet with the expression of someone trying to be gentle—said, "I thought you wanted to be a mother."

Connor was always too skinny, from his infancy to when he was a toddler, stick-legged like a lamb. He was little different as a ten-year-old sitting on the studio floor, body hunched and thin. He slowly ate pasta while his sister, five years younger yet weighing as much as him, asked for more. "I miss Daddy," Stella said. "What is he eating? Where is he being?"

"He's at home," Connor said.

"I miss home. I'm bored of sitting crisscross applesauce on the floor. I'm bored with this old place. It was fun but now it's boring. It's not like camping. You said it was like camping but it's not."

"I miss him, too," Connor said. When Emily brought their empty plates to the sink, he followed her, silent and anxious. He touched her elbow and said, "Is it my fault?"

The first contraction of his birth had made Emily seize Jack's arm. She told Jack that she was frightened. He brushed hair from her sweaty brow and told her not to be. They had the best doctor, the best hospital. Everything was going to be fine. She would have a safe delivery.

No, that wasn't the problem. Panic rolled over her flesh. She wasn't ready. She couldn't do it. Another contraction stole her breath. When the pain lessened, she said, ashamed, "I don't know how to be a good mother."

He had heard this worry before and reassured her again. He said that he knew how she had been raised and it wasn't going to be like that, not with their baby. Emily was not her mother. "You will love our baby so much," he said. "Trust me. You will do anything for him."

Connor was born and Jack's promise came true. It was true when she heard Connor's first cry, true when he was given to her, small and warm. It was true now as he looked up at her in the studio's kitchen. "No," she said, and hugged him, wishing that he were an infant again so she could hold his entire body and make him feel the safety she had seen on his face when he slept in her arms. "None of this is your fault."

She didn't want the children to be with Jack. But she also didn't want Connor to believe that he was the source of the problem. She had to make a choice. There were no good choices. She waited until Connor and Stella fell asleep. In the darkness, she texted Jack and said that Saturday morning would be fine.

Let me tell you about New York in the fall, she imagined writing to Gen after she dropped off the kids with Jack, who waited for her to come inside and, when she didn't, said, "Let's be adults about this, Em." He said this in front of the children, who had leapt at him, hugging whichever limb was closest. Emily wanted everything to be normal for Connor and Stella, so she came inside the house. She could smell freshly baked banana bread. The kids did, too. They hurtled down the hall toward the kitchen.

"Stay," Jack said to Emily, voice soft. "Please."

It was strange to be home yet not be home. It felt like she wasn't really there, as though she had become a flat image of herself, painted onto one of the transparency sheets used with overhead projectors in high school, the sheer copy of her face cast upon the walls of her foyer, upon Jack's face.

I told him I would pick the kids up tonight, Emily wrote to Gen in her mind. Then I shut the door behind me. I walked south. Orange leaves fanned out on the sidewalk. A ginkgo dripped yellow.

I didn't say goodbye to Connor and Stella because it felt like I had cut my heart out of my chest. How do you speak after that? I walked all the way downtown. I passed delis with their flowers lined up outside in buckets. I watched a man talk into his cellphone and remembered how, in college, when cellphones became somewhat common but not very, it was unnerving to see someone walk alone, talking to the air. For a second, I'd wonder if the person was crazy. Now, when everyone uses their phone to optimize everything, and a walk means time to make calls, it's rarer to see someone walk in silence like I'm doing, and I only appear to be doing that, since inside I am talking, and I am talking with you.

This is different from the beginning of freshman year at college, when I would write real paper letters filled with my new life. There is a museum of glass flowers here on campus. I went to Walden Pond. I am learning Latin. I am better at Greek. I miss you, I would write. When will you be here, when will I see you? I folded the pages, I stamped the thick envelopes.

Now you are unreachable. You're not the sort of person whose address can be found in the phone book, even if phone books still existed. I have seen you in magazines. On television. I stared at you—how you had changed, how you had remained the same.

At the end of freshman year, for months after you left, I wrote letters that I stacked like a mason, one on top of the other, my anger an invisible mortar. I had no intention of sending them. I would keep them for myself. Why should you get to know what they contained? Even the ordinary things, like how one day I hated coffee. It tasted like burnt wood. All of a sudden. I never drank it again. I wrote that down, but I mailed nothing. Did I say anger? I meant hurt. But it was a plan, anyway: the pencil, the paper, the hoard of words I refused to share. Now I don't have any plans. I don't know what I am doing. I don't know what to do.

Washington Square isn't far from the studio. My feet hurt. But I don't want to stop walking. If I do, I will think about Connor and Stella eating banana bread. But it's just for the day. I will see them tonight. I pass through Washington Square's arch and watch the park's dusty brown squirrels. Connor carries almonds for them in his pockets. Once, a squirrel touched his knee with its paw.

I left the park and entered my new building. I dumped my keys on the studio floor and when my phone buzzed with a text from Jack, I sank down next to my keys and closed my hot eyes, fists pressed against them. C+S want to stay the weekend, Jack had texted. I'll bring them to school Monday. We are making mini burgers! Come join us.

I nearly called him. Instead, I called Jocelyn.

"Emily, calm down," she said. "Be reasonable. He hasn't seen his kids in a month. You can survive a weekend without them. Unless you *do* want to go home."

"I can't."

"Then come to my place. I'm having a party. A fundraiser. It will distract you." Her fundraisers for charity are legendary, attended by celebrities invited to make the party more exciting for donors. "Put on a dress. Put on some lipstick. Pull yourself together."

I should have known. I should have asked about the guest list. I should have guessed that when I entered the parlor, more than eleven years since we last spoke, fifteen years since we last touched, I would look straight through the crowd and see you.

8

They say you're really smart," Gen said as they ran along a harvested cornfield with its yellow lines of cropped stalks. It was small, like many farms were in Washford, close to the foothills of the Appalachian Mountains. Emily didn't reply to Gen because she needed all of her breath to keep up. Gen nodded at the field. "Looks like a poem."

Emily gave her a sidelong look, unsure what she meant.

"Because of the lines," Gen said. "Each field is a big stanza."

Oh, so its shape. Emily liked that. Unbelievably, Gen increased the pace. Gen said, "They say you're going to an Ivy. That you'll be valedictorian." Emily huffed, cutting the air with a dismissive hand. Maybe she'd be valedictorian, but the best colleges turned down many valedictorians every year. Their admissions boards didn't necessarily want valedictorians. They wanted something special. Gen said, "They say you're obsessed with Greek stuff."

Emily stopped, chest heaving as she bent to brace her hands on her knees. "Why"—the words came between gulps of air—"are you talking with people about me?"

"I'm not talking, I'm listening. I'm curious."

"Why?"

"You want hard things."

"I don't think of them as hard." At least, not things related to school. Emily had discovered that school was easy as long as she paid attention. It felt good never to be confused. There were clear expectations and she met them. She enjoyed staying after school in the library, where it was warm and brightly lit and the librarian always asked if she needed anything. But it was true that Emily wanted hard things. She wanted to leave home and go far away.

"I want hard things, too," Gen said. No one talked like Gen talked. She made Emily feel like an egg without its shell. It concerned Emily that Gen was going around talking like this: immediately intimate, as though it were normal to ask personal questions and make personal comments. No wonder Gen was a loner. People at school gave her a wide berth. Emily was breathless. "Please," she said. "You're going too fast."

"Sorry. Want to walk?"

"Yes."

"Not too long, or you won't want to run again."

A car passed as they walked. Then a trailer with horses. A stray bit of straw flew from one of the open windows and darted around in the trailer's wake.

"So what's up with you and ancient Greece?" Gen said.

No one had ever asked. Emily's fascination had begun with reading myths; as a child she'd been unable to look away from the page. She had traced illustrations of Pegasus and Hydra. She didn't know, then, the word *etiology*, how it meant a story of origin, one that explained the existence of a rainbow or spider, but even though she didn't know the word she had taken comfort in the idea that everything came from something, that a spider had once been a girl who liked to weave. This is why there is a moon, that is why there is a sun. She explained this to Gen, and said that she liked how far away in time ancient Greece was, that its culture survived in ruins, its lyric poetry in fragments. She liked the incomplete nature of her understanding, because she could imagine what she didn't know, and she wasn't the only one who didn't know. Even experts didn't. The uncertainty was true for everyone alive, so it was okay for Emily to guess.

Gen listened. She didn't suggest that they run again. The sun struck Gen's shoulders and flung a long shadow behind her. In the east, the mountains were a bank of fog. "What do you guess?"

"That reality was different then. Special. Wouldn't it be, if you believed anything could be a god in disguise?"

"Maybe they didn't actually believe in gods. Maybe the myths were just stories, even to them."

"Maybe," Emily said happily. This was what she loved: that Gen didn't know any better than Emily, and Emily no better than Gen.

"Do you think I could graduate in the spring?"

Emily—tentative yet feeling that she *could* ask, because Gen was so ready to ask anything—said, "Why are you a year behind?"

"There was a custody battle."

"Oh," Emily said as if she understood, when she didn't.

"My gran won. I was out of school for a while." Gen kept her gaze on the mountains. "I want to catch up. I want to graduate when you're graduating."

Emily felt something delicate move inside her, as small as the straw flown from the horse trailer's window, lifted by the wind. "I could help you," she said.

"You could?"

The silence of her house was stale and familiar. Emily didn't expect her mother to be home and she wasn't, though Emily saw signs of her existence: a coffee mug on the table, a terrycloth robe spread over the couch in a shape that made it look almost like a person, as though Emily's mother had finished watching TV, unbelted the robe where she sat, and stepped right out of it. Emily pulled her sweaty, cold hair into a tighter ponytail and poured an enormous glass of water. She had run so much that she felt shaky.

The light on the answering machine blinked. "Hey, Ladybug," her father's voice said. "I want to take you out to dinner tonight. Ask your mom and give me a call, okay?" Emily felt a leap of excitement at this rare invitation. When her parents divorced, her father had said that nothing would change his love for her. He would see her lots. Eight years old, she had reported this immediately to her mother, who said, "We'll see."

Emily called him. "There's my girl," he said. "Did your mom say yes?"

"She's at work." Emily's mother was a registered nurse whose schedule was a mystery. She had a beeper but Emily hadn't used the number since she was small and woke in the middle of the night to discover that the house was empty. Her mother called back to say that the beeper was for emergencies only.

"I'll pick you up in an hour," her father said.

She wore a pink and white dress that he had given her last year and she hadn't quite outgrown. Her long hair, still damp from the shower, was brushed straight, though it would buckle into waves once dry. She had used a little strawberry lip gloss. He liked her to look pretty and she was always proud when he said that she did. He opened the restaurant door for her and asked the waitress to bring an extra basket of breadsticks. Emily didn't like them as much as when she was little but ate two while they waited for their pasta.

Her father carried the conversation easily. His real estate agency was doing well, especially now that he was handling commercial properties as well as residential, and his church, the United Methodist church on Sycamore Street, had appointed him chairman of the Vision Board, and she knew what an honor that was. She nodded, pretending a comfortable inclusion in all this, a skill that she didn't realize until years later *was* a skill, one that allowed time for her to catch up on what other people knew before they understood that she didn't. She ate her pasta. She had ordered alfredo out of concern for the dress, though staining it wouldn't really matter because it was already tight around her ribs and she would outgrow it soon. He told her how much he had missed her, how hard it was to get away. But he always thought about her. Every day. Emily's stepmother and half sisters were away, he explained. Denise had pulled the girls out of school for a long weekend at her parents' home in Florida. "Just paradise down there." He ran a hand through his sandy-colored hair, a favorite gesture of his that drew attention to how thick it was. "I would have loved to go, but work, you know? Gotta take care of my family." He smiled, which meant that he meant her, and child support. "One day I'll take you on a trip. Just you and me. What do you think of that?"

"Great," she said, but saw that she had disappointed him by not expressing the excitement she usually did when he proposed something. What he proposed rarely manifested, though he always meant what he said while he was saying it. *I owe you one,* he would tell her later when what he had imagined unraveled. He'd shake his head, so sad that she knew he did miss her, which always made her feel guilty for having doubted it. Still, she had the sense that she was easy for him to forget, that she needed to work harder to hold his attention. That she wasn't a room he wanted to spend time in but a hallway to a different, better room.

"Of course, you have school," he said, "so a trip would be hard to pull off."

Emily sipped her Coke. Its bubbles were harsh.

"Everything good at school?"

"Definitely." Her father appreciated positive language. He once told her that whenever his boss asked him to do something, he said *absolutely*.

"Any boys I need to scare away?"

"Dad."

"Is that a yes?"

"I'm too busy."

"Smart cookie." He cut into his steak. "So what's new? I haven't seen you in forever." He looked happy, and Emily understood that he expected her to feed his happiness, so she chatted about Kim and Meredith and prepping for the SATs, how she wanted a scholarship (she *needed* one, but didn't use that word, out of care for his pride), and that she didn't like AP Chemistry as much as she had liked AP Bio. She didn't mention Gen, though her limbs still felt loose and buzzy from the run; she would be sore later. At first Emily thought that not talking about Gen was a harmless, invisible rebellion, a decision to keep one thing private when he wanted to be the kind of father whose daughter told him everything. But as Emily talked about track and said nothing of Gen, she realized that her father wouldn't want to hear about Gen, that something about Gen would invite his disapproval—maybe the obvious poverty to her appearance, or that Gen was too skinny, too tall, too angular, too odd. He wouldn't like it if Emily liked Gen . . . and she did.

There was that feeling again: light and quick as wind-borne straw, a golden stem that flicked around inside Emily's chest as she reached for her icy glass and thought about how she would see Gen the next day.

9

Would you go to space?"

Emily wrapped the phone cord around her finger. "I've never even been on a plane."

"Let's say you are guaranteed to come back alive. But it will change you. Astronauts say that it does: to see the Earth from far away. It does something to your brain. You'll come back but you'll be always different."

"From everyone else, or from who I used to be?"

"Both."

"But I would see the moon."

"You would see the moon."

"And the Earth. And come back alive."

"Yes."

"Okay. I'll go to space."

"Me too," Gen said. "Let's study today." They had fallen into a rhythm in the past month: afternoons in the school library, then a run. Emily was running faster and longer than ever, but Gen still beat everyone on the team and at all the intermural competitions against other Ohio teams. Sometimes Emily and Gen studied while they ran, though that made Emily crazy because she liked having paper and a pencil and Gen didn't care where they were or how they talked about the helical structure of DNA or logarithmic functions. Gen could hold a lot in her head and had a talent for responding to a question in a way that made it larger than what it was asking.

Emily had taken Gen to the guidance counselor and explained

their idea: Gen could graduate in the spring by doing two years of classes in one. She would attend half of each class and get notes about what she missed. The guidance counselor said that was impossible, but Emily had made Gen take a practice SAT, and when she showed the counselor Gen's score and he reviewed her grades, he decided that the plan was possible and that Gen should apply for college. Outside his office, Gen looked worried when Emily thought she'd be glad. Gen confessed that she hadn't considered college, only graduating. But Gen could get into college, she could go somewhere good, Emily knew it. "I want to go somewhere free," Gen finally said, and wouldn't hear about loans. Emily gave Gen her notebooks from junior year and talked with her senior-year teachers, who didn't mind the unusual arrangement of Gen coming in and out of class as long as she kept up, which she did.

"I can't study today," Emily said. It was the weekend. "I have to work."

"Want to come over after?"

Emily had never been to Gen's home. She imagined Gen's room, the color of the walls, the bedspread. She suspected that Gen was messy. She imagined Gen on an unmade bed, one arm beneath her head, phone held against her cheek, long legs stretched out and crossed at the ankles. Emily immediately wanted to go to Gen's house, before remembering that she didn't know where Gen lived. Emily wasn't sure how she'd get there without a car. She had her license but there had never been a discussion about whether she could use her mother's car. Emily worked at IHOP because it was walking distance from her house.

"I'll pick you up," said Gen. "I'm a great driver. I learned when I was twelve."

"Twelve?"

"The perks of living on a farm. You can drive pretty far without crashing into anything."

"What about cows?"

"No cows. Corn and soybeans. But the crops aren't ours. My gran rents out the land."

"Not even chickens?"

“Yes, we have chickens.” Gen sounded amused. “I’ll show you the chickens. I’ll show you my favorite place, if you come.”

“I already said yes.”

“I don’t think you did.”

“Yes.”

“Great.”

“Hey, Gen.”

“Hey, what?”

“Who’s the sun and who’s the moon?”

“What?”

“You and me. Which one’s the sun and which one’s the moon?”

“I’m the sun,” Gen said promptly. “You’re the moon.”

“You’re right,” said Emily, pleased.

“I know.”

“How do you know?”

“I just do.”

The clapboard farmhouse’s white paint was dingy. From a distance, it looked like a scrap of frayed cloth. When Gen parked the pickup truck, three large dogs nosed their way out the screen door to weave around Gen’s legs. They jumped up and planted paws on her thighs, muddying her jeans. The porch had an uncertain, collapsible shape. Inside, the wooden floors had a dull gleam and smelled of orange oil, and the furniture’s upholstery was covered in clear vinyl. Gen’s grandmother, Nella, exclaimed over Emily as if she were a child and served her a glass of milk and fudge-striped cookies. The clock on the kitchen wall was enormous and ticked loudly. Nella was tiny and gray-haired, but younger than Emily would have thought, with a straight back and a warm snap of a smile.

“Gran, sit down.”

“Why should I? *You* are not sitting down. Be a good girl, like your friend, and sit at the table.”

“I’m making sandwiches,” Gen said.

Nella’s expression, as she placed her palms against Gen’s cheeks and gazed up at her, held such affection that it clutched at the loneliness inside Emily. “Let me,” Nella said, and Emily thought, *Let her, let her*. Emily found that she couldn't look at the two of them anymore. It felt like being in space. It felt like looking at the whole Earth, green and blue, and not being on it.

A dog's head rested on Emily's foot. From the kitchen doorway came the sounds of Nella watching *Wheel of Fortune* in the living room. Emily was reading about the Treaty of Villafranca and taking notes, hand cramped. Gen had her American history textbook open on the Formica table, but glanced up when Emily shook out her aching hand. "Who's the match and who's the lighter?" Gen said.

"I'm the match."

"Wrong."

"I'm not a *lighter*."

"Don't be mad! Not a *Bic* lighter. A nice one. An old-timey one. Classy."

"Fine, I'll be the lighter." The clock ticked. It was late. "You said you were going to show me your favorite place."

"It's too dark."

"You said."

"It's better in the light."

"Promises, promises," Emily teased, but Gen didn't smile. She looked anxious, lower lip bitten. Emily said, "You don't have to."

"I wanted to," Gen said quietly.

"You can show me another time." Emily added, "This is a great place to study."

"Not too loud?" Gen glanced toward the living room. Televised applause rose and fell like the long pulse of cicadas.

"It's nice." Emily rubbed her tired hand. Gen lifted hers, and for a moment Emily thought that Gen might touch her. Gen's hand dropped back to the book, but Emily saw, as though it were really happening, how Gen might have reached across the table to take Emily's hand and rub a thumb into the spot that was sore.

10

For Christmas, Emily's mother gave her usual gift: another pearl on Emily's Add-a-Pearl necklace. Housed in a green velvet box, the chain was a delicate gold thread with seventeen pearls gathered in a thin line. Emily gave her mother slippers. They didn't have a tree. Emily's mother had seen little point; she had to work her shift at the hospital later that day and Emily's father had arranged for Emily to go with his family to church in the evening. Emily fastened the necklace carefully and touched the pearls where they lay against her red dress, just below her collarbone and above the swell of her breasts.

"When you were born, I couldn't believe the hospital let me leave with you," Emily's mother said. Emily kept her fingers still against the necklace. She didn't dare move, in case that might make her mother stop speaking. Emily's half sisters had come home from the hospital wearing the same special outfit: a white hand-knitted sweater and a white cap topped with a pompom. Emily had seen pictures. She didn't know what she had worn, or how much she had weighed, or the exact minute she was born. "It felt like I was stealing you," her mother said. "Like an alarm would go off. Now look at you. All grown up."

This didn't feel true yet was said with finality, as though Emily were a completed project. Emily knew that her mother meant this as a compliment, so she thanked her.

In the church lobby, Emily's father asked someone to take a photo of them. "My whole family," he said, smiling at Emily and her half sisters, also dressed in red. Courtney, the younger one, smiled back, but Sara-Lynn, who had a solo to perform that night with the choir, looked pale. They all stood together, pleasant and stiff, until the flash went off. Emily's father promised that when he got the film developed, he'd make copies for her. Denise told Emily how glad she was that Emily could join them, that she had grown into quite the mature young lady. She asked if Emily was interested in babysitting the girls from time to time and Emily said that she was. When Sara-Lynn wasn't looking, Emily's father opened his loose suit jacket to reveal a small bouquet of flowers and winked at Emily. The little girls filed ahead to find seats as Emily whispered to her father and stepmother that she didn't get anything special for Sara-Lynn's solo, just a regular Christmas present, but Denise said not to worry: the flowers were from all of them.

There was a reading from the book of Luke. Emily listened as the angel appeared to shepherds in the field and frightened them. "But the angel said to them, 'Do not be afraid, for see, I am bringing you good news of great joy for all the people.'" Emily felt warm and happy, seated between her father and her youngest sister. She could smell the hidden roses in her father's jacket. Sara-Lynn stood. Denise squeezed Sara-Lynn's hand before the girl made her way with quick steps to the front.

The choir began to sing. Emily braced herself as she recognized the song. She hadn't known the solo would be "O Holy Night" and was upset that such a difficult piece had been given to a child: the exposure of the long phrases, that octave jump. But Sara-Lynn's voice was clear and starry, and Emily felt like one of the shepherds, surrounded by a dark plain. She saw her father's face as he watched his daughter sing—his rapt pride—and Emily understood that while she was a welcome guest, this was another way of being an outsider.

When the solo was over, Emily whispered to her father that she didn't feel well. She slipped out to the lobby, where a long table bearing punch and cookies awaited the congregants. Here, the pastor's voice was muffled by closed doors; she couldn't distinguish the words. On a small table sat a black rotary phone.

Gen picked up. "Hello?"

"Hi."

"Are you okay?"

The receiver was wet with Emily's tears. They slid down her wrist. "Yes."

"Why don't you tell me where you are," Gen said, "and I'll come get you."

Nella made Coca-Cola ham and mac 'n' cheese. The frozen Tater Tots were baked until they were crisp, their insides steaming. Dessert was chocolate box cake topped with frosting that Gen made from scratch. They watched *Rudolph the Red-Nosed Reindeer* and laughed at how the stop-action puppets moved their heads like owls. Nella gave Emily an afghan crocheted in Emily's favorite colors and Gen gave her a wrapped box slightly larger than a shoebox. Emily hadn't gotten gifts for them because she hadn't expected to receive anything, but when she tried, haltingly, to explain this, she was told to be quiet and eat more cake.

She unwrapped Gen's gift while Nella went to make tea. It was a diorama, its box polished wood, showing a mountain made from thick, layered paper that had been soaked, molded, and dried. In front of the mountain stood a tree made from twist ties painted brown, its branches delicate. One branch held a red apple.

"It's Mount Olympus," Gen said. "I wanted to make something ancient Greek-y, to show a myth, but all the stories seemed kind of messed up so I thought this was best."

"You've been reading Ovid. You should try the lyrics instead." *The love poetry*, Emily almost added.

"Hmm," Gen said.

"I can't believe you made this."

"It's a hobby."

"You've made others? Are you going to show me?"

"Sometime," Gen said, "when it's not Christmas. Do you like it?"

"I really, really like it."

Gen asked if she wanted to stay the night and when Emily said yes, Gen looked awkward and asked whether sharing her room was okay. "There are two twin beds. I mean, we have other bedrooms, but the house is old and drafty and my room gets good heat."

In the dark of Gen's room, in their separate beds, they lay silently awake. Emily thought about the diorama. She kept returning to the tree with its one apple. Gen *had* been reading the lyrics, Emily realized. There was a fragment of a poem about an apple that hung too high for anyone to reach. The poem had been written, Emily remembered, by a woman. It had been written by a woman who loved women. Her face grew hot. She was glad it was dark.

"Gen?"

"Yes?"

Emily decided the apple didn't mean anything—or at least she was afraid that Gen would say that it didn't. She abandoned her question and said instead, "Who is the slipper and who is the shoe?"

"I'm the shoe."

Gen believed she was the shoe because she wanted to be resilient, but Emily knew better. Gen was a softness that Emily could slide right into.

Gen said, "Will you tell me what happened tonight?"

Emily shifted in bed so that she was looking into Gen's face even though she couldn't actually see it in the solid dark. She told Gen about the pearl necklace; the roses; the song; the shepherds; the large, shining red planet of the punch bowl in the empty church lobby. Emily said, "I want to be somebody."

"You *are* somebody."

"I want to be somebody people pay attention to."

"*I* pay attention," Gen said.

11

New leaves were bright green froth on the trees when Gen showed her the hayloft. She opened the barn doors wide. The barn, when they first entered it, seemed unexceptional, filled with equipment: a tractor, cultipacker, and plows, a broadcast seeder. Gen named them and showed Emily the milking stalls where cows had once been kept. They climbed the ladder to the hayloft, which did not, in fact, hold hay but was an open room with a table and chairs, as well as a small bed tucked into an alcove and half hidden behind a green velvet curtain held back by a tasseled tie. There was a bookshelf stacked with paperbacks and dioramas, some crude in their design, the work of a child. Emily recognized many of the dioramas' scenes from books, like the streetlamp in the snow from *The Lion, the Witch and the Wardrobe*. A lamp stood next to a recliner, but Gen didn't turn it on. They could see clearly in the borrowed light coming from the open barn doors.

"My mother made this for me." Gen said that her mother believed that every child should have a hideout, a special place, a favorite one, and that her mother had built the furniture. She had been a carpenter until she had gotten hurt on a job and the doctor prescribed a medication that she couldn't stop taking, even after the pills ran out, and that she had to have no matter what. Gen had been in fourth grade. By fifth grade, when Emily met her, Gen was moving from place to place. Gen remembered many strangers. She remembered sleeping in a bathtub. On the floor. Gen hadn't understood what was wrong. The wrongness gradually became normal. Hunger was normal. Sometimes she was okay. Sometimes there was pizza or her mother braided her hair. Sometimes she got to sleep next to her mother, in her arms, and her mother slept very soundly, her face peaceful. Then Gen's grandmother sued for custody. "I'm glad she did," Gen said, "though at first I wasn't. I don't know. Sometimes I'm still mad. It wasn't my mom's fault. The case went on for a long time."

"Because your mom wanted to keep you."

"She died of an overdose the summer before freshman year. It's good that Gran won."

Emily touched Gen's back. When Gen didn't move away, Emily let her palm rest between Gen's shoulder blades.

"I miss her," Gen whispered.

"I think it's important that she wanted to keep you."

"Yes," Gen said eventually. "You're right. It is."

There was a senior trip to Orlando in March. Emily hadn't filled out the forms in the fall because she hadn't wanted to ask her father for money, even though Kim and Meredith were going. Now Emily was glad not to go. She called Gen. "Let's do something."

"What do you want to do?"

"Do you want to go to the mountains?"

"Like, hiking?"

"Maybe camping, too."

"I love that idea."

Emily's mother brought a tent, a camping stove, and sleeping bags up from the basement. "Who's this Gen? I haven't heard you mention her before."

"She's my best friend," Emily said.

The mountain trail was chilly, sunlight falling through the trees in thin shafts, the emerald moss damp. Moisture trickled over rocks although it hadn't rained. They passed a gushing creek. Wildflowers grew in darts of white. Years later, Emily found their name in a book: trillium. It was early in the season, and Emily and Gen were alone on the trail.

They reached a clearing and could see straight across the raw valley. Although Gen said that the preserve must be amazing in fall, she didn't add that they should come back then. They didn't know where they'd be. Letters from colleges would arrive by the end of the month. In November, Emily had offered to help Gen with her applications but Gen had said that she wanted to do them on her own; she wasn't applying to many places anyway. She wanted to stay close to home. Emily had applied widely, and nowhere in-state. She said, "Which one do you want to go to most?"

"The free one, Emily. You keep asking but the answer is always the same."

"You never ask me."

"I know where you're going."

"Come on."

"You'll see."

"I don't want to disappoint you."

"You won't."

They cooked canned soup over the camping stove, facing each other across the small fire. Emily unzipped a sleeping bag and wrapped it around her shoulders. Her heart beat as hard as it had when they were on the steep trail.

"Are you tired?" Gen said.

"No."

"You're really quiet. Like, *weirdly* quiet."

"I want to see you," Emily blurted. "Wherever we are in the fall. We can visit each other."

"I want that, too."

"I want us always to be friends."

When Gen didn't respond, Emily felt sick, sure that she had said something wrong. After a moment, Gen said, "Me too."

What else do you want? Emily wanted to ask. *What else*, she thought as they switched on the lantern and entered the tent. *What else*, as she zipped up her sleeping bag, and Gen zipped up her own, and they lay down next to each other on the cold ground, warmth rising between them. *What else what else*, as their hips nudged against each other. Gen apologized and shifted away.

Maybe Gen wanted nothing. But what Emily wanted spread in her chest, between her legs. She lay there, silent, her body crowded with desire.

12

Harvard wait-listed Emily. Gen was going to Ohio State on a full athletic scholarship. Emily told her every place that had accepted or rejected her, but Gen said nothing more about other schools she might have applied to, only that she had made her decision. While Gen's reticence suggested that her decision hadn't been entirely without conflict, that she might have been tempted in some way or let down in another, Emily didn't ask for details, just tied her sneaker's lace and tied it again, better this time, remembering how this act had once felt like an accomplishment, one that she had believed she must master before going to kindergarten or they wouldn't let her through the doors. She remembered how, as a child, she had fumbled with the laces. Emily wondered whether she would ever again feel that same high pride at an ordinary thing—a double bow, the lace sliding through—or if, each new year of her life, she would confront some version of how she had felt when she had opened Harvard's letter, and what she felt now: a sunburn of disappointment, stinging all over, the heat of having wanted something huge yet seemingly possible—had it ever been possible?—and discovering that it wasn't. So no, she wouldn't ask Gen, because she didn't want to risk making Gen feel the same way. "That's amazing," Emily said.

"Gran can't believe it."

"Free! You always wanted free."

"I hadn't planned on leaving home."

"You don't want to go?"

"It's just confusing. It seemed like a simple thing to want to graduate this spring."

"Not that simple."

"Okay, but it *seemed* that way. But I decided, and then that decision meant other decisions. I didn't expect to go to college. I didn't expect this." She flipped a hand, palm up, toward Emily, then closed it. "I will miss home. I will miss Gran. I will miss you."

Emily looked down the long road. Farmers were out in the fields on each side, putting seed into the ground under a fresh April sun. A friend could miss a friend. That was normal. She thought that people always talked about hope like it was a good thing and no one warned that it could hurt. "I will miss you, too."

"They didn't say no."

Emily didn't want to think about the wait-list. She didn't want to think about Gen. She didn't want to think about anything. "I thought we were going to run. Do you want to run?"

Gen said, "I always want to run," so they did.

The acceptance letter arrived in late May, when the redbud outside Nella's farmhouse was in bloom, a fevered pink. Gen picked Emily up and swung her until they fell on top of each other and the dogs climbed over them, thwacking them with their tails. Nella poured 7UP into champagne glasses. As Emily drank, she felt the memory of Gen's weight on her.

"Well," said Emily's mother when she came home, "don't you look like the cat that caught the canary."

Emily and Gen decided that they should say goodbye to their favorite places in town, so they visited the bronze duck in the park; the hardware store that surreally housed, next to rotary saws, a bakery, its shelves lined with red and white gingham-checked paper; the tracks where freight trains went by, the latched-together railcars so different, with different purposes: gondolas, covered hoppers for grain, center beams for lumber, flatcars, boxcars shut up tight. They went to town hall to see the old-fashioned phone booth with its penny-tiled floor and walnut trim. The black telephone was plastic, its surface softened by use. It had the texture of soapstone. Emily was amazed that plastic could feel nice.

High school ended. The days grew warm enough that when they saw *Legends of the Fall*, which was showing even though it had come out two years before, they stayed in the movie theater to watch it again, for the air-conditioning. End of June was unusually steamy, so that even Gen, who didn't like sweets, craved ice cream. They went to Culver's for sundaes and as soon as they stepped outside into the heat, they went back inside for lemonade to go, with extra ice.

The distant sky was thick with thunderclouds. Gen drove to the farmhouse and into a fallow field so that they could sit in the back of the pickup truck and watch the storm come in. There was no wind.

Gen rattled the ice in her cup, then pressed the cup against her flushed cheek before setting it down on the truck's hot bed. They heard far-off thunder. "I can't believe it. I actually graduated."

"Why did you want to? You didn't *have* to finish high school in three years."

Slowly, Gen said, "I'm not sure I should tell you."

"Gen!"

"I mean it."

"Okay."

"Okay?"

"I don't want to make you tell me."

"I was kind of hoping you'd make me."

"You're impossible."

Gen laughed but it was a nervous laugh. The storm had rolled across the horizon, but the rain hadn't reached them yet. The wind lifted and it felt good. The truck's metal bed baked Emily's thighs beneath her cutoffs. Gen said, "I worry you won't actually want to know."

Gen's nervousness made Emily nervous. "I do."

"Well, to be honest, I didn't care about graduation at first. I just wanted an excuse to talk to you."

"Why?"

The wind blew Gen's hair across her face. She pushed it back. Tentatively, she reached for one of the frayed threads on Emily's shorts. She was careful not to touch Emily's skin but Emily felt as though she had. Gen pulled the thread taut, then tugged on it. She said, "I really like you, Emily."

Emily kissed her. Gen's mouth, fresh and tangy, opened beneath hers. Emily had never kissed anyone, but this was easy, maybe because she had imagined it so many times. Gen's hands went into Emily's hair. The cup of ice spilled, slushing across the flatbed, down their legs, the shock of it a pleasure. Gen said, "Not here," but kept kissing her. Maybe *not here* meant the coming rain or the open field or that the truck sat in view of the house, but Gen didn't say it again. It was as if she had never said it, had never even thought it, when Emily slid a hand up Gen's shirt.

Here became the hayloft, hidden behind the green curtain, fully dressed and sticky in the heat, not daring to take anything off. Emily licked Gen's nipple through Gen's thin T-shirt and the white fabric grew wet and dark. Gen's hands twisted in Emily's hair. She pulled Emily onto her lap, then pushed her thigh up between Emily's legs, denim against denim. The tight contact and grind of Gen's thigh almost hurt, yet felt good, too, though not quite good enough. Emily wanted more. She curled her fingers down into the waistband of Gen's jeans and Gen opened her eyes, the pupils blown so wide that the irises looked black. "Touch me." Gen's words were phrased like an order yet shakily said.

"Are you sure?" Emily said. Gen nodded. Emily undid the button on Gen's shorts.

A call came from the yard. It was Nella, calling them to dinner. The dogs barked. Emily yanked her hand away, face flushed. She ached between her legs. The rain came down suddenly; fat, fast drops splatted against the barn. They drummed the roof as the barking got louder. Emily and Gen broke apart, then clattered down the hayloft's ladder and flung themselves out into the rain. Gen's T-shirt was quickly soaked to the skin, flattened against her small breasts and hard, tight nipples.

They didn't talk much during dinner. Emily felt a constant thrum of desire. She crossed her legs beneath the table, but the ache wouldn't go away. It deepened. She barely listened to what Nella said. Later, she couldn't remember what had been served. Gen asked if Emily could sleep over, and Nella said yes.

The hallway to Gen's room seemed longer than usual—higher, wider. Emily's pace slowed—not because she didn't want to be alone with Gen but because she wanted it too much, and knew that what happened next would change her. She set a hand against the worn wood of the doorframe. Maybe tomorrow she'd find the same burl in the wood's grain, but it would be different, because she would be different.

Gen locked the bedroom door behind them. She kissed Emily hard, driving her toward one of the twin beds, but she still seemed shy. They stood, Emily's calves pressed against the mattress's side. Gen said, "Do you want to stop?"

"Do you?"

Gen shook her head.

"Tell me what to do."

The words erased Gen's hesitation. Emily, though she had imagined this moment before, hadn't guessed the effect of seeing Gen filled with eager purpose, how that would expand Emily's own need, fed by the idea that anything could happen. Gen could do anything to her, require anything of her. Emily sank into a greedy state of anticipation. "Take these off." Gen pushed down at the top of Emily's shorts. Emily helped her, shoving them down, but when she began to do the same with her underwear, Gen stopped her hands. "Not yet. Get on the bed." Gen knelt on the floor. "Will you let me?" When Emily nodded, Gen said, "Lie down."

The bed was so narrow that Emily couldn't lie back fully, but set her shoulder blades against the wall, half reclined . . . and she did not in fact want to lie back, she wanted to see Gen brush her cheek against her knee, to see Gen's mouth as it trailed a wet path up her inner thigh. Gen touched Emily through her underwear, stroking her through the thin fabric. Gen brought Emily's fingers down to feel the damp cotton and then, just when Emily had begun to touch herself the way she had done before, alone in her bedroom, Gen thrust Emily's hand away. Gen pulled the underwear to one side. Emily felt more exposed than if she were fully naked. She felt Gen's breath first, a hot fog. Gen's tongue fluttered against her. Emily pressed a palm over her mouth to mute the sounds she was making. The seams of Emily's underwear dug into her flesh. She vaguely heard Gen telling her to tell her what felt good, but Emily couldn't answer. She came so hard that her body jolted away from Gen's tongue.

"Was it okay?" Gen asked.

Emily hauled Gen up onto the bed and kissed her. Stretched out limply along the mattress's length, Emily laughed, breathy and astonished, then was quick to explain how good it had been. "That wasn't what I meant when I asked you to tell me what to do."

Gen flushed. "Maybe you don't want to."

"I want to make you feel how you made me feel."

Gen straddled Emily's hips and unzipped her shorts. She pushed Emily's hand down past the waistband so that her fingers skidded into the fluid heat between Gen's legs. "Touch me here." Emily obeyed, finding the pressure Gen liked best until her fingers were working quickly and Gen bumped against them in an irregular rhythm. Emily rose up onto her own knees for better purchase. Gen had one hand in Emily's hair and one clamped hard over Emily's wrist when she shuddered. She pushed Emily's fingers inside her. Emily slid in and out as Gen came.

Emily didn't know how late it was when they finally stopped and got under the quilt, Gen's breasts soft against Emily's back as Gen held her, their bodies knit together. Somewhere outside, an owl hooted, its tones rich and hollow. Hunting, maybe. Mice scrambled under the corn. Emily closed her eyes. Gen drew her closer.

Emily learned, as everyone does, that happiness is often colored by worry or set-aside grief, even in the moment of happiness. It is rarely pure. But what Emily felt that summer, until the end of it, came close. It was the kind of happiness whose only worry is the loss of that happiness.

13

Emily's father wanted to take her out for a family dinner to celebrate her eighteenth birthday. "Why don't you invite Kim or Meredith? Make it more fun."

Maybe it was the sullen August heat or because Emily hadn't seen him since Christmas, but although she sensed that he wanted her to say she'd have more fun with just him and his family, the sound of his jovial voice on the phone provoked her. It made her seek to thwart him by choosing what she wanted instead. "Can I take my friend Gen?"

"Haven't heard that name before."

"Can I?"

"Sure, I suppose. Tell her to bring her parents, too, why don't you, so that Denise and I will have someone to socialize with, since I bet you kids won't want to chat with us old folks."

"Gen lives with her grandmother."

"Huh," said her father. "Well, okay."

Gen, sitting in the hayloft's recliner, eyed Emily warily. "What am I supposed to wear?"

"Whatever you want."

Gen pressed her knuckles against her mouth, winced, then opened her hand with a flourish that indicated skeptical, yet good-humored, surrender.

"You could borrow one of my dresses."

"Nope." Gen smiled. "But maybe you should, you know, remind me how they work." She touched the hem of Emily's sundress. "For example: buttons. What do you do with all these buttons?" Gen undid them, one by one, from the bottom up.

They went to a restaurant with an all-you-can-eat buffet because Sara-Lynn and Courtney loved getting multiple desserts. The little girls sat on either side of Denise, well-behaved as they ate, though their expressions held compressed impatience when their mother said that they needed to finish their vegetables before they could have ice cream. They did as they were told, then went to the buffet on the far side of the restaurant and returned with their first round of dessert.

Denise told Nella how much she admired her earrings, which were small, gold drops. Nella said that they had been a gift from her father to her mother for their golden anniversary. "You can't get things like that anymore," Denise said. "That quality. Such a sweet tradition. We gave each other themed gifts for the first few years, didn't we, Phil, but gave up around leather or wood or—what was it? Copper?"

"I get you gifts," said Emily's father, irritated.

"Of course you do. Just not *themed* ones, is all I meant." To Nella, Denise said, "Fifty years of marriage! Your father must have been proud to see your mother wear those earrings."

"I don't know," Nella said. "I think he wished they were real gold."

"Oh."

"She loved them, though."

"Well, they are beautiful."

"They are indeed."

Gen, across from Emily and next to her grandmother, shifted in her seat. Gen's silence seemed watchful. She had, in the end, chosen to wear suit pants and a white, ironed, button-down shirt. Her light brown hair, which Emily had never seen fully loose before, was longer than she had realized and brushed to a shine. Denise asked her where she was going to college and Gen told her, but the answer was cut short when Emily's father set down his fork and said, "I want more chicken. Emily, don't you?"

Dread flashed across Emily's chest. Unsure of what was coming, yet worried that it would be worse if she didn't obey, she joined him at the buffet. Rectangular piles of meat and vegetables steamed. The stiff green beans were cut at sharp angles.

He said, "I don't like how she looks at you."

"What?" But she knew exactly what he meant.

"This was supposed to be a nice dinner. Your sisters are here. You couldn't think for one moment about them and the example you set?" He tossed the tongs onto the pile of chicken, then must have seen the panic on Emily's face, because he said, his manner softened, "Oh, Ladybug. You're so young. You didn't know about her, did you?"

After an awful moment, Emily nodded, then saw that what had taken all her courage to admit was misinterpreted as the answer her father had wanted. His relief was plain. Yes, Emily didn't know. Of course not. How could she? A thing like that. Although Emily had been nervous when she had nodded, she realized only now, when she saw her father's open disgust for Gen and his relieved belief that his disgust needn't include his daughter, that she had hoped that her simple nod—yes, I knew—would change her father's anger to understanding. Yes, I know, and I'm like her, Emily could have said after she nodded. Then his disgust would disappear, because he loved her. He would think differently, for her sake.

But he didn't. He wouldn't. She was ashamed.

"You had me worried," he said. "Maybe I shouldn't have said something. But you've got to know about the world sometime, the way that it is." He led the way back to the table, where Emily, empty-handed, realized she hadn't taken her plate with her to the buffet.

"So, Gen." Her father's expression indicated that he had decided to be polite and weather the situation, yet resented his decision. "You're going to Ohio State on a full ride."

"That's right."

"On an athletic scholarship."

"Yes, for track."

"Seems you beat everyone, don't you? Everyone on the team, even the whole state. You must be pretty fast."

"I guess."

Nella said, "She doesn't like to brag."

He said, "It must be easier for girls like you to win."

Emily was filled with fear. It was exactly as if someone had poured a pitcher of it into her, right up to the crown of her head. She didn't know how to stop what was about to happen. No—that wasn't true. She knew. She could interrupt, draw attention to herself. Change the subject. Or tell her father to stop, just stop, shut up, shut up. But Emily said nothing. She wanted to hide, even if that meant leaving Gen exposed.

"Girls like me?" Gen said.

"You know." His tone was conspiratorial. It could even be mistaken as friendly. Gen drank from her water glass, and for a moment Emily thought that her father would say nothing more and everything might still be okay. He said, "Girls with a bit of boy in them."

At first, Nella looked confused. Emily saw the moment when Nella shifted from not knowing about Gen to knowing, and to knowing about Emily, too.

Gen set down her glass. It was the first time Emily had seen her angry. Gen's gaze flitted sideways to her grandmother, then to her own hand on the glass. She released it and her fingers wobbled for a moment before she placed her palm flat against the table. "You mean I win because I'm gay."

"I didn't say—"

"The fact that I'm gay has nothing to do with it. I win because I'm good."

Silence spread like cold water.

"I'm sure that this is not an appropriate topic for conversation." Denise looked meaningfully at Sara-Lynn and Courtney, who had progressed from ice cream to cake.

"No, it is not," said Emily's father.

Gen looked at her grandmother, eyes anxious. Emily's fear compounded: she felt Gen's fear now as well as her own. Emily pressed her mouth shut. She wanted to protect Gen, but wanted more to protect herself. She hadn't known before how it felt to betray someone.

Nella placed her hand over Gen's and held it, the gesture gentle and firm—steadying, as though helping Gen find her balance. "I want to make a toast." Nella raised her glass. "To my granddaughter. I love you. I love everything about you. I am so proud."

Then she said that she was tired and wanted Gen to take her home.

—

Emily saw her mother's car in the driveway when her father dropped her off. Her mother's bedroom door was shut. She took her mother's keys.

—

Maybe Gen had seen her drive up, headlights cutting across the high corn. Gen sat on the porch, waiting, the farmhouse windows lit behind her.

"Can I come inside?" Emily said.

"I don't know."

"Can we talk?"

"What do you want to say? Are you here to break up with me?"

"No! Gen, I'm really sorry."

"I'm not sure—"

"Please." *I'm not sure that's good enough*. "Don't."

"I felt really alone. Like you weren't even there."

"If my dad knew, he wouldn't love me anymore."

Gen rubbed her eyes. She looked tired, her long frame hunched, elbows propped on her knees. Emily wanted to say, *You're not being fair*, because even with her keen sense of fault, she was jealous of Gen: that toast, Nella's glass lifted in the air.

"That was awful," Gen said, then added slowly, "but it was awful for you, too. It makes me sad."

"Are we okay, you and me?"

"Yes," Gen said, and Emily believed her—out of need and because, at least then, Gen seemed to mean it. "We are."

14

Emily's mother drove her to Massachusetts, the trunk full of Emily's things. Her mother had worked overtime at the hospital for much of August, even though it was Emily's last month before leaving home. At summer's end, her mother told Emily to make a list of everything she wanted for her dorm room. "Pick whatever you want," her mother said. "I can afford it." Emily had wanted to hug her but her mother wasn't the hugging type. Instead, they went shopping at Walmart, where Emily, despite her mother's words, was careful with her choices.

They woke up at four in the morning for an early start on the long drive. At dawn they reached Lake Erie, where the sky over the water was a soft pink. They didn't stop except for lunch at a Perkins in Pennsylvania. The Allegheny Mountains sloped around them. Emily's mother was a silent driver who refused to let Emily take a turn at the wheel.

She greeted Emily's roommate with suspicion, as though Florencia's cheer was proof of mockery. She wouldn't stay to help Emily unpack; the drive home lay ahead. Emily was so used to her mother's icy efficiency that she recalled only belatedly how odd it was to other people. Florencia, usually well liked, looked puzzled by Emily's mother—a puzzlement that was, Emily would later learn, as close as Florencia got to awkwardness. Emily and Florencia's suite was composed of two rooms joined together. Florencia explained that this kind of suite—a bedroom attached to a common room that opened onto the hall—used to be meant for one student. Florencia said that she didn't mind taking the common room. She would probably be in and out a lot, and Emily struck her as a quiet type who probably liked her own space. Emily's mother looked at Florencia like she was nuts. "You *want* the room people are gonna walk through, waking you up?" Emily's mother asked Florencia.

"We can switch midyear," Emily said hastily.

"I don't get you," Emily's mother said. "Neither one of you."

Florencia excused herself, saying that she needed to speak with someone down the hall.

Emily's mother brushed her palms together, the gesture of someone whose work was done. Before she left, she told Emily that she ought to know something. "Your father called me, soon after your birthday. He said he didn't approve of that Gen."

"Why? What did he say?"

"Just that if I knew what was good for you, I'd put a stop to you seeing her."

But her mother hadn't, nor had she said anything about Emily taking the car that night. Emily had believed that her mother hadn't noticed that the keys or the car had ever left their places. Now Emily wasn't so sure.

She gave Emily a satisfied grin. "I told him that you were an adult, and he could mind his own fucking business."

Emily wrote letters to Gen about her classes: the work was hard but she loved it. She wrote about how, while she was studying in the grand, gray marble library, next to a window that overlooked the Yard, a hawk swooped down to perch on the other side of the glass and swiveled its head to stare at her with amber eyes. Emily described the Lowell House bells, taken from a monastery in Russia; the largest was called Mother Earth. Emily wrote that Florencia had the winning quality of genuinely liking everyone and attracted a crew of friends within the first week. Florencia introduced her to Violet Okoro, a quiet pianist who had turned down Juilliard for Harvard, and Elizabeth and Rory Ryall, identical blond twins from Connecticut who were inseparable yet drove each other crazy. The five of them ate meals at the same end of one of the long tables in Annenberg, beneath chandeliers and an old, arched wooden ceiling that made Emily feel as though she sat inside the belly of a big ship.

Florencia had gone for more cinnamon toast when the Ryall twins decided to interrogate Emily. "Anyone you've got your eye on?" said Elizabeth. "So many cute boys."

"I beg to differ," said Rory. "*Some*, yes, but most of them are social infants. I swear, a full quarter of the incoming class is autistic."

"*Rory*. You can't say that!"

"I'm not interested," said Emily.

"You see!" Rory told her sister.

"I'm not interested in boys." Emily thought of Gen, at that birthday dinner, flattening her palm against the table. Emily wished that Gen were here. She wished that she were more like Gen: brave. "I have a girlfriend."

Violet glanced up from her book. Her brown eyes had heavy lashes, which, lowered again, made thick black fans against her brown cheeks. She turned a page.

"Oh," said Elizabeth. "A girlfriend? Um, okay. Cool."

Rory said, "Is she hot?"

"Yes."

"I like this lesbian turn of events," Rory said to her sister. "Less competition for us."

"That's a compliment," Elizabeth told Emily. "You have our look."

"But not our brand," said Rory.

"God, Ror, you are such a bitch!"

Emily said, "I don't want to have your brand."

They looked affronted, which made Emily realize that they hadn't meant straightness but wealth.

Florencia returned, her plate piled with fragrant toast. "What did I miss?"

Violet looked up again from her book. "Emily is telling us about her hot girlfriend."

"So what did you say?" asked Gen on the phone.

"I had to censor some things."

"I'm sure you did."

"You are a little X-rated."

"That's funny, coming from you."

"I said that you're the smartest person I'll ever know."

"Oh," said Gen.

"I told them how much I miss you."

"I miss *you*," said Gen softly.

"When can I see you?"

"I'm coming to visit."

"I can come to Ohio."

"No, I want to be where you are. See your whole world. Let me."

"When?"

"Soon."

"You promise?"

"Yes."

Emily arrived too early at South Station to meet Gen's bus and sat in the waiting area for the trains, listening to the rapid flicker of numbers and letters shifting position on the arrivals and departures board. She tied and retied her ponytail. She was nervous, though she didn't know why.

Gen stepped off the bus, weary-eyed and smelling of exhaust. The ride had been twelve hours from Columbus. She buried her face into the crook of Emily's neck.

Florencia had made herself scarce, saying she'd sleep on the sofa in Rory Ryall's triple. She left a note on Emily's pillow: *We want to meet Gen! Dinner tomorrow night? Let's go out!* The note crackled beneath Emily's head as she turned to press her cheek into the pillow, Gen between her legs, the pressure of Gen's shoulders nudging against Emily's inner thighs, pushing them wide open. Emily wanted Gen so badly it was like how people want what they can never have. Gen asked if Emily was going to be quiet, and Emily said yes, not because it was true but because they both enjoyed the lie. Gen tasted her, so lightly and at such length that Emily almost couldn't stand it. Emily told Gen to fuck her and was told no: this was her punishment for lying. Emily cried out, so Gen did what Emily wanted. The window was open to the warm autumn air. Someone in the Yard called to his friends to catch up.

Gen was deep inside her when Emily came. Breathless, radiant, unwilling to wait, Emily brought her fingers to her own mouth to lick them before touching Gen, but Gen caught her by the wrist. "You don't need to do that," Gen said. "Feel how much I want you." Emily marveled at how warm Gen was, how wet, the way she slid against Emily's fingertips. A door down the hall slammed. They always found themselves in the smallest beds, yet Emily never wanted a large one; she wanted things with Gen to be exactly like this: their bodies blurred together, Gen's gasp against her skin, pleasure filling each inch of space.

Gen, wrapped in a sheet, walked barefoot around the suite. "You have a fireplace."

"It doesn't work. None of them do anymore. The college had them closed up because of the fire hazard."

"You mean this room isn't special? All the dorm rooms are like this?"

"More or less." Uncomfortable, Emily recognized in Gen her own early astonishment at how saturated with privilege the campus was. While Emily was still frequently astonished—the astonishment could arrive at any moment, by seeing a framed, handwritten poem by T. S. Eliot hung on a wall, or learning that one of the clubs had a museum-worthy collection of Delft tiles, at which club members would chuck plates during parties—she had learned it was important not to show surprise, but rather to accept Harvard's abundance as normal and deserved.

Gen studied a photo of Florencia and her mother, who looked alike: the same long black hair, plump cheeks, huge smiles, eyes crinkled at the corners. "I didn't know Florencia was pretty. You didn't say that on the phone."

"It didn't matter."

"It doesn't?"

Emily stepped toward her, opened the sheet around Gen's body, and stepped into Gen's shrouded arms. "No."

The tension in Gen's body slackened. "It's been hard."

"Classes?"

"No, that's easy."

"Track?"

"Easier."

"You're crushing the competition, aren't you?"

"Hmm," said Gen, which meant *yes*.

"It's been hard to miss you."

"Yes," said Gen. "It's been hard to miss you."

Emily kissed her. "Be with me," she murmured into Gen's mouth. Gen pressed the heel of her palm between Emily's legs. The sheet slipped to the floor.

They stumbled out of Thayer the next day. It was sometime in the afternoon and it had rained; the Yard glittered. Emily showed Gen the red-figure vessels in the Sackler Museum and a silver coin from Knossos stamped with the Minotaur's maze. They stopped at a café for hot cocoa so rich that they didn't believe they could finish their cups, but of course they did. Outside, mist rubbed away anything in the distance. Gen stopped in front of Emerson Hall, her head tilted as she read the inscription on the philosophy building's façade, above its columns: *What is man that thou art mindful of him*, with no punctuation. Gen said, "They left off the question mark."

"That inscription wasn't supposed to be there at all. It was supposed to say, *Man is the measure of all things*. Protagoras said it. Or, I mean, he said something else, more complicated."

"Tell me the complicated way."

"He said—but in Greek—'Man is the measure of all things, of the things that are, that they are, and of the things that are not, that they are not.' "

"Definitely too much to fit on a building."

"Maybe a really big building."

"If it went all the way around the top, people could circle the building and read it in a never-ending loop."

"Dizzying."

"Appropriate."

"I like the short version better," said Emily. "The rest is just elaboration."

"Not really. The first part is about how we create and define the existence of everything by judging it. The second part is about how we *uncreate* things, how we decide what doesn't exist, or that some things don't exist because we don't know them. But I guess your mind can supply the rest of the quote, because you *do* know it."

"Do you believe the first part is true? Like if I say the hot cocoa was good and you say it was bad, both of us are right?"

"About cocoa, maybe. Not about everything. Not everything is relative. Some things are good or bad. Right or wrong. Is that why *Man is the measure of all things* didn't make it onto the building?"

"The college president thought the inscription should be about God."

It began to drizzle. Gen said, "That missing question mark bugs me."

"Maybe it's like the missing part of Protagoras's quote. It's there, but invisible, because your mind can supply it."

"Only if you've read the Bible. Feels unfair. Pretty rude to non-Christians."

"Why do you want the missing question mark?"

"With it," said Gen, "the psalm seeks an answer from God, so what it really wants to know is *What is outside of me, bigger than me, that would choose me, that would care about me?* It's wondering about the nature of God, and a relationship. Otherwise, it's just *Let's talk about me.*"

"Humans, humans, humans."

"Men, men, men."

"You should go to college here," Emily said. "You could transfer. People do that." Even as she spoke, she knew how rare transfer students were. They usually came from abroad or from eccentric colleges, not state schools like OSU. A sophomore in her Latin class had transferred from Deep Springs, a tiny college in California that had only thirty students and they all knew how to butcher a cow.

Gen shook her head. "A place like this isn't for me."

"It could be."

Gen looked tired. "I don't want it to be. Being able to play with words doesn't mean I belong here. Look, you wanted me to talk like you, so I did for a minute, and it was okay and kind of fun but honestly? I think the inscription answers its own question because apparently the nature of humanity is showing off what a nice building you can have with the right amount of money. I like OSU. Notice that we are not talking about you transferring to OSU."

The drizzle turned into rain. Emily felt guilty—caught, even. She opened her mouth, then shut it.

"It's okay," Gen said. "We don't have to go to the same college. It's great that you're here. The chance of a lifetime."

"So are you." Emily said it apologetically.

Gen brushed rain from Emily's face. "Aren't you cold?"

"Yes."

"I'm starving."

"Me too."

"Is it time yet for dinner with your friends?"

"We can make it time."

They arrived before anyone else at the sushi restaurant that the Ryall twins had chosen. Emily ordered edamame, which, when it arrived at the table, made Gen's eyes widen. "These are soybeans," Gen said.

"Well, yes."

"The menu could just say soybeans." Gen split open a pod to reveal its bright green beans. "Weird."

"Why?"

"It's weird to be served something that grows on our farm. Ohio doesn't even grow them for eating. They're for oil." Gen looked at the menu again. "The markup is crazy. This little plate is three dollars. Soybeans go for six dollars a *bushel*."

"We can order miso soup instead." Normally Emily would be anxious about wasting food, especially at a restaurant, but she had saved for this weekend.

"Do you like this place?"

"I've never been here before, but—"

"Heyyyy," said Elizabeth Ryall. She kissed Emily on the cheek before taking the chair next to Gen. Rory flanked Gen's other side. Florencia swept rain from her black hair and said to Gen, "I worried that Emily might keep you to herself all weekend."

"Hi," said Violet, her posture perfect, and shook Gen's hand.

"Edamame, yum." Rory helped herself.

"So," said Elizabeth, accepting a menu from the waiter, "what have you two been up to?"

"Oh, I think we know," said Rory.

"I don't see any toro on this menu," Elizabeth said to the waiter. "Do you have toro?"

"We have tuna."

"Okay, but that's not the same thing, is it? Can you ask the chef?"

"Tuna's perfect," said Florencia, and asked the waiter for a few minutes. When he left, she told Elizabeth, "If it's not on the menu, it's not on the menu."

"I always order off menu."

"How about not this time," said Violet.

"We went to a museum," Emily told them, hoping that the skeptical expression on Gen's face would fade. "And walked around the Yard."

"You should take Gen to the Vineyard," said Rory.

"Ror, don't be stupid! The Vineyard, in this weather?" To Emily, Elizabeth said, "You have to come when it gets warm. We have a house there with a private beach." Elizabeth smiled around the table. "You're all invited. You too, Gen. We have lots of room."

"Thanks," said Gen. "Is the Vineyard . . . a winery?"

The twins laughed.

"Look," Emily said, "I don't know what it is either."

"Martha's Vineyard is an island off the Cape," said Violet. "Like Nantucket."

"It is not like Nantucket," said Rory. "Nantucket is *provincial.*"

"What's your concentration?" Elizabeth asked Gen.

"What?" said Gen.

"Your major," said Emily. "Instead of majors, Harvard has concentrations."

"Is this like calling soybeans edamame?"

"No," said Rory patiently. "*Edamame* is Japanese for soybean."

"But we're not in Japan. We don't speak Japanese." Gen glanced around. In a more tentative tone, she added, "Or . . . do you?"

"I know a little," said Violet. "My father was ambassador to Japan."

"We call it edamame," said Elizabeth, "out of respect for Japanese culture."

Gen looked at the menu. "But this menu calls rice *rice* and mackerel *mackerel*."

"You didn't tell us Gen was so pugilistic," Rory said to Emily.

"Can we order?" said Florencia.

"Yes," said Emily and Violet.

"Gen hasn't answered my question," said Elizabeth.

"I don't know what I'm going to major in," said Gen.

"But what do you want to *do*?" said Elizabeth.

"I want to run."

"For what? Congress?"

"I'm ready to order," said Gen.

"Gen's an athlete," said Emily.

"You look it," Rory told Gen.

"Rory!" said Elizabeth.

"What? She *does*. Since when is it a bad thing to look like an athlete?"

"People's bodies aren't topics of conversation," said Violet. "Are we next going to talk about how I do or don't look Black?"

"No," said Elizabeth, shocked.

"Of course not," said Rory.

"That's different," said Elizabeth. "Listen," she said to Gen, "we didn't mean to offend you. We're just surprised."

Gen lifted her brows. Coolly, she said, "By what?"

Rory said, "We thought you'd be more like Emily."

Emily felt, for a moment, everyone's regard. Their faces became mirrors, reflecting Emily back to herself: her smooth beauty, blond hair, greenish eyes, quiet poise. But she didn't feel quiet or beautiful. She wanted to do something ugly. She had anticipated this weekend, had made it perfect in her mind, and it *had* seemed that way at first, but then her happiness had evaporated. Now she felt like she had at her birthday dinner, except that instead of being afraid of her father she was afraid of herself. Someone was going to say something unforgivable, and it might be her. "What do you mean, more like me?"

"Rory, can you *stop*?" said Florencia.

"Why does everyone always yell at me," said Rory plaintively, "when Elizabeth is just as bad?"

"Tell me what you mean," said Emily.

"Let it go," said Gen. "Please."

"You told me you were into girls," Rory said to Emily, "so I assumed that meant girls like you. You know—"

"You're looking for the word *femme*," said Violet.

Rory raised her hands defensively. "And I was wrong!" To Gen, she said, "I like you. You're great."

"Thanks."

"Also hot. In your own way. Not that I mean anything by it."

"I wouldn't think that you did."

"Would you like to order?" said the waiter.

"Yes," everyone said. Emily pointed blindly at something on the menu. Florencia and the twins ordered vast quantities of sushi. Violet ordered a dish called chawanmushi and Gen ordered noodles. For a while, it seemed like everything was okay. They talked about classes and which house they wanted to live in next year, and Gen didn't comment on how they called dorms *houses*. Elizabeth and Rory described summers on the Vineyard, their childhood of sand dollars and the velvet of the pool after spending all day in the salty waves.

The waiter returned with their dishes, which he presented, sliding a pair of chopsticks beside each one.

"Can I have a fork?" Gen asked him.

Rory widened her eyes. “Were you raised by *wolves*?”

“Fuck you,” said Emily. Silence struck the table. Her chest hurt with anger.

Rory said, “It was a joke.”

“You are not funny. You are a piece of shit.”

“Excuse me?” said Elizabeth.

Florencia put a hand on Emily’s shoulder but Emily did not want to be calmed, did not want to be cajoled out of her anger—which, she realized, she had held within her ever since her birthday. Anger had been part of that night, too, nestled below the shame, a creature so timid that Emily hadn’t recognized it earlier, because she didn’t know that anger could be meek or helpless. She had thought anger was always how it felt now: destructive.

“Don’t,” said Gen, and it took Emily a moment to realize that Gen had addressed her and not Rory.

“Don’t *what*?”

“Don’t embarrass me.”

It was as though Emily had fallen out of a tree. She couldn’t breathe. She felt her face pale, then flush. “Okay,” she said. “Okay.” She stood, Florencia’s hand sliding from her shoulder. She walked through the restaurant, walked down the street. It wasn’t raining anymore but it was cold, the sidewalk shining, cars slapping up puddles.

A hand touched her arm. Gen held out Emily’s coat. Emily was freezing but she ignored the coat and kept walking, though Gen’s long legs easily matched stride. “*I* embarrassed you,” Emily said. “*Me*.”

“It wasn’t a big deal. You made it a big deal.”

“I can’t win with you.”

“You got mad because I don’t look like your idea of success and they saw it.”

“That’s not true.”

“Isn’t it? I don’t like being your secret.”

“You’re not,” Emily said, though the lie was obvious. She added, “Not to them.”

"I know why you can't tell your parents. That doesn't mean it makes me feel good."

"I'm sorry. I said I was sorry."

"You want to fuck me but you can't take me to dinner."

"I *did* take you to dinner. I defended you."

"I don't want you to defend me. I can handle myself in front of your friends." They stood outside Thayer. Its redbrick bulk held grids of lit, rain-streaked windows. Students heading for the entrance glanced at Gen and Emily but not for long; they wanted to get inside.

Panic rooted in Emily's belly. She said, "You were mad at me before for saying nothing. Now you're mad because I spoke."

"Two totally different situations. It bothers me that you can't see that. It bothers me that you tried to talk me into transferring to Harvard, like OSU is a crappy school."

"I didn't say that."

"It's a Division I school. I'm happy there."

"*I'll* transfer," Emily said wildly. "I'll come to OSU."

Gen looked startled. Quietly, she said, "I don't want you to do that."

"We'd be together."

"I'm not sure that would help." Gen studied her feet. She still had Emily's coat, held in the crook of her elbow, hands shoved into her pockets, shoulders hunched. A crowd of boys passed, laughing. "I need to tell you something. I got into Harvard. I was accepted when you were wait-listed."

Gen's words made no sense. They sounded out of order, wrong.

"I turned the offer down," Gen said.

Emily still didn't understand. "Are you making fun of me?" She had never known Gen to be mean, but maybe this was a satirical way for Gen to point out the snobbery of edamame and concentrations and quotes on buildings by pretending that she was above it all—had always been.

"I would never make fun of you."

"But . . . you didn't apply."

"I did." Gen looked so worried, even . . . *afraid*, that Emily realized with belated clarity that this was real. She knew it was real because her body did: she felt a boil of betrayal, right below her sternum. "You lied."

"No, I kept something from you."

"You kept a secret, and your *secret was a lie*!"

"Emily, listen. Will you please listen?"

"Did it make you feel good to know how much I wanted what you already had, that I was second-best, waiting on the sidelines, stupid me, to think that I deserved it?" Emily could see, as vividly as if she had been in the room when it happened, the admissions board's decision. They weren't going to take *two* students from a no-name high school in rural Ohio. Whom did they prefer? The girl who taught herself ancient Greek out of a library textbook or the girl whose grades and scores were also excellent, and achieved in the face of adversity that was poignantly, yet with no trace of self-pity, described in the personal essay: the double-mortgaged farm, the loss of a mother to addiction? Look: a state champion in track. Look: *this* girl was finishing high school in three years.

"You are not second-best," said Gen.

Emily didn't care that Gen's eyes were nakedly unhappy. Emily couldn't remember being angry before tonight, or being allowed to be angry. Now it was all she wanted to be. "You used me."

"I just wanted to be close to you. For years, I saw you in the halls, so . . . I don't know . . . alone, like your mind was always somewhere else. And it was. Everyone knew how much you cared about school. You convinced the history teacher to do a solo AP prep course for you. The librarian gave you literal *home-baked cookies*. I said one offhanded thing about wanting to graduate in the year I would have if I hadn't been held back. I said it to make conversation. That was all. I didn't know what else to say and I'd wanted to talk to you for so long. I didn't expect to get swept up in your ideas. I didn't plan for this, and if I'd wanted to go to some hotshot college, I would have gone. I wouldn't have even applied, except that I had this crazy hope that we'd be together."

"Then why did you turn down the offer?"

"Well."

"You thought you'd just *give* me the spot? That's not how admission works!"

"Except that kind of is how it worked."

"Maybe I would have gotten off the wait-list anyway, even if you had accepted the offer. We could have both been here."

"Maybe." Gen drew a ragged breath. Though the rain had stopped, water dripped from the trees. On a chilly night like this, decades ago, Thayer's chimneys would have breathed woodsmoke. Beyond Thayer's roof stood the white spire of Memorial Church, sharp as a tool. "I thought about that. It wasn't obvious what to do."

"We could have discussed it."

"Wasn't it my decision where to go to college?" Gen's voice was small. "My life?"

Emily felt like her own coat, still draped over Gen's arm, flattened under one long hand that worked the lapel between anxious fingers, an object placed here or there, hung up on a rack, sometimes worn, nice enough but not ultimately valuable. Sadness washed away her anger. She and Gen were returning, Emily knew, to the moment earlier when Emily had offered to transfer to OSU and Gen had refused. "Yes, of course," said Emily, trying to make her voice neutral. She didn't want to cry.

"I had other reasons for saying no."

"Okay. Tell me."

"OSU has a great track team. And I didn't want to go into debt for a degree. You knew that."

"What else?"

"Emily. We weren't together then, when I got the acceptance letter. You were just a crush who probably wasn't even gay."

That hurt, too: to be judged as less authentic. "I see."

"Even now . . . I don't know how much I should put into this." Gen flipped a hand between herself and Emily.

It was humiliating to love someone who didn't feel the same way, someone who was gingerly seeking a way out. "Because of tonight? Gen, what can I do? I'm sorry. I'm sorry."

"Maybe sorry isn't enough."

What *was*? Emily felt the impossibility of ever being what

someone wanted. There were standards; she always tried to meet them. There was a promise of safety in meeting them, because that's when people kept you, when they said, *You're mine*, and you weren't someone else's, or no one's, because you fit exactly into a specific hope. It should be easy. She would do whatever Gen wanted. Why wasn't that enough? Gen wanted nothing that Emily could do. People's standards shifted; Emily inevitably outgrew their ideals. The pain of this was impossible to master; she had never been able to master it, her whole young life, and she was, suddenly, too exhausted and wounded to try. "Then go," she said.

"Go?"

"I want you to leave."

In the terrible silence that followed, Gen gave Emily her coat and went inside to pack her bag. She left to catch the next bus to Ohio.

Florencia made certain that Emily attended class. When Emily refused to go to the dining hall, Florencia smuggled food back to their room. She even stole a plate and cutlery. Emily stared at the food. Florencia cut everything into bite-size portions. "Just a little," she said, and kept saying it until Emily had eaten enough. Every day, Florencia handed her a Tylenol and a glass of water. That first morning after Gen left, Florencia had said, "Did you know that research has shown that heartache actually hurts your body? Apparently, acetaminophen helps."

Emily took the pill and swallowed it.

The Ryall twins stood outside Emily's door. "We are not pieces of shit," said Rory.

"*We?*" said Elizabeth. "*You* were the problem, Ror."

"I wish I hadn't said anything. I'm really sorry, Emily."

Emily, who felt acutely that forgiveness should not be so hard, that she did not want blame to be unending—no one could live like that, with the constant cut of regret—and anyway, how can we not make mistakes, what are we, all-knowing, immortal, capable of averting the future and rewriting the past?—atonement had to end, it should be simple, just ask, just give, this should be a grace—said, "It's okay."

"Florencia said you're not leaving your room." It was Violet this time.

"I go to class."

"You look terrible."

"Well."

"I'm going to practice. Do you want to come listen to me play?"

Years later, when Emily had season tickets to box seats at Carnegie Hall, she always hoped she'd hear again what Violet had played. She didn't know, that day in the practice room, the name of the piece or the composer, but she believed that she would recognize the music if she heard it again, by how gentle it had been, and kind.

Emily found a sheet of paper.

I went to the river this morning, she wrote, and watched the crew team scull across the water. I watched traffic go over the bridges. It was cold enough that I wore a sweatshirt beneath my coat and pulled up the hood. Thayer, when I returned, was quiet at that early hour, the hallway on my floor empty, and I saw something—understood something—that made me want to write to you, though as I'm writing this I know I won't mail it, because if I think about you reading my letter and worry about how you might respond, it would be too hard to explain what happened.

I stood, looking down the windowless hallway, closed doors on either side, and thought that this was how I have always felt: like a corridor, a space people pass through to get somewhere else.

A muffled voice behind a door got louder and the door opened, letting a conversation into the hallway, and although no one stepped from the room, sunlight came from its interior, from an unseen window. The light cast itself on the door opposite the open one and lay on the hallway's floor.

No one, given the choice, prefers an enclosed space with no window, but there was something special about the combination of this hallway and the kind of light I saw, loaned by a window from an adjoining room. The light wasn't reliable or enduring; that wasn't its nature. Shut the door and it's gone. But it was beautiful. It glowed. No matter how things ended, Gen, I'm grateful for you. You were my borrowed light.

15

Jocelyn's parlor was dense with people. Servers threaded through the crowd, offering canapés. Gardenias and white freesia stood in black earthenware vessels with rough patinas that promised that each vessel was at least one hundred years old. Emily didn't absorb these details, nor did she notice Jocelyn's smile of welcome from across the room, where she was engaged in conversation with a senator. Emily couldn't look away from Gen.

Gen accepted a glass of wine. Her white dress shirt was rolled at the undone cuffs and looked sharp, hewing closely to her body. Gen had been impatient about clothes when they were younger, but Emily once read a profile of her in a glossy magazine that described her closet: extensive in its wardrobe and meticulously ordered. It was a small detail—the news that Gen had become tidy and now cared about clothes—but it had given Emily a pang to look at the photos and realize that she didn't know Gen anymore. Emily wondered whether Gen had grown into her fame and accepted that designer clothes came with the territory, or if, long ago, she had hidden a wish for better clothes because she couldn't afford them. Emily wondered what else about Gen might have changed . . . or been revealed. Emily had read that profile about four years ago, so maybe that wardrobe had been given away or left behind with yet another ex-girlfriend. Emily was at a spa when she had read the profile, the appointment booked by Jack as a Mother's Day present. Gen looked good in the photos. Confident. The sight of her—and the fact that this was just a flat image, that Gen was now a stranger—squeezed Emily's chest. She stole the magazine. It felt hot in her hand. She wanted to read the profile again later, but when she left the spa, it occurred to her that Jack might find the magazine and leaf through it. She dropped it into a bin on the street corner.

Gen had been recruited out of college for the U.S. track-and-field team. She competed in the Olympics in Sydney in 2000 and in Athens four years later and won a series of medals that felt foreordained to Emily, even though during each televised event, she had been so nervous that she could hardly breathe. Broadcasters at the Sydney Olympics began to talk not just about Gen's talent but also her looks. In the magazine profile, Gen expressed annoyance about that, but Emily understood the commentators' fascination. Gen had an allure that people didn't expect. She was arresting. Part of Emily didn't like that everyone could now see what she had always seen: Gen's odd beauty. It made Emily feel anonymous, one of many other unimportant people—which she now was, to Gen. Features that had made Gen seem strange to others as a teenager in rural Ohio—the long limbs, too-large eyes, lean features—became striking on television and in fashion spreads. "People can't take their eyes off you," the interviewer had said to Gen in the magazine profile. "Can you not put that in the piece?" Gen had replied.

In 2004, Gen transformed from an object of curiosity into a celebrity. *Apotheosis* was the word for this, from the Greek, for when a mortal becomes a god. Gen became famous not for winning but losing. In the 1500-meter race, not far from the finish line, Gen was favored to win. Another runner tripped and fell. The fall was brutal. A collective gasp rose from the stadium. Gen, slightly behind the fallen woman and gaining, stopped. Her feet stuttered along the track as she ground her body to a halt. She went to the woman, crouching to see if she could help, as other runners surged past.

"Okay, but she broke *bones*," Gen told the interviewer when asked how she felt about being celebrated for that moment. "I get why people are interested in what I did but it's stupid for me to be the focus when she literally broke her body in her determination to win." The interviewer said, "Does this mean you believe that what you did was nothing?" "No," Gen said, and Emily, as she read the profile, could hear the dogged tone in her voice. "I'm saying there are different ways to be *something*. I don't know why you're not interviewing *her*."

Gen's past became a national story. Her small-town midwestern origins. Her mother's addiction and death. Her love for her grandmother, who attended every competition. Her queerness. In the 2008 Olympics in Beijing, she swept the middle-distance categories and won several medals. She charmed in television interviews. She dated one actress, then another. Half hoping, half fearing, Emily waited for Gen to mention her—perhaps in passing, as a footnote to her youth—but she never did.

Even now, in Jocelyn's parlor, Gen didn't acknowledge Emily's presence. Emily couldn't tell if she had been seen and ignored or if Gen hadn't yet noticed that she was in the room. Gen smiled guardedly at a man speaking to her. When Emily approached and their gaze met, Gen's smile fell.

"Hi," said Emily.

"Hello," said the man, ruffled by the interruption.

"Will you please excuse us?" Gen said to him. "This is an old friend."

"Of course. I'll find you later, Ms. Hall."

They waited until he had moved away. Determined to keep her voice light, Emily said, "How are you?"

"Ah, fine." Mouth flat, Gen said, "I don't know how to make small talk with you."

"It's not so hard. You can say, 'It's been a while,' and I'll say, 'Too long,' and I'll ask how you know Jocelyn."

"She accosted me at the Met Gala."

"And I'll say, 'I bet she was charming. She always is.' "

"True."

"And it's for a good cause."

"I should have written a check and stayed at home," Gen muttered. "I wasn't made for this sort of party. Not like you."

"We're not so different."

"If you say so."

"I always thought we had a lot in common. Not just where we grew up. I guess it's because, when we were younger, you were the only person who really knew me."

Gen's stiffness eased. "Yeah. I thought that, too. But that's not small talk."

"I'll say, 'Where's home these days?' "

"Here. New York. For now."

Emily's pulse, which had jumped when she met Gen's eyes across the room, kept its quick pace.

"Any more questions in your small-talk repertoire?" Gen said. Emily hesitated, unsure if Gen had had enough of her company and this was a way to indicate that the conversation should come to an end. Gen added, "I like your questions. I want to answer them. You surprised me. I don't mean to be rude."

"How's your gran?"

"Good," said Gen fondly. "Stubborn. I tried to buy her a place with a pool. She's got arthritis and I thought this might help, but she told me, and I quote, to save my pennies. She said she had no use for a pool, unless it was for the chickens to swim in. Then she reminded me, in case I had forgotten, being so far from my roots, that chickens can't swim."

"They can't?"

"They sink after a while."

"That is hilarious and sad. I bet chickens are jealous of ducks."

"I mean, *I* am. Ducks have such nice feathers and people feed them bread."

"So Nella's still on the farm?"

"I paid off the mortgage."

"When you got the Nike endorsement?"

"You've been keeping up on me?"

"Gen. Everyone keeps up on you."

"You're not everyone."

"I always wanted to ask . . ." Emily trailed off, unsure if a question that was more than a decade old was one better left unanswered. "Was Nella mad at me, on my eighteenth birthday?"

"She was mad, but not at you. She thought you were in a tough place. Said we were both too young." Emily heard the double meaning of this: too young to know what to say or do, and too young to be together forever. "We were," Gen added.

Emily spoke quickly, while she still had the courage: "I'd like to see you again."

Gen looked into her wineglass, then set it down on a console. "I don't think that's a good idea. It was nice to run into you. I have to find that guy from earlier before he finds me, so I don't get cornered. I'm going to make him donate a lot of money."

Emily watched Gen leave. A server whisked away Gen's half-finished glass. Emily felt a solitary distress.

"You made it," Jocelyn said, kissing her cheek. Then she looked more closely at Emily's face. "What's wrong?"

Emily didn't stay long after that. She returned to her empty studio apartment. She left the lamps off, the apartment visible enough in the city light cast through the windows. As she set her keys and phone on the kitchen counter, she glanced down at her hand. She still wore her wedding ring. She had been wearing it, she realized, while she had spoken with Gen. She took it off.

The next morning, as early as was socially acceptable, she called Jocelyn. She had a favor to ask.

Emily was about to use the number Jocelyn had given her, but Gen called first. "I still remember your home phone number back in Ohio," Gen said when Emily answered, "but I had to ask Jocelyn for this one."

"That's funny. I asked her for yours." Emily leaned against the wall. She could see the texture of its paint. She shut her eyes. Had she always been capable of this—speaking in a carefree tone when something was too important? As if she hadn't flushed the moment that she heard Gen's voice, hadn't felt the pink stain her cheeks as though she were a piece of fruit gone ripe. Emily was filled with a hot, private anticipation. "Why did you call?"

"I *do* want to see you."

"Even if it's a bad idea?"

"Yes."

16

For their first date, Jack took Emily to the Boston Public Library. He showed her the marble lions, their stone pale against the warm tones of the pedestals, their unpolished paws the color of buttermilk. The sky outside was a bright haze—no snow, but the promise of it.

She had been surprised when he proposed visiting the library. She had expected that he would reserve a table at an upscale restaurant and order stupidly expensive things, though at that time in her life she wouldn't have been able to name those things. She didn't know the word *truffles.* She didn't know that oysters were better in winter, or that a glass of Meursault looked like mellow sunlight. Over the phone, after he had suggested they meet at the library, Emily had said, "Do you like books?" She had had the idea that maybe he collected them and owned rare first editions.

"I hate them," he had answered cheerfully, which made her like him more. His frankness surprised her, as did how he expressed his dislike good-naturedly—almost with affection, as though he were fond of his dislike. Florencia, who hadn't met him yet, referred to him as "the hot hedge fund bro," implying that he wasn't intellectual—and maybe he wasn't, but he wasn't *simple*. Emily almost asked Jack why he wanted to take her to a place dedicated to something he hated, but she liked not knowing. They agreed on a date and time, and Emily was surprised again, this time by the early hour. "A day date?" Florencia said when Emily told her. "Maybe he *doesn't* want to get into your pants."

"Oh, he does." Rory sipped her third cup of coffee. "He's playing the long game. He wants to prolong his hard-on."

"Maybe it's not a game," said Violet.

"Ha!" scoffed Elizabeth, and Emily agreed with her. She found, however, an appeal to being the object of Jack's game. She liked being pursued. She liked being perceived as a challenge, something he needed to strategize. It made her feel important.

In the end, there *was* an elegant meal. After they'd viewed the library's art and architecture, Jack ushered her into the courtyard tearoom, which was empty except for them and one waiter, who stood near a table heaped with peonies.

"Why are we the only ones here?" Emily whispered to Jack.

"I booked the whole restaurant. Have you ever had high tea?"

"You don't have to try to impress me."

"It makes me happy to try to impress you. You should let me." He brushed a hand down her arm. She wore a blue alpaca sweater Florencia had loaned her, so Emily didn't quite feel his hand on her, just the gentle nudge embedded in the gesture, directing her toward the table. The pressure of Jack's touch quickened her curiosity. How would this feel if she wore nothing, and his fingertips slipped down her bare skin?

Emily and Jack were served towers of pretty sandwiches and pastries. They had Darjeeling and champagne. Jack asked Emily question upon question. When he learned what Emily studied and asked whether she preferred Greek or Latin, she answered that she couldn't choose, but had known Greek longer. Latin had a raw, angular quality. It was a tool less easy to handle, whereas her knowledge of Greek felt like an old wooden spoon, smooth in her grasp. He asked what she wanted to do after graduation. She told him that she was prelaw. "Becoming a lawyer isn't exciting, but it's well-paid, and I'm interested in how verdicts are delivered based on precedent. In law, the past accretes selectively: one decision connects to another decision to another. I like that."

Jack set down his teacup and was silent. The flowers on the table exhaled their rich fragrance. The silence went on long enough that Emily thought she'd said something to offend him. "What are you thinking?" she said.

"That I've never met anyone like you."

"What am I like?"

"Perfect."

Emily hadn't known how much she had wanted to hear someone say this. Jack was the first.

The mix of tea and champagne and sweet and savory tastes made Emily relaxed yet alert. She had questions of her own for him.

He had an affinity for numbers but didn't read books aside from those he paid people to read aloud to him, something he didn't like. He could never forget the presence of the reader. There were audio book CDs, yes, but they embarrassed him. They made him remember how, as a child, his tutors had recommended books on tape and his parents threw them away, telling him that he didn't need them, that if he worked harder, if he weren't so lazy, he would finally be able to finish a book, just *one*. That was years before he was diagnosed with dyslexia. Jack shrugged as he spoke, his gray eyes cool, his mouth curled in a helpless smile that was sad yet wise and slightly far away, managing to convey that he was no longer bothered by his disability *and* that he was, that he had outgrown a cruel imperative to succeed *and* kept it close. Emily felt a tenderness for him. It seeped from her like honey from its comb.

Jack had suggested the library because he liked making moments; he wanted Emily's time with him to be memorable. He had noticed her reading at the bar and had thought a library would please her. His mother would respect her, he said; she would appreciate that Emily attended Harvard. She had always wanted Jack to go to Princeton, his dad's alma mater, but it didn't matter that Jack was a legacy applicant, or that his parents had donated enough money for him to be added to several director's lists at Ivies. It didn't matter that his parents paid tutors to write his application essays. His poor grades and scores spoke for themselves. He didn't get into any elite colleges. He was accepted by some state schools, but his parents refused to let him go. His attendance at a state school would be more embarrassing for them than no college at all. "I guess because skipping college looked like a *choice*," said Jack.

"Did you think about going anyway?"

"Sometimes I wish I had, but they would have cut me off financially. I was scared to strike out on my own. They didn't believe in me, so it was hard to believe in myself. My father's hedge fund hired me out of high school. In the end, I did find something I'm good at: money. Now I'm not financially dependent on them. Makes me proud—and honestly, they are, too, at the moment."

One day he would make partner. If his parents nursed an old disappointment, they didn't reveal it. His father's hedge fund had offices in New York and Boston, so Jack kept apartments in both places. "The commute's not so bad," he said, "especially when I think about you."

Outside, the barometric pressure had dropped and the sky was white, but it hadn't begun to snow. She could feel the cold pavement through her thin shoes. She said, "Why did you want to meet so early?"

"Don't laugh."

"I'm not going to laugh."

"Before, I always saw you at the bar. Late at night. You were so beautiful. I thought, *She must be even more beautiful by daylight.* It's true. You are."

Emily kissed him. He made a sound low in his throat and deepened the kiss, reaching into her coat to draw her hips toward him. He hardened against her. His need for her was so obvious that it made her want him more.

"You have to stop," he whispered into her mouth.

"Take me back to your place," she told him, "and make me stop."

Emily wasn't very aware of his Back Bay apartment, just of a disorienting sense of spaciousness. His bed was a vast plain. He kept saying that he wanted to go slow but that was not what she wanted. She had missed being caressed, had missed being under someone's weight. She put her thumb against the head of his taut cock. It leapt at her touch. She brushed away a milky bead of fluid and ignored his surprise when she brought her thumb to her mouth. It tasted bitter. He pulled her hand from her mouth and pressed it back into the bed.

She knew, more or less, what to expect after years of talking with her friends, but when he pushed into her, she gasped. It hurt. She tried to open wider for him and heard him exclaim over how tight she was, but she found it difficult to shift at all underneath him. She was neatly pinioned and he was heavy. He was moving too fast and too hard, but she gave in to it. She wanted the pain it gave her.

—

Afterward, when he pulled out, he groaned into a pillow, his fiery hair striking against its white. He lifted his head, eyes hazy, but quickly squeezed them shut. "That wasn't how I meant it to be. Do you want water? Let me get you water."

When he returned from a distant recess of the echoing apartment, he had a towel wrapped around his waist and held two glasses of water that clinked with ice. Emily pulled the sheet up over her, shy now, knowing that Jack was frustrated. She hadn't come—which hadn't surprised her, although she'd never before had sex without an orgasm.

"I'm sorry," he said.

"It's okay."

"I couldn't stop myself."

"Really, it's not a big deal."

"I don't do things halfway," he insisted. "It's not my style."

Emily drank from her glass. The cold water shot down the hot core of her like a steel arrow. "I should have told you something earlier." She explained about Gen. Jack listened, sitting beside her, his initial surprise growing into bewilderment. "Wait," he said. "*She* broke up with *you*?"

"Yeah." Although Emily had been the one to tell Gen to leave, Gen's rejection of her had been clear. "My roommate says it was a classic freshman breakup: two people from the same high school think they can make a long-distance relationship work but it falls apart as soon as college starts."

"You've never been with anyone else?"

"I dated, but didn't like anyone else enough to sleep with them." He was silent for a long time. "You look shocked."

He touched her cheek. "I would have done things differently if I had known. I'm shocked because I can't believe anyone would break up with you."

"Not because I had a girlfriend?"

"Yes, that is a little shocking. I'm also flattered that somehow I'm the lucky guy you chose to be with. But who cares that you had a girlfriend? That was a long time ago, right?"

"Yes," she said, though it didn't always feel that way.

"Do you want to be with another woman?"

She smiled. "Not at the moment."

"And you like men?"

Her tone was arch. "For now."

He took the glass from her hand and set it on the bedside table. "Maybe you could like me even more, under certain circumstances." The towel around his waist had shifted. Emily could see that he was aroused again. "I have an idea. Do you trust me?"

She didn't, not quite—she barely knew him—but she was curious. "Yes."

He pulled the sheet from her breasts, drew it all the way down to her toes. "Get on your knees."

She did, upright, arms loose at her sides, unsure what might come next. He got behind her, his hard chest flush against her back. "I want to find out what you like," he murmured in her ear. "Do what I tell you." A heat grew between her legs. It was impossible not to remember Gen, whose orders Emily had loved to obey. "Okay?" Jack said.

"Yes." The word came out in a sigh.

He brushed her hair away from her face and held it. He tugged, gently, and when she made a small sound, he let go, set his hand flat against her back, and bent her toward the bed. He stroked the inside of her thighs. He told her to open for him. He touched her, lightly, and told her how wet she felt. He traced where she was still sore. When he found her clit, he told her to tell him that she liked it. She did. He was still touching her when he slid into her. He stuffed himself in, then didn't move. He held her against him, his fingertips swifter now. He told her to tell him when she was going to come, but she didn't—she couldn't. Pleasure gripped her too suddenly. Her face was against the mattress and he was beginning to thrust when she fully burst against his hand, her cry muffled yet deep.

He charmed her friends. He and Violet talked about a Rachmaninoff performance he had seen in New York. He ordered the steak and said it was delicious but nothing like steak in Buenos Aires, and when Florencia asked him if he had been to Argentina, they talked for a long time about her favorite childhood places and where she liked to ski. Although the Ryall twins didn't know his family, they discovered that his parents and theirs had mutual friends. He picked up the check at dinner, batting away everyone's thanks, and kissed Emily, saying that he had to catch the train back to New York so that he could be at the office the next morning, but they shouldn't let his departure break up the fun.

After he left, Florencia reached across the table and seized Emily's wrist. "Oh my *God*."

"He adores you," said Violet.

"And you said the sex was good, right?" asked Rory.

"Honey," Elizabeth told Emily, "you need to land him like a *plane*."

Emily and Jack had been dating for a month when Emily caught a bad case of the flu and had to cancel their weekend together.

"Are you sure?" Jack said over the phone. "Maybe you'll feel better by Saturday."

"I can't even get out of bed. Florencia has been joking about painting a plague cross on our door."

"I wish I weren't stuck in New York. I miss you."

Despite the ache in her head and chest, Emily smiled. She missed him, too.

The next day, an armful of flowers arrived. Roses ended up in coffee mugs and tulips in empty soda bottles, the tops sawed off. A Waterford crystal vase arrived later. The next day, a new delivery: a hot-water bottle inside a cashmere cover. Then two silver boxes of chocolates and pâtes de fruits, one box labeled with Florencia's name. It hurt to swallow, so Emily gave her box to Florencia.

"I hate him," Florencia said. "He's ruining all other men for me."

Emily couldn't smell the flowers, but loved the tulips' dramatic swoon and the roses' slow, pornographic spread. She and Jack talked every night on the phone until she coughed too much to continue. "Will you keep talking?" she said, throat raw. "I like the sound of your voice."

"You do?" He talked about everything—the pressure of working for his father, how he wished he weren't an only child, the plots of his favorite movies, learning to sail on the Charles. A young boy, he ran away from home and crossed traffic to the Common, where he joined a kids' soccer team and played until dusk and the police came. Drowsy from Theraflu, Emily drifted to sleep as he described his childhood home in Beacon Hill, where his parents still lived. Emily found herself wandering into a dream of it, opening doors, touching the green majolica fireplace tile. She lit an oil lamp. Later, she asked him what had been real. The oil lamp? No. The green tile, yes.

On Saturday morning, Florencia said, "I think you should shower."

"Later."

"Or now?"

"Leave me alone, I'm dying."

"At least change your pajamas."

"I like them." They were fleecy ones from Kohl's, a gift from her mother. Emily blew her nose.

"Brush your hair? Look, I don't want to spoil anything but maybe you can fake surprise, because friends don't let friends look like mushrooms. You look kind of spongy and pallid. Did you know that mushrooms are older than land plants? They are millions of years old. Older than dinosaurs. What is life? Basically, at its origin, spores."

"Why are you going on about mushrooms? Why am I supposed to fake surprise?"

Emily did not, in fact, have time to shower before Elizabeth and Rory knocked on the door, accompanied by Jack, freshly shaved and carrying a pot of homemade chicken soup. Florencia grabbed a packed duffel bag and disappeared with the twins. Emily, still in bed, pulled the blanket over her head. "I'm a mess," she groaned.

"That's okay. You're sick."

"You're not supposed to be here."

"Do you want me to go?"

"No."

"Good. Can I see you now?"

Emily emerged from the blanket. Her nose was running. She reached for the tissue box, but he reached it first and passed it to her. "I thought, if you wanted, I could spend the weekend here," he said. "Florencia said it's okay with her if it's okay with you."

"In my dorm room?" He had seen it only briefly; they always spent weekends at his apartment. She looked at the room through his eyes. It looked embarrassingly young. There was a dirty coffeepot and an unkillable pothos plant. On the walls were a poster of the original cover of *To the Lighthouse* (Florencia's) and another of Alfred Sticglitz's photograph of Georgia O'Keeffe's hands (Emily's). Books filled the shelves; others towered in stacks on the floor. Greek and Latin phrases were taped above Emily's bed. The only beautiful thing, other than the flowers Jack had sent, was a wooden antique incubator for chicks that Emily had found at a flea market. She and Florencia often left notes for each other in the incubator, tucked inside plastic Easter eggs bought at CVS. Emily wasn't sure what her room smelled like. Laundry hadn't been done in a long time.

Jack took a bowl from a collection stolen from the dining hall and gave her chicken soup. "Let me take care of you."

Emily no longer cared about being gross and disheveled or about the state of her room. She felt warm inside. The soup was good. A kind, handsome man sat on the edge of her bed and said, "There's a *Simpsons* marathon going."

They watched Homer Simpson invent a chair impossible to tip over. They watched him eat his pet lobster. They watched Lisa cheat on a test. They watched Marge hold the family's one remaining possession: a washcloth. Clouds appeared in the cartoon blue sky over and over as they heard the three opening notes, then a trumpet's phlegmy buzz. At first, Emily and Jack were wedged together in her narrow bed, but when it got late, he made Emily another cup of Theraflu in the microwave, took Florencia's mattress from her bed, and set it on the floor next to Emily's. Near sleep, Emily reached down to hold Jack's hand. "Why are you so good to me?"

"Because I love you."

He had never said this before. Few people had. Her parents—her father often, her mother rarely. Her little sisters out of nowhere—a surprise, almost like a hiccup. When Emily and Gen had been together, she had believed that their love was certain—knit into the muscle, marrow at the bone. But that was over, and Emily, remembering that time, had the impression that she had been very young then, and that now, though only a few years later, she was on the brink of becoming a new person. She saw her new self in the eyes of Jack, looking up at her from the floor, his smile tender in the muted television's light. She realized that she wanted to become a new person, and that she loved him, too.

"Well done," said Elizabeth when she saw the ring after the trip to Positano.

Rory agreed. "It flirts with ostentation but stays classy."

"That was fast," said Violet.

"I am in awe," said Elizabeth.

"What about law school?" said Florencia.

Emily had gotten into Columbia. "I can be married and still go to law school. Jack says if I want to, I should. He supports whatever I choose."

"Ugh, he is such a dream. Violet's not wrong, though: it's all happening pretty fast. No one we know is getting *married*. And you barely dated anyone before him."

Elizabeth said, "Nothing wrong with a whirlwind romance."

"You can always divorce him," said Rory. "Just don't sign a prenup."

"Let her be happy, you killjoys!" Elizabeth shouted. To Emily, she said, "He's the One, right?"

"Yes," she said, and was sure.

Then, less sure. Years later, looking back, Emily could find no singular, obvious moment that created doubt. During their first dinner with his parents in their Victorian townhome on the south slope of Beacon Hill, Jack behaved beautifully. He interrupted his mother's cold politeness by telling Emily about his favorite window seat as a child. His father wasn't unkind to Emily but kept directing the conversation toward Jack's career. Jack patiently steered the conversation away, asking Emily to tell his parents about her favorite Greek lyric poets. Jack made sure to display Emily's excellent education. He dwelled on it, even. This gave the impression that Emily's identity was her prestigious diploma. But wasn't it good to be proud of a partner's accomplishments? He had chosen Emily's dress for that night—this, in hindsight, possibly foretold his domineering nature. But hadn't she asked what she should wear?

He assumed control of the wedding, spending hours on the phone with the planner. Emily's friends said how lucky she was. Men never wanted to do their share of wedding planning. How incredible: all Emily had to do was show up and enjoy the best day of her life.

Would it be the best day?

Emily had moved into Jack's Back Bay apartment after graduation, though this was a temporary arrangement; he would sell the place after the wedding and they would live full-time in New York. Emily would go to Columbia. He had already had her things shipped to his New York City apartment. Meanwhile, Jack commuted, coming to Boston on the weekends. During the week, alone in the echoing white space of Jack's living room, Emily joked on the phone with her friends about being a kept woman. She joked because it felt a little true. When she said the words out loud—laughing—it seemed less true. Violet had rented an apartment in Somerville for the summer and Emily could have moved in with her instead, but Jack said, "We're going to spend the rest of our lives together. I don't want to miss one minute. Let me come home to you." When he arrived on Friday night, he told her everything he'd been thinking about her while on the train. He always had a gift: Guerlain perfume, tickets to a performance. "I will never take you for granted," he promised. Emily believed him.

And yet: a wrinkle of doubt. After years of not communicating with Gen, Emily wrote a letter. When she began writing, she believed that this was the correct thing to do. She was informing Gen of something momentous in her life. Gen should know about the engagement. Emily would want to know, if she were Gen. But as she continued writing, she realized that she was, in fact, expressing uncertainty about marriage. Jack was incredible. But was all this—as Violet and Florencia had suggested—happening too quickly? She was twenty-one. Maybe that *was* too young. Yet she had been younger with Gen . . . and still, even while in love with Jack, Emily couldn't quite forget her. Emily mailed the letter.

Then came Gen's reply: terse, congratulatory. Uninterested.

Maybe this had been what Emily had needed. Maybe her sense of doubt had been a need for closure that Gen's reply had given.

There was, still inside her, a thistle of hurt that Gen had planted. A burr. Emily plucked it out. She folded Gen's note. She ironed that wrinkle of doubt flat. She tidied the edges of herself. She brushed away the thoughts and questions that marred this moment. The best moment. Yes, her wedding would be the best day. Of course it would, like people promised. It was the day when she would become somebody.

Maybe her doubt had been distrust that Jack's love was real, that she deserved what had happened: someone she had chosen had also chosen her.

Not long after the wedding, Emily discovered she was pregnant. She took a second test, then a third. Impossible. She was on the pill. But a doctor confirmed it.

Emily had just moved into Jack's apartment in New York. She was at home—her classes at Columbia would start the following week—and he was at the office. She knew that she should tell Jack first. Instead, light-headed, she called her mother.

"You don't sound too happy about it," her mother said.

"I'm not ready. It's so soon. Mom, I'm scared."

"I thought you were going to become a lawyer. How long does that take?"

"Three years." She was supposed to receive her JD in 2003.

"What're you going to do, quit law school?"

Emily was silent. She didn't know.

"Do you want an abortion?" The question was posed matter-of-factly.

"How can you say that?"

"I guess you don't."

"That's not why I called."

"I'm a nurse. I've seen it all. You could have been calling about that."

"I wanted—" Emily had made the mistake of going to her mother as though she were still a child, but her mother had never acted like the mothers on TV or in the homes of Emily's friends, even when Emily had been a child. "I want you to talk to me like I'm your daughter."

"Obviously you're my daughter."

"Just tell me that everything's going to be okay."

"Sure it will. You're twenty-one. Older than lots of your high school friends when they had babies. You're married. You're rich. But I guess it's true that some people just don't want children."

"Like you?"

"You always get this way. Emotion doesn't help a problem."

"I'm not a problem."

"I didn't say you were."

But that was how Emily had always felt: like her mother's problem.

Her mother sighed. "Don't worry. It's going to be okay."

Though that was what she had asked for, Emily said, "Maybe you should tell me what you really think."

"If I'm honest, I thought you'd make something of yourself."

"Meaning?"

"You were never satisfied. Always wanted more. Another book. Another piece of cake. Didn't want me to say good night."

"That's *all* children."

"You were different. You know it. You wanted to leave Washford. You left Washford. You wanted to go to a fancy school. You got into one. You married up. You decided to become a lawyer. Well, okay. What happens now? Having a baby and going to school and working is hard. I should know. But that's not my worry for you. My worry is that you *won't* do that. That you'll give up your plan. You'll be just some man's wife. Some baby's mother. That's not the Emily I know."

The anxiety Emily had had at the start of the phone call worsened: a loud panic in her ears. "I'm sick of this." Emily had called home because she had been afraid and hoped for comfort. In the course of the conversation, she had discovered that her fear over having a baby was a trapdoor to another, long-held fear: a question whose answer was now so clear that Emily stated it. "You never wanted me," she said, and hung up.

Emily was already her baby's mother. There was nothing wrong with that, even if her mother thought otherwise. It was a good thing. It was, Emily decided, the most important thing. She wondered when she would feel the baby flicker inside her. The phone call had, in the end, helped. It showed her who she wanted to be, and who she didn't.

Jack was overjoyed. When he saw, however, that Emily was quiet, he sobered and asked what was wrong. She mentioned law school. He didn't think that was an issue. Couldn't she postpone a year? What would be so bad about graduating in '04? Anyway, did Emily *want* to become a lawyer? That had been her plan to pay back loans and have a good income, not because she was passionate about law. Maybe the pregnancy was a sign that she shouldn't go. They certainly didn't need a second source of income. But really, whatever she chose, he supported.

"That's not all." She told him about the phone call.

"Emily, you're not going to be like her."

He had just articulated another aspect of her fear. She wanted this baby, even if she wasn't ready, but she worried that a baby might reveal that she couldn't be a good mother. "How do you know?"

He held her hand between both of his. "You're the sort of person who doesn't hold back when you're in love. You're going to love our child. And you will never be alone. Not like your mother. The divorce probably made parenting hard. It won't be like that for you. I will always be by your side. I will never leave you."

And it was true.

17

Jack loved her pregnant body. He always beckoned her to him when she stepped out of the shower. He wanted her even more as she grew. She often orgasmed quickly, trapped between two pressures: him, inside her, and the heavy weight of her belly. She was nearly six months' pregnant and almost as many months into their marriage when he said, "Pack your bags and clear your social calendar. We're going on a babymoon!"

She wasn't entirely surprised. On their first date, Jack had said that he liked to make moments, but as she knew him better over the year that they had been together, Emily came to understand that this trait was a need. He was sunniest whenever he had a plan. Soon after the plan had been (as always) beautifully executed, he could be touchy—prone to irritability, though he denied his bad mood. She felt better once he began humming around the apartment again. It meant that he had a new idea. "Really?" she said. "I can't wait! Where?"

"It's a surprise. Bring enough warm clothes: that's your only clue."

Snow hissed against the apartment's enormous windows with their view of the Brooklyn Bridge, which had become blurry strands of light. When he had said "babymoon," she had imagined someplace tropical, not a destination where she'd need warm clothes, but she knew not to reveal this. He would be hurt. He might accuse her of ingratitude—which she understood. How would she feel, if she had planned something for him and he suggested it wasn't good enough?

She *was* grateful. How had she deserved this life, this husband? When she told her friends about Jack's surprises, they were impressed. "I can't even get Yasar on a train to visit me," said Elizabeth, still dating her college boyfriend, who had a serial devotion to becoming talented at a skill until he mastered and abandoned it. He became a champion archer, a day trader, and an amateur pilot, completed a double major in geology and computer science, and was still in Cambridge doing his doctorate in biology. "He says I'm the one thing he wants forever but honestly I think he doesn't break up with me because he forgets I exist. You're so lucky."

Emily had learned the importance of making sure that Jack knew that she felt lucky. He was sensitive, yes, easily wounded . . . because he felt things deeply, including his love for her. After all, we can't peer into each other's minds, so if he needed to witness her appreciation of him, what was wrong with that? It was better than not caring. Better than turning away. Better than measuring, as Gen had measured, how much Emily had been worth only to decide that it wasn't enough. Emily liked how much her opinion mattered to Jack. She said, "I love the cold." She didn't, but the lie was harmless. "You're the best. Do I need my passport?"

"Not this time." He placed a hand on her belly and smiled when the baby kicked.

She didn't want to express any reluctance, not when he was so pleased with his plan, but if he had asked before booking a babymoon, she would have said that she'd rather stay home. She pushed away the wish that he had planned the trip *with* her. That wish was petty—wasn't it?

"Meet me at the airport on Friday at six p.m.," he said. "I'll be coming straight from work. We'll land kind of late, but that's okay. We'll get a fresh start the next morning and the dawn will be beautiful on the snow—" He covered his mouth, but his eyes were merry.

"Snow?"

"We are going to have the best time ever."

They agreed to meet at the first-class check-in counter at JFK. Emily arrived early. She saw him before he saw her; his height and red hair were distinctive in a crowd. As he strode toward her, his expression and rapid pace suggested a barely controlled anger. He met her gaze and tried on a smile, but it was pinched with effort. He embraced her, sighing against the crown of her head. "Am I glad to see you. What a shitty car ride."

"Was there traffic?"

"The driver told me not to talk on my cell. Can you believe that? He said I was too loud."

"Maybe he's sensitive to noise. Or wanted to concentrate on the road."

"My car, my rules."

"Except it was *his* car."

"Whose side are you on?"

"I just don't think this is something to get mad about."

"That phone call was with the CFO. I had to take it."

"So what did you do?"

"I told the driver to mind his fucking business."

"Oh."

"Took my sweet time on that call. The driver was really rude about it. Silent—but, you know, *rude*. I could feel how much he hated me. For a totally normal thing. For doing my job, just like *he* is supposed to do *his*."

"His job is to drive you, not obey you."

His mouth flattened. He took a deep, steadying breath, then shrugged. "Well, you weren't there." She was relieved that he wanted to forget the incident. It was true: she hadn't been there. She couldn't know how the driver had actually behaved. Better to let this drop. She said, "Should we check in?"

He brightened. "Ready to hear what I have in store for us?"

"Absolutely."

"We're going to the best ski resort in Jackson Hole!"

Emily's chest became breathless—very still, save for a flicker of anxiety. "You're going skiing?"

"*We* are going skiing. Isn't it great?"

"You mean you're going to ski while I relax in the lodge?"

"Are you okay? Did you not get enough sleep? *We* are going skiing. You and me. Together."

"But I'm not good at skiing." She had learned only last winter, with him patiently teaching her how to snowplow and make wide turns. It had been fun. When she tumbled, he helped her up and praised her effort, brushing off snow. After a few trips to Vermont, she had gotten the hang of skiing, more or less, and could do any green slope and some blue ones.

"I don't mind doing bunny slopes with you," he said. "We can work our way up to more exciting trails at the end of the trip."

She was bewildered at how he seemed to have forgotten the obvious. "But I'm pregnant."

"That's why we should do this now, before the baby comes and we're too busy."

"I'm *six months'* pregnant. It's not safe."

"I wouldn't do anything that would put you at risk. You'll be fine. The internet says that the safest time for a pregnant woman to travel is in her second trimester." Jack was frustrated, his positive words thinly covering a growing impatience with her incomprehensible hesitation, her childish—yes, let's go ahead and say it—childish reluctance to be happy. Most people would love a vacation like this! Her reluctancc, now that he thought about it, resembled a power play, as if Emily were trying to manipulate him by making him feel as though he had done something wrong.

Emily wasn't sure what bothered her more: that Jack felt this way or that she could read his thoughts. Sometimes it seemed to her that she even *anticipated* his thoughts. That she considered his thoughts before she had formed her own.

Maybe there had been a miscommunication. "Jack, I could fall."

"You've gotten pretty good at skiing. Anyway, you just began to show. You won't be skiing fast. Even if you fall, which you won't, snow is soft and your body is built to keep the baby safe." He patted her belly. Unthinking, she pushed his hand away. "Seriously, Em? Are we going to have a problem? I worked my ass off booking this trip *for you*." His voice raised. People began to stare. “I am trying to be supportive, to *encourage* you, and you treat me like dirt.”

“I’m not trying to be mean. I’m trying to tell you that I don’t feel safe skiing.”

“Give me some credit. I checked. The doctor says it’s fine.”

“You called my doctor? My obstetrician?”

“Yes. Well, yes, I called her, but she said that she couldn’t talk to me because of doctor-patient privilege. Which is ridiculous. I’m your husband, not some stranger. So I called my doctor, and he said it was okay.”

“Your doctor, who is not an obstetrician.”

“He’s a GP. *General practitioner. General* means he knows everything about medicine, *generally*.”

“What did you say to him? The exact words.”

“I said, ‘I want to surprise my wife with a trip to Jackson Hole and she’s six months’ pregnant. Is it safe to go?’ ” He released his carry-on handle to fold his arms across his chest, regarding her with the defiance of someone who has presented irrefutable evidence and is offended that evidence was necessary.

“You didn’t ask whether I could *ski*.”

“For fuck’s sake!” he shouted. The woman behind the check-in counter glanced up from her computer in alarm. “It’s Jackson Hole! Everyone knows that you ski at Jackson Hole! It’s *obvious*.”

The baby turned in Emily’s cramped belly. Her pulse was fast. Jack was so upset. But he loved her. He told her so, every day. No one had loved her like that, not even her parents. All couples fought. Marriage wasn’t easy. Everyone said so, and she carried his baby inside her. They were going to become a family, a real one, the kind she didn’t have growing up. She was grateful to him for giving her a family. He would give her anything—he always told her this. If she apologized, their fight would vanish.

Yet she didn’t want to apologize.

If Jack calmed down, he would understand her point of view. That’s what couples did: they tried to understand each other. If he really would give her anything, why couldn’t he give his understanding? “I’m so happy you planned this trip. It’s such a nice idea. I’m going to love the scenery and you’ll have a great time skiing. I'll read by the fire and we'll have wonderful dinners. But I'm not comfortable skiing. It's too risky."

"*I'm* not comfortable shelling out a bunch of money to be alone the whole trip. *I'm* not comfortable that you can't even manage a thank-you."

"I *have* been saying thank you."

"Actually, you haven't."

"I've said many times how glad I am. That I'm grateful."

"You don't act like it."

What could dispel the horrible tension between them, besides capitulation? It didn't matter that she didn't deserve his anger. It felt so awful to make him angry that the feeling was indistinguishable from guilt. "Thank you so much. I know how much effort you put into this."

He took the handle of his suitcase in one hand and the handle of hers in the other. He refused to look at her. "Let's check in and go to the gate, or we'll miss our flight."

Emily had bought two books in the airport bookstore but needed more. She needed to occupy not only the empty time spent seated before a view of jagged mountains but also the strained hours after Jack returned from skiing, face windburned. He answered her questions and responded to comments, polite yet curt. Her efforts at conversation failed. Part of her understood that he had decided that her refusal to ski meant that she was ignoring him, so he would ignore her, too, yet be civil in order to show that he was the better person. Another part of her knew that this was bullshit. A final part of her believed that it didn't matter what she knew or understood, because the situation was intolerable. She hated being the object of his resentment.

On the first day, she tried being cheerful. She told him about her books and the gorgeous view. "Must be nice," he said, "having such a good time without me."

The next day, she said nothing about herself but instead asked how the slopes were. He said, "You would know if you could make room in your reading schedule to see for yourself." The baby roiled inside her. The bulge of a small foot distended her maternity shirt. She considered booking her own room. She could fly back to New York. But if he was this upset about her (normal—it *was* normal, wasn't it?) hesitation to ski, what would he do if she left?

Instead, she read. She read *Bridget Jones's Diary*. She read a new translation of *Snow Country*. In it, people dyed fabric white by laying it on the snow in the sun. Emily began to feel like that fabric: bleached by exposure.

Then Emily read nothing. She looked at the mountains and drank hot chocolate. She swam in the hotel pool. What would Gen do, if she were Emily, here in Jackson Hole? Gen wouldn't have found herself in this situation . . . not just because she wouldn't have married a man. If Gen didn't want to do something, she'd refuse. She wouldn't care what other people thought. Gen was good at saying no. She had said no to Harvard. What she had said to Emily's father at the birthday dinner was also a way of saying no. Unlike Emily, Gen hadn't pretended to be straight.

Emily wrote all this down. She wrote about how Jack was devoted to her. Gen had said no to Emily, too . . . and that was okay. Loving Jack had made it okay.

Thinking about Gen made Emily's throat ache. She threw the letter into the lodge fire.

On the final morning of their trip, Emily told Jack she would try some easy slopes. His mood immediately lifted and she was rewarded with deep relief. Their fight was over. He kissed her cheek and zipped her coat, offering to fasten her ski boots. "We'll go slow," he promised. They spent the day on green slopes, with him calling out compliments on her form. After they made their final run to the lodge, he said, "You were incredible! You didn't fall once. I get that you were scared, but you can't let fear rule you. You were perfect, Em."

She wondered what else she might have to do to become his idea of *perfect*. She wondered what would happen if she couldn't.

She called Florencia, who had moved back to Buenos Aires soon after graduation.

Ever since Emily and Jack had returned to New York, he had been so attentive to her—he brought her tea in bed, he massaged her lower back—that Emily began to second-guess that she had been in the right. She was half aware that self-doubt made her life with Jack easier. If, as he believed, she had been in the wrong, and had been so paranoid about safety that she had belittled his gift of their vacation, then he was a good man with a good heart. That meant all was well, so long as she took greater care with his feelings. Maybe she hadn't been sensitive enough to how he felt. Emily's half awareness whispered that her life with Jack could continue, uninterrupted, if she submitted to his point of view. She would reach the end of her pregnancy secure in her marriage to the father of her child. Their little family would be safe. She would avoid his anger and keep his love.

Emily's half awareness was a convenient teacher, one that vanished once the lesson was learned. It was with a breezy tone that Emily told Florencia that she had gone skiing.

"You did *what*? Emily! You could have hit a tree. If you fell hard enough, the force could have torn your placenta. You could have given birth on the slope. You could have lost the baby. I can't believe Jack let you do that."

"I wanted to ski."

"Then the pregnancy hormones have rotted your brain! When I see Jack, I'm going to tell him what I think of him."

"No," said Emily quickly. "Don't."

From the first moment Emily held Connor in her arms, she loved him. He was dear to her, dear not just in the sense of cherished, but also in its older, forgotten meaning, the one that people didn't use often. *Dear* as in costly. Something that came at a high price. Whatever the price, Emily would pay it.

18

Look at you," Rory cooed at Connor. "Those big eyes! You are going to make the girls *cry*."

"Or boys!" said Elizabeth, with a quick glance at Emily, then an even quicker glance at Jack. "Or whatever!"

"Can I steal him? Just for one photo shoot?" Rory had become a talent agent for models. She had a surprisingly big roster of clients for an agent fresh out of college, but her parents had connections. "You have got to have a vision," she had told Emily when the twins first moved to New York. "Mine is apartments in Paris and London. Oh, and a spot in the Caribbean—nothing extravagant, so long as there's an infinity pool." Elizabeth, who had a degree in mathematics, had been hired by Goldman Sachs right after graduation but hated it and quit. She was living off her trust fund and taking ceramics classes. She had presented Emily with a hollow clay sculpture of Connor's head that was so fragile that she hadn't fired it, out of worry that it would shatter in the kiln. The likeness was very good, down to the thin strokes of the eyebrows.

After the twins left, Jack said, "Who gives someone a copy of their baby's head? It's like a voodoo doll."

It *was* a little creepy, but beautiful, too. Emily knew better than to say this.

"How about you see them on your own time," Jack said.

"I thought you liked them."

"If I said half the things Rory said, you'd never forgive me."

Of her friends, Elizabeth and Rory Ryall had the most in common with Jack, and Emily said so.

"Because we come from money? Not fair, Em."

She supposed he had a point.

"They look down on me," Jack said.

"That's not true."

"I'm not saying you can't see them, just that I don't want to."

This was reasonable. There was no rule that a husband had to be friends with his wife's friends. Although the twins were Emily's closest friends in New York, along with Violet, who had been accepted into Juilliard's master's program, Emily began to see less of them. At first, she would ask the nanny to stay later and met the twins for a cocktail, but Jack complained that Connor was fussy whenever she went out. It became easier to stay home. Then Elizabeth decided to break up with her boyfriend and travel the world. "I'm sick of living in Rory's shadow," she said. Rory's career accelerated; her free time dwindled. Most of Rory and Emily's communication happened over texts.

dude why doesn't Jack like me?

he does!

omg you liar. last time we all hung out he looked like he was getting an enema

are we still on for Fri?

yes if u dont cancel again

Emily strapped Connor into the baby carrier and went to the store for diapers and some formula, which she planned to stash behind the detergent in the laundry room cupboards. She wasn't producing enough milk. After thirty minutes at her breast, Connor would wail, but she had found that if she gave him a little formula after nursing, he would suck blissfully at the bottle until his mouth slipped from the silicone nipple and his eyes closed in heavy sleep. Jack had resisted the idea of formula, but this was only a little, a top off, so Emily thought it best to keep this practice to herself. She stroked Connor's downy head. He chirruped and curled his fingers in and out of her shirt as she walked back home. When she returned, she would nurse him, take a shower, and get ready to meet Rory. She decided that she would wear her favorite red dress.

But when she entered the apartment, singing to Connor, who bounced excitedly in his carrier, Jack called from another room, "Is that you, Em? Come see!"

She followed his voice to find that he had laid the table with an elaborate dinner. A bottle of champagne sat at a jaunty angle in ice. Jack kissed her. "I thought I'd knock off work early and cook a few things. It's been a while since we've had a date night. I sent the nanny home." Emily set down her shopping bags. She felt light-headed: trapped, then guilty for feeling trapped . . . and anxious, because she was about to disappoint him.

"I'll put Connor down in his crib," he said. "You relax, have a glass of champagne. I'll be back in a sec."

"I can't."

"Can't what?" he said distractedly, reaching for Connor.

"I can't have dinner. I'm meeting Rory in an hour."

He froze, then his hands swung down to his sides. "Are you serious?"

"I told you I was going to have a drink with her."

"No, you didn't."

"I did."

"It's not in our shared calendar."

Connor struggled in the carrier, impatient to get out. "This is a misunderstanding," Emily said. "I *did* tell you, but I should have put it in the calendar and I'm sorry. How about we have a quick dinner? I'll nurse Connor while we eat, and if I skip a shower, I should be able to meet Rory in time."

"Wow, Em. Way to make me feel second-best."

"You're not, it's just that I've canceled on Rory a lot, because you asked me to. I don't want to do that again."

"This is *my* fault?"

"There's always some reason you don't want me to see her. You've said you wanted to watch a movie together. Or that the apartment was lonely without me. That Connor misses me too much."

"I can't believe you're complaining that I want some family time."

"But it always gets in the way of me seeing my friend."

"Fine." Jack fumbled with the baby carrier straps and took Connor, who squawked. "Go ahead." He shifted Connor to one arm and reached for the shopping bags, then paused. He lifted out a canister of formula. "What's this?"

Panic swarmed inside her. She was ready to say that she had bought formula in case of an emergency, but the intensity of her panic stopped her. Panic wasn't normal. For this? Lots of parents bottle-fed. "Sometimes I give Connor formula. A little, after nursing."

His hand tightened around the canister. "How long has this been going on?"

"About a month."

He slung the canister at the table, shattering the champagne glasses. Emily flinched. Connor began to cry. "What the *fuck*, Emily."

"Give me the baby."

"You've been lying to me?"

"Please, you're upset. Give me the baby."

"You think I'm going to hurt my son? *You* don't trust *me*? I'm not the one keeping secrets."

"I didn't tell you because I knew you wouldn't like it."

"If you knew, don't you think that maybe you shouldn't have done it? He's my child, too." He advanced on her. She backed away. He closed the space between them.

"You're right," she said abruptly. "I'm sorry, I won't do it again. If you give Connor to me, I'll nurse him right now."

Jack glanced down at the screaming baby in his arms, then took in the wreck of the dining table. He seemed stunned. He passed the baby to Emily. Quietly, he said, "I scared you."

"Of course not," she lied.

"The idea of you keeping secrets . . . baby formula is a small thing, but it made me think, *What else don't I know?* What if I lost you? I can't lose you. You're everything to me."

Connor cried despairingly. His face bobbed against her chest.

Jack said, "I get it if you want to see Rory, but please stay? Can we talk about this? I want to talk about this. Let me make things up to you."

She felt dizzy. It was hard to think. Bits of glass glinted up at her from the floor. Connor was hot and squalling.

"I fucked up," Jack said. "I know that. But I can be better. Will you give me a chance? Please."

Emily pulled up her shirt to nurse Connor. Jack gazed at her, shaken and desperate. He was so sorry. He had lost his temper, but didn't everyone sometimes? Doesn't everyone fuck up? How could she not give him a second chance when they loved each other?

I can't make it

???

Rain check?

uhh i'm already at the bar

Yikes. Sorry!! Kind of had a crisis at home

Three dots appeared on Emily's phone, then disappeared, then reappeared.

what sort of crisis? Rory said.

Emily tried to explain, editing the story so that it sounded like a common spat. She didn't want Rory to think badly of Jack.

has it occurred to u that u married a manchild

he just wanted to be part of the decision about formula

um it's YOUR boobs

Can we try for the same time next week?

A moment went by before Rory wrote again. i'll be in LA

When are you free?

i actually canceled plans with a client tonight so I could see u

Emily had a sinking feeling. She guessed what Rory would say, so when the words appeared on her screen, it was as though Emily had written them herself. i'm not saying this to make u feel bad, Rory texted. it's so u understand. let's meet when I'm back in NYC. yr my friend and i love u but it sucks to get stood up all the time and tbh my calendar is packed. we can catch up on the phone later, ok?

Emily was in the bathroom. She had wanted a place where she could be alone for a few minutes. She sat on the floor near the oblong marble tub. She tried to think of how she could make this problem right. She wrote words and erased them. She set the phone down on the tiles. What apology, without the full truth, would Rory accept?

What would be wrong, said a voice in her mind, *with telling her the truth?* The voice was Gen's.

Emily was twenty-two years old. Four years had passed since she and Gen had broken up, and they'd barely communicated since. It was pointless to imagine what Gen would say. Gen was gone. They had different lives. They would probably never see each other again.

Emily lifted her phone from the bathroom floor and told Rory that she understood.

Jack took cooking classes and became even more skilled in the kitchen. On the weekend, Emily woke to the smell of French toast. She would walk sleepily into the kitchen and find Jack giving Connor a bottle of formula. When Connor was ready for solid foods, Jack prepared the baby food himself, steaming vegetables that he made into purees and froze in ice cube trays for Emily to defrost later. At night, he was immediately hard for her, but took her slowly. Emily began to forget the smashed plates and glasses . . . or, she remembered, sort of, but in the way that people described remembering a car crash. She knew the facts but they felt detached from reality, as if that evening had happened to someone else. The more she thought about it, the less she wanted to think about it, because they were happy again. What a happy family, people said to them on the street, and they were right.

The day had been hot but there was a breeze right around sunset. Jack suggested they take Connor to the Central Park Zoo. Connor, just over a year old, was toddling. Jack held him high to see sea lions leap out of the water. Connor gurgled, excited. He wobbled down the zoo path. He stared at lemurs. He lifted his arms to Jack to be carried and then fell asleep as Jack held him. Jack asked Emily, "Want to take a boat out onto the lake? I've never done it before because it's so touristy, but look at that sky." It was soaked in color.

Connor woke up when they put the life jacket on him, and cried. Jack soothed him. He pointed to a turtle basking on a log. He sat Connor between his legs and placed the baby's hands on the oars. While Jack rowed, Emily praised Connor for doing such a good job. Connor's expression grew serious, intent. He watched his small hands on the oars rise and fall as Jack rowed. Then Jack stopped rowing and they floated. The water was pewter, like the sea lions' skin. Connor grew restless and Emily said that maybe he was hot, so Jack took off Connor's shoes and socks and dipped the baby's feet in the water. Connor squealed with joy and grabbed Jack's face with both hands. He looked at Jack with pure adoration. Emily memorized the sight of how much her son loved his father.

Jack wanted to buy Emily a diamond bracelet for her birthday.

Each piece of jewelry at Artem's was one-of-a-kind. Jack had made the appointment with the designer himself, and Artem presented his work on black velvet boards while assistant jewelers helped other customers. Emily tried on several bracelets, Jack clasping each one and then shaking his head until one bracelet dripped over Emily's wrist in a watery streak. "Perfect," he said.

"What if you didn't buy me this, but instead gave the money to charity?"

Artem, expert at discretion, kept his expression neutral.

"But, Em," Jack said, "we *do* give to charity."

"This bracelet is too much."

"It's yours." He held her hands in his. "It's done. If it makes you feel better, I'll also write a blank check for whatever charity you want." He turned back to the jeweler. "I'd like some earrings, too. Christmas gift for my mother." He loved getting his parents expensive gifts. It was a point of pride. Although he'd been able to access his trust fund since he turned thirty, he didn't touch it. They lived on his income from work, and it pleased him to show his parents how well they lived.

The two men drifted to another corner of the shop. Emily looked down at her wrist. Her suggestion that they donate money to charity wasn't wholly selfless; she dreaded the responsibility of owning the bracelet. It was stunning . . . and a disaster waiting to happen. What if she lost it? Or damaged it? There was insurance, yes, but that might not make Jack any less upset, especially because a one-of-a-kind bracelet was irreplaceable. Everything had been going so well between them lately. Emily could predict, though, how their happiness might sour. Maybe she wouldn't wear the bracelet enough. Or if she wore it every day, he might say that she treated it like an ordinary object. Didn't she think it was special enough? What more could she possibly want?

Emily bit her lip. She was being unfair. If she lost the bracelet, Jack was so generous that he would probably say not to worry, that it gave him the opportunity to give her a better one.

"I cut those diamonds."

Emily glanced up from her wrist to see a woman who looked a little bored, ready for a break in the routine of her job. Her brown hands were tidy, resting lightly on the wooden frame of the glass case between her and Emily. She had a friendly expression, wore her short hair in close twists, and her suit fit her well. Emily guessed that the woman was gay, and guessed that the woman didn't think that Emily was. Emily felt something like homesickness, the way a ghost might, drifting unseen into its old life. She had never looked gay—not in a way that straight people recognized. Not even, sometimes, when they had seen her with Gen. But she missed the recognition from queer people. Sometimes it came in the form of a glance on the street, when she was walking alone, one of mutual acknowledgment. This had gotten rarer since she married Jack.

"Artem designed the bracelet," the woman said, "but I cut the stones."

Emily had never considered what a jeweler's workshop looked like. She realized that, as at a restaurant, there probably was a front of the house and back of the house for everything. Most people only saw a jeweler's front of the house: the display cases and reverent quiet. Emily asked, "What kind of tool did you use?"

"Tool*s*. First, a diamond saw for the cleaving stage. For bruting, I used a laser."

"Cleaving?"

"When you make the first cuts."

"And bruting?"

"Second cuts. Sometimes Artem uses an artist called a brilianteer to do the last facets, but I'm good at that, too."

"Where did you do this? Here?"

"Not *here* here. In the back there's a workshop. It's specially sealed."

"Why? So no one steals anything?"

The woman smiled. "No, because of the dust."

"You need to keep dust out?"

"We need to keep it *in*. Cut diamond dust is valuable. We let it accumulate and then sweep it up and sell it. The dust from the diamonds in your bracelet got mixed with other diamond dust that was probably used to make saws or other high-precision tools."

"It's like my bracelet has an alter ego," Emily said. "Its dust went out into the world to accomplish things."

The woman's dark brown eyes reevaluated Emily. "Do you think your bracelet is jealous?"

"Em, we're ready," said Jack, his voice tight. He stood at her side. She hadn't noticed him approach. She revisited everything she'd said to the jeweler. Once, she would have felt reassured, knowing that there had been nothing objectionable in the conversation, but she had learned that he could always find something to blame.

Outside the shop, he said, "Seems like you were more interested in dust than the actual bracelet I gave you."

"That's not true."

"Maybe it was the sweeping. If I sweep the floor when we get home, could you manage to pay attention to me?"

It was rush hour. Yellow cabs inched up the cobbled SoHo street. A driver laid on the horn.

"You can be so selfish." Jack seized Emily's wrist. She dragged back against his grip. The streetlight changed from red to green. His grip softened. She tugged free, removed the bracelet, and flung it at him.

Slowly, he bent to retrieve it from the sidewalk. He straightened. In a low voice he said, "I wish you wouldn't treat me like that."

She immediately felt terrible. He was looking at the pool of diamonds in his palm, face twisted in sadness. What had she done? She'd thrown the bracelet at him in a flash of anger—almost in self-defense, as if the bracelet had been a grenade that she needed to get away from her. But it had been a gift—a thoughtful, generous one. She apologized.

"*I'm* sorry," he said. "I got mad for no reason. I promised I wouldn't do that anymore. Did I hurt you?"

She was rubbing her wrist. "No." It was technically true.

"Will you please put it back on?" He offered the bracelet. "Can we forget about this?"

She wanted to forget about it, too. She put on the bracelet. The sidewalk was narrow. People wove around her and Jack, eager to get somewhere else. "I wasn't attracted to her," Emily said, though she had been.

He was confused. "The assistant jeweler? Why would you be?"

Emily realized that Jack either had forgotten about Gen or had decided that Emily's relationship with her didn't mean anything. Maybe he thought that it had been practice for Emily's relationship with him, and that Emily's queerness had ended once she began dating him. Was that right? She had married a man. Was she still queer? If she was, maybe it didn't matter, even if she wanted it to matter.

Jack said, "I got mad because I called your name and you ignored me."

"I didn't hear you."

"It hurts when you ignore me."

"I'm sorry," she said again, because he was right that she had been ignoring him. Even if he hadn't realized why, talking with the assistant jeweler *had* been Emily's favorite part about shopping for the bracelet, not just because of the jeweler's appeal but also why she had been appealing: the woman's skill and confidence had reminded Emily of Gen. Emily had liked learning from someone. She had liked seeing something in a new way.

But Jack was her husband. She loved him, and told him so.

Years later, after she left Jack the second time, the bracelet was one of the first things she sold.

That night, Connor, who was teething, woke up crying. Emily went to his room and held him until he fell back asleep. His hand clung to a lock of her hair, his small weight snug in her arms. She didn't want to put him back in his crib. She stayed in the rocking chair, thinking about how she used to write letters to Gen and then destroyed them. That first year in college, before she and Gen had broken up, Emily had printed out Gen's emails in the computer lab, but no one did that anymore—there were too many emails from too many people. Emails lived forever in inboxes that nobody emptied.

Not many letters survived the ancient world. Those that did had mostly been inscribed on clay tablets. She wondered what kind of letters had been lost. She thought about the diamond dust, the extra matter of things, the side stories. The dust was a kind of B plot to the A plot of the diamonds. It occurred to her that even though *The Odyssey* was focused on Odysseus's journey home, a shadow story ran beneath the narrative: the story of Athena, the goddess of wisdom and Odysseus's patron. Athena eventually begged the king of the gods to help Odysseus return home to Ithaca. Why had Athena taken an interest in him? Why did she wait so long to help him? Did she, in fact, *want* Odysseus to return home to his wife, or had she struggled with the idea of letting her favorite mortal go?

Emily supposed that Homer's point was to make a human his main character and cast the gods as minor ones, but it also seemed that he hadn't given the goddess his full attention. Athena's story was at least as compelling as Odysseus's, if not more so.

Emily put Connor back into his crib. She went into the living room. The sky brightened. The huge windows became planes of pink and yellow. She wrote a letter from Athena to Odysseus.

—

"You didn't come back to bed last night," Jack said in the morning.

"I was writing."

He drank his coffee, still sleepy-eyed. "Writing what?"

"I don't know." The idea seemed silly by daylight. "Maybe the beginning of a book."

"What kind of book?"

"A retelling of *The Odyssey*."

"The book you were reading when we first met?"

"Yes." She added, "It's not such a new idea. Other people have retold *The Odyssey*."

"But not like you." He smiled at her over his coffee cup. "My brilliant wife."

—

Emily saw little of her friends.

Elizabeth sent photos and brief, cryptic messages that read like reports sent back to a home planet from an alien scouting out Earth.

Swans are menacing. Bandit eyes. Like raccoons! But their FEET. Love their feet. Black and flexible.

Hello from Tanzania. The stars are so bright they ATTACK you.

Went hiking near Kashmir, totally off the grid. Fell but no broken bones. People who live in the mountains put BUTTER on my cuts. Nice!

OMG. In Majorca a local said worms grow in pine trees. Grow in balls (nests??). Hatch and WALK AROUND (these worms have legs??) and are POISON. Will sting, will SHOOT STINGERS AT YOU and BLIND YOU. WILL KILL DOGS. Leaving tomorrow.

The water in the Maldives is so clear I can see into my next life

Gonna buy a baby lemur, name him Marvin

Never coming home!

The surreal nature of the messages began to make Elizabeth seem like someone Emily had made up: an imaginary friend.

Emily hadn't seen Rory since she canceled their drinks night. Rory had expanded her client list to include rising-star actors and split her time between New York and L.A. When they talked on the phone, Emily made her life with Jack seem ideal. Sometimes her life actually looked that way, and she sensed that if she described how Jack could behave, Rory—mouthy, loyal Rory—might say or do something unpredictable that would make it impossible for Emily to continue the pretense, even for herself. Once Emily had started lying to Rory, it was necessary to keep lying. She tried to recapture the overwhelming gratitude she had felt two years ago on September 11, when Connor was four months old and Emily, panicked, couldn't reach Jack—it was impossible for her calls to go through—and then he came through the front door covered in dust. He had walked the whole way home. Emily relived that stroke of luck, the awe of momentous reprieve. How awful: the threat of losing him.

Florencia would visit in a few months, in summer. She would stay with Emily and Jack for a week, a prospect that made Emily slide between an excitement that made her check her calendar every day and a nervousness that the visit would go wrong. But Jack was looking forward to the visit, too. He had told Emily that he would cook dinner for them every night.

Between classes and practice, Violet wasn't often free, but came over occasionally to spend time with Emily and Connor, who was toddling more confidently and saying small words. One day, Violet brought him a plastic plane that lit up and made take-off noises. Connor grabbed it with both hands and plopped down onto his diapered bottom, mesmerized. It was a weekend. Jack had gone to the gym. Relaxed, Emily sipped sparkling cranberry juice while she watched Connor play and listened to Violet gossip about Juilliard. All the drama students were hooking up with each other. "It's nonstop," Violet said. "Their bodies are sources of infinitely renewable energy, like solar panels."

"Sounds fun," said Emily. Violet's expression shifted slightly, just enough to make Emily realize that although Violet had been talking at length, it had never been about herself. "Are you having fun? Do you like your program?"

Violet grimaced.

"It must be a lot of pressure," said Emily.

"It's not that, not exactly. Being a professional musician is always intense. I wasn't sure I was up for that, but I regretted not going to conservatory for undergrad. When I auditioned for the master's program, I hoped I'd get into Ilse Visser's studio. Now her studio is everything I worried Juilliard would be."

"I'm not sure what you mean by *studio.*"

"Each teacher chooses students to form a studio. Ilse Visser's is legendary. Any student she likes has big potential, because she's close with music directors at every major symphony orchestra and her good word means a lot. But she pits us against each other. We're in constant competition. We know our rank based on studio 'assignments.' The worst is scooping her cat's litter. My rank's not so bad: I have to bring her a half-caf latte every day. If you rank high, you're constantly afraid you'll fall. Plus everyone resents you. If you're on the bottom rung, you feel worthless."

"Can you report Visser to other professors?"

“She’s so respected that they say her methods build character.”

“Go to the president of Juilliard. Ask for a transfer out of her studio. Say that if you don’t get one, you’ll take the story to *The New York Times*.”

“They’d never publish it.”

“Abuse of power at an elite school? They would.”

“Maybe I should quit.”

“Don’t quit.”

“You make everything sound easy.”

Emily brushed away lint from her white pants. “It’s not,” she said slowly. “It wouldn’t be for me. I guess I’m giving advice I’d have a hard time following, but I believe that you can do it. If you’re ready to quit, you have nothing to lose.”

Violet watched Connor walk around the coffee table, gripping its edge for balance. “Can we talk about something else? Tell me about your book.”

It had become more than a retelling of *The Odyssey*. Emily treated the original myths and Homer’s poetry as incomplete, supplying other sides to the stories as if those interpretations had been lost, and she was restoring them instead of creating them. At that time, she was working on the myth of Arachne, whom Emily had cast as Athena’s lover in an early section of the narrative, as a flashback told before Odysseus is taken captive by Calypso.

“But she hated Arachne,” Violet said. “In the original myth. Right? Athena was jealous that a mortal could weave better than she could, so she hit Arachne on the head with a shuttle and turned her into a spider.”

“First, Athena loved her. At least, that’s how I’m writing it.”

“I didn’t know you wanted to be a writer.”

Emily hadn’t either, but the more she wrote, the more she liked writing. She liked how each sentence was an artifact of time, an insect suspended in amber, one that she had placed there, in an exact shape and gesture. She chose each word, the order, the inversion of expectation or its satisfaction. Then her task was to dissolve that amber and make the insect whir to life.

“It makes me happy,” she said.

"Why?"

"In my book, I can make anything happen. I can do whatever I want."

The front door opened. The sound was loud and startling. Emily spilled cranberry juice onto her pants.

"Hi, sweetheart!" Jack called. He came into the living room, sweaty. "Oh, hey, Violet. Good to see you! Em, do you want to go change? I'll keep an eye on Connor."

When Emily returned, wearing fresh clothes, Violet was gone. Jack sat on the floor next to Connor, zooming the plane around him. Connor giggled and reached for the plane, which Jack lifted too high for him to catch.

"Where's Violet?" Emily said.

"She said she had to go."

"Why?"

"I don't know." Jack swooped the plane down again, and this time let Connor catch it.

"Did you say something to her?"

"I asked if she had any performances coming up. I said I hoped Connor would play the piano one day. That's it. Then she left."

Connor, the plane in his hands, looked between his parents.

Emily said, "It's not like Violet to leave without saying goodbye."

Jack shrugged. "I guess she remembered something she had to do."

But it took a while for Violet to answer Emily's text thanking her for the visit, and whenever Emily invited her over to the apartment, Violet always had a reason she couldn't come.

White hydrangeas sat on Emily's lap as she listened to Violet play. She had seen on Facebook that Violet was performing Liszt at a recital hall in Midtown. Emily wasn't invited but surely anybody could come. The announcement had been public.

Violet's long fingers slowed, then sank into the keys. Applause scattered across the hall. The tissue paper wrapped around the flowers crinkled beneath Emily's grip. As people began leaving the hall, she went to Violet to congratulate her. "Oh," Violet said when she saw her.

"I hope it's okay that I came."

Violet was polite. "Of course."

"Could we get a drink?"

"My parents are here," Violet said. "We have dinner plans."

"Will you please tell me what happened?"

Violet said that Jack had told her that he hoped that Connor would play the piano, so she suggested that he start young. "I want him to play like you," Jack said. People often expressed some version of this to Violet. She understood it. After all, she wished that she could play like Martha Argerich. But she reminded Jack that it was difficult to reach her level. Few could. Jack insisted that all it took was enough practice and the right teachers. "You can be his teacher," he said. When she replied that she didn't teach little children, Jack offered to pay whatever she wanted, adding, "Come on, I know you need the money."

She asked Emily, "What did you tell Jack about my background?"

Violet's parents were diplomats. Violet, their only child, had been born in Geneva and had lived nowhere for longer than a few years. She grew up knowing multiple languages and had studied with world-class pianists. She never talked about money, but it was easy to guess that she didn't need it. "I didn't tell him anything," Emily said.

"Maybe you should have, since he thinks I need his charity. I know I shouldn't be mad at you. *You* didn't say it. But you married someone who did. We both know why he did. I've got to go, Emily. My parents are waiting." She didn't offer to introduce them. "Thanks for coming." She hesitated, then said, "Call me, okay?"

Emily was partway home before she realized that she still held the flowers.

Jack touched the hydrangeas, which stood in a vase on the dining table. "Pretty. Did you have a nice time?"

"You offended Violet."

"What? No, I didn't."

Emily repeated what Violet had said.

"What's the problem?" said Jack.

"You acted like her talent could be bought off the shelf."

"I gave her a compliment."

"You treated her like she was poor. You wouldn't have done that if she were white."

"Wait a minute. This is not a race thing. I would have offered to pay anybody for teaching Connor. Her being Black had nothing to do with it."

"She didn't invent this."

"Maybe she's offended, but that doesn't mean I did anything wrong. She's probably sensitive to this sort of thing. She must have had some bad experiences in the past. It's nice of you to want to protect her."

"I'm not trying to protect her, I'm trying to make you see."

"There is nothing *to* see. You're twisting yourself into knots over nothing. Call her and I'll explain."

Emily, who during the course of this conversation had alternated between doubting what she believed and disliking herself for that doubt, knew one thing for certain: Jack's explanation would make things worse. She didn't call Violet.

Jack invited a fellow partner at his hedge fund over for dinner. He meticulously planned the courses and ordered the freshest ingredients for delivery. "I really want David to like this rack of lamb," he told Emily while she kept him company in the kitchen. He refilled her glass of rosé. "You're going to love his wife. Jocelyn is smart and pretty and always says and does the exact right thing."

The dinner was a success. Jocelyn's smooth social grace had a lot to do with how she asked many questions and listened to the answers. This let Jocelyn keep herself at a distance, but she never gave the impression that she was hiding something, only waiting for the right moment to share, with the right person, which made Emily want to be that person. Jocelyn was also an animated storyteller. She could command an audience and sprinkled a story with enough details to give her listeners the sense that they had been there with her. She described a long drive to the Hamptons the previous weekend, bumper-to-bumper traffic. A rabbit ran in the field by the side of the road. A trucker in his cab took off his hat. There was a crash, probably, on the road up ahead. Traffic slowed, then stopped. "I couldn't stand it anymore," Jocelyn said. "I called a helicopter and had it land in the field to pick me up."

Emily was startled that one could simply *call* a helicopter. "What did you do with your car?"

"What do you mean?"

"You abandoned it in the middle of traffic?"

"Honey, *no*. I had a driver, of course. I wasn't going to drive to the Hamptons *myself*. The driver drove the car to our house."

Since leaving Ohio, and especially after meeting Jack, Emily had learned a lot about wealth. She had learned that it could make anything beautiful, even a kitchen sink drain. It could liberate, like the trust fund that let Elizabeth quit her job and travel. Wealth was a kindness, one that Emily portioned out into an account for her half sisters' future college tuition. That night at dinner, Emily learned that there was always something more to learn. Money always found new ways to express itself.

"The poor driver," Emily said. The table went quiet. Jack cleared his throat. "It seems hard," Emily said, "to be stuck in traffic for no purpose."

"You're right," Jocelyn said. "I was a pampered jerk in a helicopter!" She didn't sound sorry. To Jack, she said, "Where did you find her? She's like a dreamy character in one of those 1950s Technicolor movies." To Emily, with fond wonder, she said, "Are you a blond Audrey Hepburn? Are you going to adopt a fawn?"

Jack said, "Emily's always ready to defend a driver."

"But there *was* a purpose," David said. "We pay him to drive the car. Whether Joss was in the back seat didn't matter. We needed the extra Porsche that weekend for guests."

"David, shut up!" Jocelyn said. "You're missing the point."

Emily felt a flash of concern for Jocelyn—what would Jack do if Emily snapped at him like that, especially in front of others?—

but David, his gaze on his wife's impatient, lovely face, smiled and shrugged.

Later, after their guests had left, Jack said, "That was a strange thing for you to say."

"I think it was pretty normal."

"You have a thing for salt-of-the-earth types, don't you?"

"Maybe I do." She shouldn't have said this, but sometimes her need to monitor herself for Jack's approval was overshadowed by her dislike of that need.

"Maybe you want to pretend I'm different." Jack brushed her hair away from her face, a gesture that would have looked affectionate to David and Jocelyn, had they still been in the room. He stared at Emily as if he wanted to dig something out of her. "I bet you'd enjoy that."

"No." Jack already seemed like two people—generous, then accusatory; affectionate, then resentful. Emily didn't want to imagine yet another version of Jack. That version could be worse.

He kissed her cheek. She had said the right thing. She felt like she had won.

She hadn't, she knew that. She had said what he wanted, but that knowledge didn't banish the good student inside her that Jack tutored. She couldn't help her relief. It ballooned inside her, stretched taut, leaving room for little else. The relief felt so close to gratitude that Emily couldn't distinguish the emotions, and therefore became grateful to Jack for forgiving her momentary defiance. There were two versions of Emily, too: the one who resisted Jack and the one who didn't.

Emily's manuscript grew. She developed writing habits. She wrote in longhand. She liked to write in Connor's room while he slept, even though she could have used the guest room, which had a desk. Using paper and pencil made the work more intimate, as though the words were for someone she knew, as had been the many letters she had written to Gen when she was younger. Gen felt distant now, like a half-finished daydream, as did Emily's youth. People often exclaimed over what a young mother she was, only twenty-four—not uncommon back home in Ohio, but in New York City,

Emily's age was astonishing and almost inappropriate, as though she were a child herself. Still, she didn't feel young.

Most nights, she would leave Jack in their bed, walk softly down the hall, and curl up with a notebook in the rocking chair by Connor's toddler bed. Connor's steady, quiet breath kept her company as her pencil scratched the page. Sometimes he woke. "Mama?" He pushed himself up. She stroked his back and told him to go back to sleep. He lay down again and sighed. Those were her favorite hours of the day: the two of them alone, a pencil in her hand, the sun below the horizon.

She filled one notebook, then another. Soon, several were stacked alongside Connor's picture books.

One morning, Jack smiled at her from the doorway as she slid another notebook into place. "Sure you don't want to write in the guest room?" he said. "We can turn it into your office."

"I like writing here. Anyway, we'll need the guest room soon for Florencia."

"Right, of course. We'll make everything perfect for her visit." Jack's eagerness to please Florencia—and, through her, Emily—made Emily glad she had never told her friend about the upsetting moments in her marriage. Florencia liked Jack. He liked Florencia. Emily wanted things to stay that way. The visit had to go well. She wanted everything to be okay.

19

"Oh my God," Florencia mumbled around her spoon. "What *is* this?"

"Passion fruit soufflé." Jack topped off Florencia's mimosa.

"Is every brunch he makes like this?" Florencia asked Emily.

"Pretty much." Emily shifted Connor on her lap so that he could better reach his strawberries.

Florencia took another bite. "I never want to go home."

"Stay as long as you like," Jack said. "We love having you here."

"In college, you always talked about living in New York," Emily said.

"I wish," Florencia said. "My parents need me, though. They want to convert some of our estancias into hotels and that means hiring architects and staff, drawing up business plans . . . I'm the oldest child, so it's up to me to keep the family business going."

"I get it," said Jack. "I made that choice. But it's a lot of pressure. Sometimes I wish that I'd told my parents no."

"Then you'd have a very different life," Florencia said. She smiled at Emily and Connor. "Your life seems pretty great."

"Yeah." Jack reached for Emily's hand and kissed it. "It is."

"Will you come visit me in Buenos Aires?" Florencia asked Emily.

"Girls' trip, huh?" said Jack.

"I'd love that," said Emily. "I wanted to before, but Connor was so little."

"You should go," said Jack. "I can handle Connor. My mother will jump at the chance to help out, and since we know *help* won't include any actual work, I'll get the nanny to stay full-time."

"Amazing!" said Florencia. "I'll plan everything. Can you come for a week or two, Emily? There's so much I want to show you."

Emily had missed Florencia. She had Connor for company, of course, and Jack spent as much time at home as he could, avoiding business trips whenever possible, but her life had formed into a narrow triangle nailed down at each corner by herself, Jack, and their son. There were days when she didn't leave the apartment building, especially when Jack was home, because he would tell her to rest while he went to run errands, and if she said she'd like to go instead to the store or dry cleaner, he'd remind her that he had just offered to do something nice, and why was it that every time he suggested something, she said no? She glanced at Jack.

He said, "Bring me back some alfajores." They discussed potential dates and settled on mid-November, which would be spring in Argentina. Jack insisted on clearing the table, then went to change into running gear. Sneakers on, Jack put Connor into the jogging stroller, tickled his cheek, and wheeled him out the door.

"I wish you'd stay longer," Emily said to Florencia after the door had shut. Her friend's visit was nearly over. They had driven to a beach where the wild water, barely warmed by the beginning of summer, made Emily's feet feel like ice cream. They went to museums and stared at Picasso's *Boy Leading a Horse*, though they knew his *Les Demoiselles d'Avignon*, his Cubist portrait of prostitutes, was considered the better work. But Emily liked the sympathy between the boy and his horse, the way the animal, with no bridle or saddle or halter, kept close to the boy's side. Florencia and Emily walked all over the city. They met with Violet and Rory, who hugged Emily as though she had returned from a war.

"Are you okay?" Florencia, curled into the couch's corner, peered at Emily.

"What do you mean?"

"Your life looks nice. Great husband, cute kid, not a financial cloud in the sky. But you don't seem happy."

Emily glanced at the front door. Jack was gone, but it felt as though he were still in the room, listening. "I'm not sure why you'd think that."

"Remember when we went to the Met and saw the mummies? They were so small. Yes, I know that people thousands of years ago were smaller than us, because of evolution and our healthier diet and bigger caloric intake, and I know that those bodies are basically bones and skin and linen wrappings, but *still*. They looked shrunken. The mummified cats and falcons, too. They were smaller than I'd expect. You're like that. I'm not talking about your literal size. I mean *you*. As a person."

"You're comparing me to a mummified cat?"

"Yes."

"Like someone removed my internal organs and put them in jars and closed me up in a sarcophagus?"

"You said it, not me."

"You're being silly."

"Good, tell me I'm wrong. I want to be wrong. I don't want to think you've shrunk into a former version of yourself."

Emily laughed. She told Florencia that she was wrong.

That night at dinner, Jack was jovial. The weather had been gorgeous on his run, he said, with a salty breeze wafting off the Hudson River. He asked Florencia if she wanted seconds. She said yes, that everything was incredible. There were only a few days left in Florencia's visit. Emily allowed herself to believe that nothing would go wrong. Things would be just as she'd hoped.

But the day before her departure, Florencia ate a nectarine.

Emily and Florencia were in the living room playing with Connor, who was tired from their time earlier in the park, yet in a too-excited way. He wanted to show Florencia what he could build with magnetic blocks. He pulled off his socks and draped them over the houses he made. It was Florencia's last night in New York. Emily had booked her ticket for November in Argentina and Florencia was describing how the jacaranda trees would be slathered in purple blossoms. It would be hot enough to go to the beach in Uruguay, but in the south, in Patagonia, they could see penguins. Connor, listening, gripped his bare feet with both hands.

Jack was out of sight but Emily could hear him in the kitchen preparing dinner. The refrigerator door slammed. A bowl was set onto the countertop with a hollow thud. The pantry door opened and closed. The sounds grew more agitated until Jack called for her. She passed a block to Connor and went to the kitchen.

"Where's the nectarine?" Jack demanded.

"Which nectarine?"

"The only one we have."

"Did you check the fruit bowl?"

"Yes, *obviously*, I checked the fruit bowl. That's where I put it. I have looked everywhere."

"I'll go to the grocery store and get another one."

"I don't want a grocery store nectarine. I want *my* nectarine, from the farmer's market, that I was saving, that is exactly ripe." Jack was flushed, his hands opening and closing. His agitation, for Emily, was glazed with the surreal. Was this possible? Or was this satire: Jack pretending to be someone enraged by a piece of fruit? Was Emily living in a William Carlos Williams poem? She laughed, not because the situation was funny but because it was absurd: a jolting somersault of the rules of reality. Her laughter was thin and wild. It was a mistake to laugh and worse to keep laughing, but she couldn't help it.

"Hello!" Florencia said brightly, standing by the open kitchen door. "Did I hear something about a nectarine? I ate one earlier and it was great."

Jack was speechless.

"This is just like that William Carlos Williams poem," Florencia said. "The one about the plums. 'I have eaten the plums that were in the icebox.'"

"'They were delicious.'" Emily's belly hurt with laughter. "'So sweet and so cold.'"

"It's his best-known poem because people relate. It happens to everyone. Everyone's always eating someone else's plums."

"I was saving it," Jack said in a harsh whisper.

"That's what we're saying!"

"For *you*." Jack pointed at Florencia.

Emily stopped laughing. Florencia had a dangerous edge to her smile. "Then there's no problem," Florencia said.

"Yes, there is a fucking problem. I was saving it for the ceviche I planned to make for *you*."

"Use a mango. Don't make it at all. I really don't care."

He continued as if he hadn't heard. "Our *guest*. It's not enough, apparently, for us to wait on you hand and foot, no, everything needs to be yours, you think you can just take whatever you want."

"Me estás jodiendo?"

"Apologize," Emily told him.

He dropped the fruit bowl to the floor. It shattered. Grapes rolled.

"What a mess," said Florencia coolly. "Some asshole is going to have to clean that up."

Emily saw Connor, standing barefoot at the entry to the kitchen with its glittering floor. "Connor, no!"

Jack rushed to sweep Connor into his arms before the child stepped on broken glass. He exhaled in relief. "That was close. The bowl slipped from my hand."

"Really," said Florencia.

"I owe you an apology," he told her. "You know, you're right about the mango. Great idea. Here, honey." He passed Connor to Emily. "I got some glass in my socks, I think, but no harm no foul. Let me clean up and I'll get dinner underway."

"I'm not hungry," said Emily.

"Or we can do delivery. Why don't you choose, Florencia?"

Florencia looked between Jack and Emily, expression slack in disbelief.

"Again, I'm really sorry," Jack said. "I was out of line. Delivery's best, I think. Faster."

"Nothing for me," Florencia said. "I'm going to my room."

Morning sun washed into the building's art deco lobby. Emily waited with Florencia for the car to arrive. Florencia pulled up the handle of her suitcase, then collapsed it. "That was unacceptable," she said. "Not just for me. For you, too. I didn't know what to do. I have never seen anyone behave like that. The only reason I didn't leave and check in to a hotel was that I was afraid he'd take it out on you."

"He has a temper, but he's always sorry. You saw how sorry he was."

"You're making excuses for him, either because this sort of thing happens all the time and it's become normal or because confronting the truth is too painful and scary. There is something wrong with him."

"He means well. He has a good heart."

Florencia was silent. Through the lobby doors, they saw the black car drive up. Florencia said, "Are you coming to Argentina?"

"Of course."

"Call me if you need anything. Anytime." Florencia kissed Emily's cheeks. "Don't be a mummified cat."

"Are you nearly finished with the manuscript?" Jack asked during intermission as they mingled with other donors at a gala for the ballet.

"Yes."

Jack was quiet, then said, "I wish I could do something like that. I wish I could write a book for you."

"You already do so much for me." She was moved by his wish. It would be difficult for anyone to write a book, but especially for him, with his disability. She also recognized in the enormity of his wish's difficulty a proportionate claim on her indebtedness. She didn't want to think like that: to slide so easily from being touched to being wary. Still, was what he said sweet or a way to make her obligated to him? Could it be both?

"So, Em, since you asked me to check in with you before making big plans, I want to talk about November."

"November?"

"New York gets so dull and cold. I thought: Saint Lucia. We

can't do the end of the month because we have Thanksgiving with my parents, but before that I can sneak a week or so off work for a getaway."

"What dates, exactly?"

"November eighth through the nineteenth or twentieth would be ideal."

"I can't."

"I found a resort right on the water. They have babysitting and a spa. Our suite would have its own pool. It'll be good for us to have some alone time."

"I'm going to Argentina then."

He seemed genuinely confused. "Argentina?"

"You saw me book the tickets. I forwarded the information to you. It's in the calendar."

"Because you forgot to remove it. You're not seriously planning on visiting Florencia. After how she behaved?"

"How *you* behaved."

"Not this again."

"I've had enough of you trying to keep me from my friends."

"What are you talking about?"

"You insulted Violet."

"We've gone over this. I wouldn't do that. You're imagining things."

"You won't let me see Rory."

"*Let* you? When did I say you couldn't see Rory?"

"Florencia probably will never visit again."

"That's on her. I was pretty nice, considering how rude she was. I even apologized. You asked me to apologize and I did."

"Then you should have no issue with me going to see her."

"Shouldn't family come first?"

"I booked the tickets! I'm going!"

"Whoa, calm down. You always criticize me for losing my temper but just listen to yourself. You're no angel. That's how you want it, though, don't you? I'm the monster and you're the angel who never does anything wrong. Meanwhile I work my hardest to make you happy."

"It would make me happy to go to Argentina."

"Go, then," he said, "if that's what you really want."

"It is."

Jack's eyes were full of hurt. "You're not the person I thought you were."

A few days later, she took Connor to the park. Summer's end that year was ruthless. Leaves were scorched and brown. Emily left the apartment early in the morning so she and Connor could enjoy a few relatively cool hours before the heat came down like a lid on a pot. Jack was home, getting ready to leave for work, when she left.

He was gone when she and Connor returned. The gossamer curtains were drawn against the sun. The AC whispered. The kitchen gleamed. Their housekeeper had come and gone. Emily bathed Connor, who had played in a sandbox, and wrapped him in a white towel, which he shucked off, running naked into the living room. Normally, she would have gone into his bedroom to fetch clothes, but she let him be naked. It was hot, and she liked seeing him proud and free and joyful. It was rare for him. Connor was a quiet child. He followed her into the kitchen, and as she prepared his lunch he pressed his feet fully flat against the tiles and lifted them, one at a time. "They stick," he told her, and pointed to his steamy footprint as it faded.

It wasn't until they had finished lunch and she was ready to put him down for his nap that she realized that something was wrong. She set him in his bed, her skin prickling. She left his bedroom and checked every room in the apartment, but nothing was out of place. Everything was as it should be. No one else was in the apartment. She even opened, with trepidation, every closet door.

Instinct drew her back to Connor's bedroom. It was here that she first had had that feeling. Connor stood in his bed. "Mama?"

Her gaze swept the room.

Her notebooks were missing. They weren't on the shelf. There wasn't even a gap where they should have been. Connor's picture books ran together in a closed line.

She pulled his books off the shelf. She emptied closets. She went to the bedroom she and Jack shared, and dragged the mattress off the bed to see if the notebooks were hidden on top of the boxsprings. She pulled Jack's clothes off hangers even though the notebooks couldn't have fit in his pockets. The suits lay limp on the floor, arms flopped as though broken. She flung cushions off the sofa, emptied kitchen drawers of every culinary tool Jack had collected. Connor called for her. She rolled up rugs. She yanked art off the walls. Bile rose in her throat and soon she was no longer looking for something she knew wasn't there but destroying things just as something she loved had been destroyed.

"Mama!"

She returned to Connor's bedroom, hands shaking. She sat him on her lap in the rocking chair where she used to write at night. His room was mostly in order; she didn't want him to see the chaos of the rest of the apartment. She called her mother. "Mom? It's me."

"I know. I got caller ID."

"Can I visit? With Connor?"

There was a pause. "When?"

"Tomorrow. Today."

There was a longer pause. "Okay. But I've got work, so if it's babysitting you're after, you're out of luck."

Stung, Emily hung up. She called Florencia and hemorrhaged the entire story, not just about how Jack had taken her notebooks but also about the past few years, the slow vise of his adoration, his skill at blaming her for his faults. It baffled her, how his manipulation was so successful that at first she didn't recognize it, and still wasn't sure he knew that it was manipulation.

"Emily, breathe," said Florencia. "You can tell me everything later, but first I'm going to take care of this. We're going to hang up and I'm going to make some calls and you're going to lock the front door *with the chain* and wait. It won't be long."

Florencia hadn't said, *I'm sure there's some explanation.* She didn't say, as Emily had feared her mother would say, *They're just notebooks.* Florencia believed, as Emily believed, that this was an act of revenge.

Connor squirmed out of her lap to play with his toys. A few minutes later, the phone rang. It was Rory. "Hey, babe," Rory said.

Emily began to cry.

"Don't do that," Rory said. "Here's what you're going to do. Take Connor's birth certificate and your passports. Don't bother with anything else. Go down to your lobby. I called a car for you. It will take you to my apartment. I'm in L.A., so my doorman will let you in. Violet's on her way there. Elizabeth's talking about coming back from India or wherever the fuck she is but I told her that I've got this. I'm taking a plane as soon as I can."

"You don't have to."

"Have to? I *want* to. I want to kneecap your husband."

Emily said the thing she feared everyone would say. "They're just notebooks."

"They were *you*. And if he could do that, what else?"

Three years later, when Emily was twenty-seven, Connor was five, and Stella was a baby sleeping in the stroller, Emily stopped at an outdoor café near their house on the Upper East Side. Connor was bored and fidgety, so she gave him a pencil and napkins. He drew something with pointy feet that was almost definitely a bird. A pigeon, he said.

"Mommy, look." He opened the fold of the napkin. Inside its flap was another pigeon—larger, with a zigzag across its head.

"What's that?" Emily said.

"King Pigeon."

"Does the little pigeon grow up to be King Pigeon or are they two separate pigeons?"

"You decide," said Connor. "It's for you."

Emily remembered her first date with Jack, how there was an Emily before and an Emily after. She wondered whether the person she was before that day at the library became the person who was Jack's wife, or if the closer truth was that they were two different people. Emily didn't know. She couldn't decide.

She would wonder the same thing about the Emily who

showed up with her son at Rory's apartment and lived there for two weeks, and the Emily who realized that she had missed her period.

The first Emily resisted Jack's calls, his frantic texts, the voice mails that swerved between blaming her for their rift and begging her to come back.

Where are my notebooks? she texted.

It is not my fault you lost them.

The first Emily watched Rory and Violet play with her son. She didn't know what she had done to deserve her friends. She and Violet cooked while Rory poured wine. "I got out of that awful piano studio," Violet told Emily. "I took your advice and went to the president." When Rory heard the story of Ilse Visser, she said, "I wouldn't have lasted a day. I would have told Visser to eat a musical dick." To Emily, Violet said, "I wish I'd known what was going on with you at home. I wish you'd told us sooner."

The second Emily walked with Connor to the pharmacy and bought a pregnancy test.

Come home, Jack texted. Ill do anything

Everything feels empty

I miss you so much

She wrote back: Give me my notebooks

Three dots appeared and disappeared. He wrote, Lydia must have thrown them out. Lydia, their Polish housekeeper, cleaned everything within an inch of its life and had an improvisational grasp of English, but made up in enthusiasm for what she couldn't express clearly in words. She must not have understood that the notebooks were important, Jack added.

Emily remembered how clean the apartment was when she came back from the park. For a moment, she believed him. Then her fingers flashed over the phone: YOU ARE A LIAR. You are a LIAR and a BASTARD for blaming someone you can fire for what YOU did. GIVE ME MY NOTEBOOKS

For a while there was no response. He wrote, I can't give you what's gone.

"I never liked him," Rory said.

"Yes, you did," said Violet.

Connor opened and shut doors in Rory's apartment. "What are you looking for, baby?" said the first Emily.

"Dada," he said.

The second Emily saw what she had known she would see: the pink line that told her she was pregnant.

Her phone buzzed. It was a series of photos of the ransacked apartment.

Ive sent these to my lawyer, Jack texted. Ive told him that youve taken our son and wont tell me where he is

let me tell you how this will play out, he wrote.

you wont get custody
you wont get my money
your fucked

The phone rang. Emily answered. "I'm sorry," Jack said. He was weeping. "I didn't mean what I said. I don't know what to do. Tell me what I can do. I made a mistake but I love you, I love you, I love you."

Several months after she went back to Jack, Emily lost the baby. She had been mid-term, late enough that she had to go to the hospital for the delivery of a baby she knew had no heartbeat. The baby was a boy. Jack grieved. Emily did, too, a double grief: for the baby, and for a different choice she could have made—could still make, though she no longer believed that was possible. It seemed to her that there had briefly been a portal of possibility that shrank to a diameter too small for her to fit through even if it was large enough to give a glimpse of an alternate life.

She thought about her choice as she sat in their Upper East Side townhome, purchased in anticipation of the new baby. Jack looked older, the way people do after loss. A nursery had been decorated, the crib built. Jack made certain that everything in the nursery was gone when Emily came home from the hospital. She hadn't known he would do that. When she stepped into the room, it was as though she had stepped into a void. The wallpaper with its colorful hot-air balloons had been stripped away. He had painted the walls white and found an antique secretary desk made from rosewood. "I thought it could be your office, for writing," he said. He meant it as a kind gesture but Emily felt it like a blow. She never used the room. She didn't write.

She didn't go to Argentina. She avoided her friends, who disapproved of her decision to go back to Jack. It was easier to forgo their friendship than to confront the mistake that they said she was making.

Connor adored his father. Jack returned from a business trip with a pin that had wings. A pilot had given it to him, he explained to Connor, because Jack had told the pilot how much his son loved planes. That night, Emily checked on Connor and saw him asleep, one hand resting loosely on his pajama shirt, covering the pin as though it might crawl away.

Emily became pregnant again and gave birth to Stella. Her marriage resumed its patterns, deepened them. When Emily thought about it, time didn't change Jack but rather made him grow more fully himself, to become even more the person at the bar in Boston, the man at the library, in his bed in the Back Bay apartment. He had always been himself. She hadn't seen clearly who he was.

Emily chose to stay with Jack because there was just *enough* to make that choice. Enough loyalty, enough habit—including the habit of love, its reflex and ingrained training—enough happiness, enough moments of the four of them together, the intimacy of family, each child with each parent.

And enough fear. She didn't know how angry Jack would become if she ended their marriage, or what he might do.

Jack, in becoming ever more himself, had learned to go unpunished. He had learned that his behavior could slip further from his control, so long as he eventually reeled it back.

One day he went too far. He pulled her son into their pool

and held him underwater an instant too long. At the pool's edge, Jack looked down at Emily, his red hair aflame. "Who are you to put me on trial?" he demanded. "How dare you criticize me, after all I've done for you?"

Emily—finally—told him to fuck off.

20

Gen chose the place: a comfortable Chelsea diner with sun-filled windows and red-cushioned seats. A photo booth in the back stood next to a vintage wooden pinball machine. Emily, who was early, dropped a quarter into the pinball machine and dragged back the spring pull that shot the ball into the belly of the game. She flipped the wooden levers.

"Hey," said Gen at Emily's shoulder. The last ball slid past the levers and down into the machine.

"Where'd you find this place?" Emily kept her voice light. "It's so old-timey."

"I've been coming here awhile. It's quiet and no one's recognized me yet."

It was unnerving to think about Gen as someone whose level of fame required a break from it. Emily knew that Gen was being careful about when to meet (brunch hour during the week; the tables weren't full and several people sat by themselves at the counter), and had assumed it was because Gen had wanted to send the message that this wasn't a date. A different reason hadn't occurred to Emily.

Or *additional* reason. This still wasn't a date. Gen, a little stiff, held herself at a distance. Shaking hands would have been weird, given their history. A hug should have been normal, considering that it had been roughly fifteen years since they had dated, but Emily dreaded that it would feel intimate and dreaded that it wouldn't.

"Want to play a round of pinball?" Gen said.

It's a mean trick to discover that many years and one solid heart stomping didn't make you any more immune to the huge dark eyes and low voice of a person who once held you down in the grass and slid inside you until you couldn't shut up, you had to say everything you were feeling, had to announce the enormous orgasm barreling toward you, had to cry out how much you loved her.

"No," Emily said. "Let's order."

The waitress dropped menus on their table and disappeared.

Gen glanced at the menu and pushed it aside. "I don't know where to start. We haven't really talked since freshman year."

Emily remembered every word of their argument outside Thayer Hall. Not long after their breakup, she saw a reality show about a skydiver whose parachute didn't open and he crashed into an empty parking lot but survived because the impact had been evenly distributed throughout his body. When the show cut to a commercial, she told herself to get over Gen. Enough already! Look at that skydiver, broken to bits. He wasn't complaining. He was grateful to be alive. Everyone fell in love for the first time. Everyone experienced heartbreak. What happened to you is nothing new. Still, seated across from Gen, Emily felt a dull ache to remember that rainy night freshman year, and it was as if, fifteen years ago, she *had* fallen out of a plane. "We talked at my wedding."

Gen made an impatient face. "That doesn't count."

"I wrote you a letter, after my engagement. You wrote back." Of all the letters Emily wrote to Gen after their breakup, she had mailed one.

"I don't want to talk about that letter."

"Well?" said the waitress, pencil poised over her pad.

Gen ordered two hot dogs with a side of potato chips. Emily ordered waffles with fresh fruit.

"Who's the boy," Emily teased Gen, "and who's the girl?"

"I need protein," Gen protested.

"I see that."

"Waffles are nothing but sugar and air."

"And so delicious."

The waitress yanked away their menus. After she left, Emily asked Gen, "What did we do? The waitress hates us."

Gen squinted over Emily's shoulder. "She's new. Maybe she's just settling in. Emily, I *like* being the boy."

"I know that. I knew."

"You did?"

"I liked it."

"Well," Gen said after a pause, "you *did* marry a man."

"I left him."

Gen's gaze dropped to Emily's left hand, which no longer wore her ring. Emily had also removed the engagement ring from her right hand. Gen said, "When?"

"I moved out about a month ago."

"Pretty recent. I mean—sorry."

"It was long overdue."

"Then . . . congratulations?"

"I think so, yes."

"Where are you living now?"

"A studio in the Village. It's small for three, but it's fine."

"Three?"

"Me and the kids."

"You have kids."

"Is that surprising?"

"I just didn't imagine it, when I imagined you."

"You imagined me?"

"Natural curiosity. Let me guess: a boy and a girl and a summer home in the Hamptons."

"Upstate."

"Where are these children?" Gen looked Emily over as though she might be hiding them in her dress pockets.

"At school." Emily showed a picture of the children on her phone. "Connor is ten and Stella is five."

"And beautiful, of course. I thought Jack was rich. Like, old money *plus* new money rich. What's with the studio?"

"His money is not my money."

"A good lawyer could fix that."

"That's what Jocelyn says."

"What does Jocelyn think of all this?"

"She's appalled by the studio."

"Well, yes."

"She offered a free spare two-bedroom."

"Jocelyn is a fucking fairy godmother."

"I said no."

Gen wrinkled her brow. "That makes no sense."

"I don't like being charity."

"Do you hate yourself?"

"Come on."

"I mean it. Do you feel so bad about leaving your husband that you need to punish yourself by living in a tiny, spartan studio when you could have a nice place owned by a friend who'd never miss the rent?"

"No." Maybe.

"You think any of us makes it without being charity at some point? I've been charity. I've been charity to *you*."

"That's not true."

"The peanut butter sandwiches."

"I didn't think of it that way."

"The tutoring."

"You just wanted to get into my pants."

"*Hoped*, Emily. Hoped."

"I didn't do that because I wanted to help you."

Gen *tsk*ed in disbelief.

"I did it because I liked you."

It was quiet enough that Emily heard the whir of the overhead fan.

"I get that it doesn't feel good to be indebted," Gen said slowly, "and I'd be lying if I said that it wasn't part of our problem."

"Our problem?"

"But the fact is that my life wouldn't be the same without you. I hated that for a really long time. Now I think that's how it is for everyone. Someone gives you the extra push you need at the right moment. If you believe that you're the exception to that rule, I'd say, A. You're wrong, and B. Do you think you're better than everyone else?"

"No."

"Than me?"

"*No.*"

"Then give Joss a call. She'll be thrilled. Otherwise, the studio, it's—"

"Spartan, yes. Self-punishing, I know."

"Temporary."

"Temporary?"

"The sort of place you move into when you're expecting to return to your marriage."

"I'm not going to do that."

"It's been a month, we'll see."

"Hey, fuck you."

"Excuse me?"

"You don't know anything about me anymore."

"I call things as I see them."

"You don't know what it took to leave." Emily heard the quaver in her voice and was horrified.

"Emily. Hey. I'm sorry. Forget it, okay? Everything I said. It's all my own shit. It has nothing to do with you."

Was the studio self-sabotage? Emily had left Jack before. This time, Jack had been surprisingly easygoing; he hadn't even objected to her keeping the children for nearly the entire month. Maybe he believed what Gen believed: that it was inevitable that Emily would return. She resented the idea that other people might know her better than she knew herself. "I didn't come here for you to psychoanalyze me."

Gen's question was genuine: "Why did you come?"

"I'm not going back to him. I can't."

"Okay," Gen said softly. "You won't."

The waitress slammed their plates onto the table. "Good luck," the waitress told Emily, and left.

Gen's hot dogs were burnt and withered in their buns. The potato chips had been crushed into dust. With a spoon, Gen scooped the chip dust and let it sift back down onto her plate, watching incredulously as it poured like grains of sand.

Emily was glad that the arrival of this vengeful meal offered an escape from exposing what a mess she was. "Should you send it back?"

"I'm afraid I'll get something worse."

"She said 'Good luck' to me. Why 'Good luck'? Did she overhear our conversation? About my divorce?"

"*Is* it a divorce?"

"My food looks fine."

Gen shook her head. "I'm mystified."

"She must know who you are. Does she think I'm on your track team? 'Good luck at the next competition'?"

Gen smiled.

"It's not a crazy theory," Emily said.

"I mean, I know you're a runner, but you're not a *runner*."

"Maybe she is, and you beat her at something?"

"I would recognize her."

"Maybe you beat someone she cares about."

"I don't think this has anything to do with track."

"Oh," Emily said, the obvious finally occurring to her.

"Yeah. Maybe it's that." Then Gen shook her head. "No, can't be. She's been nice to you. Relatively. If this was a homophobic thing, we would have gotten equal treatment."

"But *you* look gay."

"So do you."

Surprised and pleased, Emily said, "What makes me look gay?"

"Your hands."

"What about them?"

"Hard to say. That's the great mystery of the Lesbian Hands. They're all different, yet every lesbian has them."

"I'm not a lesbian."

"True," Gen said thoughtfully. "Queer Hands, then," she amended. "You also look gay by association. The waitress must assume we're together. 'Good luck' meant 'Good luck with *her*.' Me."

Emily flushed. "Here." Moving quickly to disguise being flustered, she split her food, sliding half onto Gen's plate. Emily pushed the sad hot dogs over to make room. "Oh God." Emily spotted some figs on her plate and swiped them onto Gen's. "Take these, too."

"Emily, are you a hater of figs?"

"Who puts *figs* on a waffles and fruit plate?"

"What do you have against the humble fig?" Gen ate one.

"Remember how Florencia was full of facts?"

"I barely met her."

"She told me something about figs."

"Am I going to want to unknow this as soon as you tell me?"

"Figs are incubators for wasp babies. A female wasp enters the fig, loses her wings, gets trapped, lays her eggs, and dies. The male larvae hatch first."

Gen swallowed. "Can we not say *larvae*?"

"The males search throughout the fig for females and fertilize them even before they hatch. Then the males dig tunnels for the females and die inside the fig while the females hatch, escape, and find other figs to incubate their eggs. Supposedly fig seeds are actual seeds, not dead wasp particles, which dissolve inside the fruit, but figs are still gross."

"Figs are nightmares," Gen agreed. "Though not for gay wasps."

"Are there gay wasps?"

"There are gay dolphins. There are gay bonobos."

"But insects?"

"Yes: doodlebugs. They will do anything. They are also called *cockchafers*."

"No."

"Yes. You should tell Florencia."

"I don't talk with my college friends anymore."

"Why not?"

"The first time I left Jack, they were really there for me."

"The first time," Gen repeated.

"After I went back, I was too ashamed, I guess, to face them."

"Figs are a metaphor for straightness," Gen said. "It's a trap."

"Some straight marriages are happy, just not mine."

Gen raised her brows.

"The fig wasn't about me," Emily said. "The fig was a fig. I'm not interested in symbols. They hide what you really mean—or show what you mean while pretending that you're not showing it."

"People like symbols. Not just because of what symbols *do*, in comparing or representing. Metaphors work because we want to believe that common ground can be found even in difference, and that everything has meaning."

Emily set down her fork. "I find you disingenuous."

"Me?"

"Do you remember what you said to me, outside Emerson Hall, when you visited me at college?"

"I remember everything, Emily."

"We discussed the quote on the building, and you said—*accused*—that I wanted you to *talk like me*, and so you did, and that it was fun for a while but not really who you were. But that *is* who you are. When you were *talking like me*, you were actually talking like *you*, then pretending that I was the only intellectual asshole present, and that there was something wrong with me or anyone loving ideas and history and books. You act very down-to-earth, but you also use that identity to hide other parts of you. *You* are a symbol. You are a symbol for yourself. You are one thing and also a hidden thing that you make other people guess. You are a faker, Gen Hall."

Gen slapped a hand over her eyes. "Ohhhhh," she groaned. "Oh shit. Emily? I kind of feel like you need a concealed carry permit for your brain. It's a deadly weapon. But also—and I'm not trying to dodge your accusation—"

"You are! I can feel you dodging!"

"I realized why the waitress hates me. I slept with her. And never called or texted. And, I guess, forgot her face and name."

"Gen, are you a *dog*?"

"Maybe? But this situation is your fault."

"Mine!"

"I would have remembered her if you hadn't been distracting me."

"With what?"

"Figs. Your life. Your *you*. Look, I might sleep around but I do have a code. I am not all bad."

"If I scratch the womanizing surface, I will find an honorable person?"

"Yes! Rule number one: I never cheat."

"Why would you need to, if you can line ladies up, one right after the other?"

"Two: I give them what they want."

Emily's cheeks were hot. Her skin felt translucent, every sexual memory of Gen visible on her face. "The waitress hardly seems satisfied."

"Which brings me to rule three: I am clear. I explain that I am not in it to last. She knew that."

"You're saying that you're honest."

"I try to be."

"Hmm."

"What?"

Emily thought of Jack and the lies she had told over the years to maintain his volatile happiness. "I think people who pride themselves on honesty don't know what it's like to be in a position where they must lie."

Gen pushed away her plate. "I want to be honest about that day at Harvard. I was mad at you."

"I know you were."

"I mean before the dinner. When we were in the Yard, looking at that stupid quote on that stupid building. You're right: I was obnoxious and trying to hide it so that *you* would seem obnoxious. I was angry because you had brought me to that art museum."

"The Sackler Museum?"

"The Sacklers own a pharmaceutical company that made opioids like the kind that a doctor prescribed to my mother, except worse, even more addictive."

"Gen, I didn't know."

"Most people didn't. I researched Purdue Pharma for an assignment, early freshman year. I almost wished I hadn't. I had told myself that my mother's addiction wasn't her fault, but deep down I believed that it was and that she had chosen it over me. When I learned how easy it is for a company to push a pain-killer they know is addictive, I felt guilty for blaming her. Mad at myself. I tried not to be mad at you, too, that day. It was just a museum. But all you saw were the beautiful things."

"If you had told me—"

Gen shook her head. "I wanted you to be able to enjoy the beautiful things. I wanted to get over it and have a nice time."

"Is the museum"—Emily studied her waffle until it became an unfamiliar object—"why you ended things with me?"

"What?"

"It came out of the blue."

"Emily, you broke my fucking heart." Gen's expression, when Emily glanced up, was stunned. "You sent me to the bus station. I slept there until I caught the five a.m. to Ohio."

Emily felt an urgent disbelief. "But you said—"

"Said *what*? What could I have possibly said to make you do that?"

"You told me that you weren't sure how much to put into our relationship."

"A normal worry. We were eighteen and going to college far away from each other."

"Don't pretend like you were being reasonable. You implied I wasn't gay enough. You criticized me for blowing up at my friends when they insulted you. I wanted to do the right thing and you made that impossible. Nothing I did was right."

Gen shut her eyes. "I was upset. But I wasn't breaking up with you."

"Oh." A long silence unrolled between them. "I misunderstood."

Gen stared.

"You made me really sad," said Emily.

"I need to step away for a minute," said Gen. "I'll be back. I'm going to apologize to the waitress. Annette. I'm feeling pretty intensely the importance of not letting stuff go unsaid." She left Emily alone with the debris of their meal.

Emily watched Gen walk up to the counter and catch the attention of the waitress, who ignored Gen but then relented, listening. Emily, shaky from the conversation and desperate not to see the waitress smile, needed privacy. She left the table and went to the back of the restaurant, where she slipped into the photo booth and drew the curtain. The glass plate dimly reflected her face. She wanted to see herself better. She wanted to know what her expression showed. Would she look as shocked as she felt? As full of regret? What was the word for a prophecy not of the future but the past—a vision, clear as fact, of what could have been? Emily positioned her face within the circumference on the screen, looked straight ahead, and pressed the button.

When the strip of black-and-white photos emerged, wet and shining, they showed Emily in nearly identical positions. She had barely shifted between each photo. If the photos were cut and stapled at the edge, they could become a tiny flip-book that animated her for a brief second. Her green eyes were gray, her blond hair nearly white. This was the face of someone who had seen a ghost. The ghost was a misunderstanding that Emily had built her entire adult life around. She felt dizzy. Like nothing was solid, nothing was real. Like the person she had believed she was didn't exist. She turned over the strip. With a pen taken from her bag, she wrote her age on the back like her mother used to do for school pictures: *33*. Then she added, *I made a mistake for fifteen years.*

Emily pulled aside the curtain. Gen was gone. Their table, cleared. Emily's hand lifted in surprise, then dropped to her side. It wasn't like Gen to leave without saying goodbye, but she had probably changed. Emily's disappointment was heavy.

Then she saw Gen through the diner's glass door, standing on the sidewalk. Gen looked left, down the street. She looked right. Emily went to join her. The bell above the door jingled. Gen turned, saw her, and was so clearly relieved that Emily wished that she could have a photograph of that relief. Trying to be casual, Emily said, "I thought you'd gone."

"Me too."

The day was sunny yet breezy, with the hint of a chill. The

autumn trees were kaleidoscopic. A man walked his dachshund past Emily and Gen, the dog old and slow, the owner patient. His patience made Emily's throat constrict. Avoiding Gen's gaze, Emily watched the man and dog reach the end of the block and turn out of sight. The wind kicked up, blowing trash off the top of an overfull bin. A crosstown bus lumbered by.

"Do you think we could be friends?" Gen shoved her short hair out of her face, eyes narrowed against the sun.

"It would depend on whether we could get past what happened."

The letter that she had sent to Gen was written soon after Jack's proposal. Emily described Jack and the qualities that made her love him: his devotion, how hard he tried at everything. *I could make a life with him*, Emily wrote, *except for you.* Could she and Gen meet? Or a phone call?

Jack sounds great, Gen wrote back. *I'm training for the USATF trials, so I'm too busy to talk, but I'm glad you're happy.*

"I already got over everything." Gen leaned against the pale brick wall outside the diner. "I'm in New York until June. I'll have free time on my hands. We could meet up, do some friend stuff. What do you say?"

On the subway, Emily wrote *Drinks with Gen* in her calendar for the Friday after next. She looked at it for a long time. Then she texted Jocelyn to ask if her two-bedroom apartment was still available.

21

Hey, girl!" Suri Hamilton weaved around other mothers at school pickup to envelope Emily in a perfumed hug. "How *are* you? I heard about you and Jack. You are so lucky. I wish I could afford to leave my husband." Suri was wearing a dress printed with lipstick mouths layered in swirls, fanned out on top of each other like a spread deck of cards. "Sweetie, listen. It's about our children's education and it's super important. As you know, some of us are fortunate enough to have second homes in the Hamptons. Blessed! But traffic on Fridays after school pickup makes me want to die and I am not alone. What's the harm in school getting out a little earlier? Just on Fridays. It's a modest ask. School could start earlier so no hours of education would be lost. Makes sense, right? Well, the parents with helipads don't agree. They have zero sense of community. They say, 'Why should we have to change our schedule?' They chopper out of the city while we're stuck in traffic. The PTA is pretty divided! I need all the support we can get, and that's where you come in. Since you've got a weekend place upstate—you and Jack are so unconventional! In the most inspiring way!—I thought you could sign my petition. I bet you don't want to be stuck on the George Washington Bridge at four p.m."

"I can't sign this."

"Do *not* tell me you're afraid of the helipad moms."

"Your Friday plan might not work for the teachers."

"*We* employee *them*. They earn more on our tuition dollars than they would ever make in a public school. They can manage one hour earlier, one day a week."

"What about families who don't have second homes? Some students live in the outer boroughs. They already get up early to take the subway."

"You mean the scholarship kids? Emily! I know things must be rough. You look withered, poor thing." Suri rested a palm on her chest, the printed lipstick mouths smiling beneath her fingertips. "But don't let single motherhood turn you into, like, a *communist*."

"At least I don't make other people miserable so I can feel better about myself."

Suri gasped. "That is not *nice*." She left, her petition flapping. Emily was glad. It had felt good to say what she thought. Maybe she had been a little mean, but it was a relief to know that she *could* be mean after years of self-censorship.

Stella saw Emily in the courtyard, ran up, and hugged her mother's hips. "Aster's mommy looks mad," Stella said.

"Aster's mommy can deal." Emily offered a chocolate croissant, Stella's favorite after-school snack. "Today's an exciting day for us."

"Are we going home to our real house?"

"No." Emily cupped Stella's round cheeks. "It's our first day in our new apartment. You'll like it. Much more room than the studio."

"Will Daddy be there?"

"Daddy and I need time apart."

"I *know* that. You *said* that. But *I* don't need time apart. Daddy misses me too much." Stella bit into the chocolate croissant, chewing moodily, a smear of chocolate on her upper lip. "It was better when we were all together."

"What did you like about it?"

"We had cereal together. We had good night together."

"You can call Daddy to say good night to him when you're with me, and call me when you're with him."

"Daddy says you're mad because I'm his favorite."

"That's not true."

"He loves me most. He said so."

"He shouldn't have said that. He loves Connor just as much."

Stella shook her head. "Connor's a crybaby."

"Don't say that." Emily's voice was sharp.

Stella licked her fingers resentfully.

Connor's fifth-grade class filed into the courtyard. He waved goodbye to his best friend, Lucas, then ran up to Emily. He snuggled into Emily's side, his head at the height of her armpit. Emily recalled the lines that Jack had marked on the walls of the playroom, measuring the children's height and age as they had grown. Emily's body was marked with invisible lines—Stella at her ribs, Connor almost to her shoulder. Those lines would shift upward until her children were adults and no longer measured themselves against her.

Connor and Stella were polite about the apartment. They said that they liked the bunk beds and didn't debate who got the top (Connor) and who got the bottom (Stella). Neither complained that they had to share a room. If they noticed that the apartment was entirely furnished by IKEA, where Emily had spent an entire dazed day followed by a night of maddening assembly, they didn't mention it. They liked the kitchen barstools, which spun. They gazed out the windows and chose their favorite skyscrapers. They behaved so well that it was as if they had colluded beforehand to protect their mother's feelings. Their care made Emily's throat hurt. No one commented that the chicken she cooked for dinner was dry, which wouldn't have happened if Jack had prepared it. She gave Stella a bath, detangling her long hair, which darkened to copper when wet. While the children read by their cloud-shaped night-lights, Emily looked at her calendar. *Drinks with Gen* was in a few days. Tomorrow, she would meet Jack at a café near their home on the Upper East Side.

"Mommy?" Stella looked up from her book. "Why is Toad scared of everything?"

"Because it's funny," said Connor from the top bunk. "I like when he goes sledding."

"He's even scared of his bathing suit."

"He's *embarrassed* of his bathing suit."

Stella shook her damp head. "He's scared the dragonflies will laugh at him and they do. And the snakes. And everybody."

"But he still goes swimming," said Emily. "Toad is brave."

"Even Frog laughs at him. That is not okay."

"Toad doesn't mind. He knows he looks silly."

"What if he minds—on the inside?"

"Usually, he tells Frog how he feels. He would tell Frog if he minded."

Stella looked unconvinced.

That night, Stella slipped into Emily's bed. Her hair had dried and smelled like clean hay. "Why can't you sleep?" said Emily. "Because the apartment is new?"

"The windows creak."

"That's because it's windy out."

Stella cuddled closer and put her cold toes against Emily's leg. Confessionally, Stella said, "It's okay that I'm Daddy's favorite, because Connor is yours."

Emily felt a stab of failure. Stella had always been the easier child, sturdy and unbothered, the one content to color on her own, who rarely whined. She was outgoing and social. She had a carousel of playdates, whereas Lucas was Connor's one close friend. Since the separation, it had become more difficult to arrange playdates with Lucas; his mother often said that he was busy. Emily had begun to wonder if Lucas's mother disapproved of the separation, and she worried that Connor was lonely. It hadn't occurred to her to worry about Stella, who was typically cheerful. Maybe she had been easy to overlook. "You are both my favorites."

"I don't mind," Stella insisted.

"You *should* mind, if it were true, but it's not."

"Okay."

"Okay?"

"I said okay, Mommy."

"Turn over. I'll draw pictures on your back to help you fall asleep." Emily drew a mermaid. She described everything she drew: a wave crashing, the pebbles sifting beneath it. She drew herself and Stella on the beach, and how Stella saw the mermaid and Emily didn't. "But I believe you," Emily said.

"How do I know?"

"I have a smile on my face." Emily drew one. Then she drew a long squiggle.

"What's that?" said Stella.

"That's you, walking your pet worm on a leash."

"A worm!"

"Worms like to go for walks, too."

"On the *sand*?"

Emily wiped away the worm and gently pinched Stella's back. "Your pet crab."

"You're weird."

Emily tickled Stella behind her ear. She drew the night falling and the mermaid diving below the waves. With little taps, she drew the stars. Then she wiped it all away and drew something Stella would easily guess. She drew the heart over and over until Stella fell asleep.

When Jack was happy with Emily, he called her "dreamy." When he wasn't, he called her "spacey," though Emily didn't recognize herself in either word. It was true that she had always been an interior person and became more interior during her marriage, because a good place to hide from Jack was inside herself. Jack replaced "spacey" with "childish" when his discontent deepened.

She *did* feel childish the morning she was supposed to meet Jack at the café. Connor and Stella, as toddlers, would go boneless whenever she tried to carry them somewhere they didn't want to go. She wished she could use the same strategy. She hadn't seen Jack since she put the kids into her SUV and drove back to the city from upstate, having warned Jack not to follow. He asked how she proposed to stop him.

"I will hate you," she said. This seemed proof of her childishness: hate is the last option of the powerless. Her threat's effect on him surprised her. He covered his eyes. When his hand fell, he spoke in an utterly normal tone, suggesting that she relax over the weekend. He would see her at home on Sunday night. "Yes," she said, "see you tomorrow." Instead, she found the West Village studio and moved in overnight. His texts called her a cunning liar—an old accusation, like "childish." In earlier years, his accusations made her muster the correct behavior to prove him wrong. This time, she ignored him.

A ball of dread sat in her stomach as she took the number 4 uptown. The subway car grew more crowded. At each stop along the way, she thought about stepping out and crossing the platform to take the next downtown train, even though she had been the one who said that she wanted to meet. At the Fifty-Ninth Street stop, Emily pretended that the dread in her stomach was a ball of yarn. She hooked it with knitting needles and made it into something else. A sweater. This calmed her.

She arrived at her stop. She knitted a hat, mittens. She exited the station onto the gusty street. She walked by the Frick Museum, which she often visited when Stella was a baby and napped in her carrier, her hair the peachy color of Turner's skies. Emily passed by Central Park, where horses pulled carriages with tourists. She knitted leg warmers for Stella and a scarf for Connor. Then she walked into the café and saw Jack, seated, waiting for her. Everything she had knitted came undone. Jack's face filled with happiness to see her.

She had expected to find him angry. His happiness was worse, because it fed her guilt and the guilt eroded her confidence in what she had come to say. When she avoided his attempted embrace, he didn't accuse her of coldness. He winced but regained his smile. He pulled a chair out for her to sit with him.

Emily began with what she had rehearsed: "Things have been bad between us for a while."

"It's my fault. I'm ready to change."

"You've said that before."

"This time is different. I have a therapist. He's helping me see destructive patterns in my behavior. He says my childhood was built on a model of feast and famine: everything that money could buy, never enough love and approval. So when I lash out at you, I act the way I wish I could've as a child."

"What about when you lash out at Connor?"

"If you mean the pool, you overreacted. Or"—he added hastily—"consider the possibility, okay? You acted like I tried to drown him."

"I know you didn't, but it was punishing. You frightened him."

"Kids get frightened. Parents don't always know what will set them off. I thought we were horsing around but I guess he didn't, and as soon as I realized, I stopped. I never hurt him and I never would."

"The way you treated me—"

"That day? Em, I was so mad. I know you were, too, but I was insulted. It's insulting how you never trust me. You always assume the worst. My therapist says I need to take ownership of my behavior and I'm trying. I understand that you assume the worst because of how I've acted in the past, but I'm not going to be like that anymore. They say that marriage is falling in love over and over again with the same person. Can't that be us? We have to break our old patterns, but I can't do that without you. We can't get better if you don't try."

"I don't want to try. I tried for years."

Jack looked down at the table, took a breath, but didn't speak. When he lifted his face, his cheeks were wet. "Tell me what I can do."

"Nothing."

"Don't talk like you're reading a script. I'm your husband. We have a life together. A family."

"I know you work hard during the week, so you can have the children on the weekends. You will put enough money in my account for us to live on."

"I'm supposed to pay for you to leave me? You're kicking me to the curb and I haven't done anything wrong. Look at our friends. Look at Arthur Hamilton. He's a drunk and he cheats. I would never do that to you. You could take ownership, too, of your behavior. Think about how you always make me into a villain. You want to talk about punishing behavior? You're ruthless."

Emily thought of how she had sent Gen to the bus station. Was she ruthless . . . cruel? A minnow of doubt darted through her, quick in its skinny vigor. The question distracted; she found herself following where it might go. She forgot, for a moment, all that she knew about Jack in pursuit of what she didn't know about herself. Was she cruel?

"You cut your parents out of your life," Jack continued. "I know they weren't perfect but they raised you. Your first move is to blame other people. Meanwhile, I'm always trying my best. Imagine what this is like for me."

Emily imagined his loneliness. She imagined herself as he saw her, and because what he saw was true for him, it was easy, when she imagined Jack's perspective, to accept it as true for her, too. This was an old habit: inhabiting his point of view. Seeing herself as bad, wanting to be good. Now, though, she wished she were ruthless. She wished she were a cunning liar. Those qualities would make her powerful.

"I came here with an open mind," he said. "You came to give me orders. Why should I obey?"

She had practiced the words so that they would readily fall out of her mouth if he confused her. "If you don't, I'll file for divorce."

Quietly, he said, "I'll do anything you want if you give me a chance. Remember how magical we were in the beginning. We could be that way again. Wait to make a decision, please."

What would waiting gain her, if she were truly ruthless?

She said, "You'll put money in my account?"

"Em, if you need a separation so that our marriage can heal, of course. I've always supported you, you know that."

She could economize with what he gave her. She would build savings. She would need it to hire a lawyer. Divorce was expensive. And for now, she would make a calm life for Connor and Stella, the three of them safe inside the snowy story she had told them, the heavy-footed bear at bay. Jack wanted time, but time was good for her, too. Cunning? She could be cunning. "Okay."

She had an hour before school pickup, so she walked swiftly into the red-orange park, through Sheep Meadow and north to the Hernshead, a promontory of rock jutting out into the pond. During good weather, weddings happened regularly at a nearby pavilion, and while Emily had thought it would be too late in the season to encounter one, she was wrong. The microphoned tones of the officiant drove her faster down the wooded path to the boulders. Two young men, one of them wearing a Fordham sweatshirt, sat cross-legged opposite each other on the rocks, eating potato chips out of a large bag. Geese dunked their heads in the water, then slid them out. Their beaks dripped. Turtles swam at the water's surface. Connor liked to come to the Hernshead and catch turtles, which impressed other kids, who watched as he waded in and caught the turtles from behind. He showed the kids how to do it, and later referred to them as his friends even though they were strangers. Once, a turtle turned its head and bit his arm, and he yelped but didn't drop the turtle. He released it into the water gently, tears leaking down his face. He told Emily that it wasn't the turtle's fault. It was the turtle's nature.

Emily sat on the rocks. She didn't know where the turtles would go in winter. She didn't think they migrated. Some amphibians hibernated, she knew. Like frogs. Would the turtles crawl into the mud? Connor would know. He watched nature documentaries obsessively.

Her breath had gotten less jagged. She had been hot when she had arrived but now the rock chilled her butt and she shoved her hands into her jacket pockets. She returned to her conversation with Jack. *Ruthless* doesn't actually mean *cruel;* it means to have no remorse, no ruth, to rue nothing, but she regretted so much. She regretted meeting with him. She should have sent a text. She should have written a letter. But she didn't write letters anymore, neither to send nor keep, and what she wrote in her mind she never committed to paper, the way you don't build again on the shore where a hurricane took your house.

She regretted—but no, there was no point in thinking about Gen. The past was done, over; it isn't a novel you can revise until you get it right.

She regretted her lost friendships. She had blamed Jack for keeping her from her closest friends, but she had made the choice to let them go.

She called Rory. Emily didn't expect her to pick up, but it took only a couple of rings. "Emily, are you okay?"

"Yes."

"In that case, can I guess why you called?"

"Sure."

"You want to model."

"I'm too old."

"Not true. I'll represent you. Or is it one of the kids?"

"This isn't about modeling."

"You're in L.A., and you want to treat me to one of those craft cocktails that come shrouded in vapor under a bell jar, so that the cocktail is drunk and inhaled at the same time. You want me to forgive you for ignoring me for years."

"I do want that, but that's not why I'm calling."

"Water under the bridge." Emily had called Rory first, among her group of college friends, because Rory never held a grudge. "Okay, okay." Rory was probably bouncing on the balls of her feet. She guessed again. "You heard about Elizabeth."

"What about her?"

"She's getting married! To Yasar, the one with the many skills and serial hobbies. He decided that what he wanted to learn most was how to find her. He traveled all over. It took him more than a year. It was like *Where in the World Is Carmen Sandiego?* except with Elizabeth. He found her in Bora Bora and proposed."

"Isn't that stalking?"

"But for *love*. Okay, from the outside it could look bad, but the fine line between stalking and romance is knowing your audience and Yasar did. My final guess, to be honest, was my first but I was trying to be discreet. Being discreet was my New Year's resolution. It's going so-so. Did you leave Jack again?"

"Yes."

"Great news. That guy sucks. Thank God for divorce lawyers."

"We're not actually divorced."

"I know, the courts take forever."

"I haven't filed. He asked for time."

"Say no!"

"If I file, it means going to war."

"So go!"

It would be horrible. Suri Hamilton once said, laughing,

"Arthur told me that if I ever tried to leave him, he would destroy me." Jack never had to say that; Emily knew. She was afraid of divorce—its brutality, the bitter fight. She was afraid of fighting. She was afraid of losing. She remembered Jocelyn's warning that Jack wouldn't simply let her keep the children. She had agreed to give Jack time, and she would use that time to save for a legal battle, but her earlier confidence dwindled. No matter what she saved, he would always be able to outspend her.

"Who's your lawyer?" Rory said. When Emily was silent, Rory said, "*Emily*. Tell me you have a lawyer."

"Can you please not explain how I'm doing this all wrong?"

"He is going to ensnare you. *Again*."

"Discretion. Your resolution. New Year's."

"You better distract me, then. Tell me something else about your life. Something good. Juicy."

"Well . . . I ran into Gen."

"Gen, your ex? Gennifer Hall, Olympic champion and dykon and occasional model?"

"We decided to try being friends."

"Noooo. Emily, do not."

"Why can't we be friends?"

"Gen Hall is a fuckboy! She just dumped one of my actresses. I had to show up on set with Xanax and play mother, and that is not my forte. My client cried for days. Gen is a menace, and if she's in New York, it's because she's already slept with everyone in L.A. Stay away."

"What about New Year's?"

"Fuck New Year's!"

"She's not interested in me like that."

Rory huffed.

Emily said, "I don't think she's the type to look back. She moves on pretty quickly." That was how celebrity magazines described Gen's relationships. "Maybe she gets bored."

"She wrecked you once. Don't let it happen again. Promise me that you will not date Gen Hall."

"Okay," said Emily, though she was already looking forward to seeing Gen again. "I promise."

22

Gen suggested that they meet at a speakeasy on the Lower East Side called the Toy Company. You'll like it, Gen texted. They serve gin in teacups like they used to in the 20s

Why teacups? Emily texted. I mean back then

I guess in case there was a raid, to fool the cops. Make them think the place was a teahouse

Or pretend to fool them. Teacups wouldn't fool anybody

Maybe the cops pretended to be fooled

Emily felt breathless, not because of what they were texting, but because of the texts' immediacy. Gen's came as swiftly as Emily sent them. Emily had the impulse to hide herself away to read them even though no one else was in the apartment. Jack, as they had agreed, had the children for the weekend.

She wrote, Why do you think I'll like the place

You already like it, Gen wrote. All this talk about teacups

That's not an answer

Gen didn't reply for a while. Emily had time to shower, dress, second-guess what she was wearing, change, and then change back into what she had been wearing before, which was tight jeans and a loose shirt. The windows darkened. The Empire State Building glowed orange. Halloween was soon.

Emily's phone buzzed. Because it's hidden, Gen wrote, and not everyone knows about it. You have to walk down an alleyway that seems to go nowhere. You tell the bouncer a password. You walk inside, and everything is beautiful. Three dots appeared, then disappeared. Finally, Gen wrote, It is very you.

Emily flushed. Her hand that held the phone felt as though it were still vibrating from the text. What's the password? she wrote.

Just say that you're with me.

On the subway, Emily's car had a group of teenagers. They were talking about classes and what they were going to do later that night. They were loud. They paid attention to no one but themselves. Emily imagined Connor and Stella becoming that age. This made her miss them, so she tried not to think about that. Instead, she imagined Gen and herself at eighteen. Some of the group, a trio, got off at the next stop and waved at their friends through the windows, shouting. They were so young, their faces bright. Emily loved them.

She got out at Delancey Street and walked swiftly down the alleyway Gen had mentioned. A large man stood in front of a door that Emily wouldn't have noticed if he hadn't been blocking it. When he heard Gen's name, he opened the door and said, "She's in the room at the back, behind the bookcase."

The wood and brass bar shone against the garnet silk-hung walls. A fire illuminated a few people who sat on an old-fashioned couch that looked like it had hips. Emily went straight toward the bookcase set deep into the wall. Maybe it was supposed to be fun to figure out the opening but, impatient, she knocked on the bookcase's frame. A set of shelves swung partly open to reveal a woman with wide cheekbones and black hair cut like a boy's. "This room's booked for a private event," she told Emily, who heard someone say, "Who're you talking to?" The speaker appeared behind the woman, looked at Emily, smiled, and said, "Come on in."

"Shipley," said the woman, "behave."

Shipley had a quick face and wore black eyeliner but somehow not in a feminine way. It went with the black-ink tattoos etched down Shipley's arms and hands. Even the fingers were tattooed between the knuckles. "I am behaving," said Shipley. "I'm being hospitable."

"I think I have the wrong room," said Emily.

"So what if you do? We're fun, I promise." Shipley, though no older than Emily, had an androgyny that looked well-worn, with scuffed boots and old jeans and nothing new, not even the watch, a metal Timex.

"Sorry," the black-haired woman said to Emily in a tone that was kind but firm. "No random hot extras tonight," she told Shipley, and moved to shut the bookcase.

"Emily!" Gen called from deep within the hidden room. She pushed past the black-haired woman and Shipley—Gen's friends, Emily realized with a deflated sense of stupidity. Gen hugged Emily—casually, as if this wasn't the first time they had touched in fifteen years. Gen smelled the same. She fit against Emily in the same way. Every response Emily had always had to Gen's body coursed through her. She felt a bone-deep, idiotic desire, no less strong for its familiarity, yet not quite the same as it had been in their past. It was sharper now, for its keen sense of impossibility, for how it revealed a longing not just for Gen but also for what they had once had, a longing so entwined with regret that the braided emotion was as tight as a whip.

Over Gen's shoulder, Emily saw that the wood-paneled room held a group of people, most gathered around a table, a few looking curiously her way.

Emily let go of Gen as soon as she could without being obvious about it. Gen's expression was relaxed and unbothered, her smile loose. She wasn't looking at Emily but around the room. "Let me introduce you to my friends."

"Oh, interesting," said Shipley.

"That's okay, right?" Gen asked Emily.

"Of course." Emily was too proud to show her disappointment. She had assumed that Gen's invitation had been for her alone. Even though she had known it wasn't a date, she had anticipated this night as though it were one. Now she confronted the embarrassing reality that she was just another name on a list.

"This would not be my move," Shipley told Gen, who ignored the comment and said, "Emily and I are old friends. We went to high school together."

"Were you this gorgeous in high school?" Shipley asked Emily.

Gen lost her smile. "Hey, Ship—"

"I'm Kate." The black-haired woman who talked like a teacher thrust her hand out for Emily to shake. "Sorry I was rude. We didn't know you were coming." Emily's embarrassment deepened. She had been such an unimportant guest that Gen hadn't mentioned her to her friends.

"Gen, my man!" A solid guy with a sweet face appeared at the door. "Come here!" He bear-hugged Gen, let her go, shook a scolding finger, and said, "Next time, give me more of a heads-up and I won't be late."

Late? Emily was on time—or at least, had arrived by the time Gen suggested. Even a little earlier. Her anger, which had been at herself, for having imagined this night differently even though Gen had never said it would be just the two of them, and there was no reason Gen couldn't invite friends—Gen *had* said that she and Emily should "do some friend stuff"—shifted its focus. Now she was angry at Gen. Had Gen invited friends so that she could introduce Emily, or had Gen regretted making plans with her and, last minute, turned the night into a group event to avoid being alone with her? Already, Gen was distracted, listening to the sweet-faced man, Adam, describe how a rat ("A literal rat—no, I am not joking") got onto the subway at Twenty-Third Street and ran up and down his subway car ("Everyone jumped onto their seats. *I* jumped onto my seat. And I *like* rats"), then sauntered out the doors at Astor Place.

"So you saw a rat," said Kate. "This is New York. I once saw a rat big enough to eat a cat. I saw a hawk dive-bomb a trash can and pull a rat into the sky."

Why hadn't Gen just canceled?

"Hey, don't go," Shipley said to Emily. The other three weren't paying attention. They kept talking about rats. “You’ve got that going look on your face. Let me pour you a drink.” Emily wanted to get away from Gen, yet didn’t want to reveal how upset she was by leaving the bar abruptly, so she let Shipley lead her to the back of the candlelit room. An ice bucket with a magnum of champagne stood near the table where other guests were seated. “I get the sense that you weren’t expecting us,” Shipley said to Emily. The champagne was cold and crisp and made Emily realize that she was hot. Her face was probably red. “But that doesn’t mean you can’t have a good time, right?”

Emily thought about going home to her empty apartment. She took another sip. The champagne felt like a snowfall against her mouth. “Right.”

“Who’s this?” someone called from the table.

“Gen’s friend from high school.”

“Come join us, Gen’s friend!”

Once she and Shipley sat, the group around the table became six. Most of them were athletes, though Paul, who was willowy yet muscular and wore a single sapphire earring that shone against his brown skin, was an honorary athlete, they said, because he was a ballet dancer.

“I am an *actual* athlete,” said Paul.

“Ballet’s not a competitive sport,” said Candace.

“Do you know how many people you have to destroy to become a premier danseur? Do not talk to me about competition.”

“Well, I’m a professional poker player,” said Becca. She sounded like she was from the south, her voice slow and cozy. She adjusted her thick-framed glasses. “That means I’m basically an athlete, too.”

Nita languidly played with her short, pink hair, which had grown out just enough to show dark roots. “Poker doesn’t get you into the Olympic Village, honey.”

“Neither does *Swan Lake*!”

“My true athleticism isn’t ballet,” said Paul. “Once when I was in the Pines—”

“Shut up!” several of them shouted.

“I am so over the Pines.” Nita zipped her Carhartts up to

her chin as though protecting herself from a rain shower. "Fire Island is an endless dickfest."

"Fire Island ain't all bad," said Becca. "I like Cherry Grove."

"Cherry Grove is a bunch of lesbians cross-stitching on the beach," said Paul.

"I clean up with the handicrafts type. Knitters love me."

"Fire Island rivalries aside," said Paul, "if they ever *did* let me into the Olympic Village, I would head straight for the equestrians. They look like lords come to demand their tithes."

"Sometimes I think y'all don't respect me," Becca said. "Poker is too a kind of sport, if you think about it."

"I bet poker requires stamina," said Emily.

"Thank you. I like you. I'll let you win once if we play."

Candace and Nita did track, and said that Kate did, too. Shipley—A. J. Shipley, though everyone used the last name like a title—played point guard for the Liberty. Emily didn't know much about basketball but recognized the Liberty as a women's team. She glanced at Shipley, who smiled lightly back. Emily was surprised to learn that Shipley played with a women's team, and Shipley had seen that surprise, the sophistication of that smile suggesting an even greater knowledge of Emily's surprise than Emily had herself. She hadn't thought of Shipley as a man, but *woman* didn't seem to fit either. Shipley raised a brow. Emily looked away, realizing that she had been staring.

Nita tipped her chin toward the bookcase door, where Adam had his arm slung over Gen's shoulders and was talking animatedly. Kate rolled her eyes. Emily had planned to leave after one drink, but she'd have to pass Gen to get out the door. She didn't want to talk to Gen. She definitely didn't want to exchange pleasantries with her. Emily didn't feel pleasant. She felt duped. But she did enjoy Gen's friends—their little dramas, their easy way with one another. It was also nice, in a way Emily had never experienced, to be surrounded by queer people, to feel an affinity with strangers. She poured herself more champagne.

"Tell us some embarrassing stories about teenage Gen," Nita said to Emily, "before she heads over here and tries to stop you."

"Ignore Nita," Shipley said. "Tell us about yourself."

"We met in fifth grade but weren't friends until my senior year," said Emily. "We were on the track team."

"Are you middle, short, long, or what?" said Candace, whose curly hair was pulled into a sloppy bun. Freckles sprinkled her wiry arms. "Who do you train with?"

"I'm not really a runner. Gen and I studied together."

"Huh," said Becca. "So you were, like, study buddies?"

"You weren't close?" said Shipley.

"Of course they were," said Candace. "We're family. Gen isn't going to bring home someone she doesn't care about."

"We're not close anymore," said Emily. "We weren't in touch for a long time. We recently ran into each other at a fundraiser."

"What do you do?" asked Nita.

"Nothing." It kind of killed Emily to say it. Surrounded by talented people, she was far from the person she had imagined she'd become. How had she gotten so far? How much of that distance was due to Jack's persuasion, and how much to her own readiness to believe that despite always wanting to be recognized as worthy of attention, she never actually deserved it? She had let that wish go. Instead, she became a wife. A mother. While motherhood was meaningful to her, some people looked down on stay-at-home moms. She liked Gen's friends too much to give them an opportunity to dismiss her.

"Are you independently wealthy?" said Becca. "Do you know how to play blackjack?"

"I wouldn't say *independently*."

"Emily married money," said Gen, pulling up a chair. "What did I miss?"

"Maybe that wasn't something she wanted to share," said Shipley.

"What's wrong with marrying money?" said Paul. "I aspire to it. My daddy is out there somewhere."

"We're separated," Emily said.

"How long were you married?" said Candace.

"A little over eleven years."

"That's rough. Especially when money's involved. How's the negotiation going? Is she being good about it?"

"He," said Gen.

In the small silence that followed, everyone looked at Emily, except Shipley, who looked quizzically at Gen.

"Oh," said Nita.

"Sorry," said Candace. "I just assumed."

Paul refilled Emily's teacup. "If you're straight *and* going through a divorce, you need more alcohol."

"Y'all still assuming," said Becca. "Maybe Emily's bi. Or her ex is trans."

There was a flurry of apology, which Gen cut through by saying, "Jack is the cis-est, straightest man I've ever seen."

"What exactly are you doing?" Shipley asked Gen in a low voice. Gen ignored the question, which increased Emily's anger. She had liked the assumption that she was gay; it had felt good to be known and welcome. Gen had diminished that, right after portraying Emily as a trophy wife, which was exactly what Emily worried she had become. A fizz of champagne sloshed over the teacup's cold rim and onto Emily's hand. She sucked it off the back of her thumb and said, "I'm not straight."

"Obviously," said Becca.

"We're assholes," said Candace.

"Maybe just one of us is," said Shipley.

"Don't worry about it," Emily told Candace.

"Why is everyone so serious?" said Adam, who joined them along with Kate, who said, "Yeah, *you* all weren't the victim of a monologue about the intellectual prowess of rats."

"And emotional skills," said Adam. "A rat will go without food rather than see a fellow rat starve." Kate put a hand over his mouth. He pulled it away and said, "What're you guys talking about?"

Shipley said, "The themes have been sex, rivalries, and self-sabotage."

"Wait, when were we talking about self-sabotage?" said Paul. Nita nudged him.

"I think we should play a game," said Shipley.

"How about not," said Gen.

"I'd love to," said Emily.

"Poker?" said Becca hopefully.

"No!" they chorused.

"It's no fun hanging out with athletes," Becca confided in Emily. "They hate losing."

Shipley placed teacups in front of everyone who didn't already have one. "Let's play Never Have I Ever."

"Ooh, yeah," said Adam. "Love that game. Never Have I Ever caught a raccoon in a Havahart trap and wanted to adopt it because of its cute, clever little paws." He looked around the table. "Nobody else? Okay." He drank.

"That's not how you play the game," said Becca. "You make *other* people drink."

"Their *paws*?" said Paul.

"They're like miniature hands. They can open Coke bottles."

"This is stupid," said Gen.

"Never Have I Ever," said Emily, "played Never Have I Ever."

Everyone else drank—even, reluctantly, Gen.

"Seriously?" said Nita. "But it's a teenage rite of passage! What did you two *do* in high school?"

Becca looked narrowly between Emily and Gen. "Never Have I Ever," she said, "had sex in a barn."

Emily and Gen drank.

"Damn," said Candace.

"I knew it," said Becca.

"I told you that in confidence," Gen said to her.

"But you didn't tell me who *with*. It's fair for me to guess—and I aim to win."

"Never Have I Ever is not a winning or losing game!"

"I feel kind of set up," said Nita. "Anyone else feel set up?"

"What's happening?" said Adam.

"Never Have I Ever," said Kate sternly, "called my closest friends and begged them to come meet me in a matter of *mere hours* for a family-only event and then surprised them with my high school girlfriend but pretended that she wasn't."

Gen sighed and drank.

"Why all the secrecy?" Nita said. "We've met your exes before. You are swimming in exes."

"Never Have I Ever," said Shipley, "left someone at the altar."

Gen's friends looked at Gen, which made Emily look at her. Gen didn't drink. "I did not," she said, "leave anyone at the altar."

"Never Have I Ever," said Shipley, "broken off an engagement."

"Dude, drink up," Adam told Gen.

"I didn't do that," said Gen.

"Oh yes, you did," said Candace. "You proposed to Maiko and took her to France and then came back and avoided her until you confessed that you couldn't go through with it."

"Maiko?" said Emily.

"Technically, it wasn't an engagement," said Gen. "Gay marriage isn't legal in Ohio."

"Oh, that is such bullshit," said Kate.

"Drink," said Adam. "Drink, drink, drink!"

Glowering, Gen drank.

"Hey," said Nita to Gen, "didn't you and Maiko go to France for a wedding?"

Becca jammed her glasses higher up onto the bridge of her nose. "Never Have I Ever gotten married in France."

Emily drank.

"Wow," said Candace.

"I was wondering," said Nita.

"I have other friends, you know," said Gen.

"Boring ones," said Paul.

"Did you break off your engagement because of my wedding?" said Emily.

"No," said Gen.

"Come *on*," said Becca.

"I'm confused," said Adam. "Why are we being mean to Gen?"

"We're helping," said Becca. "She should live her truth."

"I hate that phrase," said Gen. "It means that nothing is true except for whatever someone individually decides."

"I think we should change the subject," said Adam.

"We are not actually talking about moral relativism, Gen," said Emily. "It was a simple question. If it's too hard to answer, you don't have to."

"Okay," said Gen. "I took Maiko to your wedding and then called off my engagement. But it wasn't because of you. I saw your wedding and realized that it wasn't something I wanted."

Quietly, Emily said, "Fair enough."

"*Now* we can change the subject."

Shipley said, "Should we talk about how sometimes people don't like the consequences of situations they create?"

Gen pushed back her chair and left the room. The bookcase door thudded shut behind her.

"I think we should apologize," said Adam. "Should I go apologize?"

"This is like that Thanksgiving when my grandma said she had her neighbor pegged and I laughed and everyone got mad at me even though *she* said it," said Paul.

"Your family understood why you laughed?" said Candace.

"Maybe they got mad because I explained why I laughed."

"I hope we haven't made a bad impression," Shipley said to Emily.

Becca took off her glasses and looked directly at Emily. "We're glad to have you here, hon."

"Do you wear those glasses when you play poker?" Emily said.

"Sure. Why?"

"Don't you give tells? You fidget."

"Not when I play. But that's in a tournament. This is life. I don't like faking around my friends . . . unless I'm parting them with their money. Back to the most important question of the evening: Know how to play blackjack? No? Lemme teach you." She produced a deck of cards from her denim jacket. It was as if she had unveiled a bomb. People scrambled away from the table. "It's a friendly game!" Becca called. "Not for money!" But the only ones remaining were Becca, Emily, and Shipley, who watched the other two as they played. The rest dispersed throughout the room, lounging on velvet furniture and drinking champagne.

At some point, Gen returned and dropped onto a sofa next to Paul. He tucked back a lock of her hair. She lowered her head to his shoulder and briefly closed her eyes, looking tired, but straightened when Kate asked her a question. Paul and Adam listened while the others talked, Gen lively now. As bits of the conversation drifted toward Emily, she understood that they were discussing the 2012 Olympic trials that would take place in June. Emily lost another hand of blackjack.

"You're not bad," Becca told Emily as she shuffled the cards. "But when you're happy about something, your eyes crinkle at the corners. When you're not, your face goes real still. Like now. Just so you know."

"Thanks," said Emily. "This was my favorite part of the evening." Then she said she was going home.

"Let me call you a cab," said Shipley.

"I want to walk." Emily was thirsty for the chilled air outside. She thought of Paul and Gen's tenderness toward each other and experienced a confused jealousy, not knowing whether she wanted to be Paul, with Gen resting against her in an easy trust, or Gen, touched with such affection.

Neither, she decided. She didn't want anything to do with Gen. Not anymore. Being around her would only go badly, like this night.

"Where do you live?" said Shipley.

"The West Village."

"I'm in Chelsea. I'll walk with you."

"You're leaving?" Gen, who had seen Emily reach for her coat, approached the table. "I'll walk you home."

"The Village is out of your way, isn't it?" said Shipley. "It'd take forever for you to get back to Brooklyn."

"Thanks anyway," Emily coolly told Gen, who, though it looked for a moment like she might insist, closed her mouth in a flat line.

"Okay," said Gen. "See you."

"Sure." Emily felt awkward. Polite lies hadn't been part of the way she and Gen were with each other before. "See you."

Wind rattled the trees. In the streetlamp-yellowed dark, the leaves were cloudy masses that churned on top of each trunk. Emily imagined how the trees would be in a week or two: undressed, their leaves on the ground. Emily enjoyed the cold for a few minutes before remembering that she didn't like the cold. It was almost funny how easy it was to forget things—whole habits, years of preferences—about oneself, even if not for long.

She and Shipley walked through Chinatown, where some markets remained open. There were crates of persimmons. Tiny, glassy shrimp flicked on beds of ice. In the cobblestone streets of SoHo, Shipley bought candied nuts to share, though they agreed that the smell was better than the taste. "It was a big New York City first," Shipley said. "The disappointment of Nuts4Nuts. I know it makes no sense to keep buying them."

Emily ate one. "Maybe you like to commemorate that first disappointment. I guess it's important: the moment when you learn better."

"But I didn't. I don't. They get me every time. They smell too good." Shipley took some more. "What's up with you and Gen?"

Emily wanted to be as dismissive about the past as Gen had been to her at the bar. "We didn't date long. Less than a year. She was my first girlfriend. Only girlfriend."

"I'm surprised at that last part."

"It's why I'm always saying things like, 'I'm not straight,' instead of what I am, because I don't know what that is, or at least I don't know what it is now."

"I think you get to decide."

"I was with a man for a long time."

"Well, now you can date anyone you want."

They reached the lower edge of the Village, where fire escapes zigzagged down redbrick buildings. A CVS displayed skeletons and masks in its windows. Emily asked if Shipley would compete in the trials for the Olympic basketball team and was told yes. Shipley hoped to get a sponsor. "The Liberty doesn't pay much," Shipley said, "at least not compared to men's teams, where the pay scale is in the millions. I'd rather not play abroad, though I could make more money that way. Of course, track doesn't pay at all, really, unless you collect enough prizes or become a coach. Or unless you're Gen."

They reached Emily's building. "Can I have your number?"

Shipley asked. Emily hesitated, surprised, though she knew she shouldn't have been. "How about I give you my number instead," said Shipley, "and you can call me if you want."

Emily gave Shipley her phone and watched the tattooed fingers move rapidly over the screen. The phone was warm when Shipley returned it. Emily slid the phone into her coat pocket, where it felt like a slim gift she wasn't sure she should open.

The apartment smelled of Stella's shampoo. Emily turned on all the lights but that didn't make her feel less alone. She avoided the children's bedroom.

Her phone buzzed. The text was from Gen. Did you get home okay?

Emily didn't really want to respond. She sent a thumbs-up.

Gen wrote, Did you have a good time?

Your friends are nice. Thanks for inviting me

How was the walk home with Ship? After a pause came: She can be a lot

Shipley's great, Emily wrote. I like her very much. If Gen didn't exist and hadn't marked Emily with the primacy of a desire still evident, as though Emily had been stamped or engraved by it, would Emily call Shipley? Yes, she thought so. And if Gen didn't exist, would Emily have stayed with Jack . . . or not married him? She saw a possible past where she dated only men because that was expected, but maybe she wouldn't have, because she wouldn't have been hurt by Gen, and so wouldn't have believed that men were a remedy.

Gen didn't reply to Emily's text. Emily turned off her phone and turned out the lights.

Halloween fell on a Sunday, which meant that Jack would have the children then. "You can come trick-or-treating, too," said Stella. "Daddy said so."

"That's your time with him."

"Please?" said Connor.

“Let’s plan your costumes. There’s little more than a week left.”

“We decided already,” said Stella. “I’m going to be a bunny rabbit. Connor’s going to be a hat.”

“A hat?”

Connor shrugged.

“Is that what you want to be?”

Another shrug.

“Why don’t you be something else?”

“No!” said Stella. “He promised to be a hat! He *has* to.”

“Why are you upset? It’s his costume, not yours.”

“We are a *together* costume! It’s supposed to be *magic.*”

“Okay, but there are all kinds of together costumes. Let’s think of others.”

“No! I’m a rabbit and he’s a hat!”

“What do you want to be?” she asked Connor.

“A zombie?”

“No!” Stella shrieked.

“Stella, stop. Are you sure, Connor? I thought you didn’t like scary costumes.”

“That’s when I was little. Lucas said at school that he’s going to be a zombie and I want to be one, too.”

Tears dripped down Stella’s cheeks.

Slowly, Emily asked, “Was a together costume Daddy’s idea?” Neither of them answered. “He can’t make you wear it.”

“He’s not!” said Stella. “I want to be a bunny!”

“That might be fun for you, but a hat isn’t fun for Connor. He’ll go as a zombie.” Now that it had been decided, Connor looked uncertain. “It’ll be a really good costume,” she reassured him.

“Come with us,” Stella said. “Come trick-or-treating like all the years.”

Emily loved trick-or-treating with Connor and Stella. Children were constantly at the mercy of adult rules; this one day was designed for children. Aware that her split with Jack was a force on her children’s lives that they were powerless to change when it was what they most wanted to change, Emily found it hard to resist spending Halloween with them. Her parents had always spent that day with her when she was little—her father, before the divorce, pretending to be scared by the costumes, and afterward, her mother, dutifully walking Emily from house to house. Emily suddenly missed her parents. She wished that they loved her like she loved her children. She dreaded that they'd prove that they didn't. Although she knew that she could call her parents, she felt entirely unable, because the only thing worse than not getting what you want is knowing that you'll never get it.

"Please?" said Stella.

"I'll stop by to see you in costume and take pictures before you head out." Stella was dissatisfied but wiped her face.

Emily texted Jack to see if her plan was okay with him. His reply was immediate:

Amazing! We were hoping you'd join us.

Not for trick-or-treating. Just pictures.

Em, please. It will be fun.

When she didn't reply, he added, No matter what, we are still a family. We should do things together. It would be good for the children.

She imagined the four of them going house-to-house, pointing at spooky decorations. Was it good to show Connor and Stella that their parents could be friendly? Or would it make them believe that Emily and Jack would get back together, and wasn't that exactly what Jack wanted?

She told Jack no. Stella didn't speak with her for the rest of the night.

A few days later, Gen texted, saying that her friends were having a Halloween party. Would Emily come with her?

Anger thick—like jam boiled down to the bottom of the pot, shining and sticky, a coagulate of Emily's embarrassment about the night at the bar and her resentment of Jack's endless manipulation—Emily lied. She told Gen that she had plans.

She shouldn't have encouraged Connor to be a zombie. She worried about it all the way uptown. Her subway car was crowded with people in costume: some sexy witches, a Santa, a Van Gogh with a missing ear, a vending machine. She wanted Connor to learn to resist his father when it mattered, and she believed that it mattered this time, that it was petty and despotic to force a child, on a day when he could be anything, to be a servant to his father's needs. But Jack would react to defiance. He usually did. When she had called the children yesterday to say good night, Connor had been quieter than usual.

She could feel the throb of Jack's displeasure. It was like the magic trick Stella and Connor were supposed to be: a sleight of hand that made something invisible only to bring it bodily forth later, solid and twitching.

Emily got off at her stop. She passed a man dressed as a spaceship walking with two little green aliens who ate candy out of their pumpkins. Sudden realization ground Emily to a halt. A *together* costume. It wasn't just that Stella was the rabbit and Connor was supposed to be the hat. Jack was the magician. He had never cared about Halloween before but he must care now. When the door to her former home opened, he would be wearing a bowtie. A red-lined cape. He would have a wand.

Emily forced herself to keep walking. Just because she had imagined Jack as a magician didn't mean that he would be one. It wasn't true. Just an idea that she had. But it felt true. The truth of it crept over her. She felt a little crazy. She stared at the front door and couldn't knock. A final realization arrived: if Stella was the rabbit, and Connor the hat, and Jack the magician, then she was meant to be the magician's assistant. The together costume Jack had planned was a family costume. When he opened the door, he would offer hers. He would tell her to put it on.

The door flung open. Stella must have seen Emily on the security camera. Stella was soft and furry and white. She had a black-painted nose. "Mommy, come in!" Emily remained frozen on the stoop.

"Hi," said the zombie who appeared behind Stella. Emily was

so relieved to see that Connor wasn't a hat that it took her a moment to think that maybe Jack, as a punishment, had decided that everyone else would wear the family costume without Connor.

"Is that Mommy?" called Jack from inside, farther down the hall. She heard his footsteps. She knew what she was about to see.

But when he emerged from the shadows, he wasn't anything at all. "Just in time," he said. "They're chomping at the bit." He wore jeans and his favorite fall sweater. He shrugged on a camel hair coat. "You okay, Em?"

"Yes," she managed. "I'm fine."

After she had taken pictures on the stoop, the other three went in the direction of the town houses where they gave out big candy bars. Emily walked back to the subway. Three years ago, in 2008, when Jack's hedge fund had made a killing by betting against the housing market, which then crashed, he had been motivated by a fat bonus and low housing prices to purchase their property upstate. Connor had been afraid of the house. He had come with them on the broker's tour, clinging to Emily while Jack held Stella. "This place is too old," Connor whispered to Emily.

"We're going to renovate it," she told him.

"I don't like it. It has ghosts."

Jack overheard. Emily worried that he would tease Connor, but instead Jack said that all homes had to be inspected before they were purchased, to check the roof and boiler and that sort of thing. If he paid extra, the house could be inspected for ghosts, too. Would Connor like that?

Jack hired a graphic designer to make a certificate that declared the house to be a ghost-free zone. The lettering was gothic and embossed, the paper creamy and thick. There was a gold-foil seal. They framed the certificate and hung it in Connor's new bedroom. Connor never mentioned ghosts again. This, too, was a kind of magic.

Emily swiped her subway card. She thought about how she had misunderstood her and Gen's breakup. She had misunderstood Gen's invitation to drinks. She had been so sure about the family costume and she had been wrong. She thought about the ghost inspection certificate. She had loved Jack that day. Maybe she misunderstood everything.

———

Emily examined Connor and Stella's candy after school on Monday, looking for anything unwrapped. Her mother had done this every year, citing bad people who put poison in candies and razors in apples. Emily passed a bag of gourmet jelly beans to Stella, who opened it and began eating. Stella offered a yellow jelly bean. "This one's buttered popcorn," Stella said. "Try it."

It had a synthetic, vaguely buttery taste. Emily reached for the bag and read it. Toasted marshmallow, sour cherry, pomegranate. The jelly beans made a lot of promises. All it took was a hint of halfway-right flavor for people to taste what the jelly bean pretended to be.

"Mommy!"

"What?"

"You're staring."

"I was thinking."

"Stop it. You always go away."

"What were you thinking?" said Connor.

"I was thinking about the jelly beans. I was thinking that it's easy to fool people into believing that a sort-of-real thing is the real thing. This jelly bean doesn't really taste like a Granny Smith."

"He*llo*!" said Stella. When had she learned that funny, rude tone?

"No one thinks the jelly bean tastes like an apple," said Connor.

"You like it because it's candy!" said Stella.

"Duh," said Connor, emboldened by Stella. For a moment, he looked frightened by what he had said, which made Emily pull him onto her lap. "Kids still say *duh*?" she said, arms around him.

"You're so old, Mommy!" Stella pushed herself onto Emily's lap, too.

"Yeah," said Connor. The children, full of sugar, giggled and squirmed. Her phone rang. It was Gen. Emily ignored it.

———

Rain flecked the windows and the children were at school when Gen sent a text: I'm going to call. Please pick up? It would mean a lot to me if we could talk

Emily remembered calling Gen from the lobby of her dad's church. How loud the dial tone had sounded. How much she had wanted Gen to answer.

Gen called.

"Hi," said Emily.

"Hey." Gen's end of the line was full of space and echoes.

"Where are you? It sounds like you're in an empty pool."

"Indoor track. I'm taking a break. I want to say something. I didn't mean for the night at the bar to be like that. Us not talking. Me being rude. Ambushing you with a bunch of strangers, even though I love them. I should have let you know they'd be there or I shouldn't have invited them. I didn't invite them, at first, but I got nervous."

"Why? It's just me."

"Yeah, exactly. I guess I'm not over everything that happened between us. But I want to be. I want us to be friends. I want to make that work. I want you in my life."

What was real? Some things Emily knew to be true. "I missed you."

"Emily. I missed you so fucking much."

23

Emily,

I can't wait to visit you at Harvard!

You asked me a question, and I'll tell you, though I don't like talking about it. So I'm kind of glad you asked me in a letter. I'm writing this in bed. My roommate is in class. I'm supposed to be at practice but I'm not because I got yelled at. No, I didn't deserve it. Had some drinks with my trackmates and I admit I went a little hard. Next day I paid for it in practice. Pulled a muscle. Coach was all in my business, asking if I thought I was such hot shit that I didn't need to put the work in, didn't need to watch my choices. Lazy, he said. Made me mad. For one night out. One little thing. But one little thing, he said, could mean everything. He doesn't want me back at the track until I "figure out what I really want."

Okay. Your question. I'm stalling, I guess.

My earliest memory is of the blizzard when I was four. You probably remember it, too. When the blizzard was over and Gran opened the door, a second door made of snow stood there. The dogs punched through. My mom and I lived with Gran then. This was before my mother's accident. She bundled me up. We followed the dogs. They plunged ahead, making a path. They peed everywhere. They'd been cooped up awhile.

Here's the part that gets me. The snow had piled in such big drifts against the house that my mom walked up one and onto the roof. She took a shovel with her. There she was on the roof, chucking snow onto the ground. She shoveled the whole roof.

She didn't need to. I mean, why? Looking back, I still don't get it. Why not shovel a path to the barn instead? The snow on the roof wasn't in anyone's way.

Maybe she did it because she could. Because it was strange. Because it wouldn't happen again. Have you ever done anything just for that? For the once-ness of it?

Watching her, I thought she could do anything. Still do, even though she's gone. It breaks me. If she could do this weird-ass, amazing, hard thing for nothing, why can't she be here—for me?

Seriously, fuck Coach. What does he know about what I really want?

Gen

Gen,

I took your letter with me everywhere. I folded it in half so that it would fit inside my coat pocket, but it wouldn't lay flat. I thought about your questions and didn't know how to answer them.

Maybe your mother wanted to make a memory for you. Maybe it was less impulse than purpose.

I imagine what you described. White clumps dropping from the roof. You below. Dogs bounding. Your mother digs snow out of the blue sky.

Maybe she wanted to be a future mirror for you.

Maybe she wanted to do an impossible thing so that one day you would believe that you could do the same.

Go back to practice.

Love,

Emily

24

Emily switched the phone to her other ear. She looked out the window of Jocelyn's apartment at skyscrapers. A crane lifted a joist.

"Take me someplace far from the center of things," Gen said, "but still New York City. I want to see the city's edges. Where it becomes something else."

"It's always becoming something else. From street to street. Like any city."

"Yeah, but New York usually insists on being itself no matter what neighborhood you're in. I want to see where it gives that up."

"Why?"

"I guess because I'm here for a limited time. I travel a lot. I don't always get the chance to know a place well and I like to. You know a place well when you recognize where it stops being that place."

Pricked by the reminder that Gen wasn't here to stay, Emily said, a little sharply, "So you want to play tourist?"

"If that's how you want to put it. My first teammates teased me. I was wide-eyed when we got on the plane. I had never flown. Did I tell you my first international meet was in Brazil, when I was in college? All I'd really known was Ohio. But you understand what that's like. Growing up small."

Emily felt a rush of kinship . . . and embarrassment that she had resented that Gen would leave at the end of spring. Who was Emily to blame anyone for leaving? "I'll take you anywhere you want to go."

Some people would consider the rivers to the east and west of Manhattan the edges of the city, but to Emily they were still the city, the East Side with its blocks of brown apartment buildings and caged baseball diamonds, the Hudson River with its newly developed piers and cheerful fake grass. Emily and Gen could go north, but Harlem was part of the city and the Bronx was, too, until it grew mansions with terra-cotta roofs and plush gardens. Emily didn't want to go north. It was too close to upstate, where Jack would be with the children for the weekend.

She and Gen went south to the Rockaways. They took the A train to Ninetieth Street and walked along a strip with a surf shop, a woodworking studio, a deli café, and a Dollar Tree. They found a short path to the beach. The porch of a weather-scoured house had a seashell wind chime that clicked as they passed.

At the beach, everything was gray. The sky, the sea. Even the sand. The crooked fingers of stubbed-out cigarettes. Bottle caps on the boardwalk. The crazy surfers far out on the waves. Their tilted bodies were the color of slate. Sometimes they looked like they were leaning into a wave and sometimes like they were leaning away from it. One got swamped. Emily shivered. Before taking the train, she had looked up a burger joint along the boardwalk but hadn't accounted for it being closed after the summer season. She suggested returning to the café by the subway, but Gen asked if they could wait a few minutes, so they sat at a picnic table as the sea pummeled the shore. Gen nodded at the surfers. "I like to watch them try."

"Even in November?"

"Especially in November."

"Why are you here until June? What's in June?"

"The Olympic trials. They'll be in Oregon at Hayward Field." Gen had decided to train here, so she could be close to her friends. Nita and Candace had been on Gen's team in college. The other friends had been collected over the years. Most of them had met Gen's grandmother. Emily tried to ignore a pang of jealousy. "Last year, I got Gran courtside seats so we could watch Ship in her final," Gen said. "She's an amazing player. Gutsy, fast." Gen peered at the water. Without turning toward Emily, she added, "I think she's into you."

Emily scooped a bottle cap from the sand. She traced its red star. The bottle cap seemed to possess the only color on the beach. She flipped it in her hand, running a thumb along its crimped edge. She thought that Connor might like it. No, he would prefer the shells and stones. The husk of a crab. This bottle cap was trash. Of course. Emily had thought that he would like it only because she missed him and Stella, and was ready to take anything home with her so that she could give it to them. "I've got too much going on," she said.

"What exactly *is* going on? You and Jack seemed solid—at least, at the wedding. Like you were made for each other. What happened?"

To answer felt overwhelming, so Emily chose one detail: how Jack sometimes left Connor alone in the hallway as a baby—briefly, she hastened to add. She didn't want to appear unjust. Yet even as she acknowledged that maybe Jack had a different parenting style, maybe it was tough love, and even though Gen said nothing, Emily began presenting further evidence to persuade Gen that she wasn't wrong to be upset. Around the time that Connor was a toddler, she might come out of the shower or kitchen to find Jack checking his email while little fists thumped on the other side of the apartment's front door. Just a time-out, Jack said. All the parenting books recommended time-outs to address bad behavior. But what had Connor done? What *could* he have done? *Come on, Emily, don't be like that. Relax. But I asked you not to do this*, she said. He sighed. *Okay, I won't*, he said, but a few months later, he did. When Emily was pregnant with their second child, it occurred to her that a house had no public hallways. Could they buy a townhome? *Yes! Great idea, Em.* Anything to make her happy. Their family was growing; they could use more space. He felt bad that he hadn't considered this earlier. Only after they moved in did she realize that a house *does* have a public hallway: the street. She prepared for the day Jack locked their son out of the house as a punishment. She installed an automatic lock with a door code, telling Jack it was for security. She made

Connor memorize the code. She set a stone planter near the door and showed Connor how he could climb up on it so that he could reach the keypad. But—had Jack noticed her efforts?—he didn't do what Emily dreaded. At least, he didn't do that exact thing. This had been a great flaw in their marriage: Emily's failure to anticipate what Jack might do.

Emily fell silent. The beach was mostly empty. A man threw a ball to his dog. A teenage girl jogged along the surf. Gen's gaze was trained on the horizon. She didn't say anything for a long time. The jogger passed Emily and Gen's picnic bench and kept going. "Maybe that's not the right way to explain," said Emily.

"I'm just having a hard time speaking." The surfers paddled out, their wetsuits black. Gen stuffed her fists into her coat. Emily turned the bottle cap in her fingers. A gull banked toward them and then cut away, seeing nothing to steal. Gen said, "I don't get how you go back to someone like that."

It was what Emily's friends had said. They dismissed the obvious reasons: her child, her pregnancy, her fear of a legal battle. We can figure it out, they promised. What she couldn't articulate was the spell of Jack's love for her. Sometimes it seemed like he might obliterate everything she cared about in order to make her his. But that's horrible! Yes: its horror captivated her. The horror was proof of his need. He needed her so much. Only she could alleviate his suffering. He would do anything for her forgiveness. She was a god. At least, for a week or so. A few minutes. A day. The lottery of her tenure of power was also part of the spell.

"That's fucked up," Gen said.

The teenage jogger hesitated by a stone jetty, then turned back.

"Maybe I asked the wrong question," Gen said. "What made you stay?"

This, Emily thought, Gen would understand even less. She told Gen about her miscarriage. Her baby had died, but he hadn't been a real baby to the rest of the world. He had been an almost-baby. He hadn't counted. Not his sealed eyes, not his tiny fingers. His body had been lightly covered in hair. That was normal, the nurse said, at this stage. He would have lost it by the end of a full term. He reminded her of a hibernating animal. A creature waiting for winter to be over. He had come out of her but people acted like he hadn't, as though he had been reabsorbed into her flesh. Gone with no trace. As though he had been—or should be—swallowed by everything that was everyday: the ATM on the corner, enrolling Connor in preschool, recycling a bottle as green as a hyacinth's blade. It piled with the other bottles in the truck. Did it break or slide whole, unseen, to the truck's bottom? Such a question—commonplace, did it need an answer?—was supposed to cover the fact of her baby's existence. His non-existence. He had never existed—except for her, and for Jack. Jack was the only one, besides Emily, who had known their son. He and Emily were the only ones who knew how real their baby was. How much he mattered.

Gen rested a hand on Emily's shoulder. She had never touched Emily like that. There had been times, like now, when Emily knew that Gen understood exactly what she was saying, but this was the first time that this understanding came from a shared sense of loss. Gen's hand was warm.

"It bothered me," Gen said, "at the bar, with my friends, when they asked what you did and you said 'nothing.' I know that being a mom isn't all you are, but it's important."

" 'Nothing' is what a lot of people think."

"Not me."

The jogger ran up the beach toward them, then slowed. When she was close enough that Emily could see that her lips were chapped, she stopped and bent to untie and remove one sneaker. She walked to them, sneaker in hand. Wordlessly, she held it out to Gen.

"Oh," said Gen. "Yeah, of course." She patted her coat pockets and found a Sharpie. As she signed the sneaker, she chatted with the girl, asking where she went to high school and what kind of track she liked best. The girl mumbled her answers, eyes glossy with adoration. She took the signed sneaker and held it with both hands.

"Put it on," said Gen. "Let's see how fast you can go."

The girl sprinted toward the water. Gen shouted encouragement. Emily joined in, clapping. Her palms stung. It felt good to shout. When the girl reached the wet sand, she turned back and waved both arms overhead. Emily and Gen waved back, then walked to the deli café to get warm.

—

A few days later, a package came for Emily as she helped Stella with her math homework. It was a box of Honeybell oranges. There was an unsigned card: *I remembered how much you hate the cold. Hope this helps.*

Emily lifted an orange to smell its vivid skin. The children clamored for some. She gave them the box but took one orange into her bedroom and shut the door. She wanted to be alone with how good this gift made her feel. The orange set her hand on fire. She thought to text Gen, but decided she would thank her when she saw her next.

—

Emily woke up wet between her legs. She didn't remember what she had been dreaming but she could guess. She slipped a finger inside and it came out slick. She traced herself, nudging her ready clit. Her breath grew short. She was wet enough that it was easy to pretend that her fingers were Gen's sliding mouth. The flick of her tongue.

Too quick. She pushed herself almost to orgasm, then stopped. She didn't want the disappointment that would come after. She clamped her thighs together, hand pressed flat between them, and throbbed.

—

She was in a sporting goods store looking for a pair of cleats for Connor, who had outgrown his, when her phone buzzed with a text from Jack.

Did you like the oranges I sent?

25

Rory called. "Where are you? I'm in town and I'm taking you out."

Jack was away that weekend for a work trip and Emily had the kids.

"Let's go to the Natural History Museum," said Rory. "Kids love the Natural History Museum. *I* love the Natural History Museum."

"What do you love about it?"

"The jewels, obviously. I'm also into the stuffed tigers. I'll see you in the rotunda by the baby brontosaurus at two p.m."

"Look at that." Rory pointed at the Teddy Roosevelt quote carved into the wall of the museum's rotunda. " 'If I must choose between righteousness and peace, I choose righteousness.' What an asshole!"

Connor and Stella stared.

"I mean, what an a-hole!"

Emily said, "You never choose peace."

"But I *should*. And I'm not a president. I don't go around carving shitty ideas into marble."

"Who are you?" said Stella.

"He didn't carve it," said Connor. "He's dead."

"I would make a great president," said Rory.

"Peace isn't always good," said Connor. "In World War II, people were peaceful with Hitler and that was bad."

"Too dark!" said Rory. "Come on, kiddos, let's go see the elephants."

They saw the elephants. They saw a movie in the planetarium. They saw a resin model of ancient hominoid footprints next to chimpanzee prints. They lay down under a life-size blue whale and looked at large dioramas of seagulls and fish, which made Emily think of Gen. She no longer had the diorama Gen had made for her. It once sat on the desk in her dorm room, but she threw it out after the breakup.

Rory declared that they should have breakfast for dinner. She took them to the Plaza, where they ate French toast flooded with syrup and buried under whipped cream.

"He sent you oranges?" Rory said over wine in Emily's living room. The kids were asleep, the door to their room closed. "Fuck that guy."

"It was nice. At least, it was nice when I thought Gen had sent them."

"Because you're hot for her. For the record, I also think it would be manipulative if she had sent you oranges."

"He's trying."

"To crawl back into your pants! He has been *too quiet* about your separation. Very suspicious. He's playing the good guy. Those oranges are proof. This is the beginning of a charm offensive. He's starting small, but watch him work his way up."

"He just wants to show that he has changed."

"That's what I'm *saying*. Look, maybe tell Gen how you've been feeling. You're not easy to read. It's not like she can see visions of vulvae dancing through your head."

"Didn't you make me promise not to get involved with her?"

"I am a sex Machiavellian. Whatever keeps you from going back to your toxic ex is an acceptable means to a noble end."

"She's not thinking about me like that."

Rory finished her wine. "Date someone else, then. Go wild. Give yourself a pat on the fucking back, because so many people stay in bad marriages. They hope it'll get better or it's too hard to leave. With my parents, I think they love to hate each other.

Gives them something to complain about besides the help. Marriage? Kill me! I want a string of adoring lovers." She put on her coat, fluffed out her blond hair, and pulled on long, black leather gloves. "Keep me updated on Gen."

Emily flushed, remembering how she had touched herself: the quick demand of her arousal. "There won't be anything to update."

"Ha!" said Rory.

On the subway ride to school, a cockroach dropped from a bench and scuttled by their feet. Stella screamed. Connor jerked his feet away. Emily stomped it.

"*Ew.*" Stella's face was pink and she looked close to tears.

"I hate the subway," said Connor. "Can we get a driver?"

"What?" said Emily. "No."

"It's still *moving*," Stella wailed.

"Daddy got a driver," said Connor. "Mr. Mike drives us wherever we want to go. Daddy said he'd get one for you, too. Mr. Mike always has candies for us. He hides them in the car and it's like a treasure hunt."

On the first of the month, Emily's bank account was replenished. It never failed to make her feel horrible and grateful. She had insisted on paying rent to Jocelyn, who had said that wasn't necessary, but Emily didn't want to depend on Jocelyn's generosity. She was aware that she escaped that form of dependence only because of her financial dependence on Jack. Her bank statement read like evidence of theft. She had to remind herself that Jack was obligated to provide a home for his children, and could well afford it. Paying rent relieved her, though it was emotional money laundering, where she shoved guilt-dollars out of her account and into Jocelyn's. But then she felt awful all over again when she set aside money for a lawyer . . . and worried, because no amount she could save would be equal to the financial force Jack could summon against her. "We're not getting a driver. Stella, stop. It's just a bug." Stella buried her face into Emily's coat.

"Daddy says we deserve the best," Connor said.

"I want a driver," Stella whispered. At their stop, she said she was too tired to walk, so Emily carried her until her arms ached, then made Stella walk a block, then carried her again. All the while, Connor praised Mr. Mike and his car, which had seat warmers and a mini-TV screen that showed cartoons. "Daddy said all you had to do was ask."

Finally, patience gone, Emily said, "Cars are bad for the environment. Subways are better. I thought you cared about the polar bears, or are you a hypocrite?" Connor was silent. When he had learned about how polar bears starved as ice in the Arctic Circle vanished, he was inconsolable. Now he glared at the ground. Guilty for making him feel guilty, and for pretending that the environment was the reason she refused to accept Jack's offer, she said, "I can be a hypocrite, too. I take planes. I don't always eat leftovers. But we're not getting a car, okay?"

"I don't care," he muttered.

"Don't worry, Mommy." Stella patted her arm. "It's Friday, so Mr. Mike will pick us up from school today. We have him all weekend. Weekends are best for cars. Subways are good for I Spy."

"Yeah, I Spy cockroaches," said Connor.

"Connor, *shut up*!" Stella shouted. She cried the rest of the way to school.

—

That afternoon, Emily texted Gen. how common is it that people recognize you?

Like the girl with the shoe on the beach?

Y

Depends on the season, Gen wrote. Or the person I'm dating

Emily so intensely disliked the thought of anyone dating Gen that she didn't write back.

Right now I'm in a fame gully, Gen wrote. If I were dating right now and she was famous, there would have been paps on that beach taking photos. Fame is weird and one of the ways it's weird is how contagious it is. But otherwise, I get to be mostly anonymous unless it's Olympic season or right after. Though queer people always 100% recognize me. Attention from everyone else will start up again in a few months

Sounds hard

Comes with the territory. It's not always bad. I mean, it's not why I do what I do. But it keeps me honest. The press can't dig up a dirty secret if I have nothing to hide. And if I'm always being myself, who cares what they photograph? I know some actors who have a public life and a private life, but ugh. THAT would be hard. Keeping your lies straight

Thinking of her marriage with Jack, Emily wrote, I see why people do it

Not me. I won't lie about who I am

The thought of letting a stranger peer into her private life made Emily shudder.

Kind of enjoying the break, though, Gen wrote. I hate when they pester Gran. Paps are relentless. Even if you give them a shot they always want a photo that you don't want them to take. An ex broke up with me over it. Said it was too much. I was too much

Too much because of the attention?

Not just that. Too driven. Gen paused. Too unsatisfied

Hard to imagine anyone breaking up with you

It is rare but it happens, Gen wrote. As you well know

I meant you have a reputation

For my handsome looks and fine mind?

I believe that "lady-killer" was the word Vanity Fair used

I prefer "rake." It's so sexy. So Regency

So Mr. Willoughby?

I wasn't thinking Jane Austen. More like grocery store romances. God I love those. The ones where there's a wallflower with glasses and a duke finds her in the garden. Or maybe she's a spitfire. No, a spinster! He unbuttons her glove and peels it down to her wrist

Will it be hard to deal with the press when spring comes?

Changing the subject?

No

I wasn't finished. I am a very attentive duke. To the scandal of the ton

I guess you don't want to answer my question

Don't worry. You won't be caught in a photo with me in Gawker. At least not until sometime in spring, close to when the trials start. You can drop me then

I'm not worried

Not worried your ex might see you with me in a magazine?

Emily's fingers hovered over the phone.

After a moment, Gen wrote, I don't even know if I'll be in the 2012 Olympics

You won't compete?

Gotta compete. I mean maybe I won't make the cut. One year, I won't. It'll all be over and I'll have to figure out what to do with the rest of my boring life

Seduce wallflowers?

The phone rang. Gen said, "Any specific suggestions?"

Emily's pulse leapt.

"I mean," Gen said, "for my post-track career." In the background, someone said, "Will you get off the damn phone? You've been mooning at it for the past half hour and now—" The phone went silent. Gen must have hit the mute button. Then the line opened again. Gen said, "I'm shopping with Becca and Ship. Becca won a tournament and wants to use the winnings to redecorate her apartment so we're helping out. She has terrible taste. Look, it's just true." Gen's voice went distant, presumably because she was now speaking to Becca. "Your apartment is a junk drawer. You toss everything in at random."

The line was muffled.

"Why hello," said Becca. "Emily, right?"

"Give me my phone back," said a faint Gen. A third person—Shipley—said something inaudible. Gen said, "Come on, this is private."

"Shopping with them was a bad idea," Becca said to Emily. "Gen's going to make me buy fancy furniture in shades of gray and Ship will insist that I get many, many beanbags. Y'all *shush*! Sorry, Emily, not you. I just want a comfy sofa. With a nice chaise lounge. I like some cush, you know?"

Gen must have seized her phone from Becca. "Let's talk later."

Emily said, "Will you meet me for dinner?"

She was in a taxi to the restaurant when Jack called. Stella had come home from school with a fever. The pediatrician was on her way; Jack had persuaded her to make a house call. "Stella's doing okay but she's asking for you."

"Will you put her on the phone?"

"Come over. Please? It would mean the world to her."

Emily envisioned Stella's feverish eyes and felt bad for not realizing earlier that she was coming down with something. She told the driver to change destinations.

Headlights from cars in the next lane caught sparse snow. The flakes lifted and zoomed. They reminded Emily of how she had felt earlier while getting ready to meet Gen. Little, deliciously chilled points of nervousness had floated across a wide space of want inside her chest.

She reluctantly reached for the phone she had set on the seat beside her. hey

Gen's reply was immediate: hi

I can't make it, Emily typed slowly. Stella's sick

!! is she ok?

I think so

Poor kid. There was a pause. I thought your ex had them on the weekends

I'm headed to his place. He asked me to come

After a longer moment, Gen said, He can't manage on his own?

Emily wrote in hasty frustration. Look my kid is sick and I need to be with her

I think you misunderstand me. Gen sent a rapid series of single-sentence texts. Of course you should be with her. I question his intentions.

Emily was home. Connor ran down the stoop. Emily stuffed her phone into her coat pocket as he flung open the taxi door. "You're supposed to be a surprise," Connor said. "Stella doesn't know." Excitedly, he pulled her by the hand up the stoop, where Jack was waiting at the top, backlit by the yellow hallway. He smiled when she reached him. Her coat pocket buzzed but Emily didn't want to know what Gen had to say, because knowing was useless. Nothing changed the essential fact of her motherhood. It didn't matter how old her children grew. She would always carry them inside her, the joy of them a brutal tragedy: their devotion, their rejection, their need, their indifference. Their inevitable departure. What else in life do you love without reason or limit, only to surrender it? What else, except life itself? Loving your children is like learning how to die. You don't learn how to let go. You learn only that you must.

Jack took Emily's coat and hung it in the closet. He had chosen the floral wallpaper in the vestibule and she had chosen the herringbone tiles. The wallpaper had one of those patterns that can appear three-dimensional with a slight unfocusing of the gaze. Jack rapped his knuckles along it as he walked into the house and called for Stella.

"Mommy's here!" said Connor. Jack shot him a furious look, then caught Emily's eye, shrugged, and ruffled the boy's hair. There was a commotion of footsteps on the walnut stairs. Stella—fuzzy pajamas, sunset hair—burst into view. She was giddy. She jumped up and down.

"I thought she had a fever," said Emily.

"Low-grade," said Jack. "The doctor just left. She said it was an ear infection. She prescribed medicine—you know, that pink stuff—"

"Bubblegum medicine!" said Stella.

"The doctor had brought a bottle just in case. That's what I call professional."

"Why didn't you tell me?" said Emily.

"You were already on your way."

"Daddy made alphabet soup." Stella tugged Emily toward the kitchen.

"Don't worry," Jack said to Emily. "I also made grown-up food. Everything's ready."

Emily resisted Stella's pull. "Stella gets ear infections all the time. If I had known—"

"Daddy doesn't like it when food gets cold," Connor reminded.

"You two go ahead," Jack said. "Let me talk with Mommy."

When they had gone, Emily said, "This is a trap."

"Look, I'm doing my best. It's not easy being a single dad. I didn't know Stella was basically fine until the doctor left, which was five minutes ago, and I'd already told Connor you were coming. If you want to leave, okay, but you'll have to explain it to the kids."

For dinner, Jack opened a bottle of Montrachet Grand Cru from the Domaine de la Romanée-Conti, a white Burgundy wine that cost thousands of dollars, which Emily knew because Jack had told her when he got the news months ago that, after a long wait, a bottle had become available for purchase. He filled her glass and said that the wine tasted like white flowers and pear and salt.

She put the children to bed. She walked softly down the hall, stopping before the door of the nursery that had been changed into a writing office that she never used. She stepped inside. There was no dust on the rosewood desk. She sat down and switched on the lamp. The drawers were stocked with blank notebooks and pencils and pens. The view was of the garden, which was too dark to see. The window held only a reflection of the lamp. The room was a lot of space for a baby that didn't exist and a book that hadn't been written.

Or maybe not enough space. The moment that she wondered how much space those unborn things required, it seemed too large to measure.

She had the impulse to take a notebook. The impulse surprised her. She hadn't written in years. But she didn't want Jack to notice that she'd taken a notebook. That would please him. She didn't want to please him. She closed the drawer.

Downstairs, Jack was waiting. She walked past him to the hallway closet for her coat. "Stay," he said. "Just for the night."

"I can't."

"Even in the guest room? I've missed you so much."

She shook her head.

"But it's not fair to the kids," he said. "Think of how they'll feel when they wake up and you're not here." Her emotions toward him had changed throughout the night, from gratitude to anger to pity to an old alliance, a worn-down, habitual love. Now back again to the sense of entrapment. She put on her coat and left.

Outside, snow came down more thickly than before. It was late. She checked her phone for the time and saw several missed texts from Gen.

I'm going to the restaurant. Don't mind a solo dinner
but . . .
if you decide you can, come join me whenever

The texts were hours old. Emily's white breath rose in the light of her phone. She wrote, Are you still there?

No answer. Nonetheless, Emily hunted for a cab.

The restaurant was nearly empty. The host told her that it was too late for dinner; the kitchen had closed. When she explained she was here to look for a friend, he said, "Ah," and led her to Gen, who sat with her back to a window swirling with snow. Her table had been cleared. She was reading.

"You waited," Emily said.

Gen looked up from the book and broke into a huge smile. She reached to touch Emily's hair and came away with fingertips dusted in snow that immediately melted. Emily shivered. Gen said to the host, "Could we have a hot chocolate?"

"Absolutely, Ms. Hall."

"I thought you were in a fame gully," said Emily.

"I thought you weren't coming! Did you text? I stopped by the bookstore on the way here and I didn't mean to read this book but between the appetizer and the main course I couldn't resist. I must have been reading for a while."

"Why wouldn't you read a book you bought?"

"It's a gift." Gen pushed the book across the table. "For Stella." It was *The Lion, the Witch and the Wardrobe*. "Being sick when you're a kid is the worst. My mom would read this to me. You know, before. It was my favorite. It's different for me now. Take Lucy. You're supposed to love her and I do, I can't help it, but she's too good, you know? She finds a *passage to another world* in a wardrobe and leaves the door open behind her. No. Just no. Who remembers to leave a magic door open so that you can go home? Not me. Fuck Lucy. I mean: fuck her embodiment of sensible good-doing."

"You aren't good?" Emily held up the book Gen had bought for her daughter.

"Terrible. I have all sorts of bad motives."

The waiter set a mug in front of Emily, who wrapped her freezing hands around it. The rich taste of chocolate coated her tongue. The heat went straight to her belly.

"I can't believe you're here," said Gen.

"I really wanted to be."

"Did you." Gen said it like a statement, her gaze roving over Emily's face.

"All night. Even before I got your last texts." Emily offered the mug. "Want some?"

"Maybe a sip." Gen reached, her fingers sliding over Emily's as she took the mug. She leaned back to drink and stretched beneath the table, her long legs brushing Emily's. "Sorry," Gen said, but Emily didn't pull away. Gen shifted forward to return the mug, her knee pressing more fully against Emily's inner thigh. Heat flushed Emily's cheeks.

Gen gave her a slow smile. She had not been sorry. She wasn't sorry at all.

Gen,

My friends and I decided to take a break from studying for finals and went to a performance at the Adams House Pool Theater. It's called that because the dorm once had an actual pool in its basement. It was drained six years ago, in 1990. These days, rows of seats line the steps of the empty pool all the way from its shallow end to the deep end, where the performances happen. I had a hard time paying attention, in part because Rory and Elizabeth were whisper-fighting, but also because I felt underwater. I thought about a question you asked in a letter: whether I had ever done something for the once-ness of it.

Maybe every moment is for once only and nothing repeats itself. If I attend another performance at the Pool Theater, even if it's the same play with the same actors, and I'm seated next to the same friends with the same sense of submersion in invisible water, it won't be the same. I won't be the same.

I remember our first kiss. There can never be another first kiss.

Or every time is a first time. I think of you inside me, filling me, the taste of you on my mouth.

You are always new to me. I can never get enough.

Emily

26

The moment at the restaurant disappeared as soon as it came. Gen slid her knee away and chatted breezily, with such nonchalance that Emily thought she had imagined the flirtation in Gen's gaze. Emily decided she had seen what she had wanted to see.

For days, she returned to the press of Gen against her inner thigh. It must have been an error. The clumsy combination of a too-small table and too-long legs. Or not an error, but the ease of an old friend, a slumber party spirit: we have known each other long enough to show affection without it meaning more. This didn't prevent Emily from feeling the memory of Gen's legs between hers, or imagining Gen's hand hidden beneath the table, shoving up the hem of her dress.

Are you free? Emily texted. It was a weekend. Hours passed before Gen texted back: Not really. I'm training

Oh ok

Wait. Gen's text bubbles appeared quickly. Can you make it to the armory in Brooklyn? I know it's far from you. But if you come around 3 I'll be cooling down. My coach will have left. You could bring sneakers, join me for a few laps

like old times?

yeah

it was hard for me to keep up even then

Don't worry, Gen wrote. I'll let you set the pace

The Park Slope Armory looked like a fortress on the outside and a train station on the inside, with a curved steel ceiling above the red-brown indoor track. Emily was glad to be indoors; it was sleeting. Christmas had passed—Jack took the children to Boston, arguing that holidays were for family, and since Emily refused to visit Ohio, he saw no reason to keep the kids from their only true grandparents. What alternate plan could Emily possibly have? The three of them alone in her apartment with a rotisserie chicken? Depressing. He was considerate—she got the kids most of the time, didn't she?—but he had to draw a line. Did she mean to take everything from him? No, he didn't want to fight about this either. She could have Christmas Eve with the kids. That was reasonable. He was being very reasonable. All he wanted was a holiday with his family. Did she realize how lonely she had made him? He added that she was always welcome to join them in Boston.

"Rotisserie chicken is fucking delicious," said Rory, who flew in from L.A. Emily made cocktails for them, garnishing the drinks with sugared cranberries and sprigs of rosemary. Gen, meanwhile, visited Nella in Ohio.

Emily found the armory's locker room. She glanced around as she pulled a sports bra over her breasts, though of course Gen wasn't in the locker room—she had been running on the track for hours already. And if Gen had been in the locker room, she probably would have looked the other way, immune to Emily's nakedness.

Gen loped around the track. Lost in concentration, she didn't notice Emily's wave. She was so swift that when Emily fell into the lane behind her and tried to catch up, the opposite happened:

Gen spotted Emily as she curved the bend ahead and closed the gap between them, drawing up alongside her.

It was like running with a racehorse.

"This is a bad idea," Emily said, breathless.

"No!" Gen slowed. "You were always good. I love doing this with you."

"Maybe if I rode a bike while you ran."

"Don't be cranky."

"Realistic."

"Don't be realistic. There are too many ways to tell yourself something won't work. Just run."

Emily ran.

Eventually, Gen stopped her. She must have been eyeing Emily, because the instant Emily faltered, Gen suggested they walk. Gen pulled off her shirt, revealing a hard abdomen and a black sports bra tight against her nearly flat chest. She was slick with sweat. Her hair was dark and damp and stayed in place when she raked it off her face. Emily thought again that running together had been a mistake—not because she would be sore later (though she would) but because of her painful awareness of Gen's body. The lines of it were familiar yet harder and tighter. When Gen ran, she looked like she was doing exactly what she had been made to do. Determined, glad. The way she ran was a kind of devotion.

In the locker room, Gen entered a stall to change. Emily did the same.

They stood for a few moments in the lobby, eyeing the sleet. Emily's lungs were blown wide open; her heart was loud. It kept saying, *What did you do to me, what did you do to me.* "Was it like old times?" She glanced to see the gladness fade from Gen's face.

"No," said Gen. "It wasn't."

Friend of my youth
Mistress of disguises
Gray-eyed Athena

Daughter of Zeus who bears the storm cloud
Tireless one
Hope of soldiers
Dear guest, who are you? Where do you come from? Where is your home and family?
Pallas Athena ran like the wind
I shall transform you: not a soul will know you
She who fights in front
Child of Power
Destroyer
Would even you have guessed that I am Pallas Athena, daughter of Zeus, I that am always with you in times of trial?

"What are you doing?" asked Connor, looking over Emily's shoulder at the notebook she had purchased earlier that day.

"Making a list."

"That's a weird list."

"It's of things poets called Athena, or said that she said, or what people said to her."

"Athena's in the Percy Jackson books. She's kind of nice and kind of scary."

"Sounds about right."

"The Percy Jackson books are awesome. They're Lucas's favorite."

"Are you still friends with him?"

"Yes."

"I haven't heard much about him lately."

Connor shrugged. "We play at recess. Why do you like Athena?"

"I'm not sure I do." Emily closed the notebook. "But I keep thinking about her."

"Why?"

"There are lots of stories about what she does and says but not much about what she feels on the inside."

"But she's not real. She's made up. She doesn't feel anything on the inside."

"I still care about how she feels. There are real things and made-up things, but the way we care about made-up things is real, too."

Connor furrowed his brow.

"I wrote a book about her," Emily said, "when you were a baby."

"Can I read it?"

Emily chose one of those lies that parents tell to make their children's world seem safer. "I lost it."

When Connor and Stella were asleep, Emily looked at the skyline. The sleet of a few days ago was gone; the air was bone-dry. Skyscrapers glittered. She recalled the obvious pleasure Gen took in running, how she loved doing what she had been born to do.

Writing had been like that for Emily. Jack had destroyed one book, but Emily destroyed the other, the one she didn't write in the lost manuscript's stead, the one she didn't pull from her memory and reassemble. This had been an act of revenge as well as self-preservation. She hated the office that had once been a nursery. She hated Jack's hope that she would blot out his crime by writing over it. She hated the pens, the pencils, the blank notebooks. Every page, written in invisible ink, was crammed with Jack's ideas. His story of their life lay neatly stacked on the desk. It was stitched into the binding of each notebook's spine. What was there to write? He had already written everything.

Emily examined the list of phrases about Athena. She no longer liked the project of her old manuscript. Retelling *The Odyssey* from Athena's perspective bored her. It had been just another way of telling the story of Odysseus. She also didn't like what she remembered of how she had written Athena—too stiff, like a talking statue. Instead, Athena should be like Connor said: kind of nice and kind of scary. A bit of a witch. Thoughtful and strange. Clever, but at risk of making mistakes. Hungry. She should want something badly—but what? If Emily wrote the book now, it would be different.

She recalled Gen slowing to run beside her. She wanted to witness Gen pushed to her limit. She wanted to know how it felt to be pushed to her own. She wanted oxygen to burn her lungs. She wanted a cramp in her side, to refuse to give up.

Emily wrote a phrase at the top of the page: *Daughter of Zeus Who Bears the Storm Cloud.* Then she wrote a beginning:

Would you like to know how to kill a god? Think first of how they are born.

Begin with me.

The story told is that I sprang from my father's head fully grown, sharply adult, bristling with armor and spear. That story is true in the way all stories are—partially.

Think behind the words you have read or heard about me. Imagine them not merely as units of meaning that carry you through time. See, perhaps, a ship. Think not of the ship but of its wake, the air that it shears with its prow, the shadow it casts. Look into that shadow. Know my story: I was born fully grown. Now guess the story untold: that I grew from a baby in my father's mind. I passed my childhood there. I spent an eon of solitude in the whorls of his thoughts.

Zeus loves me best of all his children. To him, I am proof of his omnipotent wisdom. He doesn't know, though, who he is on the inside.

What was my milk but the flow of his intentions and dreams? What was my cradle but his stratagems? How did I learn to walk but by studying his memories? I know him better than he knows himself.

They say I gave him a headache when I was born. The pain came from the thrust of my spear.

Again, think behind the story.

He was unaware of me until that moment. Occult, I had winked into existence inside him. An infant, I wailed and he did not hear. My childhood unfolded, hidden from the king of the gods.

Would you like to know how to kill a god? First, find out what he doesn't know.

It's not surprising, perhaps, that Zeus didn't recognize the thrust of my spear as a warning. He forgave me the pain of birth. Every child wants to be born. Every birth comes with a pang. He didn't see me as a threat.

He doesn't know that I, in the cloister of his mind, grew to hate him. I schemed. I crafted weaponry. At last, I burrowed my way out, buzzing like a wasp, with a plot to overthrow him.

Would you like to know how to kill a god?

Watch me.

27

Gen said that she had something for her. Could Emily meet up? Gen suggested a new place near Emily's apartment called Eat Me / Drink Me. Emily arrived early to find that the restaurant was very New York: a visual brag, from the twining vine wallpaper to chandeliers flickering pink above an empty dance floor. The tables were crowded. A Cheshire cat had been painted on a photo booth near the bar—photo booths, Emily guessed, were a trend that year. She recalled the black-and-white photos of herself taken on the day she had met Gen at the diner. She had hidden the strip of photos in a book. She would occasionally examine the strip, then tuck it carefully back between the pages as if it had been sleeping and she was sorry to wake it.

Emily stood with a cluster of people by the host. It would be an hour-long wait for a table.

Gen brought the cold with her: a whoosh from the opened door. Instead of saying hello, she touched cold fingers to Emily's cheek. Then Gen slid past to talk with the host, who, after their indistinct conversation, told Emily that two seats at the bar had just opened up. Emily resisted the urge to press her hand against her cheek, which tingled as though slapped.

"I didn't know what a zoo this would be," Gen said as they sat at the bar. "Paul recommended it. He's a foodie and to be honest I stop listening when people describe what they had to eat. It's like listening to someone narrate a dream. I can't enter the experience. So all I really absorbed was that he loves it here—which he would, he is such a maximalist—and that it's close to where you live." Gen looked at the menu. The dishes were named after cards. "I should get the King of Hearts. Right? It's so me."

"Not the Ace?"

"Well, we don't have to *announce* it. Let me be a little incognito."

"I notice that you magicked us to the front of the line."

"I called ahead."

"And gave them your full name."

"Was I supposed to give a fake one?"

"Your 'off-season' theory of fame doesn't really hold. Or you have misrepresented things."

"I was speaking *relatively*. Relatively, for now, I'm easy to ignore."

"Hmm." *Easy to ignore* had never been one of Gen's main attributes and it certainly wasn't now. Gen's eyes were even darker than usual in the low light from the bar.

"What?"

"Never mind. You said you had something for me?"

Gen gave her a yielding, butcher-paper-wrapped package that had been tucked inside her coat. "From Gran."

It was a crocheted green hat with a matching scarf. Emily rested her hands on the soft pile. She started to speak, swallowed, and then said, "This is so nice."

"She's glad we met up again."

"She said that?"

"Not quite those words."

"What words?"

"Will you try them on? She chose green to match your eyes."

Emily touched the scarf around her neck. "She remembered."

Gen was quiet, then said, neutrally, "The color is very memorable."

"Tell her thank you."

"Can we take a photo? She'd like that."

Emily took out her phone.

"No, I want to mail it," Gen said. "She likes real mail." They ordered food, left their coats on the barstools, and went into the photo booth. Emily considered saying that she'd taken her own photo that day at the diner, and why, but when Gen pulled the curtain shut and moved to sit next to Emily, fitting snugly against her, Emily lost her breath. Gen slung an arm over Emily's shoulders. Instead of facing forward, Emily turned to look at Gen's sharp profile. Despite Gen's chummy posture, her expression was unsmiling. The camera flashed.

Outside the booth, Gen took the photo strip and watched it develop. The restaurant was loud. "How do we look?" Emily said.

Gen muttered something.

"What?"

"We look like good friends," Gen said shortly. She folded the strip and tucked it into her shirt pocket. "We didn't order drinks. Do you want a drink? I want a drink."

At the bar, Gen asked, "Where've you been lately?"

"Here." Gen had been the one traveling. Soon after her return from Ohio for the holidays, Gen had gone to Arizona for a 1500-meter race, less to win the purse—which she won—than for the competition practice. "I've been around."

"I meant I haven't heard from you much."

"Oh. I've been writing." Emily described the project as Gen drank her gin and tonic. The music grew louder. "You know how something feels all-consuming when it's new?"

Gen set down her glass. "Yeah."

"It's been like that. Except this idea isn't entirely new. I wrote a version of it before."

"Why are you writing another version?"

"The other one was a sort-of fresh copy of someone else's story. This time, I want to make it mine. Unusual. Voice-y. Less like a plot, more like a memoir. I guess I'm saying that I want to write the memoir of a god. Which sounds arrogant. But not boring. Not what's already been done. Anyway, the first manuscript is gone."

Some people moved to the dance floor. Seats cleared at the bar.

"Gone, how?" said Gen.

"Jack took it."

"What?"

"He destroyed it."

"Wait." Gen held up one flat hand. "When did this happen?"

"When Connor was a baby."

"Before Stella was born?"

"Yes."

"I see."

"I know what you think you see, but it's more complicated than that."

"It really isn't." Gen caught the bartender's eye. "Can I have another?"

"You don't get to drop into my life after fifteen years and act like you understand everything."

Gen finally looked at her. "I understand nothing."

"Then let me explain."

"'Be careful.' That's what Gran said. She told me to be careful."

Emily felt as though the barstool was no longer solid beneath her—like one of its legs had a slightly different length than the others or that there was a dip in the floor.

"I don't need to hear the rest of this story," said Gen. "You might want to tell me. You might want to explain how your husband took something important from you and you went back to him and had another child with him, but it's not good for me to hear."

"Can I have this seat?" a man asked Emily, pointing at the free stool next to her.

"Sure," she said, impatient. To Gen, she said, "Then what would you like to discuss? Your pathological need to date and discard women?"

"So," the man said to Emily, "how come you're wearing a hat indoors? Is it a fashion thing, or are you cold?"

Emily pulled the hat from her head.

"Don't do that," he said. "You were adorable. I liked the pom-pom. Can I buy you a drink?"

"No."

"We're having a conversation," Gen told him.

The man noticed her for the first time. "You look familiar."

"I'm not."

"Do I know you?"

"You don't."

"Maybe a dance?" the man asked Emily.

"Classic," Gen said with a flick of the hand that paintbrushed the space between the man and Emily. The word could have labeled only the man were it not for the disdainful gesture. Emily, too, it seemed, was classic. Conclusions had been reached. Verdicts delivered. Emily thought about how the largest number in ancient Greek was a hundred million, or *myriad myriad*, which was written as a double *Mu* with an overbar: $\overline{\text{MM}}$. Gen had a way of making Emily feel like the highest known number, a peak of great intensity. Gen could say one word—*classic*—and it was as though she had scratched an overbar above Emily. She was too angry to speak. She grabbed her things, flung on her coat, and stuffed the green hat into her pocket. Gen dropped a pile of cash in front of the bartender, but Emily didn't wait for her to settle the bill. She pushed through the crowd. Walking into the cold of the street was like walking into a wall.

"Hey! Wait!"

Emily quickened her pace, but of course it was easy for Gen to catch up. She wasn't even out of breath. This made Emily angrier. "Go away."

"Why'd you leave? Why did you say that about me? You think I'm some dick who brags about her conquests?"

"*You* say it. *You* think that. You talk that way about yourself all the time."

"As a joke!"

"And 'classic'? Was that the same kind of joke, the kind you actually mean?"

"That guy? Don't defend him. He *was* classic, and yeah, not in a good way. He was a straight cliché." Gen weaved around a group of NYU students waiting in line to get dosas. "Won't take no for an answer. Oblivious to anything but what he wants."

"You meant me, too."

"What? No."

"You think I'm a straight cliché, too."

"I don't think you're like him."

"What are you doing, Gen?"

"I'm walking you home."

"What are you doing *with me*? You're playing some game. You say you want to be friends, then avoid me. You shut down conversations. You act like I have more in common with a random idiot than I do with you. You're being a brat."

"A brat!"

They entered Washington Square Park, where the dead fountain was empty of water. Trees were scribbles against the night.

"Listen," said Gen, "I do not think you're a straight cliché."

"I wasn't gay enough for you even when we dated."

"It's not a competition."

"You make it into one."

"To tell the truth, you're a bit of a princess. You are! Like, yes, of course if we go out, a man will hit on you. It *is* classic. And yes, it is classic you. People want to get close to you. All the fucking time. They want you to like them. It's not even just because you're beautiful. You're smart and kind and secretly weird. So they teach you poker. They take your side. They give you things. My *gran* gives you things. You need a place to live and it just so happens a friend has a free apartment."

"I pay for it now. You advised me to take it."

"Well, you do the princess thing to me, too."

"I'm not doing anything to you. I never asked you for anything."

"I am well aware that you don't want anything from me."

"Right, because I'm so straight." They had reached Emily's apartment building. Emily would have gone through the lobby doors and left Gen on the sidewalk, but what she had said brought Gen to a halt. The surprise of Gen going still beside her made Emily stop, too. Gen said, voice low, "You broke up with me and married a man."

"I didn't break up with you."

"I had to *watch* you marry him. I watched you promise him the rest of your fucking life. He isn't even a nice guy! I get to be a brat about this. Don't tell me I can't. You're not even interested in Ship and she's the whole package. It upsets me. It upsets me that I wasn't enough for you and yet you ended up with someone so obviously worse. I always wondered what would happen if I saw you again and this is not it. Nothing is how I want it to be."

The frank pain in Gen's voice made Emily's anger ebb. Emily saw what she hadn't seen before. It was as though Gen's words had torn away the wrappings of Gen's typical cocky assurance to reveal what had lain hidden beneath: hurt . . . and longing. "Gen."

"I don't enjoy feeling like I was an experiment. I don't enjoy hearing about the shit that happened to you. It makes me feel helpless and I'm not sorry if that means I'm a brat. I don't enjoy the constant distraction of you. I don't enjoy being your afterthought."

"You're not. You never were. No one was you."

"I don't know what that means."

"I always wanted you."

Gen's mouth closed. Her face was shadowed; Emily couldn't read her expression. But the silence seemed unsteady, a spinning top that had lost its speed and tipped itself out of its own tight orbit and spun wide.

Emily said, "I still do."

Gen hesitated, then reached for the collar of Emily's coat. She sank her fingers into the collar's open throat, just above the first button. The gesture was tentative until she suddenly gathered the material into a fist. Her knuckles brushed Emily's neck. Icy fingertips flexed against Emily's breastbone. The chill of it ran through her. Gen released the coat, then seized the fabric again, harder this time, and pulled Emily to her.

Gen's mouth was hot and soft and greedy. She tasted like juniper and lime. Emily licked at the taste of the cocktail that had slid down Gen's throat earlier. She was jealous of the lime that she had watched Gen squeeze into the tall glass at the bar, jealous of the drops of citrus trickling between Gen's strong fingers. Emily had watched her do it; it had been the smallest of moments. Then it had been over; the rind dropped down onto the ice. Emily was jealous of the rind, too. She was jealous of everything and everyone Gen had ever touched. She kissed her harder.

"Stop, stop," said Gen, but when Emily paused, Gen's lips returned to brush lightly against hers. She tongued Emily's mouth in a promise of how she would lick her sex: light and teasing. Thorough, then deep. "Take me upstairs," Gen whispered into Emily's open mouth.

They didn't wait for the elevator doors to shut behind them. Gen pulled Emily's coat open and yanked up her skirt. She wedged herself between Emily's legs. The elevator whirred upward. Emily unzipped Gen's jeans and tried to slide her hand down them but the fabric fit too tightly. Gen took her by the wrist to pin her hand to the elevator wall and rubbed the rigid denim of her thigh against her. Emily loved the pressure, the near pain of it. "Look at me," said Gen. Her eyes were large, her mouth a slick blur. "Look at me and think about what I'm going to do to you." Need deepened between Emily's thighs. The erotic promise between her and Gen was different from when they were teenagers—darker, wilder. There was nothing playful, as there had once been, to Gen's commands. There was no sweet, young clumsiness to her greed. Part of Gen was still angry, Emily realized—and realized that *she* was, too, and that she didn't care. She didn't care what might happen. What would Gen do to her? Anything. Emily wanted it all.

The elevator dinged. Gen stepped away. They had reached Emily's floor. Emily's dress was hiked up to her hips and the sudden distance between her and Gen's body felt punishing. The doors opened, but Gen didn't move. The intensity of her expression had changed, shifting from hunger to something wary. "I have rules."

"I remember your stupid rules. Let's skip to the one where you give me what I want."

Inside the apartment, Gen shucked Emily's coat and unbuttoned her dress, nibbling a line down soft flesh. This time, it was Emily who stopped her. She did it by sinking to her knees. She tugged down Gen's jeans and briefs. Emily nuzzled her, barely brushing her mouth between Gen's bare legs. Emily delved her tongue inside her. Gen's hands twisted in Emily's hair. Emily ran her mouth over Gen, her tongue marking a snail's path almost to Gen's clit, skating close: an almost-nudge, almost-lick, almost—

Gen's voice was guttural. "Don't tease me."

Emily did what she was eager to do. She remembered, as Gen twitched beneath her tongue, how good this had always felt. Emily reached to touch her and knew that if she slid her fingers inside her now, she would be rewarded with a sharp cry, then a sudden judder. She pushed the tip of one finger inside.

"Wait," Gen gasped. "I don't want to come too soon. Take your dress off. Everything off, right now."

Emily paused, Gen's words echoing in her head. How many women had heard her say this? Emily imagined them watching: a host of rivals. She sensed her past self in this room, too. It was maddening that she was jealous of the person she used to be. She wanted to make Gen need her—*her*, no one else—as badly as she needed Gen. She drew Gen's fingers into her mouth and sucked them. Gen made a sound deep in her throat.

They found the bed. Gen removed her shirt the way a man would, reaching behind to grab the back collar and drag the shirt forward over her head. Their nakedness was so different—Gen all lean muscle except for her small breasts, nipples like little treats. She leaned into Emily, pressing her into the mattress, and murmured, "Touch yourself."

She was drenched.

Gen asked if Emily wanted her mouth on her and Emily said yes, weakly, still touching herself, bucking against Gen's weight. Gen asked if Emily wanted to stop her and Emily said no. Gen asked if she promised and Emily said yes. "Anything I want?" "Yes."

If Emily had teased Gen before, this was exquisite payback. Emily hovered on the edge of orgasm, Gen knowing when to drag her tongue over Emily and when to pause. Finally, Emily begged.

Gen fucked her hard as she came. She drove Emily from one orgasm to another.

Her body singing, Emily barely heard Gen tell her to turn onto her belly. She felt Gen's weight again, this time on her back, and then the warm, fast slide of Gen's pussy rubbing against her ass. A hand clenched Emily's shoulder. Gen's breath was jagged. She came quickly against Emily, the rock of her body uncontrolled. Then she slowed.

Emily turned to face her. Gen kissed her deeply, out of breath. Emily laughed. She wasn't sure she'd ever seen Gen out of breath.

A smile curled Gen's lips. "I'm not sure what you find funny, but you'll stop laughing soon."

"Oh?"

"I'm not done with you."

"No?"

"I can never get enough." The words plucked at some faint memory—something Emily thought she herself had said, or had almost said, long ago—but Emily couldn't remember exactly, and in a moment, did not care to.

Emily woke to find that Gen was no longer lying next to her. It was still dark and the sheets were snarled.

She found Gen standing just outside the children's room, looking in. Emily said, "I thought you'd left."

Gen gently tucked back Emily's tousled hair. "Just disappear? I wouldn't do that."

But Emily didn't know what Gen would or wouldn't do, now.

"I should have listened earlier," Gen said, "when you wanted to tell me about Jack and your manuscript. It's important for me to know. I want to know everything that happened since we broke up."

Emily let herself believe that their reckless pursuit of each other's bodies had meant more than mere lust. She tried to forget her certainty, when she had woken alone in the bed, of abandonment. She was not *nothing* to Gen. She knew this. At least, she knew it in that moment. She answered Gen's questions. She told Gen about her heartbreak, her marriage, her motherhood, her mistakes. Emily fell asleep again somewhere near dawn, held in Gen's arms under thick covers, unaware that her words had slowed, that her voice was hoarse from so much talking, that she drifted into silence while Gen still listened, wide awake.

In the morning, Gen said she had to leave. "I can't skip training."

The restlessness on her face made Emily's lungs shrink with hurt and pride. "Last night doesn't have to mean anything."

Gen didn't speak for a moment, then said, "I just need to run. I don't have the right shoes here."

Emily stepped toward a window. It was sunny outside. The February sky was polished by the cold, gleaming with it. Emily saw the day's future: a long, empty Sunday of missing the children. Missing Gen. Hours pendant with disappointment. How the thin air would feel primed to crack and snap open at any moment and issue a near despair that Emily had managed to ignore since leaving Jack. After having wanted, in youth, not to be lonely, she had made choices that ultimately isolated her. Where was the good faith of life, that you try, you do your best, and yet can be undone in an instant? How does a night together become someone saying that they need to leave? She couldn't look at Gen. "I'm worried."

"About what?"

"That this was a bad idea."

"We can stop. Do you want to stop?"

How do you un-want what you want? "No."

"I don't want to stop either."

"I worry that you're going to regret this."

"Will you look at me?" Gen held Emily's gaze. "I don't regret this and I never will, even if it's a bad idea."

But Emily couldn't forget that the most important of Gen's rules was that she didn't begin anything that would last.

28

Emily consumed the weekends. When Monday came, Emily wanted more of Gen and was forced to wait. She worked on her manuscript, writing feverishly, filling the empty time when the children were at school. Sometimes she woke at night and wrote until the gray hours before dawn. She wrote and rewrote the moment when Athena first sees Arachne: *I wanted to soak into the fibers of her being. I wanted to dye her wool with my permanence. I wanted to be crimson on her skin, in the way of cherries and pomegranates. I loved her arrogance.*

The season began to turn. Days stayed lighter longer. The cold grew less desperate. Gen always slept at Emily's place; Emily hadn't seen her Brooklyn apartment. She wasn't invited and didn't ask. She tried not to be hurt by this. Gen kept a pair of sneakers in Emily's closet and would, each Saturday and Sunday, go for a ten-mile run and return sweaty, her expression faraway, altered, as though instead of running she had visited another dimension. She opened the closet door before she did anything else, even before she poured a glass of water, and tucked the sneakers at the back, lining them up neatly amid Emily's shoes. Gen kept a toothbrush in the bathroom Emily shared with her children, yet the toothbrush was placed back in its original packaging so that it looked unopened, brand-new, and was then stowed in a drawer beneath Q-tips and Star Wars Band-Aids.

"You don't have to do that," said Emily. "They're not going to wonder about two adult toothbrushes in the medicine cabinet. Even if they did, they won't guess what it means."

"Maybe you don't want to have to lie, if they do."

Emily bought a supply of new toothbrushes. At the end of each weekend, Gen threw hers away. On Monday mornings, Emily looked around her apartment and saw no trace of Gen, only caught her scent. The regular wiping away of evidence made the time she and Gen had been together seem unreal. The smell of sex on the sheets, imagined. Sometimes Emily opened the closet door to reassure herself that the sneakers were there. Emily and Gen didn't discuss what they were doing—not their hunger for each other, not the ritual of Gen's self-erasure. It was true that Emily didn't want the children to know about Gen, who would leave New York in June. This—Emily didn't have a name for what *this* was—might end even before then. She couldn't ask the children to keep a secret—she had taught them not to keep adults' secrets, in part because she had always worried about what Jack might do that they would feel compelled to hide. If Connor and Stella knew about Gen, then Jack would know. She couldn't predict the course of his response, only his anger.

"It's okay," said Gen. "I'm not ready for them to know about me either."

Emily didn't know if it really was okay but she couldn't ask. If the answer was Gen's third rule, it would hurt too much. *Not yet*, she thought. *Not now.*

They continued hiding shoes and throwing away toothbrushes. Gen's running clothes were washed, folded, and mingled with Emily's.

One Saturday morning in early March, Gen didn't go on her usual run. Restless, she poked through the books on a mostly empty shelf. The apartment still looked half lived-in, the odd piece of furniture flimsy and almost timid, as though aware of its disposable nature. Gen drew out *Memoirs of Hadrian*. "A good one."

"You've read it?"

"In college." Gen set the book back on the shelf. "Mostly because I thought it was something that you'd like." She went into the kitchen and found a mug.

"Do your friends know that you're a closet intellectual?"

"They did tease me about the *Sports Illustrated* cover. Something about misleading femmes into believing I was an uncomplicated jock." Gen poured ground coffee into the maker but spilled some on the floor. She bent to clean the coffee grounds, then straightened stiffly.

"You're injured."

Gen wiped her hands on her jeans. "I'm old."

"You're thirty-three."

"Ancient, for an athlete. London will probably be my last Olympics, if I make the trials."

"You will."

Gen grimaced. "Eventually the body won't do what you tell it. It betrays you. I did something yesterday—didn't stretch enough, set my foot wrong, didn't ease off when I should have, I don't know. Isn't it crazy, how you can make a mistake and not even know it?" The coffee burbled. "What's especially hard is that I've really needed to run. Not just to train. To think. It helps me. I have needed to think about us."

Emily's throat went dry.

"I haven't been clear with you," said Gen.

"You have." She wanted Gen to stop talking. She knew how this would end. *Not yet*, she thought. *Not now.*

"No." Gen dragged a hand through her hair. "I don't want to fuck up again. I'm not good at this. I have a gift for saying the wrong thing. Or maybe that's just with you. I want to say it right. Because this really fucking hurts." Gen swept a hand from her temple toward the floor, a gesture that seemed to reference her entire body. "You said that first night didn't have to mean anything. Is that true?"

Not yet. Not now. Reluctantly, Emily said, "No."

"What did it mean to you?"

The intercom buzzed. Emily ignored it, but it buzzed again, and again. It buzzed in Morse code. Dot dot dot, dash dash dash, dot dot dot—

Emily pressed the receiver. "*What?*"

"Mommy!" came Connor's happy shout.

"Oh shit," said Gen.

"Hi, Mommy!" said Stella. "We're here with Daddy!"

"Fuck," said Gen.

"Hey, Em," said Jack. "We were in the area and thought you might want to get pizza. I tried texting, but you didn't answer."

"Daddy never lets us get pizza!" said Connor. There was the sound of the front door opening—had a neighbor entered the lobby?—and a *ding*. Connor's voice came again, farther away: "Stella, get the elevator!"

Jack chuckled. "I guess we're coming up."

Emily released the receiver.

"I can't believe this," said Gen.

Emily had a moment to be grateful that they were both dressed, then small hands hammered at the door. Connor and Stella leapt at Emily. "Can we get pizza? Can we?" they cried. Jack appeared in the doorway with a rueful expression that didn't suit his grin. "Sorry," he said. "I couldn't hold them back." He kissed Emily's cheek.

"Hi," said Gen.

Jack, who hadn't yet noticed her, flinched in surprise.

Stella untangled herself from Emily and looked up at Gen. "Are you a boy or a girl?"

"Girl."

"Stella, that's rude," said Jack.

"I don't mind"—Gen's voice had a touch of warning—"when it's a child who asks."

"You're tall," said Stella.

"Who are you?" said Connor.

"I'm your mom's friend," said Gen. "I came by for coffee."

"Smells amazing," said Jack. "Mind if I have some?" He went into the kitchen. Gen lost her smooth, friendly expression.

"Aren't you glad to see us?" Connor asked Emily. He hadn't let go.

She returned his hug and said, "I'm always glad to see you and Stella."

"Can I get pepperoni? Daddy said yes if you said it was okay."

"Want a cup, Em?" Jack called. He hadn't recognized Gen. Though she had been at their wedding, the reception had been enormous and they hadn't been introduced. Nor had he placed her as the sort of person who'd been invited to the White House. Then again, Jack hadn't really looked at her. You can't recognize someone you don't see.

"Em? Coffee?"

"No."

"I'll take some," said Gen.

Jack gave Gen a mug and moved into the living room to sit on the couch. The children joined him, snuggling close on either side. Gen, with an incredulous glance at Emily, drank from her mug and sat opposite Jack, who said, "Really sorry to interrupt."

"So can we go?" Connor asked Emily.

"I can't. I have a guest."

"But, Mommy!"

"That's not fair!" said Stella.

"Come on, kids," said Jack. "Mommy didn't know we were coming."

"Don't let me stop you." Gen settled into her chair with a casual grace that made Emily see—as she hadn't seen before, at least not in person—the Gen that did interviews and posed for photos. This Gen was comfortable in any company. There was something unnerving about this Gen, because Emily knew that she was upset—angry even, possibly as angry as Emily felt—and that no one else could tell. "I was going to leave soon anyway."

"Don't go," said Emily.

"I'll finish my cup first."

"Do you want to come with us?" asked Stella.

"No, sweetheart," said Gen, "but thanks."

"How do you two know each other?" said Jack.

"From school." To the children, Gen said, "I've known your mom a long time, since I was about your age. Connor, you're ten, right? I met Emily in fifth grade."

"What was Mommy like?"

"She was good to me when not many people were."

Stella nodded. "Mommy's nice."

"She cries when there's a sad part in a movie," said Connor. "The happy parts, too."

"She cries during *commercials.*"

"Okay, okay," said Emily, aware that her quelling tone would make the children hunt for other embarrassing habits of hers that they could reveal. Which was fine. She wanted the conversation to be about anything but Gen. Jack appeared relaxed and pleased, so she didn't think that he had connected Gen with the story she had told him, long ago, about dating a girl from high school.

At least, not yet. It occurred to her that he might have imagined someone very different from Gen. Possibly, he had imagined the kind of woman he liked, and had assumed that that was what Emily liked.

"Commercials get me, too, sometimes," said Gen. "Like when someone comes home after a long time away. Or a person works hard and another person cares."

"I like ones with dogs," said Stella. "They don't make me cry but they give me a funny feeling like I might cry."

"I know that feeling."

"Commercials just sell stuff," said Connor dismissively.

"Well, they're about wanting things, so they remind you of what everyone wants, even when it's not about money, like having a nice mommy. Commercials are boring to make, though."

"What do you do?" said Jack.

"I'm a runner."

"I mean for work."

"That is what I do for work."

"You're a courier? A messenger?"

"I'm an Olympic athlete. I won a silver in Sydney and a gold in Beijing. Other medals, too, but those are the ones I'm most proud of."

"Wow," said Stella.

"Will you be in the 2012 Olympics?" said Connor.

"I'm going to try."

"Can I see your medals?"

"Sure, someday."

"Em, how come you never told me about your talented friend?" To Gen, Jack said, "She never mentioned you."

Gen set down her mug.

Emily said, "We weren't in touch."

Gen stood. "Thanks for the coffee." She gave a brief wave, as though the others were an anonymous crowd gathered in the stands and her mind was focused on an event to come.

Emily wasn't sure, when Gen left, if she'd see her again.

In the crowded pizzeria, Jack let the children order soda and smiled at their shocked joy. "Just once in a while," he warned. They cheered.

Emily remembered how, before Connor and Stella were born, she and Jack went on a trip to London where he ordered bespoke shoes made by an exclusive cobbler. Emily's feet were traced, her arches and ankles and heels measured. The cobbler carved and sanded wooden lasts of their feet, so that, in the future, when Jack and Emily wanted a new pair of shoes, he could fit the leather to their lasts, which were stored in his shop. She imagined the cobbler holding hers: cream-colored wood as smooth as soap. She imagined her last accepting the leather and forming a space for the real foot. She imagined that she was the last, breeding leather vessels for the jointed foot, the one that flexed and felt, that had a ripple of toes. Emily was the wooden body double. Her job, to be handled and shoved into place.

"Mommy, you're not eating your pizza."

Jack smiled. "Dreamy Emily."

What a fool she was, to be sitting there, thinking about shoes so that she wouldn't think about Gen. What a fool to eat her pizza, and know that the shoe last was not symbolically herself, but Gen, dismissed, made to feel lesser in the company of what looked like a real family, and that Emily had been thinking about her all along, while pretending that she wasn't.

Gen sent a text. Will you come over when you're done? There was an address in Williamsburg. We need to talk.

29

Gen's apartment was in a building by the East River. Emily walked along the water, the wind scouring her face as she delayed. She wanted a few more moments before Gen put an end to things. She watched joggers go by. Fawn-colored grasses waved between bushes studded with red berries. Beyond them, across the river, stood Manhattan's skyscrapers. Emily wondered if a pane of glass reflected her image and if someone behind that window could see her, hands stuffed in her coat pockets, passing a golden retriever. She would be tiny, the dog a blond dot. She envied the dog. It looked sure of itself.

Are you nearby? Gen texted.

Emily didn't answer.

just want to make sure you're not lost

Too sick with anxiety to put it off any longer, Emily keyed in the code that Gen had given her and went upstairs.

Gen opened the door and pulled Emily into her arms.

"I'm sorry," Emily said into the crook of Gen's neck.

"It's not your fault."

"I pretended like you weren't important."

"What were you supposed to do? It was a bad situation. It was bullshit." Gen leaned back and reached to touch Emily's cheek. "Super manipulative. And pathetic! Who uses their kids to get what they want? He manipulated them into manipulating you. He manipulated *me*, because I sure wasn't going to be the bad guy who kept two kids from their mom. If that was a taste of what your life with him was like, then *I'm* sorry, I'm furious, I don't even know where to start with how mad this makes me—for you."

"That's not what I thought you'd say."

"Will you come in? You're freezing. I'm making you tea. I don't like that you thought I'd say anything different. Don't you know me?"

"I don't know who you are now."

"I'm *me*. The person who always wanted the best for you. He is not it."

Gen's apartment was a loft with enormous ceilings and Doric columns. It had been a factory. It was probably rented—it had an impersonal quality, with inoffensive abstract art on the walls and neutral tones, as though staged by a real estate broker. There was, as Becca's comment about Gen's taste had predicted, an awful lot of cool grays and midcentury modern furniture. Emily took the corner of a sofa that looked like it might have some give, but didn't. Gen busied herself in the open kitchen. The windows let in the sunset. While Emily knew what had made Gen choose this place—the view, the space, the nearby footpath for running along the river—it felt like a chic hotel where Gen had checked in and would check out. The only evidence that she lived there was the collection of running shoes arranged on open shelving by the door. Several of the sneakers had spikes on the soles.

Gen placed a mug of tea in Emily's hands. "I need to say something. I've been going over it in my head so that I don't lose my nerve and do something stupid out of fear of getting hurt, like when I told you I had rules. I did have rules, but not for you. I don't have any rules for what you are to me. When you asked if I didn't marry Maiko because of you, I said that it was because I saw your wedding and knew that marriage wasn't what I wanted, but the truth is that I knew I couldn't love her as much as I had loved you. So I need to know what's going on between us, because if it really doesn't mean anything, I don't think I can bear it."

Sometimes happiness feels like an animal relief, like you've been let off your leash, told that you are good when you worried you'd been bad, allowed to run. To dig—for what? For nothing. Who knew. For the feel of the upturned earth, the rich coolness of it, the smell of rain stored beneath sunny grass. Happiness streaked across Emily's chest. She said, "Being with you means everything to me." She kissed Gen's familiar mouth. She confessed that she had been afraid, too.

Later, in bed, Gen said, "I wish I'd been honest earlier. I want us to try being more honest. I want to say things that I mean."

What was there to do but be brave? Emily had waited long enough. "I never stopped loving you."

30

Gen described the bus trip from Boston to Ohio after their breakup. The hills in Pennsylvania. Big-box stores along the highway. Gen saw everything clearly and then it would blur again. She used the sleeve of her hoodie to wipe her eyes. She had left her coat somewhere, maybe in the bus station, she wasn't sure. She kept shivering but not from the cold. At a rest stop, the driver walked up to her. "Do you have someone you can call?" he said. Gen told him that she was okay. He nodded but not because he believed her. He tried to give her two dollars. Gen said, "Don't worry, really, I'm fine, I have money." He said that two dollars wasn't much and to take it anyway, even if she didn't need it. It would make him feel better. She accepted it because you don't turn down a gift like that. When everyone got back on the bus, he said, "Even if you're not okay, one day you will be." Gen spent the next few years trying to believe him.

She was reckless. She didn't behave well. Candace and Nita, teammates at OSU, told her so. They knew nothing about Emily and Gen wanted to keep it that way. She managed heartbreak by ignoring Emily's existence as best she could, largely by bedding anyone interested. Nita said, "You don't have to sleep with everyone who wants to sleep with you." Candace said, "Nothing wrong with being a slut, but how about being an ethical one?" What she really wanted to know was when Gen was going to get serious about track. Two things were obvious to Candace: that Gen loved to run and that it was too easy for her. Gen should be winning more. It was insulting to Candace that Gen *wasn't*, because Candace knew that if she had Gen's raw talent, she would be training hard to be the best. "Like in the fucking world," Candace said.

"Me?"

"You, asshole, yes."

Gen was wary of ambition. That was Emily's thing. But running made Gen feel good when nothing else did. When she won, she felt even better. She began to wonder if her wariness wasn't actually fear, because *ambition* is just a word for wanting something badly. It's basically getting open-heart surgery while fully awake and looking down at your red, wet torso, thinking, *Am I going to make it?*

Who wanted that? Not her.

But . . .

She remembered telling Emily back in high school that they both wanted big things. Gen had to reckon with choices of hers that screamed ambition. Graduating early. Acing the SATs. Applying to a prestigious college. Maybe Gen was the sort of person who needed to put herself on the operating table of ambition over and over. Maybe, if she had to want big things, she should choose the very biggest thing.

She went to her coach and said that she wanted to train for the Olympics. He told her it was about fucking time.

She won several races at the USATF trials. She set records. She was dating Maiko, a girl she really liked from the OSU track team. And eventually, she was okay.

"I watched you," Emily told her, "at the trials."

"You did? What did you think?"

Emily couldn't think. She had held her breath. Gen stayed in the pack, hemmed in by other runners. The announcer didn't mention her name, not at first. He focused on the women in the lead until Gen worked her way out of the middle of the pack, then tucked herself behind the front-runner. Emily's heart was a drum. The announcer, in a confiding tone, mentioned bits of news about Gen that Emily hadn't known: she had recently changed coaches, she had a promising reputation in the 1500 meters. The final bell rang. The announcer discarded facts for sheer admiration, his voice rising as Gen tugged past the lead in the home straight. She dropped everyone behind her. The tape broke across her chest.

She didn't follow Emily's life. When Gen went home to visit her grandmother, she avoided driving past Emily's house. The hardware store they liked, the one that sold sour cherry pies, had gone out of business. Washford helped Gen avoid memories by having changed. The Main Street, where high school students used to go after school, was deserted and on winter days became a lonely wind tunnel. Most of its buildings were closed. The movie theater where she and Emily had seen *Legends of the Fall* was open only on weekends, and then not to show movies but to sell discounted items people had returned to Amazon. Nella went there sometimes. When Gen asked why, saying she would buy Nella whatever she wanted, Nella said she never knew what she might find for sale at the old movie theater, and she liked that the place still smelled like buttered popcorn.

Gen didn't sleep in her old bedroom. Anyway, during the farmhouse renovation, Gen had made certain to get rid of the twin beds.

But the loft in the barn remained the same. It had been her mother's gift to her. If there was another reason hidden below that one, a reason that had to do with a reluctance to erase every last trace of Emily, if sometimes Gen looked at the bed behind the green curtain and felt a dull ache in her belly, as though she'd been hungry for so long that the hunger had become fatigue, she ignored it. Her mother was the larger loss. It was easy to pretend that it was the only one.

Usually easy.

Last year, Becca came to a charity auction of Gen's childhood possessions. "Those dioramas are something," said Becca. "Didn't figure you as the artist type."

"I'm not. My mom was, though. She taught me how to make them. Felt I should keep making them after she was gone, as if she could still see them. Of what I liked, what happened to me. What I was thinking. They're a secret diary, I guess."

"Am I looking at the complete story of the misadventures of young Gen Hall?"

"Almost. I gave one diorama away."

Becca peered at the glass box containing the loft with its bed and bookshelves. "What's that one about?"

"I took my high school girlfriend there."

Becca adjusted her glasses and looked again. "Lucky dog. Not every teenager has a sex barn."

"It wasn't like that."

"Uh-huh."

"Okay, sort of like that. But I loved her."

Gen was glad when the diorama sold to a stranger.

Once—only once—Gen looked up Emily on Facebook. The first photograph was of Jack kissing Emily on the cheek. Gen scrolled through photos of glitzy vacations. Emily with Rory and Elizabeth at brunch, clinking mimosas. The twins wore matching diamond tennis bracelets, outshone by the one on Emily's wrist—bright as a comet. Jack on a ski slope. Scenes from college. Emily and her friends at graduation. Emily, Florencia, and Violet at Fenway Park, wearing baseball caps. Jack on a boat in Positano. Gen shut her laptop.

"It looked like a pretty great life," Gen told Emily, her voice echoing in the large apartment. They had taken the duvet from the bed and brought it to the couch, watching the sky over the East River go gray with the coming dawn.

"I had to make it look good."

"I know that now."

Gen and Maiko broke up when Gen was twenty-two. "Can we stay friends?" Gen said. "Fuck you," said Maiko, which Gen decided she deserved, though now she wondered. Was she obligated to marry her college girlfriend even though she knew it would be a mistake?

Gen threw herself into training. She rose to national prominence in track and field. Sponsors came calling. Her agent counseled for Gen to keep her relationship with Shira, a sportscaster, quiet. "I'm not asking you to lie about your sexuality," the agent said. "Just don't confirm it." Gen fired her agent and came out to *The Advocate*. Sponsors dropped her. Shira lost her job. "It has nothing to do with your relationship," the network told Shira when she asked. "We know you'll thrive elsewhere."

Then came the 2004 Olympics in Athens, where Gen lost a race to help a fallen runner . . . and Nike made Gen an offer.

Gen winced and looked away from Emily, who reached over the duvet to touch her knee. "What is it?" said Emily.

"The ads."

"I've seen the ads."

"They made me into more than I am."

"You *are* talented. You *were* brave."

"Stopping to see if someone's okay isn't bravery."

"Why not?"

"My gran was watching. If I hadn't stopped, I couldn't have faced her."

"Right. You put your self-respect first."

"It got blown out of proportion." Gen rubbed the heel of her hand against her forehead. "It was a rough time."

Although Shira had supported Gen coming out and had believed she was prepared for the consequences, she hadn't anticipated that their fates would look so different. Gen was a star. Shira was nothing. "Why does everyone call you courageous while I'm unemployable?" Shira said, and told Gen that their relationship couldn't continue. It was too hard. Gen said, "But I care about you." It didn't matter.

Gen told Emily, "After that, I decided to accept that maybe some things weren't meant to happen for me."

"Your mid-twenties is early to give up on relationships."

"It didn't feel early. And I was never, you know, normal. Not as a kid. Not when we were together. Your dad saw that. Then I got famous and that is really not fucking normal. It made sense that I wouldn't have a normal relationship. And there were all these women. I'm not saying I made good choices. I had the feeling I was cursed. Like because I got to win so much in track, I had to lose in some other way. It felt . . . fair? Or not fair, exactly, but inevitable. Like if I was cursed, I might as well *become* the curse. Face it. Organize around it. Be as bad as I inevitably would, and as good as I could. Have rules. Take my losses. Sorry, I don't think I'm explaining it right. Remember *Dirty Dancing*?"

"Yes."

"Remember when Johnny told Baby about sleeping with women at the resort, how they stuffed money in his pockets and he couldn't say no?"

"But you weren't poor, not after the Athens Olympics."

"I'm not talking about money. I felt like Johnny because I was missing something that other people had and they were offering it all the time. They gave me hope and then I lost it." Gen moved under the duvet to rest against Emily. "I'm tired."

"Do you want to sleep?"

"I want to watch the sun come up."

"This couch is horrible."

"It's nice."

"It's uncomfortable."

"I like it."

"Come here, you masochist."

They shifted so that they were stretched out together on the couch as though it were a bed. They barely fit. Gen lay her head against Emily's chest. Emily pulled the duvet up to Gen's chin. "Better," Gen said, and was quiet for long enough that Emily thought she had fallen asleep. The skyscrapers grew pink, the water orange. Gen murmured, "Then I saw you at Jocelyn's party." She sighed. "Trouble."

"Why?"

"You know why."

"Because I have children?"

"No. I mean, yes, in the sense that your kids make the stakes really high. I don't want to mess with their lives. I want to be really careful about them. You're trouble because you're married."

"Separated."

"Emily. I'm just saying what's true."

"Recently separated," Emily admitted, "with a history of going back to him."

Gen nodded. "And you're *you*. You're trouble because of everything you've always been for me. I tried." Her voice slowed.

"Tried to be good . . . to myself. To stay away. But like I said, I'm cursed."

"You don't have to be."

"It's not so bad. Look at me. In your arms. Lucky."

"I thought I was trouble."

"The best kind."

"Gen, the sun's up."

But Gen was asleep.

A buzz woke Emily. Gen murmured and shifted under the duvet but kept sleeping. Emily reached for her phone. There was a text from Jack: I had such a great time with you and the kids.

31

Where'd you go?" said Gen over breakfast. It was a serious spread, nothing elaborately prepared but all of it hearty—eggs, seeded bread and lox, bananas and almond butter, avocados—and ready to provide for far more than two people. "You're super quiet. What's wrong? Last night, did I say something I shouldn't've?"

"No, no. It's this." Emily showed Gen her phone. Gen read Jack's text and frowned, then glanced up at Emily, brows raised queryingly, so Emily said, "Go ahead."

Gen scrolled through the texts, the furrows of her expression deepening. She set the phone down hard. "Will you tell me why you haven't filed?"

Emily could have explained how she was saving for a legal battle, and her wish to not destabilize her children's lives, but she said the largest reason, which was also the sum of her other reasons: "I'm afraid of what he'll do."

"I get that," Gen said, "but I'm right here."

"You are?"

"Yes."

The lawyer that Jocelyn had recommended, Sophie Martinez-Day, wore a white silk blouse beneath her blazer and no jewelry. She was a stark contrast to Gen, seated next to Emily in the waiting room in jeans and immaculate Nikes. Emily closed her writing notebook and rose to shake the lawyer's hand. As she followed the lawyer into her office, Emily glanced back at

Gen, who smiled encouragement and settled in her chair with a magazine, giving the impression of a guard dog relaxed across a threshold.

Sophie told Emily, "I've reviewed your prenup and I don't think it protects Jack as much as he would like. You signed it soon before your wedding, which suggests that you were under duress to agree."

Emily hadn't felt under duress. She had seen signing the prenup as a point of pride. She had wanted to prove that she wasn't with Jack for his money.

"You also used a lawyer that your husband chose and paid for," Sophie said. "There are grounds for a challenge."

"I'm not sure I want to challenge it. I just want my kids."

"And they are accustomed to a certain way of life. That takes money. The law is the law for a reason, and New York State doesn't like to have a rich house–poor house situation, where the kids go on ski trips to the Alps with Dad and live in a tiny apartment with Mom. That's not healthy for children or their relationship with their parents. You've been out of the workforce for over a decade, and while society might undervalue a stay-at-home mom, I do not. It's work and you deserve compensation. Let me fight for what you need."

Emily took the offered pen. Signing the document felt like when she went for the last time, at eighteen, to the field near her childhood home and found the log by the creek, and saw how the log looked smaller than it had when she was little and called it hers. Her secret, her landmark. Stripped of its bark by the years, the log was salt-white in the August sun, the creek more mud than water. Her boxes were packed for college. She thought, *Everything will change.* It wasn't just leave-taking that overcame her in the lawyer's office, or fear, or elation. She was surprised, too. There was her name on the page. The date. She would never be the same. People talk about coming of age as if it only happens when you're young, as if entering adulthood means inhabiting a final era with no more moments when you say goodbye to an old life, but that couldn't be true, because she just had.

Sophie neatened the papers into a perfect stack. As Emily

watched her do it, she was filled with a huge sense of relief. Sophie said, "I have to ask: Are you seeing someone?"

Still buoyant, Emily told her about Gen.

"That was Gen Hall reading *People* in the waiting room?" Sophie said. "I thought she looked familiar." She was silent, then said, "You might want to be careful about how public you are with this relationship. Your description of Jack makes him sound volatile, and knowing about Gen could make him more so. I'd rather not negotiate with a volatile person. And, I hate to say this, but there are homophobic judges and we might get one of them."

"But this is 2012." New York had just legalized gay marriage.

"Officially, yes, discrimination is illegal. Imagine, though, that your husband sues for full custody—which he might do if only to avoid paying child support—and argues that your 'lifestyle' isn't in the children's best interests. His legal team doesn't have to say the word *gay.* They can talk instead about Ms. Hall's fame and argue that the children will be exposed to public scrutiny. They can use *fame* when they mean *gay* to give the judge an acceptable reason to rule in Jack's favor. I'm not saying this will happen. It's a risk. Ultimately, it's your call whether to keep your personal life private, and my job to protect you whatever you choose."

Outside, standing in a cold wedge of sun that fell like a brass sword between the buildings, Emily told Gen what the lawyer had said. A rare uncertainty stole over Gen, dragging at the features of her face. Then her mouth firmed into a line. "I think we should listen to your lawyer."

That wasn't what Emily had thought she'd say.

"I was in Star Tracks," Gen said. "You know, that celeb thing with photos in *People*? I saw it while you were talking with the lawyer: a shot of me and Nita vintage shopping. Nita's holding a shiny top. The caption was like, 'Hall and fellow athlete take a break from training to go for the gold lamé.' Harmless. But someone *will* get a shot of you and me. It's a matter of time. If we're seen, it should be as friends. I don't want to give Jack evidence to use against you."

"We're supposed to hide everything—again?"

"In public."

"Hiding is hard for you. You hate it."

"What's the alternative? That I cost your kids their mom?"

"I can't lose them." The thought was annihilating.

"You won't." Gen's tone was clipped and hard. "Look, it's not you I'm angry at. It's not your fault. I'm being an asshole, maybe, talking like it's my decision. I know it's not. But I need you to understand that I can be a secret this time, for this reason, okay?"

Emily slowly nodded. Gen was right: it was safer. *But you—* She couldn't finish the thought. She remembered Gen saying, when they texted about the press and how it hungered for morsels of Gen's life, *I won't lie about who I am.* She saw Gen's face as she sat on the farmhouse porch, eighteen and gutted, looking at Emily in disbelief, her eyes saying what her mouth didn't: *How could you pretend to your dad that I'm nothing? Am I nothing? Is that what I am to you?*

Emily couldn't lose her children. But what if she lost Gen? She saw how that might happen—the embittering secrecy, the one-too-many lies. Emily felt something inside her pried open like an oyster, exposing one living word: *you.* She crushed Gen's hand. Gen gazed steadily back. Emily said, "I don't know if I can hide how I feel."

"You can't?"

"Isn't it all over my face?"

No longer agitated or lost-looking, Gen smiled. "You've got a mystery face. Like, 'Oh, nothing to see here.' I know better."

"You know me."

"I do."

Passersby wove around them, busy, inattentive, jackets fluttering, and it seemed as if they were all pieces of ticker tape, and she and Gen were the only real people.

"We can be careful," Gen said. "I want to be careful with you. With your life. I don't want to be something you regret."

Because it was a weekday and Emily had hired a babysitter, she left Gen's apartment in time to make dinner. It was dark and the walk to the L was cold. Stores were closed. The street was empty. Emily hunched her shoulders.

She was a few blocks from the L when she heard footsteps. The tread behind her was heavy and fast. Emily turned the corner. The footsteps followed. Her throat tightened as she remembered the lawyer's warning. She quickened her pace, picturing the subway platform full of people. She was close. Nearly there. But the footsteps behind her quickened, too.

Was it Jack? Had he followed her to Gen's . . . or hired someone to follow her? Maybe it was a photographer chasing a story and she had been seen leaving Gen's building. If she turned around, she'd be blinded by a camera's flash. She imagined the pop of sudden light: harsh enough to strip paint. What would the image show, what would the caption say?

She ducked into a bar. Loud, humid. Safe. As she caught her breath, she saw, through the window, a person rush past—the one who had been following her. It was a young woman in her twenties wearing combat boots. She didn't even glance at the bar. She was, Emily realized with foolish relief, probably just hurrying to catch the next train.

Still, the anxiety didn't fully leave. It leached into Emily's bones and lingered even when she called a cab, buckled herself into the nicotine-scented back seat, and Brooklyn fell behind her as she went over the Williamsburg Bridge.

Stella sat on newspaper covering the wooden floor, where sunlight lay in beams like extra planks. She was painting a small cardboard rectangle while Connor did his homework at the kitchen table and Emily leafed through her notebook. The living room was peaceful. The only sounds were the scratch of Emily's pencil and the musical *plop* of Stella's brush in a cup of water. Emily was reworking an earlier section of the manuscript. Writing made her feel like an inchworm, a blind thing that lifted almost its whole self into the air, sensed where to come down next, then pulled forward the part of itself that it had left behind. She forgot her lawyer and the empty Williamsburg street. She forgot Jack.

Stella set the rectangle down to dry and returned her attention to the large cardboard structure she had assembled with packing tape.

"What's that?" said Connor.

"A fairy museum."

"There's no such thing."

Stella shrugged. "So?"

"Mom, Stella said I was stupid."

"No, she didn't."

"She did," Connor said, "with her voice."

They ignored him. Stella painted a purple door onto the museum, which was an impressive structure for a six-year-old. The building had two stories, the bottom story accessed through the top one, whose floor opened like a book to reveal, below, a gallery of a royal fairy family. The bottom level of the museum was for art and the top one was for "arti*facts*" (Stella liked finding small words hidden inside larger ones). The upper level had aluminum foil wands and a Play-Doh sculpture of a black cat (fairies loved black cats, Stella claimed, and scoffed when Connor said that *witches* did).

In the quiet, Emily reread what she had written. Earlier that day, a copy of the divorce filing had arrived in the mail. Emily had read it, feeling again that surge of buoyant relief, even pride. Then she imagined Jack's reaction. Dread crept over her skin. She hid the manila envelope in her closet. Jack had been served the papers, but she hadn't heard from him. His lawyer hadn't responded to hers.

"Where do visitors to the fairy museum go to the bathroom?" said Connor.

Stella cut him an annoyed look but drew a wobbly toilet on the wall of the second level. She brushed the toilet seat with rubber cement and sprinkled it with glitter. "That's fairy pee." She glued shiny bugle beads in the toilet bowl. "That's fairy poop."

"Mom?" said Connor.

Emily brushed bits of eraser from her notebook.

"Do you think there are aliens?" Connor said.

"Yes."

"Really?"

"The universe is a big place."

"What if aliens have super hearing, and they can hear us talking from far away?"

"With technology, or with something like ears?"

"With ears."

"They might not have ears. They might listen with their bodies differently. But they couldn't hear us from far away, because sound has to travel through a medium, like water or the atmosphere. If they have super hearing, they could hear everything on their planet up to the limit of its atmosphere, but nothing beyond that, because sound can't travel in outer space, where there is nothing."

"So if I were on a spaceship and I crashed into an asteroid, it wouldn't make a sound?"

"Inside the spaceship, yes, because there would be oxygen inside it. That air would be a medium for sound. But if you saw another spaceship in the fleet explode, you would hear nothing."

"Okay, but—"

"Connor, I'm working."

"You are?"

"I'm writing."

"That's not working."

"Writing is a job."

"But you don't get paid."

"Work is work whether you get paid or not. Some people get paid for doing nothing."

"No one gets paid for nothing."

"When you inherit money, it grows in your bank account even if you do nothing." Emily closed her notebook and looked at it. "Maybe I could get paid. If I sold this. If someone wanted to read it."

"Lots of people will want to read it."

"Why do you think that? You don't know what it's about."

"You tell good stories."

"Maybe," she said, "there's an entirely different kind of sound that we don't know about, that doesn't move in waves and doesn't need a medium. Maybe aliens do hear us with their something-like-ears. Even through outer space, from really far away."

"I think so, too."

Emily's phone buzzed.

We can get pizza again soon, Jack said. Or get a sitter and go to Per Se, just the two of us

Or wherever you want

I can't sleep. Or eat. I cook big meals and stare at the plate and can't even try to be hungry

I miss you

I miss being a family

Think of what your doing to the kids

Your ruining their lives

Do you know how lonely I am

Give me another chance

Can't you see how hard I'm working for you to forgive me

Emily hadn't intended to respond, but her phone kept erupting with texts, and as she read them, her incredulity grew. Although the texts were full of blame and anguish, they pretended as if nothing had changed. She wrote, I know your lawyer received the papers filing for divorce.

For a moment, her phone was silent, then he said, We're not getting a divorce. That's crazy. I love you and you love me

Stella painted. Connor read. Emily felt like an explosion in space, unheard: all that fire against all that black.

32

Emily rose from Gen's bed, her limbs heavy with well-fed desire. She thought about summer: a lush day where no one wants to move, only lie on the grass and inhale the trees' green breath. But they had been invited to a party at Becca's. She wanted Gen's friends to like her and didn't want to be late. She reached for her underwear.

Gen, propped up on an elbow, watching her dress, said, "White panties won't make you innocent."

"But I am."

Gen laughed.

"I'm a virgin," Emily said.

"Very curious how you explain that, since I was there when you were one."

"What is time? When you think about it."

"That got deep fast."

"Albert Einstein wrote in a letter, 'People like us who believe in physics know that the distinction between past, present, and future is only a stubbornly persistent illusion.' If Einstein says that I'm an innocent virgin, who are you to disagree?"

Gen pulled her, half dressed, back into bed, and they were very late to the party.

They didn't hold hands in the cab or when they walked into Becca's East Village apartment building. They kept space between them in the elevator, in case someone entered. Emily was glad that they could let their guard down around Gen's friends. Gen had told them about Emily well before the lawyer's warning, and said that she trusted them.

Jack had stopped putting money in Emily's account. She sold her jewelry. She didn't tell Gen. She didn't want to seem helpless . . . and she wasn't, she would be okay for a while. She wasn't surprised that Jack's first move was financial. For him, money *was* emotion. Withholding money was a plea as well as a threat: *Come home*.

Gen opened Becca's door without knocking. The apartment was loud and cluttered with several beanbags that were probably Shipley's fault. Becca shouted a welcome and weaved around Paul and Adam to offer cold beers—just opened, smoking at the throat. Emily took a sip. "I haven't had a beer in a while."

"Yeah, you don't seem the beer type," said Becca.

"It's nice."

"I'd offer wine, but it's all crap because I buy based on how the label looks. I'm a sucker for a cool label. And I can't make cocktails."

"I can make cocktails."

"Can you make some to impress our friends and say it was me? I don't impress them."

"You impress me," said Gen.

"Liar."

"You do. You're a cutthroat teddy bear."

Emily asked where the liquor was and Becca led her to the kitchen, shooing Gen in the direction of Paul and Adam. Becca's kitchen was very disorganized. Emily found the sugar in the fridge. Becca retrieved a bottle of Midori from behind a stack of canned cat food—and she did not have a cat. "Sorry, sorry, I know," said Becca while Emily made lime cordial on the stove. "It's my ADD. My brain keeps track of fifty-two cards damn near to perfection but everything else is catch-as-catch-can. *I* know where I keep everything, though."

"Where do you keep eggs? Do you have eggs?"

Becca did, so Emily foamed egg whites, added cordial, and

made Midori sours: greenish, ethereal, frothy drinks. "Lord help me," said Becca. "Those are pretty. Those are some high-femme beverages. How'd you learn to do that?"

"College job."

"No one will believe I made them."

"I won't tell."

"They'll know it was you."

"I'll leave the kitchen first. After I go, shake some ice in a cocktail shaker so you sound hard at work. Throw a kitchen towel over your shoulder before you bring out the sours on a tray. The towel will convince them."

Becca tipped her a friendly wink. "That's a real nice lie."

In the living room, Gen and Paul were deep in serious conversation. Nita and Candace, who must have recently arrived, were listening with Kate as Adam told a story that required wild hand gestures. Shipley had arrived, too, and was seated on a beanbag alone, off to the side, looking at her phone. She'd gotten a haircut with a tight fade that made her face look lean. She glanced up, saw Emily, and patted a nearby beanbag.

Emily sat. "Hey."

"Hey."

The metallic rattle and slide of ice in a cocktail shaker came from the kitchen.

Emily said, "I should explain why I didn't call."

"No need. I know the score. Knew it, even when I gave you my number." Shipley smiled. "Thought I'd try, though, just in case. But I'm glad you and Gen figured things out."

Becca appeared, bearing the tray of foamy, pale green sours.

"Hot damn!" said Adam.

"Wow, Becks."

"You made those? They're beautiful!"

"Emily made them," said Becca, then caught Emily's surprise. "I can't lie! I just can't!"

"Invite Emily to all the parties," Kate told Gen, who said that she would.

Becca passed out the drinks and Gen pulled a beanbag up to

Emily and Ship. "I can't believe you talked Becca into buying these," Gen told Shipley.

"*You* abandoned us at the furniture store."

"Where you were supposed to buy *furniture*. A beanbag is not furniture."

Emily laughed.

"What?" said Gen.

"You've become a snob," said Emily.

"No, I haven't."

"We got into a fight once," Emily told Shipley, "about chopsticks and edamame and how *I* was a snob. But look at her now: a *bean*bag is not *furn*iture."

Gen smiled. "Okay, okay." She tucked a lock of hair behind Emily's ear. Emily's skin thrilled at her touch. "Beanbags are comfortable, I admit."

"I love being right," Ship said, then brought up the Olympics, which made Gen let out a huge, excited breath.

"Emily, why don't you come over here?" Becca called from a gaming table in the corner of the room, where she sipped her Midori sour. "Y'all talking about the Games? I can tell by Gen and Ship's faces. Get out while the getting's good. They'll go on forever. Anyway, we never finished your blackjack lesson."

Gen claimed a long kiss before Emily rose to join Becca. Emily forgot her purpose. She fell into a great vat of desire. The room went quiet for a moment, then got loud again when the kiss ended. She was flushed, stupid with want. Gen smiled. Emily didn't care how obvious they were to everyone around them. She liked it.

At the table, Becca shuffled the cards. "Remember how to play?"

"Did you mean it when you said you had ADD?" said Emily.

"Why wouldn't I?"

"I wasn't sure if you were joking. Exaggerating. Like when someone's forgetful and says, 'I'm losing my mind.'"

"I wouldn't joke about a disability. Now, look at that. Jack and five. Want another?"

Emily took another card. The eight of spades. Becca made a chiding noise and swept aside Emily's losing cards.

"Is it hard having ADD?"

"When I was a kid, sure," said Becca. "Not as hard as growing up gay in an evangelical household. Why do you ask?"

"My husband has a learning disability."

Becca gave her a sharp look.

"My ex," said Emily.

"Still married, though. From what Gen said."

"We're divorcing."

Becca offered Emily another card. Emily said she'd hold, and Becca won the round. "Can't speak to your husband's experience," said Becca, "but I decided to accept myself, because what else you gonna do, right? I'm happy. I got skills, I got friends, I got this fancy cocktail. I'm killing you at cards. Life is good."

"Where'd Gen and Ship go?"

Becca glanced at the empty beanbags. "Probably challenging each other to a push-up contest."

"Seriously?"

"No. But also yeah, I wouldn't be surprised." Becca flipped over a card. "Gen told me a bit about your husband." Her use of *husband* had become pointed. "Seems like you're wondering why he's the way he is. Lots of things shape people, but we choose who we are." Becca won and dealt again.

"You believe that?"

"Let's say that I choose to believe it, which is kind of my point."

Becca made it sound simple. Emily wasn't so sure. She thought about how much Jack valued his job and used money to craft his sense of self. She had never heard his parents say a kind word to Jack except during a visit to the new town house, which he had bought in cash he'd earned. His father liked that Jack hadn't touched his trust fund. He told Jack, "You've done well." Jack had looked so much like Connor then—eyes shining, like a boy who had found the moon through a telescope.

Becca said, "I'd like to ask a favor."

"Okay. Want another cocktail?"

Becca's hands, which had held the cards loosely, firmed them into a stack that she set down on the table. "Don't hurt her."

"She's the one with the reputation. Don't you think that it's more likely that she would hurt me?"

Slowly, Becca shook her head. "She can be devoted."

"She has a million exes."

"Look at her friends, hon. How she runs. Her gran. You've known Gen longer than me. I thought you already knew what she's capable of. How she can love."

Emily realized that in her fear that she was just a game to Gen, she hadn't considered that Gen might have a similar fear. "I would never hurt her."

Becca adjusted her glasses, her expression one of acceptance without belief, and dealt another round.

After the party, Gen and Emily walked through Saint Mark's and past tiny vegan restaurants and thrift stores. Emily wanted Gen's arm around her. She wanted to slide her hand into Gen's back pocket. The way that they didn't touch seemed glaring, neon. "What did you and Shipley talk about while I was playing cards?"

"The trials. We went into the kitchen so we wouldn't bore the others. I really hope Ship makes the basketball team. It'd be nice to have a friend in the Village. Gran says she can't come to London. She's in good health but her arthritis makes travel hard." A passerby stared into Gen's face and did a double take of recognition, but Gen didn't notice or ignored it. He turned his fascinated gaze to Emily. It was uncanny. It was like becoming a character in her novel. Like being rewritten. Shaped into an idea of a person. She stared back at him until his gaze slid away.

Gen said, "Ship and I talked about you, too. She said that she hoped everything would work out with us."

A few warm days came to the city. It was a false spring—in March, it might snow again, but the weather made people giddy. They wore thin jackets. They chose café tables on the sidewalk. The weather made Emily think of Ohio, of the blue squill on her mother's front lawn. She thought about calling her mother, but after many years of not speaking with her, Emily wasn't sure that her mother would pick up. The estrangement that began when her mother had suggested an abortion was finalized on the day that Emily discovered that Jack had taken her manuscript and she called her mother in panic. Emily's mother hadn't asked what was wrong. She had acted like Emily coming to visit with the children was an imposition. She would have taken Emily in, but who wants home to be an obligation? Emily's mother always did her maternal duty, but this had felt to Emily like being offered an ice cube and holding it until her hand ached. Easier to let go.

Jack had always found Emily's mother stony and odd. Emily's decision to cut ties with her father was harder for him to understand. "He's a nice guy," Jack said. "Remember that speech he gave at the wedding?"

Her father had held notecards. He apologized to the guests for them and said that he wanted to get the speech right. His daughter deserved the best. He told the guests that when Emily was born, he called the radio station and asked them to play "What a Wonderful World." He couldn't believe how tiny and perfect she was. "Jack, I know you'll take care of my precious girl. Seeing the two of you together makes me so proud." He raised his glass. "To my daughter."

Emily remembered the dinner on her eighteenth birthday and how Nella had made a toast to Gen. At eighteen, Emily had worried that her father would reject her. Gen's queerness repulsed him; how could Emily's not do the same? Emily had longed for him to love her like Nella loved Gen. Surrounded by wedding guests who smiled at her father and his raised glass, Emily understood that her father wasn't proud of her. He was proud of his idea of her.

On their honeymoon, Emily tried to explain this to Jack. "It was a nice speech," Jack said. "I think you're making too much of this. Your relationship with that girl—it was just for a few months, right? And a long time ago."

Emily funded her sisters' college education, sent her father's family cards, and made the occasional phone call. But after the wedding she saw him as she believed her mother saw her: as an obligation.

Maybe, though, Emily hadn't given her parents a chance. She remembered how her mother had wrestled a tent up from the basement so that she and Gen could go camping. She thought again about Ohio, of the likeness of houses and the hoarse cry of a neighbor's rotary saw on a sunny day. She thought of her mother's note on a paper lunch bag: *Have a nice day, Emily!* Where was that lunch bag? Emily wished that she had kept it. She looked at her mother's phone number but was too afraid to call.

She and Gen were in a Williamsburg restaurant on the weekend when someone finally photographed them. It wasn't subtle. There was that video-gamey sound of a camera shutter that a phone makes even though it has no functioning shutter. Then giggles. The source of laughter was a pair of twentysomethings cultivating a Brooklyn chic of jumpsuits and shredded denim and terrible, adorable haircuts. Emily tried to shrink out of their line of sight. Gen, however, smiled at them. "Hi."

"Um, us?"

"You," said Gen. "Wanna come over?"

Before Emily could ask what Gen was doing, the other two were at their table, freaking out.

"I love you," said one.

"I want to have your baby," said the other.

"I mean, not *really*."

"But also: say the word and I will follow you to the nearest IVF clinic."

"That's not okay," said Emily. "You can't talk to her like that."

They fell silent.

"No, hey, it's cool," said Gen. "Let's get some selfies. But without my friend in them, all right? And can we delete that picture you took of me and her earlier?"

The three of them abandoned the table, and after an eternity of phone swapping and poses, the two fans left, shrilling gratitude. "Sorry," said Gen when she sat back down. "It seemed like the best move. That photo of us is gone."

"The entire restaurant is staring."

"You don't have to be afraid of people like those kids. I hated it at first, but then I thought a lot about it. Everyone's trying so hard, all the time. To get through a normal day. To feel like we did something okay. Something that matters. And it typically doesn't, not the way we want. Then someone wins. There's a medal on their chest. At least for that one person, all that trying paid off. Everyone's cheering. It feels so fucking good. When an audience sees an athlete win, I think they feel like they won, too, just by watching and hoping. They want to be a part of it. The fame thing, that's all it is: people wanting to get close to someone they believe matters, so they can feel like they matter, too. But we all want that, you know?"

Gen meant to be encouraging, but Emily could sense in her relaxed shrug that many years had gone into this perspective, which made Emily aware of how long it might take her to feel at ease in Gen's world.

---

what are you up to, Gen texted.

Just picked the kids up from school. We're in Central Park

good idea. So nice out

Connor wants to see if the turtles have come out of hibernation

oh me too. Where do they go in the winter?

He says that they go down to the bottom of the lake and bury themselves in mud

what if I came to the park?

To see the turtles?

to see you. And Connor and Stella

Emily hesitated. Stella said, "Mommy, can I have a hot pretzel?"

I could get there in half an hour, Gen wrote. But no pressure. Maybe it's too soon. Or too weird. But I would like to know your kids

In the spirit of an early spring day, when people eager for winter to be done wear clothes that will be too thin if the sun vanishes, Emily said yes.

The turtles were still hibernating, so Emily took the kids to the playground. They went straight for the swings. She was reading when Gen jogged up and dropped onto the bench next to her. Gen wore running gear and was sweaty, shoulders heaving. She rested an arm along the back of the bench and lightly touched Emily's shoulder with a few fingers that fell instantly away. Of course, they couldn't kiss. "Do you have water?" Gen asked when she had caught her breath.

Emily handed her one of the kids' water bottles. "I'm not sure I've ever seen you like this."

Gen, drinking, gave her a questioning look.

"You always made running look easy," Emily said. "That drove me crazy sometimes, but after we broke up I missed it. But I like this, too."

Gen raised one brow.

Emily smiled. "I like seeing you hard at work."

"I ran fast."

"From where? Not from Williamsburg!"

"I didn't want to be late." Gen looked at her watch. "I'm a little late."

Stella jumped off her swing and came up to them. She ignored Gen. "Mommy, Connor is annoying me."

Connor heard. "Am not!"

"You are so annoying!"

Emily said, "What is he doing?"

"He's picking on me."

"Connor, get over here."

Connor came. He ignored Gen, too. He protested his innocence. "I was *correcting* her. She was wrong. She made a mistake and I told her."

"I didn't make a mistake!"

"I was *helping*."

Gen said, "Did she ask for help?"

Connor and Stella looked at her in surprise.

"Hello," said Stella.

"That's my water bottle," said Connor.

Gen gave it to him. "It isn't help if someone doesn't want it."

Connor said, "Stella said she was going to swing high enough to go over the bar. She said she was going to go all the way around. That's not possible."

"I *know* that," said Stella.

"But you don't know why. I was explaining."

Gen untied a long-sleeved shirt from around her waist and pulled it over her tank top. She asked Stella, "Why did you say it?" Then she glanced sideways and said to Emily, "Sorry, I'm overstepping. I'm just curious."

"I'm curious, too," said Emily, who had been quiet because she wanted to see how the children responded to Gen's questions.

"I like to *imagine*," said Stella. "I know it can't happen but I like to pretend."

Gen nodded. "That makes sense."

"You're Mommy's friend."

"Yes."

"I forgot your name."

Connor said, "She never told us her name."

"I'm Gen."

"You're a runner," said Stella.

"An athlete," said Connor.

"That's right," said Gen.

"Wanna race?"

"Umm . . ."

Emily said to Connor, "Honey—"

"I know she'll win. But I want to see."

"Me too," said Stella.

"Is this a good idea?" Gen asked Emily.

"Yes," said Connor.

"Will you stop yelling at each other?" Gen said.

Stella shrugged. "Okay."

"Let's go to the meadow."

The meadow was scrubby with dead winter grass. Gen pointed

to a tree. "We'll run there and back. Connor, want to start us off?"

"Ready, set, go!"

The race was soon over. When Gen jogged up to the finish line, which was where Emily stood, she turned back to see that the kids hadn't yet made it to the tree. "Should I have let them win?" Gen asked Emily.

"No."

"I like them."

"They've been fighting so much lately."

"Probably not an easy time for them." Gen watched the kids reach the tree. "Not easy for you, either."

"Or you?"

"Don't worry about me."

"I miss you." Emily could still feel the soft greeting of Gen's fingers against her shoulder. Gen's gaze met hers. Desire wafted over Emily. She wanted Gen to kiss her. She could tell that Gen knew this and wanted the same thing.

"What if I came to your apartment tomorrow morning," Gen said, "after school drop-off? I could take care of you."

"Is that what you call it?"

"I could lay you out on the bed. Undo all the buttons. Be so nice to you."

Emily shivered.

"Would you like that?"

"Yes," said Emily.

"It'll be a reward. For both of us, for being so good. Look at us: two old friends out in public with nothing to hide. Who would guess how quickly I can make you come against my tongue?"

"The kids are getting closer."

Gen sighed. "I should have let them win. I want them to like me."

Connor and Stella ran up to them, gasping. Connor said to Gen in awe, "You're *fast*."

"That was extra*ordinary*!" Stella said the word as if it were two words.

"Thanks," said Gen, "but you know, nothing is ordinary."

"What do you mean?"

"Well, that." Gen pointed at the sky. "That's pretty extraordinary."

"That?" Connor pointed at a bird.

"Definitely."

"That." Stella pointed at her pink shoes.

"I love a good shoe," Gen agreed.

"That." Emily swooped Stella into one arm and Connor into the other and tickled them until they giggled and thrashed. They toppled her over. The earth was cold and damp; she was going to get dirty. They tickled her, too, and their squirming and twisting reminded Emily of when they had turned inside her pregnant belly. Emily looked up to see Gen gazing fondly down at them, the sun over her shoulder. *This could be my life*, Emily thought. *The four of us. It could always be like this.*

33

Mommy!" screamed Stella. "Mommy!"

Emily, who had been taking a shower, came dripping into the living room, a robe flung on and hastily tied, to find Stella throwing things at Connor. She pelted him with markers, a book, her backpack. Emily snatched a plastic bowl out of Stella's hand.

"She hurt me!" said Connor.

"You ruined it!"

"Ruined what?" said Emily.

Connor had ransacked Stella's fairy museum. Aluminum foil fairy wings had been torn. The black Play-Doh cat was missing. The royal family gallery was graffitied, with black pointy hats drawn on the fairies' heads and cackling grins drawn on their faces. "It's because the fairies stole the witches' cat," said Connor.

"It is *not* their cat!" said Stella.

Emily pulled Connor into the kids' bedroom. "Why did you do that? You know how much that museum meant to her."

"I made it better."

"That's not true and you know it."

"Before it was just a fairy museum. Now it's a *story*."

"If it's a story, it's a mean one."

"*You're* mean!"

"Tell her you're sorry."

"I'm not sorry!"

"Tell her anyway."

“This is your fault! I miss Daddy. I’m bored here. I hate it here! I want to go home!”

Cold water had seeped from Emily’s hair into her robe. Her pulse was electric—in the unsteady way of old houses, as if a circuit might break. “You *do* go home,” Emily told him, “every weekend.”

“Without you.”

“That’s just how it is.”

“I want you to come home. Daddy’s better now. He’s nicer. Come home, you’ll see.”

“Baby, I can’t do that.”

Connor began to cry.

Emily said, “You have to apologize to Stella.”

When he did, in a timid voice, Emily believed that he meant it. He told Stella, “I’ll help you fix it.”

“I hate you!” Stella threw the bowl at him.

Emily couldn’t sleep. The dark space above Gen’s bed was cavernous. The high ceilings went on forever.

Gen shifted beside her but slept deeply.

Emily worried about Connor. She didn’t think that he believed her when she told him that the separation wasn’t his fault. Maybe his efforts to persuade her to mend the marriage came from a conviction of his guilt. She hadn’t told the children that she had begun divorce proceedings—and neither, as far as she could tell, had Jack—but the other day, Emily had opened the manila envelope to look at the divorce papers, mostly to reassure herself of their existence, because Jack was continuing to pretend that she hadn’t filed. The papers were upside down in the envelope. They hadn’t been that way when the document had arrived. Had she slipped the papers back into the envelope upside down—or could it have been one of the children?

Emily left the bed and entered the fanatically clean living room with its wall of windows. Manhattan glinted. Connor and Stella were upstate with Jack. The daffodils that she had planted last fall must have come up. The upstate house was still full of her things—her pajamas, her face cream. She imagined Jack opening her tin of tea and couldn't help a wave of pity. She struggled to escape her sense of responsibility, but couldn't, because she had been trained by him—had trained herself—to accept responsibility. *I shouldn't have lost my temper*, he would always say, then explain how she had provoked him. If she didn't agree with his narrative, didn't share the blame (she hadn't trusted him, she kept secrets, she lied, she refused to speak with him, she leapt to conclusions, she didn't love him enough), he became worse, so it was important that she accept blame to prevent him from becoming worse. She understood how powerful Connor's guilt might feel even when he had done nothing wrong.

Emily heard the tread of feet. Gen touched the nape of Emily's neck. "Can't sleep?"

Emily shook her head.

"Bad thoughts?"

"Yes."

"Tell me."

"Who's the clean room and who's the mess?"

"I'm not a clean room, and you're not a mess—or if you are, I am, too. And I love your mess. Won't you tell me what's wrong?"

When she had heard what Emily had been thinking, Gen said, "I get that you don't want to feel guilty, but I don't see your alternative. To have stayed with him and let him hurt you? To exist in a state of half peace that's only half peaceful because he's on his best behavior out of hope that you'll come back to him? You might feel better if you just admitted to yourself that a divorce means it's him or you. Choose yourself. He's fucking around with your lawyer and taking forever to answer her requests for bank statements? Fine, take him to court. Have a judge force him to negotiate."

"It'll get ugly."

"Let it get ugly. Are you worried it's going to scare me off? I keep telling you I'm right by your side, and you keep not believing me."

"But you're leaving New York."

"Well, yes, I'll go to Oregon for the trials in June and then, if I'm A-graded, to London. But the Olympics won't last forever. I'll come back to New York after that." Gen searched her face. "Do you want me to?"

Emily stepped into Gen's arms and rested her head in the crook of Gen's neck. She remembered holding Gen in this same way, when she had stepped off the bus in Boston's South Station. Gen smelled clean, like cut grass. Emily felt a kind of wonder. She wasn't sure she deserved it: this luck, this person. "Yes."

"Hey," Gen whispered, "what if you came to London?"

Emily tried to read Gen's expression in the dark.

"The kids will be out of school then," Gen said. "You could bring them with you. I'd love to have you there. All three of you."

"And the press?"

"What's there to see? A friend supporting a hometown friend. So wholesome. And taking kids to the Olympics is, like, educational."

"Doesn't it bother you, being 'friends'?"

"It's not forever. It's for a good reason."

"What are we doing, talking about going to the Olympics?"

"Figuring out what a future together could look like."

The morning opened Emily's eyes. A huge slice of sun lay on the bed. It fell over Gen's back. Gen slept, face buried in the pillow. She wore an old T-shirt and thin cotton boxers. Emily wasn't sure if she'd ever seen Gen so still, or the limbs of her body this clearly. Gen was someone who worked her body hard and it showed, but in sleep there was a softness to her.

Gen's eyes opened a fraction, then closed again. Emily started to slip from the bed, but Gen stopped her. "No, no, come here." Gen pulled her close. "I'm awake, too."

"Not really."

"Go on, ask me something."

"What's my middle name?"

"Trick question. You don't have one."

"Astrological sign?"

"You hate that shit."

"Gen . . . can I think about London?"

Gen opened her eyes. "Of course."

"I want to go, I just—"

Gen nodded against the pillow. "It's a big thing. Anyway, we're getting ahead of ourselves. I might not make it to the Olympics."

"You will."

"I wish I didn't want it so much. I get to do what I love for as long as I can and that's more than a lot of people get. But it's hard. I don't know who I'll be when I can't compete anymore."

"You'll be you."

"You don't know that."

Emily was silent because Gen was right: no one knows who they will become. "Maybe just let yourself want the wanting. It's not like you can help it."

"Ugh! I want it so much that I'd have to get hit by a truck to stop wanting it."

"You'd have to be kidnapped by a bear?"

"An ocelot. I've always liked ocelots."

"You'd have to be sent into space to find an inhabitable planet. Your body hibernates on board the spaceship for hundreds of years. You land on a planet and it looks exactly like Earth. Same oceans. Same continents. You look up at the moon and it is the same moon. You're not sure if you ever left home."

"You're a good writer."

"You've never read my writing."

"Only because you won't let me look at your novel. But I still have your letters. I loved getting them. You think your talent wasn't obvious? Isn't? Listen to you: making stuff happen with words. You made *me* happen. No, I mean it. Making me take the PSAT. Telling me to go back to practice when I was ready to quit. It's like you told a story about me and it came true. Hey. If you can't come to London, it's okay. I asked you because I wanted you to know that I'm serious about you. About us."

"You are?"

"Yeah."

Emily kissed her.

"Mmm," said Gen, turning onto her back. She reached to

stroke Emily's hair and pulled her into another kiss. "Do that again."

Emily did, slowly. Hope opened inside her. Maybe this was possible. She remembered thinking, *Not yet, not now*, sure that nothing with Gen would last. But what if it did? What if it lasted their whole lives?

Gen drew Emily on top of her, so that Emily was astride Gen's hips. Gen touched Emily between her thighs and Emily gasped at the delicate pressure. But she took Gen's hand and rested it on Gen's belly. Gen raised a questioning brow.

"Show me," said Emily.

Gen knew what she wanted. Gen reached into her boxers and touched herself. Head thrown back on the pillow, eyes tightly shut, she shivered as her hand gained momentum.

"Show me more," said Emily.

Gen looked at her hazily, then pushed down her boxers. Emily watched Gen's fingers slip over herself, diving in and out, then return to the point where she concentrated speed. Emily grew hot with need. Gen said, the words caught in her throat, "I want you." Emily lowered her mouth to her. Gen cried out. Emily let her mouth rove over Gen's folds, the fruit of her. Sun blazed on the sheets. Gen shuddered.

When Gen nudged her onto her back, Emily was already on the brink of orgasm. She saw, beyond Gen's messy head and strong shoulders, the wall of windows. It occurred to her, in a half thought, that anyone high up enough could see into this room. Emily could be seen, legs spread. She imagined someone seeing this. It felt good to feel witnessed. She saw herself wrung out with pleasure.

Spent, she held this person who belonged to her and wished that everyone could see how she belonged to her, too.

The café was loud and Emily was wholly focused on her notebook, her pencil bounding to the margins, so she didn't notice the person who approached her. She wasn't aware of being studied by the woman, who finally came close, dragged out the chair across from Emily, and said, "Mind if I join?"

Emily's pencil clattered to the floor.

"Didn't mean to startle you." The woman sat. She had hair the color of flint and wore impeccably fitted clothes. The pencil had landed near her boot. She lifted it from the tiles but didn't give it to Emily. She inspected it, rubbing a thumb over the bite marks. She made a charmed noise. It was a run-of-the-mill pencil but the woman acted as if it weren't, as though its length were meaningful, and its nearly flattened eraser. "I prefer pens, personally."

"Who are you?"

The woman held the pencil like a ruler and set it in a horizontal line in front of her. "I'm Natasha Crane. Gen Hall's agent. And you're Emily. I hoped we could talk. Did you know that Gen missed an appointment with her strength training coach? Her head coach called to let me know."

"She has more than one coach?"

"She has a whole support team. She lifts weights with her strength training coach. She has a nutritionist. A yoga and Pilates instructor for balance and core. PT specialist. A running coach, of course . . . and me. And I have a problem. The problem is you." Natasha gave Emily the pencil. "Gen dates famous people. They understand her. They know what it means to pursue a passion. They are skilled at living in the public eye. But you—what is it that you do? A rich, married mom, right?"

"You should leave."

"There's nothing wrong with being a rich, married mom, but it doesn't equip you for how things will be if this relationship goes public. You'll be hounded. So will your children. And what will it mean for Gen? Can you imagine how hard it would be for her, always trying to protect you—and your kids?" Natasha continued, her voice reasonable, corrosive. "How will the media treat *her*? Don't underestimate the tricky calibration of being queer and edgy enough to be exciting, but not *bad*. Not a homewrecker."

"She isn't."

"We are talking about how she *seems*. And what London means to her. How much effort and time it takes to create a star. How it can all be undone in an instant. Don't you want Gen to win? For her to be able to focus on her dream? She's never missed a practice in all the years I've repped her. That worries me. *You* do."

Emily's face was hot, her cheeks red.

"I know you and Gen go back a long way," Natasha said. "She's come far . . . and in a sense, so have you. No one comes from nothing, but some people come close. Me too. So believe me when I say that Gen's heart might be in the race, but I am looking out for everything that keeps her heart free to do that. The money that means she doesn't have to worry about her grandmother. The deals that give her the respect that people like us don't always get. Emily, sponsors don't like losers."

"They did when she lost in Athens."

"To help that fallen runner?" Natasha's smile had a trace of pity. "Gen was young. Full of promise. And choosing to lose is different from failure."

"She will drop you."

"Because you're going to tell her about this conversation?" Natasha tipped her head, considering. "She might . . . if you were that selfish. Will she get another agent of my caliber? Even if she does, *she* might get dropped. Everything could go in her favor in London and she still could lose. Not all agents are loyal. Sponsors will fall away. Eventually, she might blame you. Or maybe she doesn't. Maybe you lie awake at night, knowing that you are the reason for her unhappiness." She patted Emily's hand and didn't look offended when it was snatched away. "I'm looking out for her, Emily, but I'm also looking out for you."

Do you know Natasha Crane? she texted Rory.

> gen's agent? oh yeah. she's what happens when power lesbians make deals w the devil. i think she might be a vampire. i like her
>
> You LIKE her??
>
> power likes power, babe
>
> Is she a good agent?

1000%

Emily stared at the screen.

y r u asking

Emily hesitated, then wrote, she doesn't think I'm good for Gen.

she spoke w u?!? BOLD

what do you think?

um do i think yr good for each other? lol no! the DRAMA the ANGST

After a long moment, Rory wrote a series of texts.

tbh
that is a u question
not a me question

34

The principal asked Emily to come to his office early before school pickup. Mr. Park's email was brief. Emily wondered if he wanted her help for the school's annual gala, whose fund-raising committee she had chaired in the past. But she thought he would have mentioned it in the email. The fact that he hadn't said what he wanted to discuss made her identify the request for a meeting as one of those cagey emails teachers and administrators send when they hesitate to put anything in writing.

It was a gorgeous late April day. Gen was out west for a set of road races, which were happening more frequently as the trials drew closer and the weather warmed. Tulips bloomed on the school lawn and the magnolia was ready to pop. Emily could see the tree through the window in Mr. Park's office as he motioned her to sit in one of the Mies van der Rohe leather chairs. "I want to talk with you about Connor," he said.

"Is he okay?"

"Do you know Lucas d'Avalos? He's in Connor's class."

"Yes, he's Connor's best friend."

"He's been bullying him."

Emily's stomach dropped. "Connor didn't tell me that he was being bullied at school."

"Connor's the one who's been bullying Lucas."

"Connor?"

Mr. Park had met with the boys separately. Lucas said that Connor had been bullying him since the new semester began, that at first he teased Lucas and it had seemed that he was joking, but the jokes turned mean. Connor began pinching him. Then pushing.

"No, Connor wouldn't do that. He's so gentle." She remembered him carefully lowering the turtle that had bit him into the water.

"I believe Lucas. I've seen a bruise. None of the teachers noticed anything wrong until today, when Lucas went missing after recess. We searched the school for him. We found him locked inside a janitor's closet."

Emily felt herself pale. At first, she had been sure that Mr. Park was wrong about Connor. She had been ready to fight for him, was assembling the words to protect him against a false accusation. Yet when the principal mentioned the closet, Emily remembered how Jack locked Connor out of the apartment and she had found him hysterical in the hallway. She clasped her hands tightly. They were freezing.

"Connor refused to speak with me," said Mr. Park. "I sent him to the nurse's office for the rest of the day. We want a positive outcome for both boys, but that requires Connor taking responsibility for what he's done. He's not allowed to have recess until he does. This wasn't an easy decision, because I don't believe in stigmatizing children, but until I'm confident that the behavior won't repeat, Connor will spend recess in his classroom while his teacher works on her lesson plan. Unfortunately, if the behavior continues, we need to examine the possibility that this isn't the right school for him."

Emily couldn't speak. Her Connor. Her child who loved nature and asked questions about deep space. Who still called her "Mommy" at bedtime. Who believed that she told good stories. Connor, who kept almonds in his pockets in case they saw a squirrel.

Who destroyed his sister's project.

Who had hurt his best friend.

Her son.

And Jack's.

The nurse left the office to give Emily and Connor privacy. Connor wouldn't look at Emily. He stared at his feet, which he had hooked around the steel legs of his chair. His knee jittered. She knelt in front of the chair and rested a hand on his shaking knee. His grip tightened around the edge of his chair's seat. "Connor, what happened?"

"Nothing."

"You have to tell me. Why would you hurt Lucas?"

His mouth trembled. "Because he doesn't want to be my friend anymore. He doesn't like me. He used to like me and now he doesn't." Tears spilled down his cheeks. "I want things to be the way they used to be."

Emily gathered him into her arms. His small body quaked with sobs. "Baby, everyone feels that way sometimes."

"I don't know what to do."

Emily held him close. "I'm going to help you."

When they returned to the apartment, Emily sought the privacy of her bedroom. She called Jack. At first he was excited to hear from her, but when she cut him off to explain what had happened at school, he became outraged: "This is a witch hunt. They let one kid accuse another and just believe him, with no proof?"

"Connor admits that he did it."

"I bet Lucas started it."

"He didn't."

"Well, the school is blowing this out of proportion."

"He gave Lucas a bruise. He locked him in a closet."

"Probably just a prank."

"Was it a prank when you locked him outside of the apartment?"

"What?"

"Connor learned this behavior from you."

"Are you serious?"

"I am."

"Emily, listen to yourself. You're obsessed with the past. You can't let go of anything. You think that because I gave Connor a few time-outs when he was little that this is *my* fault? Is no parent ever supposed to discipline their child? When have I ever lifted a hand to my kids? I'm a good dad. You never give me credit for it. Have you considered the possibility that Connor's behavior is because *you* left, because *you* broke up our family?"

"Yes, I have."

"Good. That's healthy." His tone became kinder. "It's good that you can finally admit your responsibility."

"Can *you*? You have been dragging your feet with my lawyer's requests. It's not actually your choice whether to give her your bank statements. It's the law."

"I can't believe you're using our son to try to manipulate me. We're talking about Connor, not you. You are so self-centered. Filing for divorce? Can you imagine what my parents would say if they knew? My colleagues? You don't want a divorce. You want to humiliate me. Meanwhile, all I ever do is try to make you happy."

"Send the bank statements or I'll take you to court."

After a moment, his voice came clear and cold. "You'll be nothing without me. You have no money, no job, no real home, no skills. What're you going to do, Em?"

"I'll be a writer." He laughed. She had surprised herself by saying it. She wasn't sure she would have said it if he hadn't told her that she had no skills. "I'll publish a book." As she spoke, the idea hardened from hope to intention. "Watch me."

His sigh was weary. Gently, he said, "We don't need lawyers. We're not getting divorced. We can make this work. Make *us* work. I'm ready to do whatever it takes."

"Do what my lawyer says."

"Is there nothing that will make you happy?"

"I would like for you to apologize to Connor for how you've treated him and me."

There was a long silence. "You need help. I don't know how else to put it. You confuse everything. I'm not the bad guy, and until you see that, I don't think there's anything I can do for you."

Emily thought of the smile Connor had around the time he was a year old. It wasn't a baby's impulsive smile but a learned one. This smile showed his little teeth and had a rectangular shape. He was trying to show the smiles he saw on other people. He looked like an alien trying to impersonate a human. It was adorable and funny but also sad, because when exactly does that start—how we impersonate our idea of a human? Does it ever stop? She had impersonated many people. The Perfect Daughter. The Small-Town Girl Who Leaves. The Intellectual. The Beauty. She had tried to be Jack's idea of a Good Wife. She knew, even now, the words she could say to him that would make him happy. The tone he expected her to take. But she thought of her baby's tried-on smile and of her child forcing another child to be his friend.

She set her phone down on the dresser and, without hanging up, backed away from it. She heard Jack say her name, but his voice was so small that he could have been three inches high. He grew smaller as she walked away, his berating voice like a hungry bird's. She wondered whom he was trying to impersonate, then decided that she didn't care. She cared about who she needed to be: someone who, no matter what the cost, even if she suffered, would always put her children first.

Stella was coloring at the kitchen table. Emily found Connor in the kids' bedroom, sitting at his desk and writing a letter of apology. His handwriting was careful but the ink was smudged. Crumpled balls of paper dotted the floor. He said, "Will Lucas be my friend again?"

"I don't know. I hope so. It might be difficult for him."

"But I miss him."

"I know that's hard. You can talk with me about it anytime. I made an appointment with a doctor you can talk with about this, too. I think she'll help."

Connor bit his lip. "I'm bad."

She touched his tear-streaked face. "I don't believe that. Everybody makes mistakes."

"Not you."

"Yes, me. Me too."

Emily keenly felt Gen's absence. She wanted to tell her about Connor's situation at school but didn't, knowing that Gen's schedule was tight with races and travel. She worried that discussing the trouble would make Gen feel like a parent, and that this would be unwelcome. Or if not unwelcome, then too much too soon, and at the wrong time. A distraction from training. It was less than two months until the trials. Natasha Crane's warning rang in her ears. Basically, Natasha had been saying, *Your life is a mess. You are dumping your mess on my client. She has worked too hard for you to come along and fuck it all up.* What did Emily have to offer Gen? A secret romance when Gen hated secrets.

When Emily talked with her on the phone, she didn't tell her about Connor. She didn't tell her about Natasha Crane. She made everything seem fine.

A smiling, middle-aged woman stood with Emily's children in the schoolyard near the fountain.

Emily, who had just entered the yard, didn't recognize her. She wasn't another mother. She wasn't a teacher. As Emily approached, over the musical chatter of children and their parents, she heard the woman say, ". . . your mommy have any special friends?"

"We went to a museum with one," Stella said. "And there's a runner."

"Does the runner ever sleep over? What's Gen like?"

"Super fast," said Connor.

"She's going to win all the Olympics," said Stella. "She's going to *smoke* the other runners."

"Really?" said the woman.

"Yeah, they suck."

"Is that what she said?"

Connor shrugged.

Emily felt nauseated. Natasha Crane's warning was coming true. Here was a member of the press, interviewing Emily's children . . . who were innocently turning Gen into a braggart. It hadn't occurred to Emily that her *children* could damage Gen's career. She listened with fascinated horror, not quite able to believe this was really happening, that a careless comment could make Gen, the image of honorable athleticism, seem like a cocky fake.

"Mom's late," said Connor.

"Mommy's *always* late," said Stella. "She *abandoned* us. We're going to have to live in a snow hut with a bear all by ourselves."

Emily forced calm into her voice: "You're making things up."

"Oh, hi, Mommy!"

"Gen never said anything bad about other runners. I'm on time like I always am."

"Must be hard," the woman said, condoling, "being a single mom."

"Connor, take your sister to the gate."

"She's not single," Stella said. "She's married to our daddy."

"*Connor.*"

When the children were out of earshot, Emily said, "Stay away from my kids."

"Maybe *you'd* like to answer my questions."

"Fuck your questions." Emily turned away, shaking a little. She heard a phone take a photo. The sound locked her body into place.

She turned back. With a plastic smile, she said to the woman, "You know what? It might actually feel good to talk. Sorry I was so rude. This just isn't the right moment. Let me give you my number and you can call me."

"Great! I'd love to get to know you, hear about you and Gen Hall." The woman grew coy. "There *is* a you and Gen, isn't there? Does your husband know?"

Emily snatched the phone. It was making an audio recording that had been started long before she had arrived at the school. She was so angry. She had been all along, but the anger, which had been pouring slowly into her like thick concrete, now became total. It suffocated her. It made her into a blind statue of herself, cracking at the edges. She threw the phone into the fountain. The woman shouted at her. Emily shouted back. Parents stared.

When she met the children at the gate, Connor said, "You said the eff word."

"You never talk to strangers! Do you hear me? You never, ever talk to strangers!"

"Mommy?"

"We won't, we promise. Mom? It's okay. Let's go home. Mom? Mommy?"

Emily was short of breath. She touched the base of her throat. She felt as though she had been running hard, like she imagined Gen must feel sometimes. Gen didn't win every race. She knew how it was to fall behind. To dwindle, lose. Gen understood failure, but Emily believed that Gen had never been overwhelmed by it. Emily was overwhelmed.

---

landed!
got an earlier flight. had to come home to see you
that last race didn't go great
um last few races
actually I'm skipping some
can i take a cab straight to your place?
really need to be in your arms
in cab line now. OK to come? Kids are at jack's, right?

Emily finally wrote back. Yes, please come.

Gen looked weary when she came through the door but brightened to see Emily, which made Emily feel terrible. She poured coffee for Gen, grateful for an excuse to look away. The sight of Gen made her eyes smart. She wanted to press her face against Gen's shirt, close her stinging eyes, and smell the hours of travel on the cotton. She was aware that she hadn't always been affected by Gen's beauty. There had been a time when she barely noticed her, but how had that been possible? She held the mug, letting it warm her hands before offering it. Emily wanted to stay in this moment forever. She thought that a lot of people must feel that way right before they say something awful. "I can't go to London."

The gladness left Gen's face. She took a sip, lowering her gaze to the mug. "That's okay. It makes sense. I know bringing Connor and Stella would be complicated and that you wouldn't want to come on your own and be away from them for so long."

"I mean that you and I can't be together for now." She hadn't intended to say this with such remove. She was anxious, and the effort to keep that anxiety at bay made her sound distant and cool.

Gen set down the mug. She was pale. "You're breaking up with me?"

"No," Emily said quickly. "I'm asking for a break."

"Why?"

Despite having rehearsed this, she struggled with words. "It's too hard."

"What's too hard? What are you saying?"

She told her about the woman in the schoolyard.

"But that—that's amateur hour. Emily, that woman can't be real press. They wouldn't go into a private school's yard. They'd get sued. And she used a phone? This isn't a professional. This is some independent operator hoping for her big break. But you destroyed the phone. It's okay, everything's okay."

"She could still write a bad story about us. About you."

"My agent can catch and kill it. Pay that woman so the story is never published."

At the mention of Natasha Crane, Emily felt a cold plunge of embarrassment. She saw how Gen had needed to define "catch and kill," how Natasha had been right: Emily didn't belong in Gen's world, she didn't even know its vocabulary. Look at her: ignorant, apt to flounder. "There will be another story."

"I already said I'd be your secret. I'll make sure the press doesn't connect you to me."

Emily imagined Natasha Crane's reaction to this: professional skepticism. "You can't make that promise. A break would be good for you, too. I don't want to get in your way."

"My way? For me? You're making no sense."

"You have the Olympics." She didn't say, *How many races did you skip to be here now?* She didn't say, *You could lose so much because of me*. Emily didn't say what she believed, which was that she would not be worth it. She didn't tell Gen about Natasha's warning. Gen would fire her even if it sent her career into a tailspin.

It was exactly the sort of morally pure thing Gen would do. "You have your training."

"Please do not pretend you're doing this on my behalf."

"It's not just for you."

"It's not for me at all!"

"Gen, I'm barely keeping my head above water." She didn't say, *I'll run out of money by the end of the year*. "Connor's having trouble at school. If my relationship with you goes public, it could jeopardize my custody. You know this, yet you're totally blowing past the fact that that woman was interviewing my kids. You don't know what it's like to worry about losing them."

"You forget that I know exactly what a custody battle is like."

"You know how it is one way. You don't know what it means to be a parent."

Gen frowned with the quick and severe expression of a person who has tasted something bitter. She dragged a hand through her hair and covered her mouth, thumb against one cheek, fingers fanned over the other. She squinted as though she had double vision and couldn't tell what was the real thing and what was its copy. She let her hand drop. She spoke very quietly: "How much time?"

"We can see where we are after the Olympics."

"Do you realize the Olympics is when I most need you? I'm not trying to be a dick. I'm not trying to guilt you. But I needed you. And after this summer? You'll probably still be in divorce proceedings. That's just how it is. There's money and kids, so it's going to take forever. I'm not an idiot. I know that. I'm not asking you to choose me over your kids. I wouldn't. But you could be choosing *us*, all four of us. You could be there for me and let me be there for you and go through the shit together and I keep telling you I'm right here and you keep not believing me or you're ignoring me. I don't know what you're doing. All I know is that if you wanted it to be us, it would be us."

This wasn't how Emily had hoped the conversation would go, but she now saw no way that it could have gone otherwise. It struck her as so stupid as to be almost funny, that even the smallest part of her had hoped that it might be possible to put Gen on hold, to dismiss her and call her back later, as though Emily's power could be that great.

Gen said, "Is there something you're not telling me?"

"No," she lied.

Gen leaned against the wall like she'd been pushed. Her shoulder blades and the base of her head made a short, dull sound as they lightly struck the wall's surface. She closed her eyes. "Choose."

"Choose?"

Gen held her gaze. She looked a little wild, almost afraid. "Yeah, choose. Are you with me or not? I'm not doing a break. I'm not doing some half-assed thing with you. We've got problems, okay. We can deal with them together. But you have got to choose. Yes or no?"

Emily felt a sticky kind of grief, a glue that made words clog in her throat. She thought *please*, but wasn't sure what she wanted to plead. *Please give me time*? It had already been fifteen years. *Please trust me*? She was a liar. She had just lied to Gen's face. She kept secrets when Gen valued honesty.

"Is it because you don't like that you're queer?" Gen said. "If it's that, I don't think this would ever work. I'm not okay with a future where you make me stay home from parent-teacher conferences."

The image of this—Gen sitting by her side in a classroom—floated before her with all the luster of a painting. She loved it. She wanted it badly. It was the kind of painting you put behind bulletproof glass so that no one can touch it.

"Say something." Gen's voice cracked. "I deserve better than this."

"You're right," Emily finally said. "You do. You deserve better. I can't."

"You can't."

"No."

"Your answer is no. You are breaking up with me."

"It's not because I don't want to be with you, or I'm embarrassed of you."

Gen's mouth twisted.

"I need to put my children first." Emily did, she always would, there was no version of this world where she wouldn't. Gen's vision—*all four of us*—was just that: a vision. A fantasy. Emily had had that fantasy, too. If you wish hard enough, you can delude yourself into believing anything. But reality always comes back. Her life was two conflicting realities. It was a camera's flash, petitions for custody, interviews, bank accounts, skipped races, the principal's office, a pulled muscle, school pickup, the Olympic Village, Stella's costume, Gen's agent, Connor's guilt, a chance to win, hounding texts, Nella's toast, her father's toast, lemonade, a lease, old letters, sold diamonds, gin and tonic, lost notebooks, milk cartons, wedding shoes, running shoes, oranges, toothbrushes, a birth, a miscarriage, a birth. You cannot live more than one life. Sometimes, you must choose.

Gen shook her head. She stared at the duffel bag, which hadn't been unzipped, where it waited near the door. "Well. I understand. Will you look away? Please don't look at me. I want to leave without—" Gen didn't finish her words.

Emily didn't look. Her vision was thick with tears. She heard the door open and expected to hear it close. When she didn't, she almost looked, and later she wished she had, so that Gen might not have said what she did.

"I think you never stopped being ashamed of me," Gen said.

The door shut.

Emily,

I'm sorry to write this in an email. It seems cold. I don't mean it to be. I went back to the airport. I'm flying to Oregon early. My team will meet me, and I have some friends I'd like to see. Being there will help me focus for the trials.

I don't want to be in touch with you for a while. I don't think I can bear friendly check-ins. The truth is, we were never really friends. Never just that.

Gen

35

Spring came into its own. Cut peonies appeared in the flower buckets outside bodegas. The air was soft and warm. Emily encountered a million things that made her want to talk to Gen. A bulldog wearing a cravat. Old running shoes on a sidewalk. *Free*, said a note tied to the laces. A roughed-up copy of *Memoirs of Hadrian* in a used-book store. She thought of texting Shipley and asking about Gen but didn't. She had to accept missing her. This second heartbreak set in like an infection, taking up a murky residence in her chest. There was no help for it. It wouldn't get better. Emily didn't want it to get better. *Let it be chronic*, she thought, *as long as it's mine.*

Whenever she remembered the last time she saw Gen, she was struck by how utterly themselves each of them had been. Gen with her uncompromising ways, Emily trying to compromise too much. She thought about that game they used to play. She could have said, before Gen left, *Who is the you and who is the me?* That game was over now. The point had never been who was what—salt or pepper, window or door. The point was the pairing. They had been saying, *I belong with you*, and now they didn't.

Jack called. "We need to talk about our future."

"Listen, Jack—"

"Let's meet, go out to dinner. I have a babysitter for next weekend."

"I don't think that's a good idea."

"Why not?" he said cheerfully.

"It sounds like a date."

After a pause, Jack said, still in that blithe tone, "I'd just like to clear the air. Go over a couple things. No matter what happens, we'll always be Connor and Stella's parents. Don't you think we should do whatever we can for the kids, including taking time for each other, and going over the big questions?"

"You need to understand that our marriage is over."

His voice, though still light, became steely. "Maybe you haven't considered all the factors."

Anxiety pierced her like a hypodermic needle that flushed her veins. "Just say what you have to say."

"It'll be better in person. It would help me find closure."

He had threatened her with one hand and offered what she wanted with the other. If he had closure, maybe the divorce proceedings would move more quickly. Maybe he would leave her alone. This had the hallmarks of a trap, but Emily agreed to meet, out of the need to know exactly what kind of trap it was, and the unreasonable hope that it wasn't.

Gen appeared on a late-night talk show. She looked relaxed, ready to laugh. The top buttons of her shirt were undone, exposing the collarbone that Emily had kissed.

The host asked if Gen was dating anyone.

Gen shook her head, never losing her smile. "Too busy with training."

"There were rumors about someone in New York." The host held up his hands in mock defense. "None of my business, of course . . . unless you want to make it my business? Don't be mad!"

"Hey, no worries. Yeah, I heard those rumors. I met up a few times with someone from back home, but we weren't together. She was just somebody I used to know." Gen shrugged good-naturedly, as if the subject were a trivial mystery or a joke that she didn't quite get.

Emily had nearly finished a draft of her manuscript. She was working in a café that played a classical radio station, the pieces selected by a man whose voice sounded like scotch and honey.

She would have dinner with Jack at the end of the week. Focusing on the notebook helped her not worry about the dinner. It helped her not think about Gen.

The music changed to something that Emily immediately recognized. She set down her pencil and listened to the lithe piano, impatient for the deejay to speak again. When the music ended, he named what Violet had played for Emily more than fifteen years ago, after Emily's first heartbreak.

Emily dialed the number Rory had given her. It included a country code, though Emily wasn't sure which country +41 was. Violet picked up. "Allô?" When Emily hesitated, unsure how to respond, Violet added, "Grüezi? Pronto!"

"Hi. It's Emily. From college."

There was a silence before Violet spoke. Her voice wasn't hostile, just curious. "Why are you calling?"

"I heard something you played for me. Schumann's *Kinderszenen*. Part of it."

" 'Träumerei,' probably."

"That's it." The word sounded like *trauma* but the deejay had said that it meant *daydream*.

"Okay," said Violet. "Well . . . it's late here."

"I wanted to thank you. I mean, to apologize. You were a good friend to me. Better than I deserved."

"Deserved," Violet repeated.

"A better friend than I was to you."

"You think friendship is like balancing a checkbook? That I see it that way?"

"No, but—"

"No one balances checkbooks anymore."

"I'm sorry."

"What exactly for?"

"I'm sorry my husband said racist shit and I didn't do anything about it. Or acknowledge it to you. I'm sorry that you gave me so much support when I left him and then I failed your faith in me. I'm sorry that I don't know about your life now. You said that it's late there and I don't know where 'there' is."

"Geneva. It's central for gigs in Europe, and it always felt like home."

"I'm sorry for disappearing."

"Why did you?"

"I thought that I must have used up everyone's patience. You were shocked when I went back to my marriage."

"Obviously."

"I knew it was a bad decision but it felt impossible to make a better one. If we'd stayed friends, I wouldn't have been able to ignore my mistake. You wouldn't have let me."

"Were you able to ignore it?"

"Sometimes. It's so stupid. When I married him, I thought that it would take away the loneliness I felt. Then I let him make me more lonely. I really missed you, Violet."

"Why didn't you say this years ago? It makes me mad that you didn't. We could have had a conversation."

"Can we talk now?"

"I don't know. I don't know you anymore."

Emily asked her to describe the room she was in. (The kitchen balcony, where Violet stood overlooking the wet street.) Where she kept her piano. (It took up the entire living room; there was no space for a couch or dining table.) What she had had for dinner. (Peanut butter and jelly. Violet had practiced until late and didn't want to cook. It was hard to find peanut butter in Switzerland—Europeans disliked it—but Rory shipped care packages.) Did she have a pet? (No.) Plants? (Many, all dead, except one that was fake.) Partner? (An on-and-off thing with an opera singer.) "She's a charismatic tyrant," said Violet. "Rory says she's a coloratura mob boss who makes me offers I can't refuse."

"She?"

Violet laughed. She and Emily talked late, until Violet could hear the hum of morning trams carrying people to work. She told Violet about Gen despite some reluctance. Her loss felt sharp, heavy, shiningly private, as though what had happened was a cut gem she had swallowed to keep wholly hers, this one thing that Gen had left, which was the pain of her absence. In college, Emily had wanted to recover from Gen. Now she didn't. She told

Violet not for comfort, sensing that comfort might diminish the loss, and then Gen really would be gone. She told Violet because of everything Violet had told her about her new life, and because she wanted Violet to trust her, which meant trusting Violet.

Violet said, "I guess some things don't work even when you want them to." Emily thought about how wanting can make a person feel deserving, as if the wanting is enough to shape reality, when in fact people want things they can't get all the time, and she was no one special.

Emily chose the restaurant, convinced that if she didn't, Jack would book an upscale one with a set menu of many courses that would chain them to the table for hours. She made a reservation at a bare-bones New American restaurant in the theater district known for how expertly they got people out the door in time for their shows. Here! Jack texted. Seated in the back. Text me a few min before you get here, ok?

Emily, unsure why he wanted forewarning of her arrival but not liking the thought of giving him time to prepare—for what?—didn't text him, which was why—had he planned to meet her at the door with an explanation?—she was confused when the host said, "Oh yes, they're already here. Right this way."

They?

The two men at the table stood to greet her. "Hi, Ladybug," said her father.

He was wearing the same suit he had worn to her wedding. It was too formal for this restaurant and had become too large for him. He had grown gaunt. His hair, always a point of pride, was still thick yet entirely gray. It had been cut and brushed in the style of a younger man. Jack, a hand companionably at her father's back, beamed.

"What the fuck is this?" said Emily.

Both men lost their smiles.

"Jack gave me a call," said her father. "Flew me out here. First class. I can't thank you enough, son."

To Emily, Jack said, "It always felt wrong: this estrangement. You don't understand the effect you have on people when you cut them out. I don't know what went wrong between you and your dad but he's a good man. Talk it out. It's never too late." Jack's gaze was earnest. "People can surprise you."

"You mean *you*," said Emily. "This is about you."

"You're always carrying the past on your back. Don't you want to stop? If you did, it would help you see the present more clearly. Everybody hopes that it's not too late to set something right."

"Won't you sit?" said her father.

Emily sat with him. "Leave," she told Jack.

"Emily," her father chided.

"It's okay," said Jack. "I'm used to it."

"You got what you wanted," she said. "Your trick worked. Now go."

Face flushed, he did.

"I didn't raise you to be cruel," her father said. "He wanted it to be a nice surprise."

"I've had enough of his surprises."

"You don't want to see your old man?"

Her love for him stung like a blister, like her skinned knees when he had taught her to ride a bike. She had missed him.

"There's trouble between you and Jack—that's plain—but can't we enjoy each other, you and me? The way we used to?"

She remembered how she would say *absolutely* to show him certainty that she didn't always have. His face had new lines. His mouth had changed shape. He looked softer, looser. She thought about how grateful she was for Rory's and Violet's friendship, how she had abandoned them and they still forgave her. "Okay."

"I'd been working so hard—trying to save for retirement, gotta have that nest egg, you know?—that I lost sight of how long it's been since we've seen each other."

"You did?"

"No, I guess I knew. I thought about it. Prayed on it. I don't know how things went wrong between us. I was always your dad. How come you stopped being my girl?"

Emily's fingers lifted, bloodless, to her head. She tightened her ponytail. She looked at her hands, now flat against the table, and was reminded of Gen's, when they were eighteen—that dinner, everything her father had said, the desperate glance Gen had thrown her grandmother before touching the white tablecloth as though for balance. Emily had thought that grown children couldn't fear their parents, but fear churned inside her: choppy, full of bits of hope. She realized that she had always felt that way about her father.

He gazed at her, and it seemed, maybe for the first time, that she had his full attention. He said, "Know why I call you Ladybug?"

She shook her head.

"You're my lucky charm. If something's wrong, tell me. We'll figure it out."

She had wanted so much to hear him say that. "I stopped speaking with you because of my birthday. When I was eighteen."

He frowned, trying to remember. "That was a long time ago."

"We went to dinner. With your family. I brought my friend."

His frown deepened. "Uh-huh."

"Gen Hall. Do you remember her?"

"I'd say everyone in town does."

"She wasn't my friend. She was my girlfriend."

He pulled away. Emily's body went still and cold, but she had started and couldn't stop. "I loved her."

"Nonsense."

"It's true."

His mouth creased in distaste. "You were a child. Confused."

"I wasn't."

"They're lonely, girls like that. They try to make good girls be like them. I wish— Well. I can see why it's troubled you all this time. Why you had to get it off your chest. I don't like to hear it but it's over. It happened long ago."

"We were with each other through this past winter and spring. Here in New York."

"But you're married." His voice rose. "You're married to Jack! You have two children! You have to fix this! Does Jack know?" When Emily shook her head, her father said, "That poor man. Trying with all his might. Didn't you see the pain on his face?

You're so young. You don't know how young you are. Thirty-three. So much life ahead of you. But you're taking all that's good and chucking it out like it's rotten. People say it's harmless. Let them be. But you let them be and this is what they do. It's worse than not being normal. They see what's normal and can't stand it. They turn everything normal inside out. It makes me sick. They make me sick."

"But I'm *them*."

"Hi, folks," said the waiter. "Can I get you started on something?"

"No, thanks," said her father. "I have no appetite."

It was all so predictable: what he had just said, how he had said it. How he rose to his feet and told her, "You have no respect for me. You have no respect for yourself."

Emily should have guessed. She could have written his words, his reaction, her own. She felt as small as a drop of water.

He left the table. He left the restaurant. She stayed alone at the table.

She could have written that, too. Anyone could have written that whole scene at the restaurant and not be satisfied with what was on the page because what her father had said and done was so common. It should have been obvious to Emily what would happen when she told him . . . and it had been, which is why she had avoided him for years, knowing that if he confirmed her fears, if he said out loud the things that she already heard in her head, she would lose a hope that she couldn't regain.

And yet she also hadn't known. She had imagined other reactions, different words, ones of comfort—just as common, just as ordinary, because it is ordinary for a parent to love a child. It is ordinary for a parent to choose a child first. This should be as simple and sure as a rock that looks like nothing and that a child carries home as treasure. Emily had thought that maybe, if she told her father, he would choose her, but he didn't.

Jack was waiting for her outside the restaurant. "Your dad wouldn't tell me what happened. He went back to his hotel. He said that you and I need to talk."

Emily's face was wet with tears. "Stop," she said. "Just *stop*."

"Calm down, Em. Hey! Don't walk away from me!"

She had pivoted. Her back was to him and she didn't see, only felt, a great tug at the back of her head, hard enough to make her fall. She cried out. She landed on her hip. A tide of pain pushed the breath out of her. He had grabbed her by the hair, she realized—by her ponytail.

"Are you okay?" he said. "I'm sorry, I didn't mean to do that. I was reaching for your arm. I guess you must have moved at the last minute."

"You're a *liar*."

"Keep your voice down."

The sidewalk was empty. No one had seen what he'd done. She scrambled away from him. She limped into the street, her vision blurred.

"Emily!"

A yellow blob came up the street. She gasped with relief and hailed the cab. She felt Jack drag at her and she shoved him, not caring if she hurt him, in fact realizing that she wanted to hurt him, that she was filled with trembling anger. She slammed the cab door and fumbled for the lock. She heard him through the closed window. "You're not yourself." His voice was muffled by the streaky glass.

"Go," she told the driver.

The next day, when the bruises had become livid, Emily photographed the continent that mapped her hip and thigh. She sent the photographs to her lawyer and said that she was done trying to negotiate with Jack. She wanted a date in court. She knew that putting the case before a judge would drive up legal fees. She didn't care. She would spend every last penny. *I want full custody*, she wrote to Sophie. Her hip throbbed. Her thoughts tumbled out in disjointed sentences. *Contest the prenup. Can we get a restraining order? Do what you need to do, so long as I get my kids. Use the photographs. Make him go away.*

36

Rory?"

"Hello! You're on speakerphone. I'm eating a taco. It's so spicy it's dissolving my eyeballs but I like it."

"I got a date in court."

"Emily." Rory was earnest. "That's great."

"It's not until late September. Jack and his lawyer refused to do it any sooner."

"Tweedle-dick and Tweedle-dicker are the worst. Still! You got a date! Did you tell Gen?"

"She asked me not to contact her." Gen had been so careful about leaving no trace of herself at Emily's apartment that nothing remained of her, not even a dirty T-shirt.

"She would want to know," said Rory, "even as a friend."

"It could distract her. The trials are in a few weeks. This is probably her last chance to make the Olympics. I think she's afraid of what comes after. She loves running and competing so much. I want this win for her."

"Ugh, fine! But your most annoying habit is how you make choices for others. Use your words! Stop disappearing on people!"

"She said she couldn't bear friendly check-ins."

"This is not a friendly check-in! Getting in front of a judge is major fucking news!"

"Can I ask a favor?"

"No. You're too annoying."

"Do you know any literary agents?"

"Your book!"

"I finished a draft."

"Yeah, I know literary agents. I can hook you up, but that's it. I love the sweet nectar of nepotism and am happy to share, but no one will sign you unless the book is good. Or unless you're an ex-president or a seamy cult leader. Or you *escaped* a cult. Cults are a thing right now. Did you write about a cult?"

"The pantheon of Greek gods was kind of cult-y. There was sex and murder and the worship of a fucked-up patriarchal leader."

"Nice! Is your book good?"

"*I* like it."

"Tell me the story."

Emily did, Rory constantly interrupting her.

"Sounds weird," said Rory after Emily had described the premise.

"I know."

"Maybe good weird. What happens in the end?"

In Emily's manuscript, Athena tricked Zeus by tempting him to live inside a mortal's mind, just as she had grown up inside his. He changed into mist and flew up the nose of the sleeping Odysseus. Athena chopped off her mortal friend's head. "I'm not saying it made me feel good," confessed Emily's Athena, "but Odysseus forgot a cardinal rule: never trust a god. Know what else about gods? It's hard to kill one, but not so hard when you make him mortal."

It was a bright day. She had taken the children to the park near their school. They were climbing on a play structure. Their shadows were cutout puppets on the ground. A bee droned near the take-out cup next to Emily on the green bench.

Jack texted, You're crazy if you think you'll get full custody.

Her throat was dry. She tried to ignore her phone.

There's no way you're getting around the prenup

You get nothing

Accusing me of abuse? That's fucked up, Em. I can't believe you'd lie like that.

She walked unsteadily to the edge of the park and called him. "You hurt me."

"You fell."

"You made me fall. I have photographs."

"My lawyer showed me photographs of a bruise you got when you slipped and fell. They don't prove anything."

Emily had the sense of being made entirely of paper. She felt very light.

"It was an accident," he said. "You have no proof it wasn't. No witnesses."

His words made everything unreal. Her own reality seemed to fall away from her. She became a schema of a person, a drawing of a mother standing in the park while her children played.

That night, while Connor and Stella were sleeping, the intercom buzzed. Voice crackling through the static, Jack said, "Can I come up?"

She recoiled from the intercom. The buzzing continued, then stopped.

Her phone rang. After it stopped ringing, the texts came.

Do you really want to go to court?
I dont want things to get nasty
We can still turn this around
Will you please let me up?
I pay for this fucking apartment
How are you paying for this apartment
You have no money
Em come on
I have something for you

He didn't write anything for a few moments, which led Emily to hope that he had given up and gone away. There was nothing he could have that she would want.

He texted a photo. It showed a set of notebooks in his hand, the closed lobby doors of Emily's building in the background.

Jack held Emily's manuscript: the first version of her book, the one she had written years ago.

Frost crept over Emily's lungs. She almost dropped the phone. She wrote, I thought you destroyed it

No you assumed that. You blamed me for something I didn't do

you've had it all these years?

I just found the notebooks. You must have misplaced them. They were in a box of old things from when we moved

There was a time when she would have believed him if only because not believing would make her life untenable. She would have believed him in order to prevent the shame of having married someone who could do and say what he did to her. She was shaken by how easy it would have been to ignore an obvious lie.

Keep them, she told him.

She made sure that the front door was locked and bolted. She slept on the floor of the children's room. When they woke in the morning for school, they were tickled to find her there. Stella, excitedly, asked if she knew how to sleepwalk. "Will you teach me?" Stella begged.

37

Emily was too nervous to watch Gen's final USATF event alone. During a commercial break, she called Rory, who turned on her television, too. Rory asked if she'd heard back from any literary agents. Emily, who had sent out query letters and sample chapters a couple of weeks ago in early June, said no. The commercial on TV became one for laundry. She watched grass-stained shorts go from green to white. She wished that Rory hadn't asked that question. Now Emily's own anxiety threaded through her anxiety for Gen.

Rory said, "You're coming to the wedding, right?"

Emily had received Elizabeth's invitation. The wedding would be in July. The invitation came with an enclosed note:

EMILY!!!!!!

Rory told me your news. I'm sure it was hard to leave Jack and I hope you're okay, but as Rory says, we're all glad you got the fuck out of it. You pulled a disappearing act on your friends but hey, me, too. I want to believe that you can disappear on the people you love and still come back. Prove me right.

I know this invitation is short notice, but you never would have been a B-list invite if you'd stayed in touch! Be my A-list friend and come.

XOXO,
Elizabeth

"Of course I'm coming," said Emily.

"Florencia will be there."

Encouraged by her reconnection with Violet, Emily had tried calling Florencia. Her many calls went unanswered.

"Hey," said Rory, "it's on again."

The camera panned over Hayward Field, then the runners. It lingered on Gen, who stretched, looking away. The announcer described her career, reminding the audience how she'd stolen their hearts during her first Olympics in Sydney: someone had given her flowers after she had won a silver. She brought them to her grandmother in the stands. Sweat-soaked, face full of joy, Gen placed the flowers in her grandmother's arms. Emily had watched this moment, in 2000. She had seen how Nella reached to cup her granddaughter's face just as she had in the farmhouse kitchen when Emily was a teenager and looked on, wishing that someone loved her like that.

Now Gen scanned the stands, which were emblazoned with the USATF logo of a star with wings. Emily knew that Gen wasn't looking for Nella, who could no longer travel—if her arthritis had, in the end, allowed her to attend the trials, the camera would surely be on her right now, for the emotional drama. The announcer sketched the highs and lows of Gen's career, adding that she had made an impressive showing at the trials thus far and was one win away from qualifying for London. He mentioned an injury Emily hadn't known about—a pulled tendon—that had kept Gen out of an international competition last year.

"You know," said Rory, "your relationship with her confused me."

"You don't know why we were together?"

"Oh, that was obvious. You fucked each other silly. The way you looked at each other oozed over everything. Like the slime in *Ghostbusters*. You were the green ghost with all the hot dogs."

"I believe you mean *ectoplasm*."

"Okay, Egon. You got your sex-toplasm everywhere. You haunted each other. No, what I meant was that I couldn't figure out your trope."

"Trope?"

"All great romances have one."

"Our romance didn't work."

"It was still great."

"Yes. It was."

"At first I thought you were the friends-to-lovers trope."

"We were always more than friends."

"Right. That trope doesn't fit. Then there was the enemies-to-lovers period, after you met again at that fundraiser."

"But we didn't hate each other. We were just mad."

"Right! Then I thought: second-chance romance."

"Those end happily."

"Love at first sight?"

"We were ten."

"Then I thought—"

"Shh!"

"Sorry, I'll shut up."

"It's starting."

"Wow," said Rory. "I don't normally feel gay but seeing them all lined up like that does do something for me."

The starter's gun fired.

"Holy shit," said Rory.

"Oh my God."

"Shh!"

"You're the one who's supposed to shut up."

"She is so fucking fast."

A bell signaled the final lap. Emily was no longer nervous. It was impossible that Gen wouldn't win. Rory was screaming in Emily's ear but Emily was silenced by Gen's stride, how her whole body became an expression of will.

Gen crossed the finish line. She was A-graded. She made the Olympic team.

Elizabeth's wedding reception took place at the Boathouse in Central Park. Her style was Old Hollywood glamour, her blond hair in waves. She flung her arms around Emily, then whirled away to another claim on her attention. Emily remembered how it was to be a bride. Everyone wishing everyone well. She thought about everything that she hadn't known then about her future. She thought about Gen, unseen among the guests, watching Emily kiss her husband. With brittle regret, she wondered what Gen had wished then, and what she wished now.

There were geese on the water near the Boathouse. The turtles, long out of hibernation, were black and shining. A family rowed by in a boat. Emily had once been a family in a boat. She had seen this very place, the one where she now stood, over Jack's shoulder as he helped Connor pretend to row. She wasn't far, either, from the meadow where Gen had run with her children. Her throat closed. She didn't want to cry at Elizabeth's wedding. She listened to the dip of oars in the water. The blue cloth of sky had no flaws. *You can't go back*, her mother used to say with a shrug, as if surrendering the past was easy.

Emily hadn't seen Florencia at the ceremony but they were seated at the same table for dinner. Violet was there, too, her opera singer not in attendance because of a performance in Berlin. Rory had also come alone, because she was hoping (as she had told Emily earlier) to have coat-check sex with a stranger. Florencia's husband was handsome, with a closely trimmed black beard, and he eyed his wife worriedly as Emily approached the table. Emily was full of apologies that she had rehearsed and hoped that Florencia would let her say. Florencia folded her arms above the crest of her pregnant belly. She stared at Emily, brown eyes furious. "Elizabeth should have seated me at a different table."

"Mi vida," her husband said gently.

"Give Emily a chance," said Rory. Violet said nothing.

"Why?" Florencia demanded. "Where were you?" she asked Emily. "When I fought with my parents? And met Damien? When I found out I was pregnant?"

"I'm sorry I couldn't—"

"You could have!"

Damien spoke to his wife, who argued with him. He persisted. She let out a guttering sigh. "He wants me to tell you something."

"A story," Damien said in English. Then he spoke in Spanish, which Florencia, still angry, translated. "He and his friend were in high school. They had gone to get pizza. Two police officers came into the pizzeria." Florencia stopped and asked something. Damien shrugged and spun his hand like a wheel. She said, "The cops went up to the counter and ordered, but of course they didn't expect to pay. Cops never paid. The pizzeria owner had to give them whatever they wanted for free. My friend and I left. We snuck around a street corner, but at a high vantage, so we could see the front door of the pizzeria. The cops came out with their pizza. We shouted—" Florencia broke off and stared at Damien. "Qué loco!" she told him. "Por suerte seguís vivo!"

"What did they shout?" said Violet.

"Mendigos," said Damien.

"He called them beggars." Florencia was horrified. "He has never told me this story." Damien continued to speak. "We died laughing," said Florencia. "They chased us. We thought, *They will never catch us, those corrupt fools*. But they did." Florencia had paled. "You have to understand that during the seventies and eighties in Argentina, many people disappeared. Anyone the government wanted gone. The police would come, people vanished. It was the nineties when my friend and I insulted the cops. The Dirty War was over, but it was still well known: you do not fuck with the police.

"They caught us and split us up. One guy took me, the other took my friend. I've never been so frightened. He asked me where I lived. I was terrified to involve my parents. He asked if I wanted to go to prison instead. He drove me home. We stopped in front of my house and he brought me to the door. My father answered. Shock carved his face into stone. The cop said, 'Do you know what your son called me?'

"'No,' my father said.

"'Mendigo.'

"My father's breath sucked in, as though he'd been punched in the gut . . . I still hear it. He started to speak. To beg. But the cop pushed me toward my father. 'Teach your son better manners,' he said. Then he walked toward his car, laughing the whole way. What a joke to fuck with two little punks who thought they were so smart!"

Violet said, "Was your friend okay?"

Damien nodded.

Florencia said, "Why did you tell us this? Dios mío, Damien."

He said, Florencia translating, "We all do stupid shit. How does anyone get through youth? You look back and you are astonished at what you survived. Not because you were good or special but because when you made your mistakes, you got lucky. It's enough to survive a mistake and be grateful. Not everyone does. Listen to what your friend has to say, my love. I know that you missed her. Look at her face. You can see how much she missed you."

The 2012 Olympics began, for Emily, in late July with the first U.S. women's basketball game. Connor and Stella, who had been out of school for a month, sat next to Emily on the couch as they watched the U.S. team play Croatia and win, 81–56, with Shipley shooting a three-pointer mid-game and, toward the end, darting around an opponent for a soaring layup. It was late morning in New York, five hours behind London, and Emily and the children ate pancakes while they watched. Later that day, Connor had a playdate with Annika, a friend he had made at a weeklong robotics day camp earlier that summer. "She has *four cats*," he had told Emily after the first day at camp. His excitement had a nervous edge to it. He spilled forth other details: Annika loved stuffies; she had lots of Pokémon, even a rainbow rare; she lived in a building with long hallways for running up and down.

Emily had signed with a literary agent. For a while, it seemed that no one was interested, but in June she received an email from Leila Alami, a junior agent at a powerful firm. "It's not bad that she's junior," Rory told Emily. "It means she's hungry." Leila invited Emily to lunch and praised the manuscript. She loved the prickly, pensive voice. Its unusual narration, too—restless, unwilling to settle fully into one way of telling a story, as though the book disliked routine. "But Zeus is too villainous," Leila said, "which makes it hard to understand why Athena waits. I get that she must figure out *how* to overthrow him. But the wait should also be emotionally driven. He should be slightly less bad. Charming in some way. It would help if we see that, in his own messed-up way, he truly loves his daughter, and she knows this and needs it." Leila had some concerns about the ending, which she said was rushed. A reader becomes a friend of a book, Leila believed; it's important for the end to be a proper goodbye. "Summer is dead for publishing," said Leila, "but I'd like to go out with this in mid-August, right before the fall submission rush. Enough editors will be back in the office by then and I want them to read your manuscript before they get swamped by a million of them. Can you revise the draft before then?"

After the meeting, Emily reached for her phone to text Gen. She caught herself and slipped the phone back into her bag.

The Olympic basketball games edged into August, when track and field began. Gen hadn't yet competed, but there was a television interview with her. She praised the other athletes and said that it was an honor to be there. No matter what happened, she was glad to be able to compete. Emily hadn't seen her face up close in so long. She stared at the familiar lines of her. The quick smile. Gen looked carefree, a picture of health and strength.

The sportscaster said, "It must be hard for you that your grandmother couldn't make it."

"That's okay. She's watching from home."

"Any special words for her—or someone else?"

Gen's smile faltered. Then she shrugged playfully. "No, I just want to make my gran proud."

The segment changed to a panel of retired athletes and coaches, who talked about the importance of Gen's first race the next day and how it would set the tone for her entire Olympics. They discussed her impressive showing at the USATF trials, though one coach noted that she had favored her left leg—the one that had been injured previously—when she slowed following a race. "We don't know how that old injury will affect her performance," said a gray-haired woman who had competed as a middle-distance runner in the '80s. "We always talk about athletes making history. What we mean is setting records. We forget, though, that athletes also make their own personal history. They measure themselves against who they were and what they accomplished in the past. Gen Hall knows she has a lot to live up to. Tomorrow could be the most important race of her life."

Yet the following day, with millions watching, Gen did not appear at the track.

Sportscasters speculated, but no one knew. Was she injured? Someone on the team took Gen's place at the starting line.

After the race, the team's coach was questioned by the media. "She had an emergency," he said. "That's all I can say."

Emily called her. The call went straight to voice mail. Increasingly concerned, Emily tried again, but Gen either wouldn't or couldn't pick up. Emily sent texts. They went green, unread.

Finally, Emily scrolled through her phone to find Shipley's number. Shipley picked up on the first ring.

"What's wrong?" said Emily. "What happened? I can't reach her."

"You wouldn't be able to," Shipley said. "She's on a plane. She's flying home to Ohio. She just found out that her grandmother is sick. Nella is dying. Gen wants to make it there in time."

38

Emily called her mother and asked if she could visit with Connor and Stella. If not, she would stay at a hotel, but the closest one was forty-five minutes from Washford. "I'm not sure how long I'll need to stay."

Her mother was silent. Emily thought that she might have stepped away from the phone. Maybe she had set it down on the kitchen countertop and walked into another room. "Mom?"

"What about Jack? Is he coming?"

"We're getting a divorce."

"Uh-huh. Makes sense."

"Why?"

"No, thanks. I'm not in the mood to get hung up on. You're welcome here anytime. For as long as you need. You know that."

Emily hadn't known that.

"I'd like to meet my grandkids. When would you get here?"

"Tonight. I just booked our flights."

There was a pause. "Okay. What made you decide to come?"

"Nella Hall is dying. She has brain cancer."

"I wondered. I'd see her sometimes, at the old movie theater, where they sell Amazon stuff. She'd buy anything for anyone who wanted it. Did that at the Kroger, too, buying groceries for folks. Last time I saw her, it looked like she was ailing. She had that face I'd see on patients. Haven't seen her for some time. But what's Nella Hall got to do with you?"

"I want to be there for Gen."

"Yes, the granddaughter. The runner. Your friend from high school. Awful lot of trouble, for you to fly out here with two kids to stay for who knows how long. Even for a friend."

"I love her."

"Well, you always did."

"You knew?"

"What am I, stupid?"

"Why didn't you say something?"

"None of my business."

Emily's voice was small: "Do you still want me to stay with you?"

"You're my daughter. This is your home."

"Mom." Her throat was sore and swollen. "Mom."

"I retired last year. Gave me time to think. I'm not good at saying things. Never have been. Never will. Things always go wrong when I talk to you. Just come home."

"What did you mean, when you said that it made sense that Jack and I are divorcing? Because you knew about Gen and me?"

"I didn't mean anything. Forget it."

"Please."

Her mother sighed. "It's not any one thing."

"Then what?"

"All right. When he looked at you, he didn't see you. I'm not saying that we don't have our issues, you and me. But I know you. You've always been different. Not difficult, I'm not saying that. Just different. I knew you were going to leave Washford. Knew it when you were little. What kind of kid wants to learn Greek? You weren't common. Talked different, thought different. Did different. I don't know the details of your marriage and I don't need to. You asked me to say what I meant and I'm trying. Here's what I mean. Jack looked at you like you hung the moon, but I knew you hung the sun."

When Emily had learned that her second baby had no heartbeat, she didn't believe it. There had been a mistake. Then she placed a hand on her rounded belly. It was so still. He was still.

It had been nice, before, to guess what part of the baby pushed against her skin—the head, a foot? Now nothing moved beneath her hand. She imagined him. His eyes sealed shut. So quiet. She didn't want to deliver him. It was impossible to pretend that he was alive, but he remained part of her. He was still hers. When she delivered him, he wouldn't be hers anymore. No, he *would*—how could he not?—but he would be forever out of reach.

She didn't want to compare her lost child with anything. He wasn't a metaphor. He was her baby. But she understood, as she looked at Jack's name on her phone, that she had taken so long to file for divorce because it is terrible to confront loss, even when what has died is a marriage.

Jack picked up the phone. She told him that she was taking the children to Ohio to visit her mother.

"Nice of you to inform me," he said. "They're my children, too."

"We leave for the airport in an hour."

"How long is this visit?"

"I'm not sure." It was mortifying to hear her voice shake.

"A week?"

"I don't know."

"My parents have Labor Day plans with the kids."

"You might have to cancel those plans."

"That's in a *month*. Are you telling me that you're going to be there for a month?"

"Maybe."

"School starts right after Labor Day!"

"I'll wait to cross that bridge when I come to it."

"What the fuck is going on?"

"Gen's grandmother is dying."

"Gen? Who's Gen?"

"You met her at my apartment the day we went out for pizza with the kids."

"The runner?"

Emily took a breath so deep that it made her ribs ache. "She was my girlfriend when I was eighteen. I told you about her a long time ago." Although Emily's lawyer had warned her not to do this, she said, "On the day you came over, she had spent the night. We were together all winter and spring."

"You *cheated* on me?"

"That's not how I see it."

"I bet you don't. You have an amazing gift for blaming other people for imagined crimes and then pretending like you do nothing wrong."

"I need to help her if I can."

"You are unreal." Jack let out a furious yet determined sigh. "Listen. I know how you were with me when things were good. You had a one-time thing when you were a teenager, but you and I have a whole life together. We can get past this. We can cancel the court date. I am asking you one last time to come home. Say you're sorry and come home to me. Say you made a mistake."

"No."

"What the *fuck*." Emily thought he would say more but he went quiet. She heard the clicking of a keyboard. He gave a short, dry laugh. "So that's who she is. Wow. Okay. Have you looked her up on the internet? She runs through women like water. I hope you don't think you matter to her. I'm sending this link to my lawyer. He's going to love it. Em, what are you thinking? You want to expose our kids to a woman who gets splashed all over trashy magazines? Not on my watch." His voice was clear and cold. "You can't take them to Ohio without my permission. If you do, that's kidnapping."

"Please let me."

"No."

"If you let us go," Emily said, "I won't contest the prenup."

He was silent, then said, "That's family money. It never had anything to do with you. I've never even touched the trust. I work hard for everything we have."

"Keep it. All of it. I don't want any money from you. Just let us go."

After another, longer silence, he said, "Fine, take the kids to Ohio. Put your promise in writing. But you're going to regret this when I see you in court."

Emily left a message on Gen's voice mail saying that she was on her way to Washford: "It's okay if you can't see me or don't want to, but I'll be there if you do." Her plane landed in Columbus after nightfall and she buckled her sleepy children into the back seat of the rental car. Somewhere along Route 33, she stopped so that Stella could use the bathroom. There was a text from Gen: I've moved gran home. Please come as soon as you can.

39

Emily tucked the children in. Her mother had insisted that they sleep in her room, which had a bed large enough to share. "I'll sleep on the couch."

"No, Mom, I will."

"I fall asleep there half the time anyway, watching TV. You sleep in your own room. Enough. I don't want to hear it. My house, my rules." She told Emily to eat before driving to the farmhouse and reheated fried pork tenderloin in the microwave. "You listen. I'm sure Gen Hall has the money to hire a round-the-clock private nurse but there are good ones and bad ones. If Nella's in pain and it's not time for morphine, she'll need gabapentin, one hundred milligrams daily. Haloperidol for delirium, once it comes. I'm writing this down. If she can't swallow good, give her glycopyrrolate, one milligram every four to six hours as needed. Stop looking at me like that. You think I worked at a hospital for fun?"

Emily accepted her mother's notes.

"Maybe Nella's got a while, I don't know, but you tell Gen to talk to her at the end. Hearing is the last sense to go."

Emily hadn't known this. It stunned her that it wasn't common knowledge. It felt reckless that she hadn't known this crucial fact.

"Don't worry about the kids," her mother said. "I'll see you when I see you."

It was late and dark. The soft, heavy summer came in when Emily rolled down the car windows. She heard crickets, the crunch of gravel beneath tires, then the rush of wind. It was dark, especially on the country roads, but Emily knew the way. She wouldn't miss a turn. Gen had always driven Emily to the farmhouse when they were young, except for the time Emily had taken her mother's keys. Even so, knowing the way was instinct. Although more than fifteen years had passed since Emily had been on this road, she had taken it many times in her mind. She had imagined the old beech at the corner, the intersection that led to town and how she would need to go the opposite way. She had often imagined driving to Gen's home, if not like this.

Gen was sitting on the porch, shoulders hunched, when Emily drove up. Two dogs that Emily didn't recognize—of course she didn't recognize them; the ones she knew were long gone—bounded up to the car. They were the size of baby deer. Gen called them back, her voice threadbare. Emily had never seen her look so tired. It seemed as if she couldn't stand, so Emily sat down next to her and held her. Gen buried her face in Emily's hair. Emily heard the flap of bats overhead. Gen's ragged breath. "She lied to me," Gen said. "Arthritis. Bullshit. She was diagnosed last fall. She didn't want me to come home. Didn't want to interfere with my training. Said she didn't want me to miss my big chance." She lifted her wet face. "I am so angry. I am so fucking mad. I feel horrible for being mad."

"She probably understands that."

"She doesn't know. I didn't tell her."

"I think she knows anyway. She knows you."

"What am I going to do?"

"I'm going to help you." Emily looked more carefully at Gen's face in the porchlight and saw deep shadows under her reddened eyes. She asked after Nella and was told that she was sleeping under the watch of the nurse. Emily remembered the advice she'd read online when Connor was born: sleep while the baby sleeps. She remembered how hard that had been to do, despite exhaustion. She told Gen to go to bed. She or the nurse would wake Gen for anything important.

As they entered the house, Emily noticed how it had changed.

The walls were freshly painted. Radiators had been ripped out; discreet vents showed that central air had been put in. The furniture was new, comfortable-looking, and bright; a poppy-red sofa was strewn with Nella's afghans. One striped blanket was unfinished, its yarn trailing into a basket on the floor. Nella slept in the living room in a hospital bed, equipment arrayed around her. Her thin hair—she had refused chemotherapy—was like dandelion fluff. Emily was reminded again of a baby; Nella's hands were curled into frail, loose fists. The skin of her eyelids, while wrinkled, had the sheer quality of an infant's: a near translucence. The nurse sat nearby, reading a romance novel.

Emily led Gen to her bedroom. Emily paused, slightly, before they entered, startled to recognize a whorl in the wood of the doorframe. She remembered noticing it long ago, that first time with Gen. She remembered being filled with desire and nervousness, and how she had thought, then, that after she followed Gen into that room and into her bed, she would change. She would become a different person. She had forgotten that. How had she forgotten? And now she was different. Emily didn't believe in ghosts, not really, but sometimes she came close to believing, and while everyone assumes ghosts are from the past, it occurred to her that they might be glimpses of the future. What would the Emily she had been think of the Emily she was now, if the teenager had seen the adult standing on the threshold?

Gen's hand tightened around hers. Nothing is ever the same again. Emily loved her more now. She led Gen to bed—the old twin beds had been replaced by a large one—and drew the light summer quilt over her. She intended to sit at the edge of the bed until Gen fell asleep, but Gen slept almost instantly. Emily wondered when Gen had last slept. Emily was tired, too, but collected dirty clothes from the floor and explored the house until she found a brand-new washer and dryer set in the basement. Then she spoke with the nurse, who stuck a thumb in her novel and confirmed Nella's medications. Relieved, Emily left the living room and tackled the kitchen.

It was almost unrecognizable—a carnation pink Aga stove, a shiny lime backsplash. The one thing that remained the same in the kitchen was the big clock with its loud tick. It ticked as Emily loaded the dishwasher. It ticked as she swept and mopped the floor. The fridge wasn't full but it had some essentials. A rooster crowed. The sky was apricot. Emily went outside—the once-sagging porch was firm beneath her feet—and let the chickens out of their coop. The feed was where it had always been. She scattered the feed, the two dogs nosing curiously and largely about her. Feeling acutely that she hadn't slept since a nap on the plane, Emily returned to the house, where she went to Gen's bedroom. She missed the twin bed that she had lain in that Christmas when she told Gen that she wanted to be somebody. She wrote a note explaining that Connor and Stella, though they had obediently packed their small suitcases to come to Ohio, were confused by their presence here and needed an explanation. *I'll be back as soon as I've slept.* She set the note on Gen's nightstand.

On the drive home, the cornfields were as high as a human. The day was clear, the mountains sharp. They looked as though they had been cut from construction paper and glued to the sky. Her car trailing dirt, Emily saw a sign along the road: EGGS. A woman sat by a stand. Eggs! Emily had forgotten to collect eggs from the coop. Later, she would do it later. Pulling over to the side of the road felt like an act of penance. The woman's eggs were pale blue. Emily realized that fatigue was making everything seem more than it was. She was going to have to be very careful driving home. She was practically dreaming while awake. She could have an accident. It was good that she had stopped. She bought all the eggs the woman had.

At home, Connor and Stella were in pajamas and sitting at the table with her mother, eating cereal. The linoleum—the same as when Emily lived here—had peeled up in places. The room was sunny. Her mother drank from a Styrofoam cup. "What's all this?" she said as Emily set the many dozens of eggs on the table.

"They're *blue*," said Stella.

"Are they robin's eggs?" said Connor.

"Take a big robin to lay those," said her mother. "A neighbor brought coffee. There's a box of it on the counter. Want some?"

Emily shook her head.

"Look what Grandma showed me how to do." Stella held up a white paper cutout girl. She stretched her hands wide and the girl became many girls, a garland of them, pleated where they joined.

"Better get some sleep," said her mother, "or you'll drop where you stand."

Emily went to her room. The sheets were clean. Emily closed her eyes and saw the paper doll chain, each girl identical—were they identical?—unfolding between her daughter's hands. Sleep was an undertow. Her room smelled like childhood.

When she woke, her mother was watching television and the children were playing outside. It was late afternoon. Through the open windows, Emily could hear that Connor was trying to catch a garter snake. "But what will you do with it?" said Stella. "What will you *do*?"

Emily went outside and said that she wanted to talk with them. They squinted up at her. "Gen's grandmother is sick and won't get better," she said. "Nella will die soon. She's Gen's only parent."

"No, she's her grandmother," said Stella.

"She's a parent, too. Gen's mother died when Gen was a little older than Connor. I'm not sure if Gen's father knows that she exists. When Gen was born, her mother lived with Nella and worked as a carpenter. Then Gen's mother was injured at work and the doctor gave her bad medicine."

"What kind of medicine?" said Connor.

"It made the pain go away but also made her want the medicine so much that she would do anything to get it. She took too much. It killed her."

Stella, wide-eyed, said, "Was it bubblegum medicine?"

"No, baby, nothing like that. Don't worry."

"Does Gen have a sister?" said Connor.

"There's only Nella. When she dies, Gen will feel very alone. That's why I wanted to come to Ohio: so that Gen won't be so alone. Will you be patient, even if it gets boring to stay here?"

"Okay," said Connor. Stella nodded.

"I'll be gone a lot but I'll take you to the playground. There's a library. A pond for swimming. A farm nearby with horses. Grandma will take care of you when I'm helping Gen."

"I like Grandma," said Stella. "She's funny."

"She is?"

"She got mad at a neighbor for roaring his motorcycle early in the morning. She opened the door and yelled at him. She was like, 'I'll fix *you*!' I said he wasn't broken. She said he would be, when she got through with him."

"She gave us doughnuts," Connor said. "She said it's a secret, though. She doesn't want to get in trouble."

"Doughnuts are okay," said Emily. "There's something else I need to tell you." The longer she avoided this, the more it felt like lying. She told them about the divorce. She explained it as a simple fact with no details. She used a tone of finality. The reaction was as bad as she had feared. Stella cried. Connor pleaded, "Mommy, don't. I'll be good, I promise."

"You *are* good. The divorce has nothing to do with you or Stella. It's about me and Daddy and how we can't be together."

"Try to be together," said Stella. "Try."

"We tried for a long time. Some things don't work no matter how hard you try."

"But we don't want a divorce."

"I know you don't."

"Then don't do it!"

"I have to."

"You have to try harder," Stella insisted. "Daddy said so."

"I can't."

"You can!"

"I don't want to," said Emily. "I'm sorry."

"Then it's your fault. Daddy said it was. He wants us to be a family and you don't."

"You are my family," she told them. "Always."

Connor had grown somber. His eyes looked older than they had a few minutes before. Stella said, "But it's not the same! It's not the same! It's not—" Connor took Stella's hand and his sister went silent. Emily realized that her children belonged to each other in a way that they didn't belong to her. It was hard to see them look to each other for comfort and to be the cause, but she also hadn't wanted them to have her childhood—that scrounging for affection—or to be like Gen, solitary in her loss. Emily had always wanted more than one child. She wanted each to be the other's ally.

Connor said, "What will happen?"

"I don't know."

"You have to know."

"All I know is that I will always love you."

They accepted this in miserable silence.

"There's something I'd like to do with you," she said. "Will you help me?"

Connor said disdainfully, "I don't want to be *distracted.*"

"It might feel good."

"Okay," said Stella, wiping her face.

Emily's mother was gone from the couch, though the television was still on. Over it, Emily heard the sounds of her mother taking a shower. She fished the coffee cup out of the trash, rinsed it, and handed it to Connor. She gave a spoon to Stella. "Will you fill that cup with dirt from outside?"

When they returned, Emily showed them the worn pack of marigold seeds. The image on the pack had faded, so Emily explained that the flowers would be yellow and orange, like little suns. "I'm not sure they'll grow. The seeds are old. But some might." The instructions on the pack were illegible, so Emily looked them up online and handed the phone to the children. Carefully, they plucked seeds from the open pack and set them in the dirt, then added water from the tap. Emily Saran-Wrapped the top and rubber-banded it. Connor poked holes in the taut Saran Wrap.

"I hope they grow," said Stella.

"Me too. Go put the cup in a sunny spot."

Connor said, "Do you think they'll grow?"

"Seeds can live a long time. We'll have to see."

Emily returned to Nella's chicken coop, collected eggs in a basket, and brought them inside through the farmhouse's side door to the kitchen, where the nurse was making coffee. "Nella's awake," said the nurse. "She's feeling pretty good. Gen said that if you came over, you should join them."

Gen and Nella didn't notice Emily enter the living room. Nella said to Gen, who sat in the chair next to the hospital bed, "The doctor shouldn't have called you."

"Don't say that."

"I could've watched you compete from here. I have that big TV. I wanted to see you do what you love."

"Why did you lie to me? Why did you do that? I would have come home sooner."

"I know."

"You shouldn't have done that! I thought you were okay!"

"Sweetheart. You're going to have to forgive me."

"I do, but—Gran. Gran." Gen's voice deteriorated. "I don't want you to go."

"The doctor said I might not speak right later so listen now. I wish I could stay for you. Sometimes I wish I could be here until it's your time, so I could make sure you're okay to the very end. But that would be too hard. It would be too hard to bury another child. I lied to you and I'm not sorry. Still, I'm glad you've come home. Maybe that's selfish. It's good to have you, even though it cost you."

"Stop talking about the cost!"

Quietly, Nella said, "Your Emily is here."

Emily had frozen while they spoke, sure she shouldn't be listening to their conversation yet worried that if she moved and they noticed, that would interrupt what they were saying, and then they might never say it. Gen looked at her. She looked lost.

"Go for a run," Nella told Gen. "You need it."

"I'm not a dog you have to let out."

"You told the nurse not to let me watch anything but Hallmark movies. You think I can't be high-handed with you, too? Go on. You haven't run since you've been home. Take your phone. Emily will sit with me. Won't you?"

"Yes," said Emily.

"Some people listen."

Gen gave her grandmother a wan smile, kissed her cheek, and left.

"You've grown up," Nella told Emily.

"I wasn't that young when I saw you last. I was eighteen."

"A baby. An infant. Bring me that blanket. The unfinished one. It bothers me." Emily brought the striped blanket to Nella, along with the pink ball of yarn attached to it. "I'll tell you how to fasten it off." Emily did as instructed. She crocheted it closed and cut the blanket free from the ball of yarn. Nella said, "I'm tired. Need to close my eyes. I want you to do one more thing."

"What is it?"

"Take care of her when I'm gone."

Emily heard the dogs outside bark. She left the air-conditioned house and stepped into the hot sludge of the day. Gen patted the excited, writhing dogs. She did it intently, as though this was work that required careful attention. She glanced up. Her expression of effort intensified as she held Emily's gaze. Emily wondered if, for Gen, being around her was hard. The thought made Emily sad. Maybe it wasn't helpful that she was there, and Gen had agreed to it only because she'd been confused by the shitstorm of grief, or she had felt obligated to offer an invitation to the farmhouse once Emily had flown in. "I'm sorry," she said.

"For what?"

Emily felt too overwhelmed to say what she had been thinking—and, once her head cleared, she believed that to say it would be wrong. She didn't want to seek reassurance from someone who was suffering. She chose a specific apology. "I'm sorry I overheard your conversation."

"I'm not. It means a lot to me that you're here. I couldn't bear this alone. I'm not sure I can bear it anyway. The doctor said we have a few weeks. That's all. That's what's left. How long"—anxiety crossed her face—"can you stay?"

"As long as you need me."

It was several days later that Gen said, "*How* are you here?" She said this as though coming out of a daze. They were at the kitchen table. Gen hadn't touched the food on her plate. "You brought Connor and Stella . . . and Jack doesn't care? You're staying with your mom? I thought you didn't talk with your mom."

"How much do you want to know?"

"Everything."

Emily told her about the conversation with her mother. She described the dinner with her father, her lost manuscript, the bruise. Gen made a sound that stuck in her throat and started to speak but Emily shook her head. Gen scraped her chair back from the table and went to the sink. She turned on the faucet and took a glass from a cabinet but didn't fill it. She stood before the running water, shoulders slouched, staring into the sink. Slowly, as though she didn't trust herself not to break it, she set the empty glass on the counter and ducked her head under the water. She remained like that for a moment, hands braced on either side of the sink, water running through her hair and over her neck until she turned it off and straightened, dripping.

"It's hot out," said Emily.

Gen's voice was rough: "You know that's not why."

"It doesn't matter anyway."

Gen stared at her, shirt wet, her brown hair black and matted to her head. "It doesn't *matter*?"

"A photograph of a bruise is no proof of how I got it."

Gen had such an awful expression that Emily went to her. Gen pulled her close, arms tight around her. A trickle of water ran down Emily's back. Gen said, "I want to kill him."

"That wouldn't be good for your image. Killers don't go on Wheaties boxes."

"Don't joke."

"What's crazy is that I used to almost hope it would happen. Then it would be obvious that there was something wrong. But when it actually happened, it didn't matter."

"Please stop saying that."

"I'm embarrassed to tell you this."

"Don't be. Listen. Will you listen? I'm sorry this happened to you. It matters. You matter. You have always mattered to me and you always will."

Emily's breath quickened.

"Even if we can't be together," said Gen. "Okay?"

"Oh," said Emily quietly. She stepped away. Her shirt was splotched with damp patches. "Okay."

"What's wrong?"

"Can we go outside? I want some air."

It was warm but not oppressive on the porch. The low sun made the green corn shine like water. Emily was silent, trying to manage the weight of her disappointment.

"I'm surprised Jack let you bring the kids."

"I offered not to take money from him in the divorce."

"You did?"

"I was surprised, too, that he agreed, especially when I told him about us, but he's weird about money. It's bound up with his sense of self-worth."

Gen squeezed her eyes shut. "You told him? But your lawyer said— Emily." Gen stared. "Why would you do that?"

"Well, there's no *us* now."

Face tight, Gen rubbed her collarbone. Her shirt had dried. She said nothing.

"We were always going to end up in court," said Emily. "He was never going to make it easy."

"You didn't have to tell him. Why did you tell him? Why did you do that? Why would you risk so much?"

Emily could have said that it was a matter of self-respect, but she wanted to give a fuller answer to Gen, whose eyes were wide and unhappy. Emily gazed across the yard to where the barn stood. She remembered its hayloft, all that had happened there, their hunger for each other, the peaceful quiet afterward, dusty light drifting up from below. A wind blew over the farm. She heard the soft applause of leaves. She looked at Gen: older now, soon an orphan. If they weren't exactly friends and couldn't be lovers, there remained one thing they could be. "You might not think of me as family," Emily said, "but I think of you as mine."

How's Gen? texted Shipley.

Not good, Emily wrote. Nella's really weak

I meant the tabloids

Emily had been too busy to watch the news or go into town. Did they find out about Nella? Gen hated the thought of paparazzi descending on Washford and using her grandmother as entertainment, which was why she had been so secretive about her departure from the Olympics.

No, said Shipley.

What's going on? said Emily.

In leaving London with no explanation, Gen had detonated her image. It kind of fucked her, Shipley wrote. On ESPN, sportscasters said she was a coward. "What's so bad that she can't at least be honest about it?" they wondered. The fundamental rule of sports wasn't complicated: you win or you lose, but you must play the game. Sponsors dropped her. Op-ed writers said that she had betrayed her nation. Tabloids speculated that she was on a bender. *Like mother, like daughter,* said one article. It's all gone to shit, Shipley texted. She should have faced the press. Told them a lie, whatever. Should have faked an injury. I told her to. Got a real fatal flaw, that one. Too proud.

Emily realized that there was never a newspaper on the farmhouse porch when she arrived in the mornings after sleeping at her mother's, even though it had been common to see them around Nella's house when she was a teenager, and to collect one from the doormat outside Gen's apartment in Williamsburg. She recalled Nella complaining that the nurse had commandeered the TV's remote control.

Emily went to Gen. "You blew up your career?"

Gen covered her face and sighed. "My agent won't stop calling. She wants to scrape me off the pavement, put me on the *Today* show or something. Cut out my heart and hold it up for everyone to see. She even said that she wanted me to *live my truth.*"

"Natasha's just looking out for you."

Gen's hand fell from her face. She narrowed her eyes. "You know her? How do you know her name? You said that like you know her."

With reluctance, Emily told Gen about the conversation with Natasha in the café.

Gen said, "Is that why you said a break would be good for me?"

"Well."

"I'm going to fire her," Gen said flatly.

"Gen, no. This is why I didn't want to tell you. She's powerful and she's on your side."

"Can I fire her for telling me to live my truth?"

"There's a reason people like that phrase."

"She messed with my personal life."

"You need her. Let it go."

"I didn't realize how bad the press could be. I mean, I knew. But I didn't *know*. I put so much pressure on you, that last night in New York. I was upset. But I'm okay now, I really am, I think I am. We can be family, you and me, if that's what you want. I don't want to lose you again. Can we make a promise? I get that people need to keep stuff to themselves, but if I ask a real question, will you promise to always give a real answer? An honest one. Like, *full.*"

"You'll do the same?"

"Yeah."

"Okay."

Gen looked relieved.

"How are you doing, with your gran?"

Gen's grief emerged like a thick thread that followed its needle everywhere. As they talked, dusk came. The porchlight went on.

Not long after, Gen asked about the divorce. Emily grimaced but gave a real answer. She told her everything.

"I have money," said Gen.

"No."

"If he tries to outspend you. Think about it."

"No."

"What're you going to do?"

"I'll get a job. I've got a degree. It'd be nice to finally use it."

"Are you scared about this going to court?"

"Yes."

"Me too. I'd be less scared if you let me help with lawyer fees."

"No." Emily shook her head, smiling a little. "You really don't give up."

Gen went quiet, as though startled, and looked thoughtful. She didn't press the issue.

—

August lengthened. Emily's agent submitted her novel to editors. The marigold seedlings grew. The children were thrilled. Emily felt the greenhouse warmth breathe from the cup as she removed the Saran Wrap cover so that the seedlings could climb above the rim.

—

"Petti*coat*," said Stella.

"*Cot*tage," said Emily's mother. The four of them were on the grass by the local pond. Connor had just come out of the cloudy, warm water.

"What's a cot?" said Stella.

"A small bed."

"*Corn*er."

"Oh, the little word in the big word game," said Connor, water dripping off his skinny body. He had Skyped earlier that day with his friend Annika, and was feeling pleased and much more grown-up than his sister.

"*Slip*per," said Stella.

"It was my turn," said Emily's mother. "S*wing*."

"Spar*row*."

"Croco*dile*."

"*Dile*?" said Stella. "That's not a word!"

"Sure it is. A dile. Sometimes I go to the dile and buy milk."

"That's cheating!"

Connor said, "There's *dial*, *d-i-a-l*. That's a word."

"That doesn't count! That's not how you spell *crocodile*! I know it. I know it from *Lyle, Lyle, Crocodile*."

"But it sounds the same."

"It's not the same. Right, Mommy?"

"Go on, Emily," drawled her mother, "pick a side."

"I can't pick a side."

"Coward."

Did *dile* count because it sounded like *dial*? When Gen had said that she didn't want to lose Emily again, did that mean that she still felt the same way about Emily, just as Emily did about her? That was how it had sounded. But her hope of what Gen had meant could have been a *dile:* an invention. A *dile:* a glop of wet clay that could be shaped into anything. "I don't know," Emily said, because she didn't. Then she grinned. "*Coward,*" she said, and the game began again.

Not long after, Emily was sitting under a tree at the farm, reading, when a truck loaded with lumber pulled up. A work crew got out of the truck and discussed something. She couldn't hear what was said. A man went to the front door. Gen opened it, and after a brief exchange, she nodded and gestured toward the barn. The crew went inside it. Emily couldn't see what they were doing, but the air became filled with the sounds of demolition.

She was so distressed that she shut her book. Since returning to Washford, she hadn't gone inside the barn because it would have been painful to see the hayloft, but it had nonetheless comforted her to believe that, as much as she and Gen had changed, this one space hadn't. She had noticed the farmhouse's improvements, and although she missed the house as she had known it, missed the bed where she had slept, the changes didn't seem to have anything to do with her. This change did. It felt pointed. Intended to scrape away the past. The sound of hammers on wood made her chest hurt. *Why?* she wanted to ask Gen, but didn't, because she wasn't sure that she wanted a real answer.

The window of her childhood bedroom was open and there was a little breeze. The thin curtains were sucked against the screen, then billowed, but the room stayed stuffy and hot. Outside, Stella called to Connor. They were drawing with chalk on the sidewalk. Her mother sat in a plastic lawn chair, watching them. Emily was getting dressed after a shower. She heard birds and a lawn mower. Her phone rang: it was Leila Alami. "Are you ready for good news?" her agent said.

When you haven't had good news for a long time, its arrival has the quality of a myth. Who would believe it?

"We have an offer for your book," said Leila.

An editor had offered one hundred thousand dollars.

Emily sat on the bed. It was so much money. It didn't matter that the sum was small change for Jack; his car had cost that much. Emily had never made even a fraction of that amount in her entire life. "Can you say that number again? I think I misheard you."

The number was the number. What Emily felt was fresh and sweet and cool: a river of relief. She felt saved. She had saved herself. She wasn't sure what she said into the phone. It seemed like she wasn't saying words, just making joyful sounds, like a puppy, like a child, a toddler, the world a bath of wonder.

Leila laughed. "I guess we're saying yes."

After Emily hung up, she flopped backward on the bed. She stared at the faded floral wallpaper. She would be able to keep paying her rent. Her lawyer. She would be okay.

As her heart calmed, she thought of the ending of her book. She had been envious of her own character when writing it. She had wished that there was a way to outmaneuver Jack like Athena had tricked Zeus. The ceiling fan wobbled as it spun. Outside, Stella asked for a Popsicle. It occurred to Emily that there was no trick that could undo the problem of her husband, but she could at least tell him something that was true.

When Jack answered the phone, she said, "I want full custody and I want to settle out of court."

"You're not going to get that."

"I have photographs of your abuse."

"We've been over this. Why would a judge believe you?"

"Why would a judge believe *you*? I have years of stories of what you've said and done. I'm not going to stay quiet. I don't care who knows. The judge. Your parents. Your colleagues. Your friends."

He was silent.

She said, "Connor and Stella will know."

"Are you seriously saying you'd try to turn our children against me?"

"I won't lie for you." When Jack was silent again, Emily said, "I know you love them. You could become a different kind of father, but they will be safer with me. Any reasonable judge will see that."

Quietly, Jack said, "I don't want our marriage to be over."

"But it is. You need to know that. You need to know that I'll fight for Connor and Stella and I will never give up."

When Gen heard about the book deal, she said, "I knew you'd do it."

"You did?"

"I'm proud of you."

"You are?"

"I'm really, really proud."

The marigold seedlings leafed into tiny trees.

"Gran doesn't always recognize me now," said Gen. "She thinks I'm my mother. Or her own mother. But she doesn't always say the right word. Sometimes she says 'other.' "

"What do you do when she thinks you're someone else?"

"I pretend to be whoever she needs me to be."

Gen's friends sent flowers. Shipley had the local store deliver groceries. Becca sent board games but Nella didn't have it in her to play. In the beginning, Gen hadn't realized that Emily was cleaning the house, feeding the chickens, and doing laundry; Gen had been too sad to notice. But one day soon after Emily had arrived, as they put away Shipley's groceries, Gen stared at the clean kitchen and then looked at Emily. Gen begged her not to do anything like that again and hired a housekeeper.

Yet Emily had the habit of tidying the farmhouse and did it when Gen wasn't aware. She didn't want to feel useless when everyone around her was working. The nurse, the housekeeper. Gen, getting through every day. Nella, trying to live a little longer. Once, when Gen was out for a run, Emily brought clean sheets to Gen's room. On the nightstand lay a strip of photographs.

They were from the night at the bar when Gen had given Emily the hat and scarf, and they fought, and ended up in bed. Emily held the photos. She hadn't seen them that night; Gen had glanced at the strip and tucked it into her pocket. *We look like good friends*, Gen had said, but that wasn't true. The black-and-white Emily looked at the black-and-white Gen with such longing that it was as clear as a word typed on a page. That didn't surprise Emily. She had expected it. But she hadn't expected the last image, where the Emily in the photograph looked straight into the camera's lens. This time, it was Gen who gazed at her. Gen's expression, too, was full of longing. They had looked at each other the same way, just not at the same time.

"Mom, where does time go?" asked Connor. They were sitting in her mother's front yard at dusk. Fireflies rose from the grass.

Emily said, "What do you mean?"

"I just asked that question—*Where does time go?*—and now it's in the past. But we can only be in the present."

"Yes."

"Did that question get mixed with everything in the past? Like the dinosaurs and the big bang?"

"I think it must have."

"Does it all keep existing?"

"What do you think?"

"Yes."

"Why?"

"Because I want it to."

"I think that's right. Because you made a memory. You're remembering the dinosaurs and your question. The past keeps existing because it stays inside us."

"Do I ask too many questions?"

"I like your questions. They are big questions. They are the ones we all want to know."

The children decorated the Styrofoam cup with drawings of the flowers that would soon open. The seedlings' color darkened, the green more robust. There were many buds. Connor and Stella counted them.

Nella slept more and more. She was rarely awake. But Emily had told Gen that Nella would be able to hear her until the end, so Gen talked to her grandmother when it seemed like she might be listening. Gen asked Emily to sit with them. Emily listened to Gen tell Nella about the first race she had won. How Nella had taught her to drive the tractor. Gen described her mother: her long, dark braid. She told Nella about getting lost at the fair. Nella had found her.

Nella opened her eyes. "Lucky."

"Gran?"

"I'm lucky I got to have you."

Gen's phone call came very early in the morning, when it was still dark out. Emily drove to the farmhouse. The lamp in the living room was on. Emily let herself in. Gen was sitting next to Nella. Even though Nella was gone, Gen continued to murmur to her. Gen's palms lay open on her own lap, limp and upturned. Emily touched her shoulder and Gen fell silent. Emily placed the cup in Gen's hands.

The marigolds were ready to flower. One of them had begun to open. Gen's face crumpled. "You were supposed to keep them," she said, "for when you needed them."

"I did," said Emily.

40

Gen didn't want a funeral for Nella. That would be too sad. Instead, Emily helped her plan a memorial brunch. They booked the local rec hall and hired caterers to come from Columbus. "I want colors for her," Gen said. "I want champagne." They collected Nella's handmade blankets to give away. The last one she made, and which Emily cut from its yarn, Gen kept.

Gen's friends flew in. They came early to the rec hall and helped with setup, arranging tables and chairs. Becca had printed out photos of Nella at Gen's meets, and when no one could decide how best to display them, Nita made a last-minute drive to Walmart for a bulletin board. Emily's friends sent flowers that Adam and Kate arranged into table centerpieces. Rory texted: how's Gen holding up?

Emily wasn't sure. Gen greeted Connor and Stella seriously, as though they were adults, and thanked them for coming. Emily and the kids had tickets to fly back to New York the following day. It was Labor Day weekend and they would make it home just in time for the start of school. Gen played the host with everyone, trying to be easy with the task; she wanted this to be a warm gathering. Shipley made her smile. When Paul arrived, though, and hugged her, her shoulders sagged. Emily couldn't see her face, only Paul's, but she saw Gen's grief mirrored in his expression.

Gen was quiet around Emily, even a little distant. They didn't speak much—Gen was busy, of course, and Emily had to negotiate with the caterers, because more people were arriving than they'd expected, and while there would be enough food, there wouldn't be enough servers. "No problem," her mother said. "Do a buffet." When it became clear that the caterers hadn't brought a long table for a buffet, only round ones for the brunch, she disappeared in search of the right kind, sure that the rec hall had one stashed somewhere. Emily and Gen talked briefly about the change in plans.

"Hey, thanks," said Gen. "Not just for today. I mean for everything." She said it awkwardly. The words were nice but Emily felt dismissed, because saying thanks is what you do when what you're grateful for is done. Gen's thanks were another way of saying goodbye.

Emily shrugged and smiled, not trusting herself to speak.

"Really." Gen spoke as though Emily had tried to argue with her. "You saved me."

It occurred to Emily that Gen seemed awkward because she was embarrassed. Emily had seen her at her grandmother's bedside, devastated and helpless. Maybe Gen wished that Emily hadn't witnessed that. She hated to be seen as helpless. Emily didn't want her to feel that way or to think that something was owed. "I came here because I wanted to. You would have done the same for me."

Gen nodded but looked dissatisfied.

More people arrived. Emily's mother and Candace put the found long table into place. The crowd surprised Emily, not just its size but also its composition. She had expected Gen's friends. The industry people, too, with their bespoke suits. Some glamorous Hollywood types. Athletes who greeted Shipley and Gen's track friends as colleagues. And she had expected yet wasn't prepared for the extent of queerness, a visual kinship that ran through the crowd like a seam of ore. Emily belonged to it in a way that she hadn't felt before. With that sense of belonging came the realization that all it took to belong was to know that she did. Maybe that should have been obvious to her, but it hadn't been.

What surprised her most, though, was how many townspeople had come. She knew a few of them—retired teachers, the high school coach—but soon the rec hall was so full that it seemed as if all of Washford were there. Young people, too. And people her age. Their kids played with Connor and Stella. She could tell who lived in town, even when she didn't know them: they wore their Sunday best. Their expressions as they glanced at the out-of-towners showed a mix of curiosity and discomfort. This could have been an aversion to the queerness on display, but Emily thought that most of it was defensive: a worry that Washford and its people would be disdained by outsiders. Still, whenever someone from home greeted someone from out of town, all she saw was kindness. The faces of the Washford High kids made her breath catch—not just because she had been like them once. Sometimes one of them looked at Gen's friends, and their entire face became a wish.

Shipley approached. "How are you?"

Her throat closed. She was leaving the next day. Gen was stunned by loss. Shipley's question felt too hard to answer. "It's amazing how many people are here. I hadn't realized how many people in town cared about Nella."

"And Gen."

"Because she's famous?" She hated the thought that Gen was a spectacle.

"Because she's done so much for the town." Shipley looked at her more closely and added, "You didn't know?"

No, Emily didn't know that Gen returned home on a regular basis to coach kids on the track team. She didn't know that Gen funded scholarships, not just to colleges but also to trade schools. She didn't know that Gen had donated to the library and that it was undergoing renovations. She didn't know that Gen came back for fairs, just for fun. The people in town knew her not only as Nella Hall's granddaughter but also as herself.

"What do you think she'll do now?" said Shipley. "Not that her career is necessarily over, but . . ."

"What do retired athletes usually do?"

"If she does interviews about why she left, she could get in good with the public again."

Emily saw Gen across the way, listening to Becca, who was speaking emphatically. She seemed to lecture Gen.

"She could do the fame thing," said Shipley. "More modeling. Do a talk show."

"I don't think she cares about being a celebrity. She just loves to run."

"Sportscaster?"

"Maybe?"

"Coaching?"

Emily remembered how Gen had been with the girl on the beach whose shoe she'd signed. "I can see that."

"Yeah."

"Maybe she tries to make the Olympics again in 2016."

Shipley nodded. "Never hurts to try. I mean, it does, of course. It can hurt like hell. But what else are you going to do? Regret a missed chance forever?" She was no longer talking about sports. "What about you two?"

Emily was tempted to answer openly. It felt like she and Gen were a story that couldn't end well, a myth where the avoidance of tragic fate produces that fate, or a plot with a cruel scramble of the timeline, Gen looking at her when she didn't see, then Emily doing the same to her. Impossible. *I have no right.* That was the thought that kept welling up within Emily: *I have no right to you.* She had broken Gen's heart twice. How could Gen return to that—to her? Look at this crowded hall. All the people who loved Gen. Emily was just one more.

"Hey, Ship," she said. "Can you spread word that the buffet is ready?"

Shipley waited a moment, then replied, "Sure thing."

Across the way, Gen said something to Becca, who flung up her hands, impatient. Becca's attitude made Emily angry and protective. Why was she berating Gen? Didn't she know how difficult this day was? Emily saw the difficulty etched on Gen's face. Surely Becca saw it, too. Emily had the impulse to cross the room and interrupt.

Not my business, she decided, watching Gen argue with Becca.

Although the rec hall was air-conditioned, it felt stifling. She went outside for fresh air.

It was not fresh. The sun had reached its height. The air was still. The trees' leaves were cupped, hoping for rain. It was the dog days of summer—named by the ancient Greeks not because this kind of heat would drive a panting dog into the shade but because the peak of summer coincided with the rise of the dog star that hunted in Orion's constellation.

There she was, doing what she always did: shifting her thoughts elsewhere to avoid confronting what mattered most. She turned away from the rec hall. She had said that she'd stay as long as Gen needed her and she no longer did. *Face that*, she told herself. Who cared about stars? She couldn't even see them. And if she could, she wouldn't be seeing them as they actually were but as they had been ages ago, when they first made the light that had traveled across the universe. The movie that she'd seen with the kids at the planetarium had said that the night sky is an image of the past. Most visible stars made their light ten thousand years ago. Some of them don't even exist anymore. She was filled with the sense of her irrelevance.

"Emily?"

It was Gen.

Emily turned and said something like, *Everything okay? Is there a problem with the food? The caterers?* She wasn't sure what she said. Some bullshit. Her voice trailed away. Gen's expression looked like it had that summer day when they drank lemonade in the back of her truck. She was taut with nervousness.

Emily was, too. She blurted, "Why did you renovate the barn?"

"What? Oh." Gen rubbed the back of her neck. "Um."

"Real answers only."

"It wasn't safe."

"Safe?"

"For Connor and Stella. The ladder to the hayloft was old, you know. I worried about them falling. I had the crew build a proper staircase, better guardrails. Some bunk beds, nicer shelves. Cubbies for toys. I wanted to surprise you. Like, I can live anywhere, but I'll always want to visit Washford, because it's where we come from. I thought maybe you'd come back sometimes, too—I mean, to see your mom, if nothing else. And you'd bring the kids. It'd be a great place for them to play. Is that okay? You look really strange."

"But your mother made the hayloft for you."

"It was mine. Then it was ours. I want it to be theirs. All kids need a secret place, a place of their own. Hey, don't cry. Did I fuck up? Why are you crying?"

"I thought you renovated the hayloft because you were over us."

"What? No."

"That you wanted to get rid of it."

"Emily. I will never get over us."

Emily was too happy to speak.

Gen searched her face and said, "Can I ask you something? Will you give me a real answer? Do you still love me like I love you? You are my friend and you are my family. But I also want you to be mine."

Emily kissed her. She said yes. She kept saying it. She didn't understand how her yes hadn't always been obvious. She wanted to be obvious. She wanted everyone to see how she felt. She told Gen this. She begged her to believe her.

Gen was hollow-eyed from lack of sleep, but she smiled. She believed her. "Becca told me you'd say that. But I didn't know."

"I hate that you didn't know. But you know now?"

"I know now."

"Always?"

"Yes."

The rec hall, when they returned, was loud. The gathering was what Gen had wanted it to be: plates heaped with food, colorful tablecloths, lively conversation, shared memories of Nella. A good day.

Later, guests began to go home. Connor and Stella, restless, left with Emily's mother. Many people stayed. They opened more champagne. Emily poured some for her and Gen. She leaned into Gen, head resting on her shoulder. Gen kissed her, mouth soft.

They weren't paying attention to the others, but the others were paying attention to them. There was a clinking sound. The room quieted. Becca stood, gaze on Emily and Gen, her champagne lifted in a toast. She didn't say anything—she didn't need to. Everyone in that room wished them well, and everyone raised a glass.

ACKNOWLEDGMENTS

Thanks to Alexandra Machinist, the best agent anyone could hope for and a dear friend. Felicity Blunt, you are incredible, too, and I trust you implicitly. I'm also grateful to my amazing editors at Knopf and Virago: Jennifer Jackson, Carla Josephson, and Caitlin Landuyt. I've learned so much from you. Thanks as well to Kathleen Cook, Lyn Rosen, Tiara Sharma, Susan VanOmmeren, Emily Murphy, Kelsey Curtis, Micah Kelsey, Celeste Ward-Best, Lilly Cox, Grace Vincent, and the entire teams at Knopf and Virago. Finally, thanks to Reagan Arthur, Jordan Pavlin, and Maris Dyer for welcoming me to the Knopf fold.

Many people helped me in the writing of this book, whether by offering advice and information, brainstorming with me, or reading and giving feedback. Thank you to Marianna Baer, Holly Black, Laura Blackett, Mary Bly, Valérie Buffet, Kristin Cashore, Kat Cho, Cassie Clare, Adam Deaton, Donna Freitas, Juliet Garlow, Yves Gleichman, Daphne Grab, Maureen Johnson, Josh Lewis, Malinda Lo, Florencia Marotta, Cindy Pon, Amy Rudolph, Carrie Ryan, Jill Santopolo, Eliot Schrefer, Robin Wasserman, Katie White, and Ashley Woodfolk. Nikki Hiltz, you are an inspiration.

Thank you to Becky Rosenthal, Drew Gorman-Lewis, Leigh Bardugo, Jason Holloway, Kate Duguid, and Gail Monaco for being there.

Thank you to Thomas Philippon, for being a great co-parent and loving father.

My parents, Marilyn and Robert Rutkoski, gave me a happy childhood that has sustained me all my life: a wonderful gift.

A final word for my sons. Thank you, Eliot, who loves the turtles at the Hernshead, and Téo, who asked where time goes. I love you both. I will always be proud of you.

A NOTE ABOUT THE AUTHOR

Marie Rutkoski is a *New York Times* bestselling author of books for children and young adults, including *The Shadow Society* and the Kronos Chronicles, which includes *The Cabinet of Wonders*. She published her first novel for adults, *Real Easy*, in 2022. Rutkoski is a professor of English literature at Brooklyn College and lives in Brooklyn with her family.

A NOTE ON THE TYPE

This book was set in Janson, a typeface long thought to have been made by the Dutchman Anton Janson, who was a practicing typefounder in Leipzig during the years 1668–1687. However, it has been conclusively demonstrated that these types are actually the work of Nicholas Kis (1650–1702), a Hungarian, who most probably learned his trade from the master Dutch typefounder Dirk Voskens. The type is an excellent example of the influential and sturdy Dutch types that prevailed in England up to the time William Caslon (1692–1766) developed his own incomparable designs from them.

Typeset by Scribe,
Philadelphia, Pennsylvania

Designed by Casey Hampton